Heinrich Kreissle von Hellborn, Arthur Duke Coleridge

The Life of Franz Schubert

Vol. I

Heinrich Kreissle von Hellborn, Arthur Duke Coleridge

The Life of Franz Schubert
Vol. I

ISBN/EAN: 9783743402188

Manufactured in Europe, USA, Canada, Australia, Japa

Cover: Foto ©Raphael Reischuk / pixelio.de

Manufactured and distributed by brebook publishing software (www.brebook.com)

Heinrich Kreissle von Hellborn, Arthur Duke Coleridge

The Life of Franz Schubert

THE LIFE

OF

FRANZ SCHUBERT.

TRANSLATED FROM THE GERMAN

OF

KREISSLE VON HELLBORN

BY

ARTHUR DUKE COLERIDGE, M.A.

LATE FELLOW OF KING'S COLLEGE,
CAMBRIDGE.

WITH AN APPENDIX

BY

GEORGE GROVE, ESQ.

IN TWO VOLUMES.—VOL. I.

LONDON:
LONGMANS, GREEN, AND CO.
1869.

PREFACE.

It is scarcely an exaggeration to say, that Schubert's reputation in England, until very recently, rested upon little more than half-a-dozen songs. We are now beginning to realise the importance of his music; and if (as many believe) a great future be in store for Schubert in this country, let us acknowledge our obligations to the joint exertions of my friend Mr. George Grove, and that admirable musician Mr. Manns, the Conductor of the Crystal Palace Concerts. Mr. Charles Halle's efforts have also powerfully aided the cause of Schubert's popularity, and Mr. Arthur Chappell, the Director of the Monday Popular Concerts, has been indefatigable in bringing forward his Quartetts, Quintetts, Octett, and others of his splendid chamber compositions. These gentlemen have done much to redeem us from that vexatious conservatism which persists in ignoring the claims of more than one great musician, and eliminating from our musical creeds such men as Bach, Cherubini, and Schubert. It would be impertinent in me, a humble worshipper of an art I imperfectly understand, to attempt to ascertain Schubert's exact position in the rank of great composers. Rhapsody is a poor substitute for criticism, and silence is more becoming when Mendelssohn, Schumann, and Liszt have recorded their opinions of the quality of Schubert's works.

A word of explanation, rather than apology, is due from me to Mr. E. Wilberforce, who has epitomised the work I have translated, and published a short memoir of Franz Schubert. I was not aware that such a work existed, until I had more than half completed my translation; but it seems to me that apart from much valuable and curious information contained in the notes, a catalogue of Schubert's works was much wanted, and that the biography in its entirety may not only be useful as a book of reference to musicians, but also interesting to the general reader.

I wish to thank Mr. Grove for his valuable contribution to this volume.[1]

A. D. C.

December 1, 1868.

---

[1] See Appendix, p. 297.

CONTENTS

OF

THE FIRST VOLUME.

——◆◆——

CHAPTER I.

(1797—1813.)

CHAPTER II.

(1814.)

CHAPTER III.

(1815.)

CHAPTER IV.

(1816.)

CHAPTER V.

(1817.)

CHAPTER VI.

(1818 AND 1824.)

CHAPTER VII.

(1819.)

CHAPTER VIII.

(1820.)

CHAPTER IX.

(1821.)

CHAPTER X.

(1822.)

CHAPTER XI.

(1823.)

ERRATA. VOL. I.

Page 29, line 6 of note; 56, line 3 of heading; 80, line 3 of heading; 303, line 11;
    313, line 13—*for* B *read* B-flat.
 ,, 128, note, *for* Josef A. *read* Josef H., and *for* Heinrich A. *read* Heinrich H.
 ,, 146, note 2, line 3, *for* H. Anselm *read* Anselm H.
 ,, 229, line 8 of heading, *for* A *read* A-flat.
 ,, 239, bottom line, *for* the original copy *read* the autograph of the Overture.
 ,, 290, note, line 2, *for* Ghost Chorus *read* Chorus of Spirits.

LIFE OF SCHUBERT.

CHAPTER I.

(1797—1813.)

SCHUBERT'S FAMILY — FRANZ PETER SCHUBERT — FRANZ SCHUBERT'S
CHILDHOOD—FIRST INSTRUCTION IN MUSIC—HIS ENTRANCE INTO THE
CONVICT—HIS FIRST COMPOSITIONS—COMPANIONS AND MODE OF LIFE
IN THE CONVICT—A LETTER TO HIS BROTHER—VISIT TO THE
THEATRE—ANTONIO SALIERI—SCHUBERT'S D MAJOR SYMPHONY, THE
CANTATA 'ZUR NAMENSFEIER'—SONGS—SCHOOL EXPERIENCES.

THE Schubert family, and the immediate ancestors of
the composer, Franz Schubert, came originally from
the province of Zukmantel, in Austrian Silesia.[1] Franz
Schubert's father was the son of a peasant, and local
magistrate of Neudorf in Moravia. In the year 1784
he came to Vienna to study, and his brother Carl, at
that time a school-teacher in the Leopoldstadt suburb,
admitted him as an assistant. Two years afterwards he
was appointed schoolmaster in the parish 'Zu den heil.
14 Nothhelfern,' in the Lichtenthal suburb.[2]

---

[1] For information respecting Schubert's family and connections I am
indebted partly to the written statements of Ferdinand Schubert, and
partly to conversations with Madame Therese Schneider (the musician's
sister) and Anton Schubert.

[2] The school-house was No. 10 (now No. 12) in the Säulengasse, on

B

His reputation as an efficient teacher was considerable, and his school was one of the most frequented
amongst those set apart for the poor of the district.
At the age of nineteen he married Elisabeth Fitz, a
Silesian, three years older than himself, and at that
time in service at Vienna as a cook.   The union was
blessed with fourteen children, of whom only five,
namely, Ignaz, Ferdinand, Carl, Franz, and Therese
survived.   A year after his wife's death, in 1812, Franz
Schubert the elder married Anna Klayenbök, the
daughter of a Viennese artisan, and five children were
born of this marriage, all of whom, with one exception,
survived. Of the children by the first marriage Therese,
widow of Mathias Schneider, a teacher in the suburb
of St. Ulrich in Vienna, alone survives ; of those by the
second, Andreas, an accountant, and Anton (under the
ecclesiastical name of Hermann), a prebendary of the
Schotten Chapter at Vienna, are still living.[1]

the Himmelpfortgrund. It belonged to Schubert's father, and is now
the property of Georg and Therese Schreder, dairy-house keepers.
The shape and arrangement of the rooms still point to the habits of
their former occupants.   The elder Schubert lived and kept his school
there until 1817 or 1818, when he undertook the mastership of the
parish-school in the Rossau.

   [1] The eldest of the brothers, Ignaz, a schoolmaster in the Rossau,
died in the year 1844 ; Ferdinand, director of the head preparatory
school of St. Anna at Vienna, in 1859 ; and Carl, a landscape-painter
and writing-master, in 1855.   Franz Schubert's half-sisters Marie (un-
married) and Josefa, the wife of Bitthan, a tutor at Vienna, died, the
former in 1834, the latter in 1861; his father died on July 9, 1830, and
his step-mother in January 1860.   The Schubert family were well

Franz Peter Schubert, the youngest of the four sons before alluded to as the issue of the first marriage, was born January 31, 1797, at Vienna, in the suburb of Himmelpfortgrund, in the parish of Lichtenthal.[1]

His early years of childhood and boyhood were passed at home, where he remained until he was eleven years old. Under the eyes of his parents, and surrounded by his brothers and sisters,[2] he lived on in the circumstances, more or less narrow, which are usually incidental to the existence of a schoolmaster blessed with a numerous family.

known as schoolmasters; Franz himself did not escape the hereditary *rôle* of tutor and pedagogue. Several of his younger relatives have adopted the same course of life.

[1] A baptismal certificate bearing date January 3, 1827, and taken from the registers of the parish 'Zu den heil. 14 Nothhelfern,' in the Lichtenthal, affirms that 'Franz Schubert, the lawfully begotten son of Franz Schubert, schoolmaster, and his wife Elisabeth, both of the Catholic religion, was born at Himmelpfortgrund, No. 72, and baptized as a Catholic in this church on February 1, 1797, by the 'Cooperator' Johann Wanzka, in the presence of Herr Carl Schubert, acting as sponsor.' The house (now the property of Madame Barbara Leithner) where he was born bears the sign of 'zum rothen Krebsen' (the Red Crab), and is now No. 54, at the higher end of the main street leading to the Nussdorf lines. Over the entrance-door there is a memorial tablet of gray marble, bearing the inscription: 'The house in which Franz Schubert was born;' on the right side there is a lyre, and on the left a wreath of laurel, with the date of the birth in relief. The inauguration ceremony connected with this memorial, erected by the 'Männergesang Verein' at Vienna, and executed by the sculptor Wasserburger, took place on October 7, 1858. A side street leading into the Nussdorferstrasse (formerly called Brunngasse) now bears the name of Schubertgasse, in honour of the composer.

[2] Of all the family circle, Ferdinand, senior to Franz by three years,

His fondness for music was remarkable in his very earliest years, and needed but small inducements to show itself. According to his sister Therese, the boy contracted a warm friendship for a joiner's apprentice, a namesake and a relative, who often took him on a visit to a pianoforte warehouse. Upon the instruments in the warehouse and an old worn-out piano at home the child studied his first exercises without any master to guide him; and when, later—at the age of seven— he began a course of regular instruction, it soon became evident that he had anticipated and mastered the principles which his master proposed to teach him.

The following passage occurs in his father's memoirs: —' In his fifth year I prepared him for his elementary lessons, and in his sixth I sent him to school, where he became distinguished invariably as the first of his compeers. From early childhood he delighted in companionship, and was never happier than when at his play-hours in a circle of merry schoolfellows. In his eighth year I taught him the rudiments of violin play-

---

was pre-eminently the one most closely attached to Franz in after life. It was Ferdinand who closed his eyes. Ferdinand Schubert, born in 1794, was appointed, in the year 1809, assistant-teacher at the Orphan Home in Vienna; actual teacher in 1816; in 1820 precentor in Altlerchenfeld; in 1824 master at the preparatory school of St. Anna in Vienna; and in 1851 director of that Institution. He was an accomplished musician, and wrote several sacred compositions for the church, besides theoretical works on music. The rich musical treasures bequeathed by Franz remained for a long time in his possession, and after their owner's death, in 1859, were finally bequeathed to his nephew Dr. Eduard Schneider, of Vienna.

ing, and practised with him till he could play easy
duetts very tolerably; after that I sent him for singing-
lessons to Michael Holzer, choir-master in Lichtenthal.
This gentleman assured me often, with tears in his
eyes, that he had never had such a pupil. "If ever I
wished to teach him anything new," he used to say, "I
found he had already mastered it. Consequently I
cannot be said honestly to have given him any lessons
at all; I merely amused myself, and looked at my
pupil with mute astonishment."'

When Holzer heard him extemporise on a given subject, the master would exclaim in rapture, 'He has
harmony at his fingers' ends!' Holzer gave him instruction also in pianoforte and organ playing as well as
thorough-bass.

His eldest brother, Ignaz, was very conscientious in
teaching him the elements of pianoforte playing. 'I was
amazed,' he says, 'when Franz told me, a few months
after we began, that he had no need of any further
instruction from me, and that for the future he would
make his own way. And in truth his progress in a short
period was so great that I was forced to acknowledge
in him a master who had completely distanced and out-
stripped me, and whom I despaired of overtaking.'

Franz Schubert, then, was one of those highly-favoured
natures, on whose brow, at the very threshold of life,
the genius of art had imprinted a sacred kiss; and if we
except Wolfgang Mozart—a real prodigy—at six years

of age, the writer, or rather the infantine scrawler, of a
pianoforte concerto, and at eight the composer of an
orchestral symphony—we shall probably find that in
none of the great musicians was the creative power
awakened so early, or made its way with such irresistible power, as in Franz Schubert.[1]

His brother Ferdinand affirms[2] that Schubert's first
pianoforte composition was a Fantasia for four hands,
written in 1810, and that in the following year he
wrote ' Klagegesang der Hagar,' his first song; but there
is no doubt he composed before this period songs,
pianoforte pieces, and even stringed quartetts, for some
of his vocal pieces, the precise date of which is not accu-
rately known, must be referred, from their comparative
unimportance, to a very early period of his career as a
composer.

At eleven years of age, and gifted with a fine soprano
voice, Schubert was employed as a solo singer and
violin-player in the choir attached to the parish church
of Lichtenthal. His performances, we are assured by

[1] Mozart's first symphony bears date 1764. See Köchel's catalogue.

[2] In the essays on 'The Life of Franz Schubert,' contained in the
' Neue Zeitschrift für Musik,' Numbers 33–36, vol. x., 1839. They contain a catalogue which embraces all Schubert's compositions at that
period (1839), either in the possession of Ferdinand Schubert, or in the
publishing-house of Diabelli; but it does not exhaust the entire number. The value of this catalogue consists in the fact that it is a record
of Schubert's compositions of the earliest period. In the lapse of time
these were lost, and, but for this catalogue, could no longer be verified
by their title, or known by name.

listeners who are still amongst us, were marked by correct and delicate expression. The father soon succeeded in getting his boy a situation in the Emperor's Chapel, and he became in consequence a pupil in the Convict of the town. It was in October 1808 that Franz was called on to give a proof of his ability before the two Court Capellmeisters of the period, Salieri and Eybler,[1] as well as the singing-master Körner.

When the other candidates saw the diminutive Schubert—who, after the fashion of the time, appeared in a kind of gray or whitish suit—they thought him a miller's son, and that he must succeed as a matter of course.

Schubert's singing on the occasion of his trial astonished, as might have been anticipated, his examiners; he explained any musical problem put before him so triumphantly, that his admission as a chorister in the Chapel Royal, and as a pupil in the Convict, followed as a matter of course. The bravery of a gold-bordered uniform—to the dazzling effect of which Schubert was by no means insensible—may have helped to neutralise the pain of separation from home, for the lad was now forced to take a long leave of all those who had hitherto been so closely connected with him.

[1] Josef Eybler, born in 1764 at Schwechat, near Vienna, a pupil of Albrechtsberger, was appointed a 'regens chori' in the church of the Carmelites at Vienna; in 1801 Imperial Music-teacher; in 1804 Vice-, and in 1825 full Capellmeister. He died at Vienna in 1846.

He was now a chorister-boy in the Chapel Royal;
and having acquired fair proficiency as a violin-player,
became a member of the school band, made up of
the lower boys at the Convict, whose duty it was to
study daily, and to execute the great Symphonies of
Haydn and Mozart, and subsequently Beethoven's works,
which were still regarded suspiciously as curiosities. Of
these orchestral works we may cite more particularly
some Adagios from Haydn's Symphonies and the G
minor Symphony of Mozart,[1] as having made a deep
impression on a lad whose great depth and earnestness
of character inspired him with no very friendly feelings
towards his ordinary associates, and this impression rose
to enthusiasm when he heard Beethoven's Symphonies.
His predilection for Beethoven was already very conspicuous; to Schubert, above all other artists, was the
lot assigned of emulating and soaring after that mighty
master, whom he regarded ever after as his bright ideal,
without forfeiting his artistic self-dependence.

The Symphonies of Krommer,[2] which, from their
brightness and cheerfulness, were favourites at the time

[1] 'One can hear the angels singing in that symphony,' ·he used to
say. (From Josef Spaun's 'Memoirs.')

[2] Krommer (Franz), born in the year 1759, at Kamenitz, in Moravia,
was a favourite composer at the beginning of this century. His teacher
was his uncle, a 'regens chori' in Turas, who educated him as an
organist; the rest of his musical education was the result of his own
industry and zeal.   On the strength of a good reputation as a violin-
player, he was admitted as choral director to Count Agrum, at Simon-
thurn in Hungary; afterwards he became chorus-master at Fünfkirchen,
then Capellmeister of the Caroly Regiment, finally, the Prince Grassal-

we are speaking of, found small favour with Schubert; but those of Kozeluch,[1] although musicians ran down his antiquated style, he would warmly defend in opposition to Krommer's works. His favourite overtures were Mehul's and those to the 'Zauberflöte,' and 'Figaro's Hochzeit' of Mozart.

Schubert, who was soon advanced to the post of first violin in the small orchestra, exercised a considerable influence over the band by virtue of his eminent artistic gifts and earnestness, so that the leadership of the orchestra, on occasions when the director Ruczizka could not be present, devolved on the first violin as deputy-conductor.

About this time, when Schubert was thirteen years old, his genius for composition awoke with irresistible strength; and he confided to his comrades, under the

kowitz took him to Vienna, and made him director. After his patron's death he retired into private life, and, partly by teaching, partly by the sale of his most popular compositions, realised a fair competency. After Kozeluch's death (1814) he became Kammercompositeur, and died in Vienna on January 8, 1831, having long outlived his reputation. He wrote a great deal of music, and aimed at a cheerful and simple style.

[1] Kozeluch (Leopold), born in the year 1753 at Wellwarn, died at Vienna in the year 1814. He was originally intended for a lawyer, but gave up all idea of such a profession in order to devote himself exclusively to music. In 1778 he settled in Vienna, where he was highly esteemed as a music-teacher, and taught several members of the Court and aristocracy. In 1792 he succeeded Mozart as Imperial Kammercompositeur. He wrote a great deal of music in various styles, but his works are now all forgotten. His daughter Katharina, afterwards Madame Cibbini, and woman of the bedchamber in the royal household, was famous for her pianoforte playing.

promise of secrecy, that he frequently put his thoughts upon paper. These musical fancies flowed from him in abundance, and for want of music-paper he was frequently unable to preserve them. Schubert's means were not adequate to purchase this luxury: a friendly hand supplied him,[1] and the consumption was something extraordinary.

Sonatas, masses, songs, operas—nay, even symphonies —are vouched for as having been finished at this period, and the majority of these works he discarded as mere sketches and exercises.

We have already stated that, in the April of the year 1810, Franz wrote a grand Fantasia for four hands (the so-called 'Corpse Fantasia'). This was followed in 1811 and 1813 by two other less ambitious fantasias. The first-mentioned work is extended over thirty-two closely-written sides, and contains a dozen pieces differing in character from one another, and each of them ending in a different key from that in which the piece opens. The pianoforte variations which he played to his father as the first specimen of his composition already bore the stamp of individuality.[2] In the year 1811 he wrote the songs 'Hagar's Klage,' 'Der Vatermörder,' several instrumental pieces,[3] and the second Fantasia for the pianoforte.

[1] No doubt that of Josef Spaun.

[2] Ferdinand Schubert. 'From Franz Schubert's Life,' 1839.

[3] According to Ferdinand Schubert's catalogue, a quintett overture composed for Ferdinand Schubert, and a stringed quartett.

'Hagar's Klage' is noticeable as being the first song of importance that Schubert composed.[1]

He wrote this song at the age of fourteen (whilst still at the Convict), on March 30, 1811, and attracted Salieri's attention to such a degree that the master at once secured the further development of the boy's rare gifts by getting him instruction in thorough-bass. This lengthy and plaintive composition is extended over no less than twenty-eight pages, and is divided into several parts entirely distinct from one another in key and rhythm. It contains two short recitatives. This work certainly suffers from its fragmentary character; the vocal intervals are at times forced, the sequences harsh, and the pianoforte accompaniment here and there reminding the hearer of Zumsteg and Mozart. Still, the work viewed as a whole has a value of its own, and never fails to make an impression when well executed by competent singers. There are some passages which breathe unmistakably the spirit of Schubert, and from these one catches, almost imperceptibly, the rustling of the wings of his genius. This song has never been engraved.[2]

---

[1] This song begins with a Largo in E-flat major $\frac{3}{4}$, to the words:—

Hier am Hügel heissen Sandes sitz' ich,
Und mir gegenüber liegt mein sterbend Kind, &c.

[2] Copies of 'Hagar's Klage,' and all the songs and part-songs that followed, are, with scarcely an exception, in the Witteczek collection (now in the possession of Herr Hofrath Freiherr Josef von Spaun, in Vienna), and, generally speaking, bear the date of their origin.

The second vocal composition bears the name of 'Der Vatermörder,' a parable[1] (author anonymous). It bears date December 26, 1811. This, too, viewed as a whole, is a remarkable effort; but 'Hagar's Klage' is the larger, more ambitious, and more valuable work of the two.

It is curious that in the list of songs there is but a single one the date of which can be ascribed to the year 1812. This is the 'Klagelied'[2] by Rochlitz, a slight and commonplace work. But church and instrumental music are all the more numerously represented.[3]

In considering these active mental efforts of a lad just entering his fifteenth year, we may fairly conjecture that in and out of school-hours he was more engaged in filling sheets of paper with musical sketches than in annotating the lectures of the professors and working

---

[1] Herr Spina, of Vienna, possesses the MSS.

[2] This is contained in Op. 131. Schubert certainly composed several songs in this year; the originals of these would give, like all his other compositions, the month and day on which he wrote them : he used to make a note on his larger works of the exact time he began and ended them.

[3] These are chronicled in Ferdinand Schubert's catalogue thus :— A Salve Regina and Kyrie (engraved); a Sonata for pianoforte, violin, and cello ; two stringed Quartetts (in B-flat and C); a Quartett Overture (in B-flat); Andante and Variations (in E-flat) ; an Orchestral Overture (in D); and thirty Minuetts and Trios, composed for his brother Ignaz, which were so much admired by Dr. Anton Schmidt, a friend of Mozart, and a first-rate violinist, that he exclaimed, 'If these works are written by a mere child, there's the stuff in him to make a master such as few have been.' These minuetts were lent about to people and lost, and Schubert, spite of oft-repeated entreaties, could never be prevailed on to write them down again from memory.

at his themes and exercises. This was the case. He composed secretly during school-hours, and wrote for the Thursday concerts given by the pupils orchestral overtures and symphonies, which were played then and there as opportunity offered. The attention of the higher powers was drawn to this diversion of Schubert's in the written reports made by the masters to the visiting committee, and as his musical progress was specially commended, it was accompanied by a more qualified account of his improvement in the ordinary branches of learning.[1]

Here, by way of preface, we may mention the names of some persons who, although of a different age to Schubert, were his contemporaries in the Convict, and several of whom, in after times, continued on intimate terms with their friend, who had become since their

---

[1] Schubert is said to have received good testimonials only in his first year's course at school; in the following years he was obliged to submit to re-examinations. The curator of the Institution at that time was Josef Carl Count Dietrichstein; regularly ordained priests, of the Order of the Piarists, gave lectures; the director was Innocenz Lang, a doctor by diploma, and rector of the Academic church; the vice-directorship was filled (from the year 1811) by Franz Schönberger. The preachers were Markus Haas, Andreas Platzer (1812), and Georg Kugelmann (1813); catechist Egid Weber and Josef Tranz (from 1811). Pius Strauch and Mathias Rebel taught the two lower classes, Alois Vorsix the upper. The other professors were Vincenz Kritsch and Benedikt Lamb (poetry), Amadäus Brizzi and Josef Walch (mathematics), Benedikt Rittmannsberger (geography and history), Josef Lehr (writing), Leopold Baille and Carl Bernard (French), Carl von Molira (Italian), Johann Votter and Böttner (drawing). Gottfried Kerschbaumer officiated as inspector.

old school-days an illustrious composer. These Convict contemporaries, if not actually 'form-fellows,' were Josef Spaun, Josef Kenner,[1] Leopold Ebner,[2] Josef Kleindl,[3] Max Weisse,[4] Franz Müllner, Carl Rueskäfer,[5] the poet Johann Senn, Benedict Randhartinger,[6] Johann Baptist Wisgrill,[7] Anton Holzapfel, and Albert Stadler. Of these gentlemen we may cite Spaun, Stadler, Senn, and Holzapfel as being more intimate with Schubert than the others.

Josef Spaun (at the present time Frh. v. Spaun) was, in the early and latter days of Schubert's life, one of the musician's truest and most disinterested friends. Schubert was his junior by nine years, and was indebted to his older schoolfellow for presents of music-paper and many acts of kindness.[8]

---

[1] Kenner, who in the year 1816 left the Convict, became subsequently Magistratsrath at Linz, and in 1854 a district overseer at Ischl, where he now enjoys his pension. He was also versed in the belles-lettres, and Schubert set several of his songs to music.

[2] Ebner still lives as Cameralrath in Innsbruck.

[3] Kleindl, Rath of the Supreme Court in Vienna.

[4] Weisse, the present professor and advocate.

[5] Carl Rueskäfer, Under-Secretary of State, now Reichsrath in Vienna.

[6] Randhartinger, born at Ruprechtshofen in the year 1802, a fellow-pupil with Schubert and pupil of Salieri, became, in 1832, chief tenor in the Chapel Royal. He was made Vice-Hofcapellmeister in 1844, and succeeded Assmayer in 1862 as Hofcapellmeister at Vienna.

[7] Wisgrill, afterwards a doctor and professor, died 1851.

[8] The following passage is taken from a memorandum of Spaun's:— 'Schubert, at that time poor and neglected, was for weeks and months supported by a friend at a small tavern. This friend often shared his

During his musical career, and when separated by long distances, his early school-friend Spaun repeatedly showed proofs of his sincere regard and esteem for the musician whose artistic powers had developed so wonderfully, and the two friends kept up an animated and constant correspondence until the musician's death. There are many proofs existing of Schubert's great affection for Spaun.[1]

Albert Stadler, (born in Steyr in the year 1794), now member of the Town Council, and living on a pension in Vienna, migrated in the year 1812 from the Kremsmünsterstift to the Convict, where he remained up to 1815, and in 1817 finished the course of his studies in jurisprudence. He was fond of music and poetry,[2] was a pianoforte-player and composer, and witnessed the origin and progress of nearly all the compositions written by Schubert at this period, and these works he was in the habit of copying for himself as quickly as possible. After finishing his studies, Stadler practised as a provincial barrister in Steyr, and in the Easter of 1821 was appointed a legal adviser to the magistrates at Linz. When Schubert, in 1819 and

room and bed with him.' Spaun himself is, without doubt, the friend here referred to.

[1] Schubert dedicated to him the Sonata Op. 78, and several songs.

[2] Of Stadler's poems, Schubert set to music a dramatic interlude, 'Fernando' (1815), the song 'Lieb Minna' (1816), a second song for Josefine Koller (1820), and a Cantata in honour of Vogl (1819).

1825, visited Upper Austria, the two old school-com-
rades met at Steyr and Steyeregg, where they passed a
happy time together at the houses of the Kollers and
Paumgartners, as well as at the castle of Count Weis-
senwolf in Steyeregg.

Anton Holzapfel was already installed at the Convict
when Stadler first entered there, and they finished
their course of studies in jurisprudence at the same
time. Like Schubert, he was originally placed on the
foundation in the Convict after leaving the Emperor
Ferdinand's school for chorister-boys, which was called
' am Hof.' Holzapfel could boast of being the oldest
of Schubert's school-friends, and it was he who, in all
the ardour of grateful enthusiasm, took possession of
those early songs, which had as yet advanced no farther
in the world than the threshold of the Convict. He
was reputed a sound musician and violoncello-player,
and had, in addition, a fine tenor voice. He was a
sincere and lasting friend to Schubert.[1]

Johann Michael Senn (born April 1, 1795, at Pfunds,
in the Tyrol) was, like several other sons of Tyrolese
guides, a contemporary of Schubert at the Convict.
He was a gifted, impetuous lad.[2] In the year 1814

---

[1] After finishing his studies he began an official life in the courts of
justice at Vienna (his native place); he became subsequently Magistratsrath, and has for several years past been living on a pension at the
castle of Aistersheim, near Wels.

[2] Kupelwieser's portrait of Senn gives him a very attractive head

or 1815, having made himself conspicuous as a ringleader in an *émeute*, which broke out in the school, in revenge for an imprisonment inflicted on one of his comrades, he forfeited his place as a foundation member. Of an obstinate, unyielding disposition, and satisfied of the injustice of the punishment, he preferred dismissal from the school rather than do penance for his fault. In the year 1823, Senn devoted himself to the profession of arms, and became an officer in the regiment ' Tiroler Kaiserjäger.' In later years his life took a more melancholy turn. At war with circumstances, with everything about him, and the censors of the press, an embittered misanthrope, without friends or support, he at last took to drinking, and died in 1857, alone and forgotten, in the military hospital at Innsbruck. Of his poems (which were published by Wagner in 1838) Schubert set the ' Schwanenlied.' Senn dedicated to his friend a sonnet headed ' To S., the Tone-poet,' and to the poet J. Mayerhofer, of whose connection with Schubert we shall speak hereafter, two sonnets headed ' In Memory of M., the Poet.' It seems that Senn did not become intimately acquainted with Schubert at the Convict, but in later years under Spaun's or Schober's roof.

There was unusual musical zeal and vitality in the Convict at that time. Dr. Josef Hauer (Surgeon to

and delicate features. Senn was for some time tutor to Eduard von Sonnleithner, and also instructor in Dr. Gredler's family at Vienna.

C

the Factory 'at the Oed'), who became a member in
the year 1816, speaks in the following language on the
subject in a letter written to me:—'I did not become
personally acquainted with Schubert until the year
1825, and we grew very much attached to each other.
I am at a loss whether I should ascribe our sympathy
to any musical capacities of my own, or to a more
probable cause—the fact of my having received, like
Schubert, my education as a chorister-boy in the
Convict. Here was a practical school for Schubert.
Every evening we had performances of symphonies,
quartetts, and vocal pieces. Besides this, his taking a
part in classical church music was not without practical
results. I remember meeting with overtures and symphonies by Schubert, which we tried to perform, and
the separate parts were put before me as Schubert's
handwriting. I myself copied a volume of his songs,
and some of these I never found, in later years, either
in print or manuscript. Unhappily, I have lost all
these treasures.'

In a treatise by Kenner,[1] there is a passage referring
to the same fact. It runs thus:—'In the instrumental
practice-room, during leisure hours after dinner, Albert
Stadler, a composer, and Anton Holzapfel, his form-
fellow, used to play Beethoven's and Zumsteg's works,
and on such occasions I represented the audience. The
room was never heated, and the cold fearful. Occa-

---

[1] Herr Stadler is my authority for this paragraph.

sionally Spaun joined the party, and Schubert also, after he left the Convict. Stadler played the pianoforte, Holzapfel sang ; occasionally Schubert sat down at the piano.' Leopold Ebner did not become intimately acquainted with Schubert until after the latter had left the Convict; for Schubert, off and on for a couple of years, used to visit his friends at the Institute, and run through with them his latest songs and pianoforte works.'

Holzapfel and Stadler often assisted at the social music in the elder Schubert's house. In the orchestra of the Convict, Holzapfel played the violoncello, Kleindl and Spaun violins, Senn blew the horn, and Randhartinger beat the drum.

It is plain from the following extract from a letter written to his brother (most likely Ferdinand), and dated November 24, 1812, that Franz, during his noviciate at the Convict, was, in the matter of the common necessaries of life, by no means on a bed of roses.[1] The language of this letter, plain-spoken but good tempered withal, shows the peculiarities of the lad now entering his sixteenth year. The poor pupil at the Convict pours out his heart in the following petition :—

' I'll come at once to the point, and unburthen my heart's secret, and not detain you by beating about the bush or circuitous talk. I've been thinking a good long

[1] Taken from an essay of Ferdinand Schubert's for the ' Neue Zeit-schrift für Musik,' 1839, and headed ' Relics.'

time about my position, and found that it's very well on the whole, but that in some respects it can be improved; you know from experience that one can often enjoy eating a roll and an apple or two, and all the more when one must wait eight hours and a half after a poor dinner for a meagre supper. This wish has haunted me so often and so perseveringly that at last, *nolens volens*, I must make a change. The few groschen my father gave me are all gone to the devil;—what am I to do the rest of the time?

'"They that hope in Thee shall not be ashamed" (Matt. ii. 4). So I thought. Supposing you advance me monthly a few kreuzers. You would never miss it, whilst I should shut myself up in my cell and be quite happy. As I said, I rely on the words of the Apostle Matthew, who says: "Let him that hath two coats give one to the poor." Meanwhile I trust you will listen to the voice, which unceasingly appeals to you to remember your loving, hoping, poverty-stricken—and once again I repeat poverty-stricken—brother Franz.'

During his school-days at the Convict, Schubert was often at his father's house, for on holidays his stringed quartetts (taken scarcely dry from his desk) were played off-hand at the meetings which were held usually on Sunday afternoons for quartett practice. Schubert the elder played the violoncello, Ferdinand the first, Ignaz the second violin, and Franz the tenor. The most sensitive performer of the party was the youngest.

If the smallest mistake was made, he looked at the
offender sometimes smilingly, sometimes sternly; if
the father made a blunder, he passed over the mistake
the first time, but if it occurred again, he would smile
and say quite timidly, 'Father, there must be a
mistake somewhere'—a hint always accepted without
contradiction. These practices were a great delight to
the performers, and gave the composer the advantage
of satisfying himself of the effect produced by his own
compositions on players and listeners.

During the holidays Franz used to go to the theatre.
Of the operas given in those days one especially interested him, the 'Schweizerfamilie,' by Weigl. It was
the first he ever heard given in its entirety, and Vogl
and Milder both sang in it.[1] Cherubini's 'Medea,'

[1] Anna Milder was born on December 31, 1785, at Constantinople,
where her father (Felix), a native of Salzburg, was in service as confectioner to the Austrian ambassador, Baron Herbert. In 1790 the
family left Constantinople, and withdrew to Bucharest; afterwards, on
the breaking out of the war between Austria and the Porte, they went
to Pesth, and finally to Vienna. Anna received her first instructions in
singing from Tull, a village schoolmaster in Hütteldorf; afterwards
S. Neukomm (of Salzburg) gave her lessons, and introduced her to his
master, J. Haydn. Introduced to the stage by Shikaneder, she made
her first appearance, in 1803, in the part of Juno in Süssmayer's
'Spiegel von Arkadien,' and was received with great applause. It was
for her that Cherubini wrote his 'Faniska,' and Beethoven his
'Fidelio,' Weigl the 'Waisenhaus' and the 'Schweizerfamilie.' In
the year 1810 she became the wife of Hauptmann, a jeweller at
Munich; in 1812 she made her first artistic tour, and in 1816 concluded
an engagement at Berlin, which lasted up to 1829. From that period
she only appeared at concerts given in the great cities; at Vienna, for

Boildieu's ' Johann von Paris,' Isouard's ' Aschenbrödl,' were all favourites with him; and he delighted in Gluck's 'Iphigenia auf Tauris,' in which Milder and Vogl played the chief parts. This last-mentioned opera always delighted him, and on account of its grand simplicity and elevation of style, he preferred it to all other works of the operatic school.

These visits to the theatre explain to some extent the fact of Schubert's extraordinary self-reliance, in applying himself at a very early period to musical efforts of a dramatic kind; for as early as the year 1813 we find him taking in hand a setting of Kotzebue's magic opera 'Des Teufels Lustschloss,' a work he completed in the following year. In the year 1815 he wrote several dramatic works and cantatas, to which we shall refer in the proper place.

Of those musicians who influenced Schubert's musical education (if in reality anyone but Beethoven can strictly be said to have had any influence at all), Anton Salieri, the Court Capellmeister in Schubert's youthful days, has a claim to the very first rank amongst Schubert's early advisers, for it was Salieri who first recognised the rare gifts of the young pupil, and who

instance, as late as the year 1836, she sang Schubert's ' Hermann und Thusnelda.' During her residence in Berlin she kept up a correspondence with Schubert, and to this reference will be made hereafter. ' Suleika's (second) Song' is dedicated to her, as well as 'Der Hirt auf dem Felsen,' composed by Schubert at her own suggestion. Milder died at Berlin in the year 1838.

for a period of several years gave him lessons in the art of composition. His attention having been roused by the ' Hagar's Klage ' and some stringed quartetts, he handed the young composer over to Ruczizka for lessons in thorough-bass. But when the lessons began, the old farce was once again re-enacted, for the master pronounced his pupil omniscient. 'He has learned everything,' said he, 'and God has been his teacher.' The result of this report was that Salieri took to Schubert more warmly than ever, and made himself responsible for the further development of these rare gifts. As Salieri plays a prominent part in the days of Schubert's pupilage, we may here give a short abstract of his life, which will throw light on his intimate connection with Schubert.

Salieri (Antonio), born in the year 1750, at Legnago, a fortified town in the Venetian territory, was the son of a well-to-do merchant, who had him early instructed in Latin and in music by his eldest son Franz.[1] At the age of sixteen, he had the misfortune to lose both his parents. A friend of his family, Giovanni Mocenigo, took him to Venice, where he applied himself with increased zeal to the studies he had already begun. Florian Gassmann,[2] a Court Capellmeister, who had

[1] See 'Life of Salieri,' by Mosel.

[2] Gassmann (Florian Leopold), born at Brüx in Bohemia, in 1729, played the harp, and sang exceedingly well, when only a boy of twelve years old. To escape being apprenticed to a trade, for which his father intended him, he ran away from home when he was but thirteen years

come to Venice to write an opera for the Fenice Theatre,
happened to meet him, treated him like an adopted
child, and continued his friend and benefactor for the
remainder of his days.

In June 1766, Salieri, accompanied by Gassmann,
came to Vienna, where, nearly six decades later, he was
destined to find his last resting-place. His industry
at this time was unremitting. Gassmann read with him
the contrapuntal studies in Fux's 'Gradus ad Parnassum;'[1] another master taught him French and German, but with indifferent success; his other subjects
were Latin and Italian poetry, elocution and verse
writing. Thus prepared, he was introduced to the
Emperor Joseph II., for whose chamber concerts he
worked at vocal and instrumental compositions, besides
sacred music of all kinds. In 1770 he composed his

old, and fled to Carlsbad, where he made a good deal of money by his
music. From Carlsbad he went to Venice, to study under Father
Martini. Two years afterwards he became organist at a convent, and
his church and stage compositions were soon in fashion. In 1763 he
accepted an invitation to Vienna, as ballet-composer. In 1766 he was
once more in Venice, by consent of the Emperor, who had nominated
him Court and private organist. He wished to bring out at Venice
and in Milan his own operas. From Venice he took the young Salieri
with him to Vienna. In 1771 (after Reuter's death) he became Court
Capellmeister, and in 1772 founded the still-existing Institution for the
support of widows of native musicians. Gassmann died in 1772, from
the effects of a fall from a carriage. Mozart himself used to speak with
admiration of his church compositions.

[1] Fux, born in the year 1660, in Upper Steiermark, became Court Capellmeister in 1715. He wrote music for the church, chamber, and stage,
and compiled the 'Gradus ad Parnassum.' He died in Vienna in 1741.

first opera, 'Le Donne letterate,' which won him great applause. This was followed in the course of the next six years by a dozen operas and operettas. In 1778 he passed some time in Italy, where he launched five operas for the theatres at Venice, Milan, and Rome. In 1781 he was commissioned by the Emperor to write the German opera 'Der Rauchfangkehrer,' which was received with great applause. By Gluck's recommendation he wrote several dramatic works for Paris, and conducted them himself in the French capital. Of these works the 'Tarare' of Beaumarchais, afterwards called 'Axur, King of Ormus,' arranged for the Italian stage, and soon afterwards a boasted ornament of the German theatres, was reckoned his masterpiece. It was this very opera which Schubert himself applauded.

After the death of the Court Capellmeister Bono,[1] Salieri succeeded to the place, the duties of which he discharged with the greatest zeal for the remainder of his life. In the year 1789, the Emperor Leopold II. relieved him of his conductorship at the Opera, which fell into the hands of Capellmeister Weigl. He then applied himself with increased industry to the composition of operas, cantatas, songs, symphonies, &c. On June 16, 1816, he celebrated his fiftieth year's service. Franz Schubert took part in the jubilee, of which we shall speak in detail.

From this period he ceased to appear in public as a

---

[1] Born in 1710 at Vienna, where he died in 1788.

composer, for he felt that the taste of the time had deviated far from what he considered to be the orthodox standard. In his capacity as Vice-president of the Institute of Artists,[1] and afterwards as head of the Academy, from which society originated the National Conservatory, ho had always a wide field of activity before him, and he found an agreeable relief in employing much of his spare time during the week in giving lessons gratuitously to pupils of both sexes. These lessons were in singing, thorough-bass, and the art of composition.

His strength failed him after he had attained his seventieth year : in 1824 he asked for his pension, and died on May 7, 1825, at Vienna, where he was buried.

Salieri's reputation amongst his contemporaries was not merely that of a deep-thinking and prolific composer, with a considerable gift of melody and invention, but he was highly esteemed as a kind and amiable man.[2] Friendly, cheerful, humorous, full of anecdote, a handsome man with expressive eyes, a quick temper, but very easily reconciled, such is the sketch given of him by Friedrich v. Rochlitz,[3] who accompanied him

---

[1] In the year 1824 Eybler, who succeeded Salieri as Hofcapellmeister, was Secretary of the Institute, of which Count Kuefstein, afterwards Count Moriz Dietrichstein, was President in the year 1818.

[2] He wrote some forty operas, twelve oratorios, cantatas, masses, a requiem, four concertos for different instruments, a symphony (1776), overtures, serenades, ballet music, and dramatic music in every variety of style.

[3] In a work headed ' To the Lovers of Music,' Leipsic, 1832, vol. iv.

to Vienna in the year 1822. He never learnt the
German language, and in the hurry of conversation
would interlard his talk with French and Italian words,
alleging as an excuse for his ignorance that he had
only lived in Germany half a century.

Salieri lived in the heart of the city, at a house of his
own in the Seilergasse. Thither (from the year 1813 to
1817) young Schubert used to come, with his musical
exercises in a roll under his arm, to submit his work to
his master's eye, and receive instructions how to write,
if he would aspire to a good position as a composer.[1]

Salieri did not agree with Schubert's method of composing, much less with the selections of poetry which
he chose for setting to music; he required of Franz to
give over attempting to set Göthe's and Schiller's verses,
to husband his resources of melody until they were
riper, and adopt the 'stanze' of the Italian writers for
his usual practice;[2] still he fully acknowledged the
rare talents of his pupil, and on one occasion, when
Schubert surprised him by a variety of compositions,
he exclaimed, 'That fellow is up to everything; he is

Towards Mozart, whose superiority Salieri instinctively felt, he be-
haved in a low intriguing manner, with the hope of hindering his
popularity. (O. Jahn, 'Mozart,' vol. iii. p. 61.)

[1] At that time the genial jovial Schubert might be seen stealing into
a wine-shop near Salieri's lodgings after the lesson was over. There he
would sip his glass, and chat for hours with his old comrade Franz
Doppler (who told me the story).

[2] A. Stadler, of Vienna, has one of these exercises, bearing date 1813.

a genius! It doesn't matter what it is, songs, masses, operas, stringed quartetts, he can compose in all styles.' His pride and delight in Schubert's first Mass (in F) we shall have occasion to allude to hereafter.[1]

There can be no doubt that Schubert derived from Salieri's teaching those advantages which every able pupil would receive from the practical hints of an artist, able and self-reliant, whose experience of his profession ranged over half a century. But the intellectual bent and taste of a teacher who clung obstinately to the traditions of the old Italian school were entirely at variance with those of Schubert, whose winged fancy hurried him along through the realms of German romanticism, and spurned all artificial checks and impediments. That these two men should run in couples for a long time together was not to be thought of. Schubert was already self-reliant; his path lay clear before him and the mission he was to fulfil. From Salieri he had as little more to learn as Beethoven had before Schubert's time, for Beethoven too had. for some time been to school for the study of dramatic music.[2]

---

[1] Herr Josef Hüttenbrenner told me a curious story of Schubert, who, when Salieri told him that he was competent to write an opera, stayed away from his lessons for several weeks, and then begged his astonished master to examine the entire score of 'Des Teufels Lustschloss' (1813-1814), which he placed before him.

[2] It is well known that Albrechtsberger, Beethoven's teacher in thorough-bass, and Salieri, his teacher in operatic composition, said of

We are not concerned to know the particular motives assigned by Schubert's contemporaries for his abrupt departure from his old master;[1] the separation was unavoidable, and the gigantic strides of Schubert's musical development were the natural consequence of this emancipation. The pupil's gratitude and respect for his master's memory was lifelong, as we gather from passages in his diary, and the fact of Schubert setting to music the ode written in honour of Salieri's jubilee festival. With regard to Schubert's musical activity in the year 1813, we must refer to the sketches of a partly written opera, besides a symphony, a cantata, some songs, and an unusually large number of part-songs and canons

The Symphony in D (the first of the eight entire or partly finished symphonies by Schubert)[2] was written in honour either of the birth or baptismal day festival of Innocenz Lang, the Convict Director, and was performed by the pupils of the Institute. It con-

their pupil, that he would learn to his cost hereafter what his disbelief in their teaching led him to discredit.

[1] For example, Herr Doppler (foreman in the musical warehouse of Herr Spina) declares Schubert's chief reason for breaking with Salieri to have arisen from the fact that the latter cut out and corrected al those passages in Schubert's Mass in B which reminded him of Haydn or Mozart. Schubert, he says, came to him (Doppler) with the altered Mass, and flung it down on the table in a passion, declaring he would have nothing more to do with Salieri as a teacher. Others, on the contrary, are of opinion that Salieri's proposals to Schubert to write music for the Italian ' stanze' induced him to quit his master.

[2] Ferdinand Schubert mentions the sketch of a ninth, which he gave to Mendelssohn in 1846.

sists of four movements,[1] and is written unmistakably
on the model of the old masters. The Cantata contains only one terzett (for two tenors and a bass)—'In
honour of the father's name-day festival. The words,
with guitar obligato accompaniment, composed by
F. Schubert, on September 27, 1813.' The terzett, a
simple tuneful melody, begins with a short Andante
(A major $\frac{12}{8}$) and ends with a lively Allegretto ($\frac{6}{8}$), expressive of the son's happiness and congratulations.[2]

[1] Introduction (Adagio) and Allegro vivace $\frac{4}{4}$, Andante G major $\frac{6}{8}$,
Minuett and Trio (Allegro D major), Finale Allegro vivace D major $\frac{4}{4}$.
The manuscript, dated October 28, 1813, is in the possession of Dr.
Schneider, at Vienna. At the end of the score are the words, 'Finis et
Fine.'

[2] Schubert's poem runs thus :—

(*Andante*)   Ertöne Leyer
     Zur Festesfeier.
     Apollo steig hernieder,
     Begeistre unsere Lieder.

(*Allegretto*)   Lange lebe unser Vater Franz,
     Lange währe seiner Tage Chor
     Und in ewig schönem Flor
     Blühe seines Lebens Kranz.

     Wonnelachend umschwebe die Freude
     Seines zürnenden Glückes Lauf,
     Immer getrennt vom trauerndem Leide
     Nehm' ihn Elisiums Schatten auf.
     Endlos wiedertöne holde Leyer—
     Bringt des Jahres Raum die Zeit zurück—
     Sanft und schön an dieses Tages Feier
     Ewig währe Vater Franzen's Glück.

The MS., which bears this heading, 'Auf die Namensfeier meines
Vaters, September 27. 1813,' is in the possession of Dr. Schneider, with a

The canons, for the most part set to fragments of Schiller's poetry, are studies in that form of composition, and were very likely written for Schiller's schoolfellows in the Convict.[1] They are nearly all of them written for three men's voices. Hölty's 'Todtengräberlied' was beautifully set as a trio (for two sopranos and one bass). Some stringed quartetts, three Kyries, three minuetts with trio for orchestra, a third pianoforte fantasia, a pianoforte fugue,[2] and an octett[3] for wind instruments, belong to this period.

Here we close the first period of Schubert's artistic career, brief in number of years, but fruitful in the production of artistic works. It was a period of incessant, almost unconscious, creative power, during which the boy, scarce ripened into early manhood, gave on the one side full play to the riches of his inexhaustible fancy, and on the other hand still adhered to the forms of the masterpieces by the great men who preceded him. In his instrumental compositions these forms

second Namensfeier (September 27, 1815), consisting of one vocal piece, 'Du Erhabener' (an Adagio in E-flat major).

[1] The great number of canons following one after another in rapid succession reminds one of Mozart, who in one day (September 2, 1788) wrote ten, one after another. (Jahn, 'Mozart,' vol. iii.) Schiller's poem 'Elisium' is set in this style, particularly the first, second, fourth, and last strophes.

[2] The MS. is in the hands of Josef Hüttenbrenner, at Vienna.

[3] The octett (dated September 19) is written for clarionet, bassoon, trumpets, and horn, and is marked in Ferdinand Schubert's catalogue as 'Franz Schubert's Leichenfeier.' Perhaps it has reference to the funeral of Schubert's mother. I have never seen this composition.

were crude and misshapen to some extent, although evidencing rare powers, whilst the individuality and character of some of his songs showed the amazing fertility of his genius.

The succeeding years may be entitled 'Schubert's probationary period as learner,' being the time when he underwent a course of systematic teaching under Salieri, and showed his usual mental activity as a creative artist in the most opposite and varied styles of music. This educational period cannot certainly be said to resemble the strong discipline to which other great masters—Mozart and Mendelssohn, for example —submitted, and in return for which their powers harmoniously developed themselves in a continued and ever well-regulated scale of progress. Schubert's wonderfully quick development reminds one much more closely of the impetuous career of spirits more allied to his nature, such as Beethoven and Schumann; on the other hand, the well-authenticated fact that Schubert in his early days, and by his own confession in a later period of his life, applied himself zealously to the study of acknowledged masterpieces in instrumental music, disproves a widely-spread belief, that in truth he never learned anything thoroughly, and can be only regarded as a genial and 'naturalistic' composer. At all events, his earliest efforts in song revealed such a masterly and original power, that in this branch of art he may be regarded as a phenomenon hitherto unique, and certainly without a rival.

CHAPTER II.

(1814.)

SCHUBERT LEAVES THE CONVICT—HIS LIFE AT HOME—FRANZ BECOMES
ASSISTANT-TEACHER—THE MASS IN F—THERESE GROB—INSTRU-
MENTAL AND VOCAL COMPOSITIONS—THE OPERA 'DES TEUFELS
LUSTSCHLOSS'—JOHANN MAYRHOFER.

SCHUBERT'S residence at the Convict lasted from the
October of 1808 to the end of the same month in 1813,
a period of full five years. He was now approaching
his seventeenth year, an age when the 'childish
treble' usually breaks, so that his employment as a
chorister-boy necessarily came to an end. Franz was
at liberty, if he had so chosen, to continue his studies
in the higher branches of the classics, for the Emperor,
who was minutely informed of the progress of the
students, permitted him to remain at the Institute.[1]
But he was not anxious to continue his studies, espe-

---

[1] This was in consequence of a resolution framed on October 21, 1813,
which stipulated that during the vacation Schubert was to improve his
studies in the highest form or class, and consequently go through
another examination. Assuming he did this, a place on the so-called
'Merveldt' foundation was to be given him. (This was told me by
Herr Ferd. Luib.) An intimate friend of Schubert's affirmed that he
ran away from the Convict, but this story is pronounced a myth by
others of Schubert's contemporaries, and particularly A. Stadler.

cially as he would have been obliged to submit to
another examination, and he left the Institution to return once more to his father's house.

   According to Ferdinand Schubert,[1] he was summoned
on military duty; by another version of the story, his
father tried to break him of the habit of composing, with
a view to his adopting other than musical pursuits; and
both these reasons have been assigned for his devotion
for a considerable period to the art of teaching. During
the educational term, 1813–14, he studied at the school
of St. Anna, with a view to qualify himself as a tutor,
and afterwards became assistant to the lowest, the A B C
class, in his father's school. With a cordial dislike to
his duties, but a zealous and conscientious discharge of
them, he stuck to his post for three long years. It is
said that he was impatient and choleric if he had to deal
with an obstinate child.[2] Considering the claims made
upon his time during this ' Dominie Sampson ' period,
in 1815, his musical fertility seems all the more remarkable. At the very outset of his tutorial career,
he found an opportunity of distinguishing himself by
writing a sacred composition which spread his fame far
and wide, and commanded the high respect of his
musical friends, and notably that of his former master,

   [1] The day of his leaving the Convict was some time between October 26 and November 6, 1813.

   [2] His sister Therese told me that Franz was strict and ill-tempered
as a teacher, and that he often kept his hands in practice on the children's ears.

Salieri. This was the Mass in F, written for the centenary festival of the parish church of Lichtenthal, the performance of which he conducted in person on the first Sunday after the festival of Saint Theresa, Mayseder playing the first violin. The soprano part was sung by Therese Grob,[1] a singer much admired

---

[1] Therese Grob was the daughter of Heinrich Grob and his wife Therese. Heinrich at that time (1814) was dead, and his widow had a silk factory in the Lichtenthal. Schubert came to this house after leaving the Convict, attracted doubtless by the lovely voice of the youthful Therese (then about fifteen years old) and the musical talents of her brother Heinrich, a capital player on the violoncello and piano. For Therese, whose bell-like voice ranged to the upper D, Schubert wrote a 'Tantum Ergo' and a 'Salve Regina.' Heinrich Grob, during Schubert's lifetime (and even later), directed, jointly with the composer, the church music of the Lichtenthal choir; Schubert generally contenting himself with remaining in the nave, in order to hear the music to greater advantage. In this very intelligent artistic family music was much cultivated, and Schubert's Masses specially were often rehearsed previous to the performances in Lichtenthal, Grinzing, Heiligenstadt, &c., under the composer's own direction. Schubert, who was like an adopted son in the house, often brought his songs there (the first Therese ever saw was 'Süsse heilige Natur'), and besides this, he wrote for his friend Heinrich Grob, in the October of 1816, an Adagio and Rondo Concertant for the pianoforte, with violin, viola, and cello accompaniments (in the possession of Herr Spina). His intimacy with the Grob family lasted until about the year 1820, when Therese married, and the musician was drawn into other social circles. About the year 1837 Heinrich Grob changed his place of business nearer to the centre of the city, where, since his death in 1855, his widow and two sons have still carried on the firm. Therese, to whom I am indebted for these details, lives still at Vienna, hale and hearty, for more than twenty years the widow of Herr Bergmann. The family of Grob are said to possess compositions of Schubert unknown to the public, but I have never been able to get a sight of them.

by Schubert, and the member of a family to which
Schubert was very fondly attached up to the year
1820. Salieri, in great delight with his pupil's work,
embraced him after the performance was over, exclaiming, 'Franz, you are my pupil, and will do me
great honour.'[1]   The Mass[2] was soon afterwards repeated in the church of the Augustins, under circumstances which gave the performance the character of a
family festival: Franz conducted; his brother Ferdinand
played the organ; Therese Grob again sang the soprano part, and the other parts were distributed amongst
friends and acquaintances; Michael Holzer officiated as
'regens chori.'   After the festival Franz was presented
by his father with a five-octave piano.[3]   To this period
belong a 'Salve Regina'[4] for tenor; a song, 'Wer ist
wohl gross,' with chorus and band accompaniment; five
Minuetts and six 'Allemandes' set for stringed quartetts and French horns; three stringed quartetts; and a
good number of songs (ten of them set to Mathisson's

---

[1] Herr Doppler, who was present at the performance, is my authority.

[2] According to the MSS. in the hands of Dr. Schneider, at Vienna,
Schubert wrote this Mass between May 17 and July 22, 1814. The
Kyrie is dated May 17 and 18, the Gloria May 21 and 22, the
Gratias May 25 to 28, the Quoniam May 28, the Credo May 30 to
June 22, the Sanctus and Benedictus July 2 and 3, the Agnus Dei
July 7, and the Dona Nobis July 15 to 22. The Mass in F has never
been engraved.

[3] Such is Ferdinand Schubert's story. Therese Grob cannot remember this second performance.

[4] Dr. Schneider has the original manuscript. The 'Salve Regina' is
accompanied by violins, viola, hautboy, bassoon, horn, and double bass.

poems).[1]   Amongst the latter there is a song with the title 'Auf den Sieg der Deutschen,' a trivial light composition of the dance order with stringed accompaniments, written no doubt as an occasional composition with reference to the happy issue of the war against France, and most probably performed by a circle of friends.   The list ends with a grand Sonata in C minor, for four hands, but it was left unfinished.[2]

On May 15, 1814, Franz finished the magic Opera of 'Des Teufels Lustschloss,' a work in three acts, by Kotzebue, which the composer had taken in hand in the preceding year.[3]   The piece, as regards the musical part of it, is written to iambics in rhyme, but there is a great deal of spoken dialogue besides.

The following is the plot:—Oswald secretly carries off from the castle of her uncle, the Count von Schwarzberg, his niece Luitgarde, and marries her.   After a long absence he returns home with her, to settle on his property.   (Here the music begins.)   The scene represents a desolate heath; the knight's carriage is broken in two in the bad roads; attendants are looking

---

[1] The Quartetts are in B-flat and D major and C minor.   The first was given, in the year 1862, at Hellmesberger's Quartett meetings, but in an abbreviated form, and with passages in other quartetts interpolated. The parts have quite recently been engraved by Spina, who has the original manuscript.   .

[2] This composition consists of an Adagio, an Andante amoroso in B-flat, an Allegro in B-flat, and an Adagio in D-flat.   The MS. of this rather obscure work is in the possession of Herr Albert Stadler, of Vienna.

[3] Dr. Schneider has the score.

after Luitgarde, and Robert, Oswald's faithful companion, is busy looking out for accommodation for her
and the whole party.   He finds it at an inn hard by,
and thither Oswald and Luitgarde follow him.   The
hostess greets both the strangers, and engages them in
conversation.   A peasant then enters, who tells the
knight that the whole neighbourhood is bewitched by
an enchanted castle, which, judging by the nightly
apparitions, can only be the Teufel's Schloss.   Oswald
determines, spite of all warning, to break the spell, and
hurries off with Robert to the castle.   They enter an
apartment fantastically furnished with statues and a
cenotaph.   The ghost then appears.   A gigantic hand
emerges from the ground, gives Robert a blow, and
vanishes, whereat he knocks one of the statues down,
and Oswald tries to do the same with the other.   But
the second statue throws a glove at his feet, which
Oswald takes up and begins a combat, in which four
other statues, brandishing drawn swords, take part.   During the fight an Amazon, dressed in black, arises from
the cenotaph and offers her hand and heart to the
knight, intimating that his death is certain if he refuses.   Oswald, mindful of his Luitgarde, refuses the
offer, whereupon a cage emerges from the ground, and,
after enclosing Oswald, disappears again.   In the second
act we find Robert lying on the earth, and bemoaning
and calling for his master ; Luitgarde, in search of her
lover, joins him.   Judgment of death awaits Robert,

who has disappeared in a gloomy cavern. A Turkish
march is heard, followed by a chorus of virgins. The
Amazon tries once more to persuade the knight, but
even now he withstands her allurements. The cry of
vengeance is heard; Oswald is to be hurled from the
rock. The death-bell tolls, a funeral march is played,
and the bier brought forward. Men and virgins join in
chorus. An attendant calls on Oswald to forget his
bride, a slave whispers to him to pretend to give in
to the wish of the Amazon, and thus to save his life.
But the slave's treachery is discovered, and the knight
ordered, as a sign of his love for the princess, to run
through the slave with the sword. He refuses to do
this, and with the weapon in his hand, cuts his way
through every one, until he gains the summit of a
precipice. There, attacked on all sides, and no longer
able to defend himself, he throws the sword from him,
and leaps into the gulf below.

In the third act Luitgarde appears, bemoaning the
loss of her husband. Robert advances to meet her.
The suit of armour worn by Oswald comes up from
beneath in the shape of a trophy. Luitgarde rushes to
seize it, and the armour disappears. Despairing of saving
her lover, she orders Robert to return to his home,
and leave her to die. Robert, however, determines to
stay with her; and, to show his courage, he rushes at a
great gate against an old wall in the background, and
gives it some violent blows. This gate falls with a

crash, the walls also, and an executioner is discovered,
axe in hand, and near him the fatal block. A second
attendant announces to the disconsolate Luitgarde that
Oswald has been executed an hour ago. Determined
on following her lover to the grave, she climbs the
rock, lays her head on the block, and awaits the fatal
stroke.

Oswald is then brought on the scene in chains, with
his eyes bound. The bandage is withdrawn, and when
he sees Luitgarde he tears himself from the custody of
his guards, rushes to the rock, seizes the executioner,
hurls him into the abyss, and clasps his wife in his
arms. The lovers, saved with such difficulty, are now
exposed to fresh danger. Floods of water, descending
on all sides, threaten everything with destruction. The
thunder roars, the rocks are rent, and in their place beds
of roses appear, the waters recede. Count Schwarzberg now appears on the scene with his attendants, and
comforts the awe-stricken lovers with the assurance
that the whole enchantment—made up of machinery,
trap-doors, masks used by his own servants, &c.—was
his own device, and was used for the purpose of proving
Oswald's fidelity to the wife of his bosom. As he has
proved himself so brilliant a knight, she receives her
uncle's pardon.

An overture precedes the Opera[1]—a stirring, charac-

---

[1] This overture was played, probably for the first time in public, on
March 1, 1861, as an introduction to Schubert's Operetta, 'Der häus-

teristic musical episode, written in the true Schubert vein.

The first act begins with an introduction, during which Robert and the servants are busy on the stage. After an interval, they are joined by some peasants, and we have a brilliant musical ensemble. The second number, written in the strophe form, is a drinking-song for Robert, followed by a duett between Oswald and Luitgarde, an air for the latter, a quartett (Oswald, Robert, a peasant, and the hostess of the inn), a bass air for a peasant, a trio (Oswald, Robert, and the hostess), an air for the hostess, and a song for Oswald. Then comes the incantation scene and an ensemble, in which Oswald, Robert, an Amazon, and four statues take part.[1] The scene changes to an ancient temple, with the cenotaph, and the first act concludes with an air for Robert.[2]

The second act opens with a grave and appropriate introduction (D minor $\frac{4}{4}$). A chain of recitatives for Robert and Luitgarde, with an air for the former, precedes some soft music heard in the distance,[3] and this gradually swells into a full and sonorous march of Turkish music. Virgins appear with lutes, flutes, and

liche Krieg,' at a concert given at Vienna, and is the only single piece of this opera that has hitherto been given in public.

[1] The advance of the statues is accompanied by horns and trumpets.

[2] This act was completed on January 11, 1814.

[3] Andante con moto, F major, with hautboys, clarionet, horn, and bassoon accompaniments.

cymbals, accompanying their own chorus. The situation is soon changed ; a funeral march is substituted for the triumphal one, and in this the men and women both join. A finale (Oswald, the attendant, the bride, the slave, and the chorus) completes this act.[1]

The third act only contains two pieces—a trio (Oswald, Robert, Luitgarde) and a final chorus. The Opera was finished on the 14th of May, 1814. It has never been given in public. In the same year Schubert reset this curious story, and his second arrangement of the work is said to have been that with which he astonished his master, Salieri.[2]

Of the three acts, only the first and last survive, the second has been lost.[3]

Towards the end of the December of 1814, Schubert made the acquaintance of a person with whom, the distinctive characters of both men being taken into consideration, he was to be associated by circumstances of a very peculiar kind. This person was the poet Mayr-

---

[1] Schubert finished this work on March 16, 1814.

[2] The first act, occupying 128 pages in the original score, was finished on September 3, the third on October 22, 1814. I am not in a position to say how far the second setting differed from the first ; the overture is the same in both, with the exception of the middle movement (a Largo), which accompanies the incantation scene. I know nothing further of the musical parts of the two separate arrangements.

[3] Herr Josef Hüttenbrenner has the original score, Schubert having made over the property to him in payment of a small debt. In the year 1848 the servants of the house lighted the fires with this second act.

hofer, well known by his works and the tragical end of his career.

Johann Mayrhofer [1] was born on the 3rd of November, 1787, about ten years before Schubert's birth, at Steyr, in Upper Austria. 'The flowers which strewed his pathway of life fell,' says Ernst Freih. v. Feuchtersleben, 'from the same brimming horn which scattered all the charms of nature over the fair land of his birth. His own poetic vein impressed him with a deep feeling for natural beauty; his own muse, his earliest recollection and faithfullest companion throughout life, accompanied him on the gloomy path of his existence. After passing the course of studies at the Gymnasium, he went through a course of philosophy at the Lyceum in Linz. In accordance with the wishes of his father, who had intended him for the church, he became a member of the College of St. Florian, where he remained for three years—an interval he employed in attaining a knowledge of the ancient languages, which in his after struggles proved of great service to him. After passing his noviciate, he determined to give up his present line of life, and study law at Vienna. This pursuit, owing to his force of character and tenacity of purpose, was crowned with success. A change came, and his inclinations, moved by vivid poetic fancies, led him to abandon law for poetry. An outer world, rich and

[1] The following sketch of Mayrhofer is made up of notices by Herren v. Feuchtersleben, Franz v. Schober, and Von Gahy.

significant, opened upon the view of this lonely, self-
contained, self-taught man, and this outer world, allied
to his innate earnestness and moral powers, could not
fail to work the happiest results. He soon formed
happy intimacies with cheerful, highly-gifted young
men, of the like ambitious nature with his own; and
one side of his character was developed—a cheerful,
bright disposition of the soundest and healthiest sort—
a quality which, in earlier days, had been kept in the
background by his existence as a sort of youthful recluse.
This formed an element in the general features of an
earnest, robust nature, and in later times still clung to
him, although it gradually became less palpable, and
partook of that less blameless character which he himself used to designate as 'caustic.' His flashes of wit, if
more rarely indulged in, were all the more pungent if
indulged in at all. 'Mephistopheles,' a poem found
amongst his papers after death, gives a perfect picture
of this bitter element of cynicism in his nature. It is the
frame of mind incidental to a gifted man, who would be
gladly on good terms with the things of this world, but
cannot shut his eyes to their destructive and corrupt-
ing influence on himself and all around him. For such
dispositions he invented a poetical formula, which he
called 'Sermone,' and in these he poured out his spleen
on that which is common to mankind, yet acted inju-
riously to his own particular nature. However stern his
character, viewed on one side, it was gentle and exqui-

sitely tender even to a fault on the other. He was extremely like Wilhelm Meyern, author of 'Dia-Na-Sore,'[1]
who exercised an enduring influence on Mayrhofer.
Both were too rigid in their exactions on the world and
themselves, and these exaggerated claims brought them
into conflict with the world and each other; both alike
were rational and sound; both were hypochondriacal—
with this difference, that Mayrhofer, by his poetic temperament, was the earlier able to harmonise with the
elements of the external world.

'For this advantage he was very mainly indebted to
the influence of Göthe, who was of the greatest service
to him at this epoch. He was still living at a time
when the king of poets was publishing new works, and
stirring the hearts of men. Göthe was his " be all and
end all," at a period when the world began to hold
aloof from the great poet; and the Göthe no longer
understood and flattered interested him more than the
Göthe to whom the whole world had paid homage.

---

[1] Meyern (Wilhelm Friedrich), born at Ausbach in 1762, studied
law at Altdorf, but gave it up afterwards for other pursuits. He entered the Austrian service as a lieutenant in the artillery, followed the
Austrian Embassy to Sicily in 1807, afterwards served diplomatically
at Rome and Madrid, and ended as a military commissioner of the
Bund at Frankfort, where he died in 1829. He had the reputation of
being a clever versatile man, whose incapacity for a settled purpose
deprived him of making his many advantages of marketable value, and
of securing him a life-long appointment commensurate with his merits.
His extraordinary romance, 'Dia-Na-Sore' (1787–1791), was a great
favourite with the public.

If Göthe in this respect was useful to him, so also was Herder, whose power of taking a grand comprehensive view of things, and reconciling the elements of the universe to one creed and one religion, was in entire conformity with his line of thought.'

'Fessler must also be mentioned,[1] whose far-seeing views and commentaries on music, womanhood, ethical and religious symbolism, contained in his work "A Review of my Seventy Years' Pilgrimage," were well calculated to lend a sort of halo to the peculiar views of Mayrhofer. These, the chief circumstances in the earliest stage of his development, exercised a marked influence on Mayrhofer. In his later studies he devoted himself to mythological research in works which

---

[1] Fessler (Ignaz Aurelius), born in 1756, at Czurendorf in Lower Hungary, entered the Capuchin Order in 1773, and ten years later became professor of Oriental languages at the University of Lemberg. Having been made a Freemason at the same time as a Capuchin, he quitted the latter Order. A tragedy of his, performed at Lemberg in the year 1787, being pronounced atheistical, he was obliged to fly to Silesia. In 1791 he became a convert to Protestantism, and afterwards (1796) lived at Berlin, where, accompanied by Fichte, he founded the 'Humanitätsgesellschaft.' In the year 1806 he lost the office he had been entrusted with—that of a consulship for the Catholic provinces, and in 1809 he went to St. Petersburg as professor of philosophy. Dismissed from this post, on a charge of atheism, he settled in Wolsk with a view of realising some philanthropic scheme. In 1817 he withdrew to Sarepta, the chief seat of the Moravian brethren, where he worked in his own peculiar fashion. In 1820 he was superintendent, in 1833 member of the St. Petersburg Consistory, and he died at St. Petersburg in 1839. He described his eventful life in a book called 'A Review of my Seventy Years' Pilgrimage' (1826).

are ascribed to the famous Hermes, and about which he would expatiate in the wildest terms.'

Such was the wonderful man who, in 1814, and therefore in the twenty-seventh year of his age, formed an intellectual friendship with Schubert, who was then in his eighteenth year. This intimacy was the central point of Mayrhofer's existence, and more than any other preceding event in his career helped to mature his powers as a poet. Seeing that Schubert's was a musical genius, the event is in its kind unique. 'My acquaintance with Schubert,' says Mayrhofer, in his memoirs, 'was brought about by a young friend giving him my poem " Am See " to set to music. The friend brought him to that very room which, five years later (1819), we were destined to share in common. It was in a dark, gloomy street. House and furniture were the worse for wear, the ceiling was beginning to bulge, the light obstructed by a huge building opposite, and part of the furniture was an old worn-out piano and a shabby bookstand—such was the room. I shall never forget it, nor the hours we spent there.[1]

---

[1] The house here mentioned as that where Mayrhofer and Schubert lived together for two years consecutively, was No. 420 in the Wipplingerstrasse. The room of ' Der Dichter und der Tonsetzer' (as these two artists were called by their friends, after the title of a then favourite operetta) was on the third floor, and their landlady was a tobacco-seller, one Sanssouci, the widow of a French emigrant. Herr Josef Hüttenbrenner lived at that time in the same house, with a certain Irrsa, and afterwards rented Mayrhofer's and Schubert's room, being the identical one which Theodor Körner had inhabited during his

' As the spring tempers the earth, clothing it with
verdure and flowers, and refreshing it with breezes,
so does she invigorate and endow mankind with the
innate consciousness of productive power ; for, as Göthe
says :—

> Weit, hoch, herrlich der Blick
> Rings in's Leben hinein,
> Von Gebirg zu Gebirg
> Schwebet der ewige Geist
> Ewigen Lebens ahndevoll.

' This depth of sentiment and mutual love for poetry
and music drew our sympathies closer and closer ; I
wrote verses, he saw what I wrote, and to these joint
efforts many of his melodies owed their beginning,
end, and popularity in the world.'

In the year 1815, Mayrhofer was encouraged to
greater efforts in poetry from this copartnership and
joint ambition.   He wrote two librettos for operas, of
which Schubert set one, ' Die beiden Freunde von Salamanka ;' the other, ' Adrast,' was found amongst the
papers of the poet after his death.

In the years 1817 and 1818, Mayrhofer joined some
friends (Spaun, Kenner, Ottenwald, Kreil,[1] &c.) in pub-

---

residence in Vienna.   Madame Sanssouci (in after years married to the
prison inspector Jaworek) took a great deal of pains to keep the household establishment of her two lodgers in order.   The house No. 420 is
further remarkable as having been originally the place of rendezvous
of the Jacobins.   In the last forty years it has been pulled down, and
new buildings erected in its place.

[1] Later on in our work (1819) we shall meet again with the two last-
named gentlemen.

lishing a periodical, the object of which was to spread
a healthy manly sense of patriotism amongst young
men, and two numbers of which appeared (published
by Härter at Vienna), entitled 'Beiträge zur Bildung
für Jünglinge.' The feelings which in the memorable
war epoch, just concluded, had animated every German
had found also an echo in the heart of Mayrhofer. The
patriotic sentiment, linked with the ideals of humanity
and individual happiness by faith in a Providence
revealed in nature and history, collected the beams of
his intelligence for a final burst of brilliancy, which
still gleamed fitfully on the ever darkening path of the
distracted poet. He worked zealously at the ancient
classics. Fragments of an attempt at a translation of
Herodotus were found in his desk; at Horace, too, he
tried his hand, but the Stoics were his model. But
the more that these contemplative pursuits counter-
acted the present, the thicker was the veil they wove
around the student's soul. The study of history,
into which he plunged with alacrity from an active
interest he took in the Austrian annals and the archives of Hormayer, was his healthiest diversion: the
stout-hearted man, by dint of strenuous official labour,
tried to raise a strong barrier against the increasing
confusion of his brain. Mayrhofer was appointed
officer to the Austrian censorship, and practised his
duties as government secretary and press reviewer
with such painful conscientiousness, that it really

seemed he was endeavouring, by a fitful discharge of official duty, to reconcile the difference between the ideal and the actual, which in happier moments he had been capable of balancing by his creative powers of poetry.[1]

---

[1] Bauernfeld gives (in a 'Book of Merry Rhymes about us Viennese,' by Rusticocampius) the following picture of this singular man :—

Halbvergessen ist auch jener
Wiener Dichter, hiess Mayrhofer ;
Viele seiner Poesien
Componirte sein Freund Schubert.
So die zürnende Diana
Philoktet und manche andre ;
Waren tief ideenreich
Aber schroff,—sowie der Dichter.
Kränklich war er und verdriesslich,
Floh der heitern Kreise Umgang,
Nur mit Studien beschäftigt ;
Abends labte ihn das Whistspiel.
So mit älteren Herren sass er,
Mit Beamten, mit Philistern,
Selbst Beamter, Bücher-Censor
Und der strengste, wie es hiess.
Ernst war seine Miene, steinern,
Niemals lächelt' oder scherzt' er.
Flösst uns losem Volk Respekt ein,
So sein Wesen und sein Wissen.
Wenig sprach er,—was er sagte
War bedeutend ; allem Tändeln
War er abgeneigt, den Weibern
Wie der leichten Belletristik.
Nur Musik konnt' ihn bisweilen
Aus der stumpfen Starrheit lösen,
Und bei seines Schuberts Liedern
Da verklärte sich sein Wesen.

In the year 1819, he shared a room with Schubert at the house of the widow Sanssouci, and continued thus until 1821, when Schubert migrated to Schober's lodgings in the Landskrongasse. 'Whilst we were together,' says Mayrhofer in his diary,[1] 'curious things happened. We were certainly both of us peculiar, and there were plenty of opportunities for droll incidents. We used to tease one another in all sorts of ways, and bandied pleasantries and epigrams for our mutual benefit.[2] His free, open-hearted, cheerful manner and my retired nature came into sharp contrast, and gave us an opportunity of nicknaming each other appropriately, as though we were playing certain parts assigned us. Alas! it was the only *rôle* I ever played.'

In the year 1824, Mayrhofer, at the solicitation of his friends, published (at Volke's, in Vienna), by subscription, a small volume of poems, which, however, under the circumstances, at that time very unfavour-

---

Seinem Freund zu Liebe liess er
In Gesellschaft auch sich locken,
Wenn wir Possen trieben, sah ihn
Stumm dort in der Ecke hocken.

[1] Printed in 'Archives,' by Hormayer.

[2] A favourite joke of Mayrhofer was to rush at Schubert with a sword-stick topped with a bayonet, and to howl at him in the dialect of Upper Austria, 'Was halt mich denn ab, du kloaner Raker!' to which Schubert would sing out, 'Waldl, wilder Verfasser!' and thrust him back. Gahy often witnessed these scenes.

able for lyric poetry, especially in Austria, met with but an indifferent reception.[1]

In the following years the stream of events and change of society separated him from Schubert, not to mention his own illness and his altered views of life. But what once had been, would reassert itself. After Schubert's death, on the very day the Requiem was sung over his grave, he revisited that very house where in earlier years he had so often visited his friend. After the death of the great song-writer he wrote poetry less frequently. At last came the actual sacrifice to real life, that sacrifice which for a long while estranged him from his muse. The harp, so long unstrung, was touched once more on the occasion of Göthe's death.

. In the year 1835 he undertook an excursion to Salzburg, Gastein, and the Fuscher-Bad, and returned so invigorated that he sketched out the plan of an epic poem.[2] Life seemed once more to be returning to him in a full healthy tide. But it was the last flickering of the expiring flame. Melancholy madness,

---

[1] Amongst the subscribers' names we find the following :—Justina v. Bruchmann, Endres, Gaby, Gross, Hölzl, Hönig, Hüttenbrenner, Kenner, Kreil, Sophie Linhart, Ottenwalt, Caroline Pichler, Pinterics, Sanssouci, Freiherr v. Schlechta, von Schober, Moritz Schwindt, von Sonnleithner, Spaun, Vogl, Watteroth, and Witteczek,—persons who all, more or less, had some connection with Schubert. In the old edition of Mayrhofer's poems, those set by Schubert are printed in their entirety ; in the new edition they are, with some few exceptions, omitted.

[2] The 'Bird Catcher,' published in the new edition of his poems.

the old demon that possessed the unhappy man, again seized upon those powers which had already failed him, and on February 5, 1836, led him to that melancholy end which snapped the thread of life asunder.[1]

To complete the sketch of Mayrhofer's peculiarities, the following facts may be added. He most strenuously avoided people who styled themselves connoisseurs.

[1] Einmal kam er frühen Morgens
Ins Bureau, begann zu schreiben,
Stand dann wieder auf—die Unruh
Liess ihn nicht im Zimmer bleiben.
Durch die düstern Gänge schritt er
Starr und langsam, wie in Träumen
Der Collegen Gruss nicht achtend
Stieg er nach den obern Räumen.
Steht, und stiert durchs offne Fenster.
Draussen wehen Frühlingslüfte,
Doch den Mann, der finster brütet,
Haucht es an, wie Grabesdüfte.
An dem offnen Fenster kreiselt
Sonnenstaub im Morgenschein,
Und der Mann lag auf der Strasse
Mit zerschmettertem Gebein.—RUSTICOCAMPIUS.

According to Herr Hölzl, Mayrhofer had once before, in a fit of melancholy, thrown himself into the Danube, but been drawn out and restored to life. To his friends' remonstrances he answered, with an air of indifference: 'He could never have believed the river Danube would have been so little chilly.' Just before the final catastrophe he came early to his office, visited one of the officials, and asked him for a pinch of snuff, and then mounted the upper story of the building, from which he threw himself headlong. He broke his neck, but survived for forty hours afterwards. It was not a weariness of life that drove him to the desperate step, but an incessant dread of cholera. So, at all events, I am assured by Herr Hölzl and Herr M. Beermann of Vienna.

The straightforward, healthy-minded man of action was one whom by preference he cultivated. The jokes and *bons mots* of a noted wag of the time, a great diner-out, and a sure find at an evening party, he refused to record next morning in his diary, which was filled with memoranda and quotations from Young's 'Night Thoughts' and 'Hermes Trismegistos.' His mode of life was extremely simple; in moderation and self-denial he resembled a Stoic. A few books, a guitar, and a pipe made up his furniture, a short nap after dinner and a walk the sum of his enjoyments. His dress was plain, almost slovenly. His employments day by day followed in the same monotonous round, and were discharged with the same unerring punctuality. There was something stiff and unbending in his exterior, which is often the case with a recluse. Fits of laughter at times broke in on his generally unbending moroseness. He walked firmly, he wrote a bold upright hand. His figure was compact, he was of the ordinary height, his features somewhat commonplace; he sometimes wore a sarcastic smile, he had eagle's eyes, sharp and piercing. Only in his heart of hearts did he hug himself in pride; he overrated other people; he was indifferent to applause, and reckoned any praise of the beauties of his poetry as an insult.

Judging by the sketch—one that emanates from the hand of a worthy friend[1]—Mayrhofer's character was

---

[1] Feuchtersleben. Preface to the new edition of Mayrhofer's Poems.

that of a sound, earnest, and moral man, but disfigured
by pedantry and a want of elasticity. We shall compare
his nature with Schubert's in the course of our work,
and the result will enable us at the first glance to
discover the qualities the two men had in common, as
well as their angularities, which, when they came in
contact, rubbed against each other and kept the men
apart. How thoroughly Schubert was attracted by the
poetical pictures of Mayrhofer, his many and frequently
his most noteworthy songs set to his friend's poetry
abundantly testify. There can be no doubt there was
plenty of mutual appreciation; it is equally certain
that Franz could never by choice have lived longer
alone with Mayrhofer, since the latter, beginning with
mere banter and raillery, ended by fomenting disputes
and collisions, which were the worry and torment of
Schubert's life.

Mayrhofer has in several poems given expression to
his feelings towards his friend, prematurely snatched
away from him,[1] but to Schubert was the task assigned
of transfiguring many of the poetical effusions of his
friend, and handing down to posterity the more perish-
able words of the bard attached and linked to his own
immortal song.

[1] 'Geheimniss,' 'Nachgefühl an Franz Schubert' (Nov. 19, 1828),
and 'An Franz,' the first and second strophe of which last poem
have been engraved with Schubert's music attached, and entitled
'Heliopolis.'

CHAPTER III.

(1815.)

THE BALLADS 'MINONA,' 'EMMA UND ADELWOLD,' 'DIE NONNE,'
'ERLKÖNIG'—VOCAL COMPOSITIONS FOR MIXED VOICES—THE MASS
IN G—SONATAS—THE SYMPHONIES IN B AND D—THE OPERAS 'DER
VIERJÄHRIGE POSTEN,' 'FERNANDO,' 'CLAUDINE VON VILLABELLA,'
'DIE BEIDEN FREUNDE VON SALAMANKA,' 'DER SPIEGELRITTER,' 'DER
MINNESÄNGER,' 'ADRAST'—SCHUBERT'S CAPACITY AS AN OPERATIC
COMPOSER.

WE now come to the year 1815, the eighteenth of
Schubert's existence, and, as regards the number of
compositions which originated at that time, the most
prolific year of Schubert's life. Over a hundred songs,
half a dozen operas and melodramas, not to mention
church music, chamber music, symphonies, and music for
the piano, all these are crowded into that period; and
how the hard-worked pupil of Salieri found the time to
produce, as if my magic, such a multitudinous heap of
musical scores, passes one's comprehension. Never
troubling himself about the form, inner meaning, length,
or conciseness of the poems, he seized on them as subjects for his cantatas and songs; sometimes the great ballads of Göthe, Schiller, Hölty, Bertrand, Körner, sometimes the short Strofenlieder of the favourite writers

of the time, Schulze, Kosegarten, Mathisson, Klopstock, Fellinger, Stollberg, &c., or the songs of Ossian, which lost nothing by the musical dress in which Schubert was wont to clothe them. Some of the songs which fall within this period may be catalogued as among the best efforts of Schubert's creative powers in this particular province; others again out of the great pile are to be found which possess, comparatively speaking, but little worth.[1] At that time he applied himself with particular energy to the composition of ballads on an extended scale, and 'Emma und Adelwold,' by Bertrand,[2] is the most lengthy vocal piece that Schubert ever wrote.

In order of time, the ballad of 'Minona,' by Bertrand (written on February 8), stands first. The composition is unmistakably steeped in the spirit of Schubert, and reminds one, especially in the pianoforte accompaniment, of the songs from Ossian, some of which were produced at this time. This is more especially the case with 'Amphiaraos,' by Theodor Körner. This great poem was set to music by Schubert in the incredibly short

---

[1] Herr Spina has the MSS. of seven songs, which were composed on one and the same day (Oct. 15, 1815). On the 19th of October following he wrote four more.

[2] Who Bertrand, the compiler of these ballads, was, and how Schubert may have come across these poems, which, it seems, never appeared in print, I have never ascertained with any reliable certainty. Possibly, it was the Franz Bertrand who, in 1787, at Halle, wrote 'Pyramus und Thesbe' for the composer Benda. The MSS. of 'Emma und Adelwold,' 'Minona,' 'Die Nonne,' and 'Amphiaraos,' are in the possession of Herr Spina.

space of five hours (as we find in the original score). The composition is a remarkable one, and never failed to make an effect, when given with the requisite expression by a competent singer.

On June 7, Schubert took in hand Bertrand's ballad of ' Emma und Adelwold.' The music written for this poem fills no less than fifty-five manuscript pages. The composition, of a fragmentary kind, contains fine passages, and teems with those strong individualities which stamped Schubert's compositions at this period. Once fairly occupied with setting ballads into music, he composed (on June 16) the well-known and gloomy poem by Hölty, ' Die Nonne ':—

> Es lebt in Welschland irgendwo
> Ein schöner junger Ritter, &c.

The Cantata, too, consists of several parts, introductions and interludes, recitatives, &c. ; the accompaniments and vocal parts bear the unmistakable mark of their author.[1]

---

[1] Besides the ballads we have mentioned, ' Die Bürgschaft' (by Schiller), ' Die Spinnerin,' ' Der Sänger,' ' Der Rattenfänger ' (by Göthe), and ' Der Liedler ' (by Kenner), belong to this year. Amongst other songs (contained in the collected catalogue) are found Schiller's ' Punschlied,' the finale of which is identical with that in ' Loda's Gespenst,' ' Mignon's Gesang,' marked No. 4 (Schubert has set this as a song four times, once as a duett, and once as a quintett) ; besides ' Der Kampf ' (Schiller's ' Freigeisterei der Leidenschaft '), of which only two strophes are set to music, and an improviso by Schiller :—

> Es ist so angenehm, so süss,
> Um einen lieben Mann zu spielen,
> Entzückend wie im Paradies
> Des Mannes Zauberkraft zu fühlen.

According to Josef v. Spaun, it was in the last days
of this year, or at the latest in the beginning of the
year 1816, that the 'Erl-King' was written, second
only in point of popularity to the 'Wanderer,' the solid
foundation of Schubert's popularity six years later,
and which, within a short time, became public property of the whole musical world.   Schubert wrote this
song one afternoon in his room in his father's house in
Himmelpfortgrund.   Spaun came to see him whilst he
was hard at work.   He had read the poem twice in a
state of intense mental excitement, and as, whilst thus
employed, the musical significance of the poem had
dawned on him, he had dashed down on a paper a
sketch which only needed some mechanical finish to
bring to perfection.   On the evening of the same day
his composition was brought finished to the Convict,
where Schubert sang it over first, and then Holzapfel
to his friends.[1]   The audience made wry faces, and
smiled incredulously at the passage, 'Mein Vater, jetzt
fasst er mich an,' whereupon Ruczizka undertook to
clear up the mystery and explain the discords, which
nowadays are reckoned so harmless an incident to
music.   As Vogl was intimate with Schubert, he immediately monopolised this song, which seemed created
on purpose for his particular powers, and sang it on
frequent occasions in private society, until at last, in

---

[1] The date is given on the manuscript, which Madame Schumann possesses.   The song was twice set by Schubert, the second time with the
triplet accompaniment, omitted in the engraved copy.

the year 1821, on the occasion of an academy being opened at the Royal Opera, the 'Erl-King' was introduced to the general public.[1]

Of this ballad there are plenty of arrangements, both as cantatas and for the orchestra. The value of the song itself was a great bone of contention; some exalted it to the skies, and one critic, in the Leipzig 'Allgemeine Zeitung,' affirmed that all the king says was untrue, seeing that womanly virtue might be destroyed by such bewitching melodies, but that the idea

[1] After the appearance of the 'Erl-King' in print, the song was used in various ways. Thus Anselm Hüttenbrenner wrote 'Erl-King Waltzes,' a profanation which excited Schubert's wrath, which he vented in some distichs in the musical journal conducted by the well-known poet and writer Friedrich August Kanne, probably with a view of Huttenbrenner's passing them on to Anselm. These lines run thus:—

1. DAS GEFÜHL.

(*Frage.*)

Sag' mir, strömt das Gefühl der jetzigen Welt nur dem Bein zu?

Antwort:

Seit sich die Menschen geschnürt, sanken die Herzen hinab.

2. KÖDER.

(*Frage.*)

Sage mir, lieblicher Kauz, was siehst in den Werken des Goethe?

Antwort:

Titelchen stör' ich mir auf;—Erlkönig—Deutsche, ich find's.

3. DREIACHTELTACT.

(*Frage.*)

Sprich, wie tanzt man den deutsch der Geisterwelt furchtbare Schauder?

Antwort:

Kann man nicht jegliches Lied tanzen der heutigen Welt?

of a child dying of terror whilst encircled by the protecting arms of a father was an impossibility.

Amongst choral part-songs we may cite 'Der Mor-
genstern,' 'Jägerlied,' and 'Lützow's wilde Jagd' (by
Th. Körner), as well as two 'Mailieder,' by Hölty,
written for either two voices or two French horns.
There are also some vocal trios, whereas the four-part
song is scarcely represented at all. Of the songs written
in this year, there are nearly half a hundred unpublished and unknown; but the most important of these
are without doubt the ballads we have previously mentioned.

The astonishing rapidity of Schubert's musical development at this period is evidenced by the 'Mignon-
lieder' and settings of Ossian's songs, which bear the
stamp of a master mind; but we would invite particular
attention to the Mass in G, written in the March of
1815, for the parish choir of Lichtenthal, and specially
intended for those of his youthful musical friends who
had been pupils of the 'regens chori,' Holzer.[1] This
Mass is one of the most solid of church compositions;
the Kyrie, Credo, and Agnus Dei are all movements by a deep musical thinker. Taken as a whole,
it has never been surpassed by any of Schubert's later
Masses; and this masterpiece is the work of a youth of
eighteen—a true genius. A second Mass (in B-flat)[2], the

---

[1] Herr Doppler is my informant.

[2] This has been engraved by Haslinger as Op. 141, and is given at
Vienna more frequently than his other Masses.

first Stabat Mater (in B-flat),[1] a grand Magnificat, and
two sacred Cantatas on a slighter scale,[2] belong to this
period. In the department of chamber music he wrote
for amateurs a stringed Quartett in G minor, the first
and last movement of which, as well as the first part
of the exquisite Scherzo, contain passages very point-
edly illustrating Schubert's peculiarities, whereas in
the second movement, and the Trio in the third, he
adheres to the forms adopted by Haydn.[3]

The pianoforte music is represented, amongst other
things,[4] by two Sonatas (in C and F)—his first great
efforts, it would seem, in this style of composition, to
be followed within a short interval by a series of fine
massive works, all of which spoke eloquently of the
energy and high gifts with which Schubert was destined to advance in this new department of his art.

But the activity of this unwearied composer was not
yet exhausted. Orchestral music and the opera were
each to claim their share of attention, and Schubert
found time enough to finish in this year two sympho-

---

[1] For a mixed choir, with stringed, organ, and wind accompaniments.

[2] These are a Salve Regina and Offertory, and the second Dona Nobis
to the F Mass (1814). Dr. Schneider, of Vienna, has the MSS. of the
first of these compositions (bearing date July 5).

[3] The Scherzo, in form and expression, reminds one of the vigorous
Scherzo of Mozart's G minor Symphony, a great favourite of Schubert's.
The manuscript of this quartett is in the library of the Musikverein at
Vienna. Herr Josef Hellmesberger gave a performance of it in the
year 18

[4] Twelve 'Deutsche' with Coda, ten Variations and Ecossaisen, dedicated to Maria Spaun.

nies and six vocal melodramas, one in three and another in two acts. The Symphonies are those in B-flat and D.[1] The first seems never to have been brought forward in public; the last movement of the Symphony in D was first given at a concert in Vienna (on December 2, 1860) as a 'symphonic fragment,' and delighted the audience by the freshness, originality, and perfection of its form.[2]

The operas and melodramas which belong to this period are the following:—'Der vierjährige Posten' (May), 'Fernando' (July), 'Claudine von Villabella' (July and August), and 'Die beiden Freunde von Salamanka' (November and December). Besides these, 'Der Spiegelritter,' 'Der Minnesänger,'[3] and 'Adrast' (the two last have not yet been discovered) may be mentioned in the catalogue of works referable to this period. 'Der vierjährige Posten,' an operetta in one

---

[1] The first of these, in the possession of Dr. Schneider, of Vienna, shows that Schubert began it on December 10, 1814, and finished it on March 24, 1815. It consists of four movements: A Largo $\frac{4}{4}$, which is an introduction to an Allegro vivace; an Andante in E-flat $\frac{3}{4}$; a Minuett with Trio in E-flat $\frac{3}{4}$; and the Finale, Presto vivace, in B-flat major $\frac{2}{4}$. The Symphony in D, the original score of which bears date May 24, 1815, has also four movements: an Adagio maestoso $\frac{3}{4}$, an Allegro con Trio, an Allegretto, a Minuett with Trio (Allegro vivace, D major $\frac{2}{4}$), and the Finale (Presto vivace, D major $\frac{6}{8}$).

[2] The other fragments were the first and second movement of the tragic Symphony in C minor (1816), and the Scherzo of the sixth in C (written in 1818).

[3] In C. M. v. Weber's 'Biography' (by Max Weber), an operetta of the same name is mentioned.

act, the words by Theodor Körner, was finished on
May 13.[1] The story is as follows:—Duval, with his
regiment, has arrived at a village on the German fron-
tier, and has mounted guard on a neighbouring hill.
The regiment marches away from quarters, forget-
ting to relieve their sentinels. Weary of his long
watch, he descends one evening into the village, and
learns that his comrades have already gone. He determines on remaining in the village, makes acquaintance
with Käthchen, the daughter of Walther, a village magistrate, and marries her. As luck will have it, his old
regiment marches through the village once more after
a lapse of four years, and here the musical interlude
opens. Duval, fearing he will be brought before a
court-martial as a deserter, thinks on the following
artifice. He puts on his uniform, and mounts guard at
the very spot from which he had waited in vain to be
relieved; and when the captain recognises him, and
orders the company to seize him as a deserter, Duval,
relying on his rights as sentinel, threatens to shoot
the first man who approaches him. Whilst the captain
and his men are exchanging words, the general appears,

---

[1] The original score is in the hands of Dr. Schneider. On the title-
page of Körner's melodrama there is the following observation:—' The
poet's intention was that this musical vaudeville should be set throughout as a finale. Steinaker set it to music in this shape, and it was thus
given on the stage at Vienna.' Steinaker (Carl), born at Leipsic in 1785,
studied at Vienna, and wrote several operettas; amongst others, 'Die
Vedette.' Like Körner, he took part in the War of Liberation, and died
in 1815.

who, when informed of the whole affair from beginning
to end, pardons the 'vierjährige Posten,' and gives
him a certificate of honour on quitting the service.

The libretto, partly prose, partly verse, contains nine
scenes, and Schubert's music, besides a tolerably long
overture (filling fifty-six manuscript pages), is contained
in eight numbers. The overture (written May 13—
16) begins with a Larghetto (D major $\frac{6}{8}$), an introduction to a lively movement, continued in the same vein
to the end of the number. The introduction (Allegretto
con moto, B-flat major $\frac{2}{8}$, written on May 8) consists of
a chorus of peasants, varied by a trio, in which Käthe
(soprano), Duval (tenor), and Walter (bass) take part.
This is followed by a duett between Duval and Käthchen,
a trio by the same with Walter, a short recitative for
Veit, and a grand prayer of Käthchen.[1] A march,
heard in the distance, and a soldiers' chorus to follow
(Tempo di marcia, B-flat major $\frac{4}{4}$, accompanied by hautboy, clarionet, bassoon, horn, and trumpets), with a
final chorus and quartett for the principals, make up
the other pieces of the operetta, in which the spoken
dialogues play a prominent part.

This operetta has never been given on the stage. The
soldiers' chorus, a lively characteristic piece, was per-

---

[1] The first part of the air (Adagio in E-flat major $\frac{3}{4}$) is accompanied
by clarionet, horn, and bassoon; in the Allegro affettuoso (E minor $\frac{3}{4}$),
beginning with the words 'Nein, das kannst du nicht gebieten,' the
whole power of the orchestra is introduced. The air is pitched very
high, and is extremely difficult.

formed with applause at an evening's entertainment
given by the Vienna 'Singverein' in 1860.[1]

Amongst Schubert's contemporaries at the Convict
was, as we have already stated, Albert Stadler, who continued there after Schubert had left the Institution, and
in the year 1815 passed the second year of his studies
in jurisprudence. He came frequently in contact with
the Lichtenthal assistant of that period; and as Schubert felt an ardent longing at the time for composing
operas, and actually set about writing one after another,
Stadler pledged himself to write a small drama for his
friend, an offer Schubert accepted eagerly. This was
the origin of 'Fernando,' a piece in which (according
to the opinion of its author) 'a chief part is given to
thunder and lightning, grief and tears, as the favourite
objects of enthusiastic youth.' The music was written
within six days. Schubert appeared before Stadler
with the finished score,[2] which they examined and ana-
lysed together. The work was afterwards put aside,
and neither poet nor musician troubled himself again
on the subject. The characters in the piece (written in
April 1815) are : Fernando de la Porta, Eleonora his

[1] The musical details of the vaudeville composed in the year 1815
are, with some few exceptions, unknown to me. The Operetta 'Der
vierjährige Posten' has been also set by Reineke.

[2] The following title appears on the original score in Dr. Schneider's
possession:—'Fernando, a vaudeville in one act, by A ... St. .... The
music by Franz Schubert, pupil of Herr Salieri. Begun July 3, 1815;
finished July 9.'

wife, Philip their child, twelve years of age, a peasant,
a huntsman, and a charcoal-burner. The scene lies in
a rough part of the Pyrenees, and the time occupied is
from nightfall to break of day. The plan of the piece,
in which, by the way,[1] there is much more talking than
singing, is as follows:—Fernando de la Porta has slain
his wife's brother, having been slanderously accused by
him of committing a foul crime, and after perpetrating
this deed is obliged to fly. The tribunal of the Inquisition sentences the murderer to death, and puts a price
on his head. Influential friends (after the abolition
of the Inquisition) contrive subsequently to get him
pardoned, but of Fernando, who has retreated to the
mountains and lived disguised as a hermit, no tidings
can be obtained. Eleonora, who is convinced of her
husband's innocence, having pardoned him the crime
committed in haste against her brother, sets off with her
son in pursuit of Fernando, with the intention of re-
storing him to his family. Within a short distance of
the hermit's retreat, they are overtaken by a storm;
Philip, going astray in the darkness, loses sight of his
mother, and calls her by name with piteous moans.
(Here the musical interlude begins.) Looking in the
background, he sees a wolf slinking away amongst the
trees, and runs off screaming and terror-stricken.

The storm passes over; Fernando, in hermit's dress,
comes forth from his cell. Tortured by conscience, he

[1] The libretto contains forty-two closely printed pages.

repeats the last words, addressed him by the victim
of his revenge. Philip advances, tells him his fate,
and asks his protection and help. A shot is heard in
the distance. Fernando promises the boy he will
stand by him in his hour of trouble; but on question-
ing him further as to the object of his own and his
mother's journey, Philip sings him a song, learnt from
his mother, the burden of which is the murderous
deed of Fernando. The hermit grows pale, but Philip
tells him that the mother has forgiven the murderer.
Then a peasant advances, carrying a blood-stained
cloth he has found in the bushes. Philip and Fernando
shudder, for they expect Eleonora has become the
prey of the wild animal that appeared a short time
since in the thicket; the peasant withdraws, Fernando
no longer veils his secret, and discloses himself to
his son. Both bewail Leonora's death. She appears,
accompanied by a huntsman and a charcoal-burner.
Fernando enjoins his son to keep silence, the son rushes
into his mother's arms. Eleonora, the huntsman, and
charcoal-burner now talk in turns, as to how Eleonora
was on the point of being torn to pieces by the wolf,
when the huntsman's bullet rolled him over, and the
charcoal-burner's axe finished him. They both withdraw. Fernando asks Leonora what chance has brought
her there, and hearing from her own mouth that she
has pardoned the murderer, he hurries to his cell, and
reappears decked out in bravery of Spanish fashion.

Eleonora, who has already learned from Philip that the hermit is Fernando, repeats the word ' forgiveness,' and, in a universal chorus of joy, the harmless and almost childish extravaganza concludes.

The musical part of this operetta opens with an introduction (Largo, D minor $\frac{4}{4}$, after 12 bars Presto), during which (at the 30th bar) the curtain rises. This introduction, representing a storm growing louder and louder, ends with a recitative of Philip, calling for his mother in wailing tones of despair. This is followed by a prayer, accompanied by orchestra, an air for Fernando, a romance[1] for Philip, an air for Eleonora, a duett for Fernando and Eleonora, and the finale, beginning with a duett for the same characters, concluding with an ensemble for the principal characters. The operetta concludes with a joyful chorus in praise of wedded love.

' Fernando ' has not yet been given on the stage. A few years after Franz's death, Ferdinand produced the Finale at one of his concerts, along with other fragments of his brother's operas.

The third piece intended for the stage is ' Claudine von Villabella,' an Opera in three acts by Göthe. From the first act of the score, which still exists, we find the story thus treated.

The two brothers Carlos and Pedro von Castell-

---

[1] The romance, arranged in strophe form, is seldom omitted in any of Schubert's operas.

vecchio have experienced cruel treatment at the hands
of their father. Carlos, the elder of the two, driven
from home by his father's cruel temper, lives a considerable time under the name of Rugantino, as a leader
of banditti in the Sicilian mountains; Pedro succeeds
after his father's death to the entire estate, but if he
can only discover his brother, will gladly share the property with him. Engaged to Claudine, the daughter
of Alonzo, Lord of Villabella, at whose castle he has
been staying for some time, Pedro leaves the family,
now that his time of leave has expired, to pay his
homage at the court of the king. (Here the music
begins.) Rugantino has a scheme for attacking the
castle of Villabella, from whence he intends to carry off
by force Alonzo's fair niece Lucinda. One lot of vaga-
bonds sticks to him, another joins Bosco, an accomplice
of Rugantino, to go after booty of another kind. (End
of the first act.)

Schubert set to music all three acts of this drama,
the original musical score of which is in the hands
of Herr Josef Hüttenbrenner, of Vienna. Unfortunately, however, the last two acts met with the same
melancholy end that befel the manuscript of 'Des
Teufels Lustschloss,'[1] so that one must reckon the

---

[1] This manuscript is also headed: 'The music is by F. Schubert,
pupil of Herr v. Salieri, 1815.' The beginning and completion of the
first act are dated July 26 and August 5. Schubert wrote it in eleven
days. Johann Andrä, in Offenbach, Göthe's friend, set the same drama
to music in the year 1774 (O. Jahn, 'Mozart,' vol. iii. p. 79). Josef

music as lost for ever.[1] The fragments of the music that remain, if lacking in power, are still characteristic and charming; those portions which are lost, in which the composer had more opportunity offered him than in the first act for the development of dramatic treatment, were doubtless sustained with equal dignity of style. Schubert himself attached some importance to this composition, the scoring of which occupied him for two months, for in the following November we find him employed with the two-act Opera, 'Die beiden Freunde von Salamanka.'

An Overture in E.[2] precedes the Operetta ' Claudine,' beginning with an Adagio, and ending with a brilliant movement (Allegro vivace $\frac{4}{4}$).

The introduction contains a trio for Lucinda, Alonzo, and Pedro von Rovero, supplemented by a chorus of peasants. This is followed by an air for Lucinda, with stringed accompaniments, an air of Claudine, another for Pedro (tenor), an arietta for Claudine, a quaint, humorous song for Rugantino, with his chorus of outlaws, and the finale (dialogue between Rugantino and Bosco, the two sets of outlaws being divided

Drechsler (1823–1829), Capellmeister of the Leopoldstadt Theatre, also set it to music.

[1] Two acts, according to Herr Hüttenbrenner, were thrown by his servants into the fire, during his absence from Vienna in the year 1848. A finished and complete copy of the work perished also in the same way.

[2] Herr Witzendorf, of Vienna, has a copy of the overture. Reineke also composed an overture to 'Claudine.'

into sections for chorus); the whole forms an animated scene. 'Claudine' was never performed on the stage, and was saved from the mass of Schubert's papers, not to be published to the world, but to perish in the flames.

The Opera in two acts, ' Die beiden Freunde von Salamanka,' owes its origin to the friendly relations that existed between Schubert and Mayrhofer: the latter wrote the libretto. The music, which took Schubert some six weeks to compose, was written between November 18 and December 31, 1815. The original score (in the possession of Dr. E. Schneider) is on a large scale, the first act alone filling 320 pages. The libretto is lost.[1] As far as we can collect from the score, a Count Tormes strives to win the hand of the Countess Olivia, with whom he has no personal acquaintance, but the fame of whose loveliness has attracted him. Don Alonzo hates the Count, and in order to throw impediments in the way of his getting hold of Olivia, enjoins his young friend, Fidelio, to execute the following plan :—Diego,

[1] Freiherr v. Feuchtersleben wished to insert it in a new edition of Mayrhofer's poems which he edited ; but, as he himself remarks, in deference to advice from many quarters, and out of respect for a large number of readers, he gave up the idea, and excluded both 'Die Freunde von Salamanka' as well as 'Adrast' from the collection. The consequence of this is, that most probably the librettos to both works have ceased to exist, as of Mayrhofer's literary remains, which came to the hands of Herr v. Feuchtersleben, some quotations from Herder excepted, nothing is to be found, and the manuscripts, as I was told, were very likely treated as lumber or destroyed by the household servants.

a friend of both parties, is to head an apparent assault
of banditti upon the Countess, whereupon Alonzo and
Fidelio are to rush to the rescue, and by this means
introduce themselves to Olivia. The lady is attracted
by some undefined longings to a solitary place, where
the Giesbach foams over the rocks—where

> Ein tiefes Roth die Beeren säumt,
> Und holder sind der Blumen Sterne ;

and in the course of her wanderings is surprised by
Diego.   Both friends rush forward in answer to her
cries for help ; Diego flies; Olivia's people advance ;
Eusebia, the confidant of the Countess, recognises in
Fidelio her lover. The whole party goes off in triumph
to the neighbouring castle.   Olivia falls in love with
her knight; after the explanation that ensues, forgives
him the anxiety which his premeditated attack has
caused her, and the lovers are married.

Count Tormes is conducted by Fidelio to Eusebia,
whom he takes for Olivia, and for whose hand he
woos as a suitor. Eusebia, initiated in the secret,
will not discover herself until, at last, Olivia comes
on the scene, and Tormes learns that he has been
deceived.

There is another complication in the fact of Diego,
a young lawyer, becoming a suitor for the hand of
Laura, daughter of the Alcalde. After Diego has
passed a successful examination in the Digests, the

Alcalde, with the consent of the Countess, hands him over his own judicial office, and gives his consent to the proposed marriage. Alonzo, disappointed, ' walks empty away.'

The opera is preceded by an overture, and there are eighteen vocal numbers in the work. Seven of these are in the first act :—an introduction leading to a trio for Alonzo (tenor), Diego (tenor), and Fidelio (bass), an air for the latter, a quartett (for the three characters before mentioned, and Tormes), an air for Olivia (soprano), a trio (Olivia, Eusebia, and a peasant), a duett (Alonzo and Diego), and the finale,—an ensemble in which the Alcalde, Laura, a chorus of men and women form the principal characters.

The second act begins in a very cheerful vein. It is the time of the vintage. Vine-dressers, both men and women, are busy picking the grapes, and in ex-pectancy of the feast to be given them when their toil is over. There is an introduction for the orchestra, written in the pastoral style (Allegretto, F major $\frac{2}{4}$). The steward comes to the vine-dressers, to encourage them in their labours :—

> Lasst nur alles leichtfertige Wesen,
> Hurtig die Trauben gelesen,
> Was soll das Grüssen,
> Das Flüstern und Küssen ?

Thus he greets the labourers, who answer him in chorus :—

Zum Moste stampfen wir die Beeren,
Der Most muss gähren,
Sich veredeln und zum Wein,
Zum süssen Blute roth und rein, &c.

A general chorus of rejoicing closes a lively pictur-
esque scene, set to music alla Pastorale.

The next number is a characteristic national Lied
for a guerilla chief (bass):—

Guerillas zieht durch Feld und Wald
In rauher Kriegeslust, &c.,

which is repeated as a couplet after the entrance of
another member of the banditti force. Then follows
an air for Tormes, another for Xilo (bass), a duett
for the two, and a second duett for Diego and Laura,
an air for Olivia, a duett between her and Alonzo, a
romance for Diego, a trio for the Alcalde, Laura, and
Diego, and an air for Laura, with a finale, in which
the principals take part.

In this opera, Schubert, although not entirely aban-
doning his individuality of style, shows, throughout
the entire work, a leaning towards the manner of the
older composers. Up to the present time, this opera has
remained amongst the musician's posthumous papers,
unnoticed and unknown.

Besides the operas and stage cantatas before mentioned, we must refer to 'Die Minnesänger,' 'Adrast,'
and 'Der Spiegelritter.' I have been assured that Schubert set 'Der Minnesänger' (probably Kotzebue's work)

to music.[1] He is said also to have set a portion of Mayrhofer's 'Adrast,' but not a trace of the music remains.[2]
He is said to have set the whole of Kotzebue's three-act
Opera, ' Der Spiegelritter,' to music, and a fragment of
this has appeared.[3] The libretto contains airs, duetts,
concerted pieces, and choruses, and is written in a
decidedly jocular vein. The vaudeville, at least the
musical fragment we have of it, is made up of the following story:—Prince Almador, son of the King of Dum-
mistan, after being reared in all the luxuries of court-
life, is sent out by his father on a journey of adventure,
with the hope of making him a man, and capable of
knightly chivalrous actions. Schmurzo, the butt of the
court wits, is to accompany him. For a motto and
watchword, the magician, Burrudusasussi, gives the
Prince a blue shield, whereon is mirrored the words,
' Der Tugend treu.' The mirror has the peculiar
power of turning white on the approach of dangers;
the secret that, should its surface ever reflect the face
of Milnis, the enchanted Queen of the Black Islands,
the lady should be rid of the curse weighing on her
of everlasting hunger, is hidden from the knight.
Almador and Schmurzo set out on their travels.

---

[1] Both Ferd. Schubert and Bauernfeld mention this opera.

[2] Probably the musical and philosophical author Adrastrus of Phi-
lipoppolis. Herr Josef Hüttenbrenner says that Schubert composed a
chorus for the work.

[3] It was found by some members of Ferdinand Schubert's family.
The Vienna Musikverein now possesses it.

The fragments of music which have been discovered contain an air for the King, 'Der Sonnestrahl ist warm;' a humorous quintett for Schmurzo and the ladies who worry and banter him, 'Wir gratuliren Dummkopf;' an air for the Prince, 'Ach es ist schön, fremde Länder zu sehen;' a duett for the Prince's parents (soprano and tenor), 'Wohl ist nur halbe Freude;' a concerted piece with chorus, 'Ein Sinnbild auf dem blanken Schild;' an air for the Prince, 'Schweigt, haltet graues Haar in Ehren;' an air for the magician, with chorus,

> So nimm, du junger Held,
> Den Spiegel im blauen Feld,

and the fragment of a song for the Prince. Under what circumstances the opera originated, and of its ultimate fate, nothing further is known.

All these operettas and musical dramas, which followed one another in quick succession, are to be regarded in the first instance as efforts, on Schubert's part, to make himself master, by independent means, of dramatic forms in music within a smaller compass and frame than those often used by operatic writers. Nor can it be doubted that the inclination for writing dramatic music, which we see so frequently the moving spirit in the early days of many of the greatest masters, worked with irresistible force on the mind of Schubert, who certainly knew how to satisfy his ambition in this particular field, by writing copiously for the stage.

The musical value of these operettas cannot be ranked amongst the more important legacies bequeathed us by Schubert, nor probably would they, viewed as stage pieces, any longer accord with the present taste of play-goers, especially when one takes into consideration the *naïveté* of some of the librettos now in vogue;[1] on the other hand, it would be a mistake to suppose that these first fruits of Schubert's dramatic music showed the mere clever efforts of a gifted schoolboy. For the musician, with his inexhaustible creative powers, his familiarity with the laws of harmony and art of instrumentation, who at that time had already written several of the loveliest songs, and had the stuff in him to produce such a work as the Mass in G, moves in these operatic works with such ease and sense of security in the management of the vocal and instrumental part, that to talk of mere scholastic efforts is an absurdity. A performance of the musical fragments of these operettas in a small concert-room would reveal many a lovely musical thought.

The passion for operatic writing haunted Schubert all his life. A long pause here and there intervened, but on the whole his fertility and activity in this line are astonishing; and although, at a later period of his career, the ill-fortune which attended theatrical management neutralised that reception of the two greater

---

[1] Certainly there is no lack of silly librettos in our own times; but the method of trifling is changed, and adapted to the period.

works he wrote for the stage, and on which he might have counted for success, we see the undaunted man nevertheless busied to the end of his days with the thought of a new opera.   Such specimens of Schubert's dramatic work as were ever represented on the stage during his lifetime, belong exclusively to the melodrama and extravaganza.

CHAPTER IV.

(1816.)

'JUBILEE CANTATA' IN HONOUR OF SALIERI—THE CANTATA 'PROME-
THEUS'—CANTATA IN HONOUR OF JOSEF SPENDOU—THE MASS IN
C—THE SECOND STABAT MATER—SYMPHONIES IN B AND C MINOR
—AMATEURS' ASSOCIATION—THE OPERA 'DIE BÜRGSCHAFT'—PART-
SONGS—SONGS—QUOTATIONS FROM DIARY—SCHUBERT APPLIES FOR
THE POST OF MUSIC-TEACHER AT LAIBACH—FRANZ V. SCHOBER.

THE year 1816 represents in Schubert's brief earthly
career a time of incessant, and, with some trifling interruptions, unbroken exercise of productiveness. Besides
the ever-increasing number of songs (for his operatic
writing at this period is represented by only one solitary fragment), the cantata, in the shape of three
'occasional compositions,' was his special subject. Of
these cantatas the one that is set to the poetical text of
'Prometheus' far surpasses the other two. The first
cantata in order of date is that for which Schubert, at
the jubilee festival of the Court Capellmeister Salieri,
prepared a harmless libretto of his own rhymes, and set
to equally unpretentious music.

On June 16, 1816, Antonio Salieri entered on the
fiftieth year of his service to the Emperor of Austria.
Both he and his family had some time previously anti-

cipated with eagerness the impending jubilee fête, and
determined on celebrating it with becoming honour,
and the Emperor himself was intent on giving dignity
and lustre to the jubilee festival.[1]

Early on the morning of June 16, the same day on
which the Emperor Francis (starting from the castle of
Bösenbeug) returned to Schönbrunn from his journey
to Italy, Salieri visited the Italian church to offer his
prayers and thanksgivings. His four daughters accompanied their father, who thought of the first walk he had
taken through the streets of the Imperial city on June
16, 1766, with his master Gassmann (who had long since
been called to his rest). At ten o'clock in the forenoon
an Imperial carriage was in attendance before the door
of his house (No. 1154 in the Spiegelgasse), which took
him to the hotel of the grand steward, Prince of Trautt-
mannsdorf-Weinsberg. This gentleman appeared in
the entrance-hall, with the Hofmusikgraf Kuefstein, and
conducted him to a chamber decorated for the occasion,
when, after a short address, he was invested with the
great gold medal and chain of honour of the civic class,
in the presence of the whole body of court musicians.
Salieri thanked the Prince for the mark of distinction
awarded him, and then the whole body of assembled
musicians for their zeal; and after many gracious words
had been interchanged, he led the way (it was on a
Sunday) to the Court chapel, to discharge his ordinary

[1] From 'Salieri's Life,' by Mosel ('Wiener Zeitung,' June 19, 1861).

duty, and conduct the high Mass (on this occasion one of his own).

In the afternoon there was a family gathering at the dinner-table, and some intimate friends were asked to join the party. About six o'clock in the evening, in answer to an invitation that had been forwarded to them, all his old pupils, of both sexes, who were still working professionally, came to visit him. Count Kuef- stein honoured the company with his presence, and when the whole party had assembled, the musical part of the festival began. Salieri, surrounded by his daughters, who were all dressed alike, took his seat at the piano. To the right of him, sitting in a half-circle, were four- teen ladies, consisting of his former and present pupils: these were Rosenbaum and Fux (the maiden name of both was Gassmann), Correga, Flamm, Klüber, Schütz, Milani, Hähnel, Canzi, Franchetti, Teyber, Fery, Weiss, and Mathes. To the left were twelve gentlemen, pupils of former days, and some still taking lessons, chiefly composition pupils:[1] Carl Freiherr v. Doblhoff, Josef Weigl, Stunz, Assmayr, and Franz Schubert. Hummel and Moscheles, who were absent on professional tours, contented themselves with sending presents of their own composition. Amongst Salieri's pupils in singing there appeared, Mozatti, Frölich, Platzer, and Salz- mann. Opposite the old man, the hero of the jubilee

---

[1] There was a pupil of the name of Liszt. Franz Liszt was then in his sixteenth year.

fête, were two prominent places reserved for the superior officials, but in the centre of these stood the bust of the Emperor Joseph II., Salieri's first patron and friend. When everyone had taken his seat, Salieri expressed his thanks to his audience, and a chorus expressive of gratitude to God, the Emperor, fatherland, family and friends was sung by the whole company. The words and music also were by Salieri. Afterwards the vocal compositions, written for the occasion by his pupils, were given, each in its turn, beginning with the work of the youngest, and ending with the presentation works of Hummel and Moscheles. Schubert himself was present at this festival, as we have already stated, with a cantata, the libretto and music of his own, entitled ' Contributions to the Jubilee Festival of Hofcapellmeister Salieri, by his pupil Franz Schubert.'

The composition consists of a vocal quartett for men's voices (Adagio, B-flat major $\frac{4}{4}$), to the words:—

> Gütigster, Bester!
> Weisester, Grösster!
> So lange ich Thränen habe
> Und an der Kunst mich labe,
> Sei beides Dir gebracht, (geweiht?)
> Der beides mir verleiht.

This is followed by an air with pianoforte accompaniment (Andantino, G major $\frac{2}{4}$):—

> So Gut als Weisheit ströme mild
> Von Dir, o Gottes Ebenbild.
> Engel bist Du mir auf Erden,
> Gern' möcht' ich Dir dankbar werden,

and a canon for three voices (Moderato, G major $\frac{2}{4}$)—

Unser aller Grosspapa
Bleibe noch recht lange da !

finishes a cantata which is more calculated to interest
people by the circumstances to which it owes its origin
than from its intrinsic value as a work of art.[1] A far
more important work was composed by Schubert about
this time, and one which commanded the unanimous
praise of the still-living witnesses of its first performance. To this work the modest author owed his
first honorarium in the shape of forty florins; and he
was so well pleased with the music, that several years
later he gave it at a public performance. This is the
Cantata called in the preface 'Prometheus,' for principal voices, chorus, and band. Several law-students,
amongst them Count Constantin Wickenburg (head of
the Austrian Board of Trade), and as Hauptveran-
stalter,[2] Herr v. Managetta, determined on surprising
Heinrich Watteroth,[3] on his name-day (July 12), with
a musical celebration, which was to take place in the
garden attached to his house in the Erdberg suburb.

---

[1] Copies of this work are in the hands of Josef v. Spaun, the music
publisher Herr Witzendorf, and the wife of Dr. Lumpe, of Vienna.
This lady also possesses a trio with pianoforte accompaniments, set to
the same words, and composed also in the June of 1816. It differs in
some respects, but not materially, from the above-mentioned quartett.

[2] Probably Hofrath Filipp v. Managetta, who died a short time
since.

[3] Watteroth was the father-in-law of Schubert's friend Von Witteczek.

Filipp Dräxler von Carin (at that time Hofrath and Kanzlei-Director of the Imperial Obersthofmeisteramt), at the request of several of his colleagues, composed the words of the Cantata 'Prometheus,' whilst taking a stroll through the mountain-valleys of Baden, and the poem was entrusted to Schubert, who had no personal acquaintance with the author. The rehearsals for the performance were held in the Consistorial Hall of the University, and were continued with vigour. The performance, which had frequently to be postponed, from the unfavourable state of the weather, came off finally on July 24.

Fräulein Maria Lagusius (who afterwards married Herr Griesinger, and died in 1861) and Josef Goetz undertook the solo parts of 'Gea' and 'Prometheus;' the students worked in the orchestra and chorus. Count Wickenburg delivered the public oration in honour of Salieri. The Cantata and other musical works followed. The performance seems to have been successful, and the impression made by the original and beautifully instrumented work was of a decided kind.[1] The music had

---

[1] A few days afterwards the following poem by Herr F. v. Schlechta (at that time chief in the head department of the Exchequer Office) appeared in the 'Theaterzeitung;'—

'To Franz Schubert, on the performance of his "Prometheus."

'In der Töne tiefem Leben,
Wie die Saiten jubelnd klangen,
Ist ein unbekanntes Leben
In der Brust mir aufgegangen.

made such an impression, that Dr. Leopold v. Sonnleithner proposed it for the programme of the Musikverein's
concerts; but his scheme failed, as the public had
no wish to hear any music 'of so young and hitherto
obscure a musician.' In the last years of Schubert's
life the work became more generally known, and, at the
request of the authorities of the Göttweih Institution,.
the score and the parts, copied by Schubert himself,
were sent to them. The Cantata, however, being wanted
elsewhere, the score and parts were, at Schubert's request, sent back again to his house (at that time No.
694 on the Wieden), but the MS. disappeared about
the time of Schubert's death, and, up to this time, has
never come to light again.[1]

In dem Sturmeston der Lieder
Klagt die Menschheit jammernd Ach,
Kämpfend steigt Prometheus nieder,
Und das schwere Dunkel brach.

Mich hat's wunderbar erhoben,
Und der Wehmuth neue Lust
Wie ein schimmernd Licht von oben
Kam in die bewegte Brust.

Und in Thränen und Entzücken
Fühlte ich mein Herz zerstücken,
Jauchzend hätte ich mein Leben
Wie Prometheus hingegeben.'

[1] The poem has been lost. In the year 1842 Herr Alois Fuchs advertised in the 'Musikzeitung,' at Vienna, for any news respecting the
missing work, but all in vain. In the 'Neue Zeitschrift für Musik,'
No. 8, for the year 1842, this advertisement was referred to, and the
remark made: 'If only the unprinted things of Schubert, which he is

A third composition of a similar kind was written in honour of the Chief Inspector of Schools, Josef Spendou,[1] to the words of Hocheisel, for solo voices, orchestra, and chorus, entitled, 'Expressions of Gratitude on the part of the Institute of the Widows of Teachers at Vienna to the Founder and Principal of the same' (Josef Spendou).[2] The composition consists of recitatives (for bass), an air, a duett, and several

known to have composed, could be brought to light! For instance, in the library at Berlin there is a grand Opera (" Alfonso und Estrella "), and in Vienna over fifty works of still greater value. These cannot print themselves : those whose chief business it is ought to give themselves some trouble, that the world may at last come to a full and correct appreciation of the value of Schubert.' Herr Frühwald undertook the restoration of 'Prometheus' from Göttweih, and Dr. Leopold v. Sonnleithner (to whom I am indebted for this communication) sent the score to Schubert, who had asked for it in a letter of which Frühwald was the bearer. Unfortunately no copy was made of the Cantata, the parts of which had been written out by Schubert himself. The score was also sent to Innsbruck, and a performance given there by Capellmeister Gänsbacher. In the year 1819 'Prometheus' was given at Sonnleithner's house, and Dr. Ignaz v. Sonnleithner sang the part of Prometheus. In the year 1816 Schubert was present at the performance, and of those who took part in it and witnessed its production were Dr. Leopold v. S., Albert Stadler, Ant. Müllner, afterwards Minister of Finance, Von Schlechta, and Herr Josef Hüttenbrenner. In the year 1820 Schubert wished to give the Cantata in the Augarten, but the idea was given up from the ill success of the rehearsals. The time occupied by the performance was about three-quarters of an hour.

[1] Spendou was Domscolasticus, a Doctor of Divinity, Privy Councillor, Member of the Royal Commission in affairs connected with German Schools, a mitred prelate, and Chief Superintendent of Schools.

[2] The Cantata is published as Op. 128, with a pianoforte arrangement by Ferdinand Schubert.

choruses. The first bass Recitative (Grave, G minor
$\frac{4}{4}$), 'There lies he stricken down by death,' alludes to
the dead father, and, in short, powerful passages, expresses the helplessness of the fatherless children. A
mournful elegy is given to the widow, accompanied by
a chorus (Andante, F minor $\frac{4}{4}$) of children consoling
their widowed mother. A second bass Recitative is
addressed to the deliverer, whose kindly interference
is the subject of a duett (Allegro mod., B-flat major) by the widow and one of the children. Another
passage in recitative follows (Andante molto $\frac{4}{4}$), and to
this succeeds a chorus of orphans and widows (Allegro
maestoso, D major $\frac{4}{4}$) in honour of Spendou, and
lastly, a short bass solo (Adagio con moto, D major $\frac{4}{4}$),
leading to a choral finale (in B-flat major $\frac{4}{4}$), which,
beginning with a quartett (widow, child, tenor, and bass),
accompanies the soprano solo to the end of the work.

The recitatives in this Cantata are finely and ex-
pressively treated. The other portions of the work allowing for smooth execution on the part of the orphan
children, move in gentle flowing melodies. The homely
nature of the libretto was not well adapted to develope a
grand mode of treatment on the part of the composer ;
but the intention of paying honour, by appropriate
music, to the benefactor of widows and orphans, is said
to have been completely answered in the public performance of the Cantata.

Church music is amply represented at this period by

the Mass in C,[1] comparatively speaking a work of less pretensions than many others; by the Grand Magnificat,[2] a so-called 'Duett-Arie'[3] for soprano and tenor, the fragment of a Requiem,[4] and the Stabat Mater, in imitation of Klopstock; finally, by two smaller contributions in the shape of Klopstock's Hallelujah (for three voices), contained in Series 41, and a Salve Regina. Of these sacred compositions, the Stabat Mater, for solo voices, chorus, and orchestra, is unquestionably the grandest, and of the most artistic value.[5] It consists of four airs

[1] This is Schubert's Fourth Mass (marked third in the title-page). It was written for four voices and orchestral accompaniment, dedicated 'Zur freundlichen Erinnerung' to Herr Holzer, and was engraved by Diabelli as Op. 48.

[2] This Magnificat is for solo and mixed voices with instrumental accompaniments (violin, viola, hautboy, bassoon, trumpet, drum, and organ). It begins with a chorus (Allegro maestoso ¼), 'Magnificat anima mea Dominum,' &c., followed by a quartett for principals (Andante ¾), 'Deposuit potentes de sede,' &c., and a concluding chorus with quartett for principals (Allegro vivace ¾), 'Gloria Patri et Filio et Spiritui Sancto. Amen.' Herr Spina has the MS., bearing date September 25, 1816.

[3] This work is one of large pretensions (Moderato G major ¼), and is accompanied by violins, hautboy, bassoon, cello, and double-bass. The words run thus :—

'Auguste, jam cœlestium Divis recepte sedibus,
Dignare te colentium piis adesse mentibus.
Omnem per orbem gloriæ tuæ eriguntur simbola;
Per te impetratæ gloriæ ubique stant insignia. Amen.'
Spina has the original manuscript.

[4] The Requiem reaches (inclusively) to the fugue of the Kyrie.

[5] The Stabat Mater bears date February 1816. The instrumental accompaniments are for violins, viola, hautboy, trumpets, and double-bass. In the year 1841 it was performed in the concert-room of the

(one for soprano, another for bass, and two for tenor), a duett for soprano and tenor, two trios for soprano, tenor, and bass, one of which has a choral accompaniment, and five choruses for mixed voices. These are the most successful portions of the entire work, and the double chorus (No. 5), given out alternately by men's and women's voices, is full of beauty and expression. The soprano solo (No. 2) and the trio (No. 10) are written in a genuine church style, the solo being immensely effective. The bass air might have been written by Mozart, so exactly is it formed on the model of that master. To the two Symphonies (in B-flat and D), which were composed in the preceding year, must be added, as the results of this year, two additional Symphonies, that in C minor (called ' the tragic '), and a second in B-flat major.[1] Of the two Symphonies in B-flat, one is known as ' the Symphony without Trumpets and Drums,' probably from the fact of there being

Musikverein in Vienna, Staudigl, Lutz, and Frl. Tuczek taking the principal parts. In the year 1858 the trio and chorus were given by the Vienna Singakademie, and the whole work was given in its entirety in the April of 1863 in the Altlerchenfelder Church in Vienna.

[1] The C minor Symphony, composed in April, consists of four movements :—an Introduction, Adagio molto $\frac{3}{4}$ with the Allegro to follow, an Andante (A-flat major $\frac{2}{4}$), a Minuett with Trio (Allegro vivace, E-flat major), and the Finale (Allegro, C minor $\frac{2}{4}$). The Symphony in B-flat has also four movements—a Largo and Allegro, an Andante, Minuett, and Finale. The second movement of the C minor Symphony was given as a fragment on December 2, 1860, at a concert in Vienna. The Vienna Musikverein possesses a copy of the B-flat Symphony, and Dr. Schneider one of the C minor.

no trumpeter or drummer in the Orchestral Society of Amateurs, for whom Schubert, at that time, was in the habit of composing his chamber and orchestral music.

The small circle of friends and neighbours, starting with quartett parties at the elder Schubert's, had by degrees enlarged its borders, and swelled into an orchestra competent to perform Haydn's Symphonies, which were reduced into a quartett arrangement with each part doubled. To the existing quartett of performers were added Herr Josef Doppler (foreman and chief manager of the musical establishment of C. A. Spina), who had been intimate with Schubert from boyhood, the violoncello players Kamauf and Wittmann, and the double-bass player Redlpacher.

As the elder Schubert's house was now too small for these meetings, Franz Frischling, a merchant, very gladly opened his doors (No. 1105, Dorotheergasse) to the musicians. Several new members joined, and consequently, in the autumn of 1815, the smaller Symphonies (by Pleyel, Rosetti, Haydn, and Mozart) became feasible, and people came to listen. The room was too small, so at the end of the year 1815 the Society migrated to the house of Otto Hatwig (originally a member of the orchestra of the Burg Theatre) at Schottenhof, and in the spring of 1818 to his new house in Gundelhof. Continued and regular practices, coupled with the addition to the band of some first-rate musicians, led to performances of the greater works of

Haydn, Mozart, Krommer, Romberg, and the two first
Symphonies of Beethoven, besides the Overtures by
Cherubini, Spontini, Câtel, Mehul, Boildieu, Weigl,
Winter, and others. It was for this Society that Schubert
wrote the two Symphonies we have mentioned, and in
the year 1818 the Symphony in C, besides, in 1817, the
Overture in the Italian style (of these we shall speak
hereafter) and an Overture in B-flat,[1] written in September 1816. The practice meetings continued as late
as the autumn of 1820, when, for want of a suitable
locality, they were discontinued and never resumed.[2]

Schubert made a strong effort to complete an Opera
in three acts, called 'Die Bürgschaft,' but it was never
finished.[3] This opera, the score of which bears date
May 2, has two acts entirely finished; of the third there
is but one air with chorus; in all there are fifteen numbers. The compiler of the book is not mentioned, and
I have never succeeded in finding the libretto. It has

---

[1] The score is in the possession of Dr. Schneider, of Vienna.

[2] The Society, after leaving Hatwig, held its meetings at the house
of Anton Pettenkoffer, a factor in the Bauernmarkt. When P. left
Vienna, and no fitting place of resort could be got without paying for
it, the Society was dissolved. Amongst the standing members from the
years 1815–1818, were Ferdinand and Franz Schubert (the last as a
player on the viola) and Josef Doppler (bassoon); Ferd. Bogner (flute)
joined them occasionally. As solo singers who took part in the
performances were Von Gymnich, Goetz, Tieze, and Frl. Josefine
and Babette Fröhlich.—See 'Essays on the State of Music in Old
Vienna,' by Dr. L. v. Sonnleithner, in the 'Recensionen' of the year
1862.

[3] The score is with Dr. Schneider.

been said to have been the work of some law-student.[1] The verses and the expressions contained in them in some passages are beneath criticism, and form a convincing proof of the easy, unexacting nature and temper in which Schubert applied himself to the librettos for his operas. If the idea as a whole pleased him, and he could discover any openings for the dramatic development of his music, he passed over the remaining imperfections with incredible ease and good nature. I do not know why he was deterred from finishing the entire opera (possibly the unmeaning character of his book may have prevented him). The treatment is in the manner of Schiller's ballads, for which Schubert at this period had written music.

The opera begins with a chorus of people praying for deliverance from cruelty and tyranny (Allegro moderato, C minor $\frac{4}{4}$), to accompaniments of violins, viola, cello, bassoon, horn, trumpets, and double-bass. Moeros (bass) enters to the assembled crowds, and expresses his intention of vengeance in an air (Allegro agitato, F minor $\frac{4}{4}$).[2] The chorus answers in a wild characteristic strain, taking for its subject the flaming volcano of Etna

---

[1] In the same year (1816) appeared 'The Friends of Syracuse,' a new play in five acts by Elise Bürger (*née* Hahn), extracts from which were printed in the 'Theaterzeitung,' in Vienna, September 1816.

[2] Amongst other pieces, Moeros sings the following verse :—

Muss ich fühlen in tiefer Brust
Tiefes Elend, tiefe Schmach,
Und mit dieser Rachelust !
Und ich bin so klein und schwach!

and the infatuated rebel, who is to be impaled and crucified that very day.[1] The tyrant of Syracuse gives the assassin one day's leave for settling his worldly affairs, for which favour the villain expresses his gratitude in an air[2] (Moderato, D minor $\frac{4}{4}$); but Dionysius, in a recitative, expresses his doubts on the subject of his return.[3]

Feste gibt es heute wieder
Bei dem König an dem Hof,
Uebermuth singt üpp'ge Lieder
Bei den Prassern zu dem Soff, &c.

[1] The chorus then utters the following frantic nonsense :—
Auf, löscht ihm (dem Etna) die schmachtende Qual,
Erfrischt ihm den brändigen glühenden Mund
Mit purpurner Welle bis auf den Grund.
Er labe die brennende Sonne einmal
Und singe bachantische Lieder.—
Es lebe der meuter'sche Thor,
Er zieret das Kreuz mit dem schönen Leib,
Er stellet die Fülle vor ;
Und langet und presset das lüsterne Weib,
Sie möchte ihn gerne für sich befreien ;
Er lebe gesund und stark, der Blüten nur schmauset,
Nicht Krankheit und Pest.
Er muss sich dem Henkertod weih'n.
Er sei ihm ein Opfer, ein herrliches Fest.
Wir schauen's noch heute am Kreuze vollbracht.

[2] Diese Gnade dank' ich dir,
Werd' sie stets dir denken,
Und ich eile froh von hier,
Mein Geschäft zu lenken.

[3] Ob er wohl zurückkehrt ?
Ich kann es nicht glauben,
Die That wär unerhört,
Sie ist gar nicht zu glauben.

The scene changes to the interior of the house of Theages. His wife Anna sings a romance about a poor lost child, recovered back once more into the fold from which it had strayed. The two children of Theages, Julus and Ismene, repeat the last verse each time with the mother. This charming piece is followed by a two-part song for the two children—the subject is a narrative of some legend. A duett between Anna and Theages forms the burden of the next number. Theages, who goes bail for Moeros, is ordered—the defendant not appearing—to be cast into prison. Anna utters loud lamentations, Theages seeks to comfort her.[1] The chorus of guards incites Theages to follow him,[2] and this leads to the concluding subject of the final ensemble of the first act.

[1]
ANNA.

Du gehst in Kerker—du,
Du eilst in Kerker—du,
Zur finstern Kerkersnacht hinab,
Das geht nimmer rechtlich zu.

THEAGES.

Geliebtes Weib gib dich in Ruh!
Ich geh' in den Kerker, doch nicht zum Grab.

ANNA.

Nein, nein, das war noch nicht erhört,
Das geht nicht an, du bürgst ihn nicht, &c.

[2] On this occasion Anna says:—
Die rauhen Männer führen ihn
Zum finstern Kerkersort,
Er klirrt in Ketten fort,

The second is separated from the first act by an
overture, which (beginning with an Andante in C
major ⅜, and ending in Allegro agitato) leads to an air
for Moeros on his return home, in which he thanks the
gods for saving him from drowning.

The scene changes to Anna's room. The lady, terri-
fied by a dream about her husband's fate, expresses her
anguish in a series of passionate recitatives. Julus
and Ismene endeavour to comfort her. Their dialogue
ends with a trio, in which Anna takes part.[1]

Philostratus, the friend of the family, enters and tries
to restore the confidence in the fidelity of the now dis-
trusted Moeros. Anna answers him in gentler accents
and style, a duett for the two characters follows. Philostratus ends the interview with the following words :—

> Liebet unbeschreiblich ihn,
>   Er gibt zehnmal sein Leben hin,
> Um Freundes Leben zu erretten,
>   Wenn nur von traurigen Ketten,

and Anna and the two children repeat that sublime
stanza.

The scene now changes to a forest. Robbers are
lurking, on the look-out for booty, and sing a characteristic quartett. The band, in a movement Allegro
furioso, describes a battle with the highwaymen. A

---

[1] Ja so sind wir ganz verlassen,
Statt des Freundes muss er sterben,
Herzlich muss ich Moeros hassen,
Da wir alle nun verderben.

number of recitative passages follow; Moeros vanquishes the robbers, quenches his thirst from the refreshing stream, and thanks the all-powerful gods. He continues to exclaim, as he enters the scene :—

> Wenn ich verbliebe!
> Mitleidiger Gott !
> Ohn' Erbarmen—wär' er todt.
> Und mir winkt ein Ziel,
> Heiliger Andacht grosses Gefühl.

And here the second act ends.

The third contains only two finished numbers. It opens with a chorus of the people, assembled in front of the place of execution; a short introduction (Andante, B minor $\frac{3}{8}$) precedes this chorus. The choral sentiment is thus expressed :—

> Der Abend rückt heran,
> Du büsst für deinen Wahn ;
> Man führt sogleich dich fort
> Zum strengen Kerkerort.

Thereupon Theages answers :—

> Schweigt, Ihr seid im Wahn,
> Durch Euch spricht der Tyrann,
> Euch wurmt mein fester Muth,
> Mein hohes Glaubensgut.

Then follows an interesting musical passage—Theages, prepared for death, appeals to the crowd :—

> Ein böser Geisterchor,
> Der sich voll Zweifel seitwärts steckt
> Nun schweigt, ich lass mich tödten,
> Und werd' ihn so erretten,

whilst the crowd replies to him in scornful language, admirably understood and illustrated by the composer:—

> Die Sonne sinkt, nun gute Nacht,
> Du hast's gebüsst, du hast's vollbracht,
> Das hast für deinen Glauben,
> Den dir kein Mensch kann rauben.
> Seht, wie der Freund zu lösen eilt,
> Und seinem Freund die Wunden heilt,
> Da ihn die Stunden schlugen,
> Die sie zusammentrugen.

From this point the solo and chorus, although without a libretto, are carried on through five pages of the original score; and a short phrase is given to Theages:—

> Wenn dreimal sich der Abend neiget,
> Und er sich noch nicht findet,
> Meint ihr, der Glaube schwindet?

The setting of this solo passage extends to the space of six pages, and thus ends the unfinished Opera, of which no single portion has ever been represented in public.

There are numbers of instrumental compositions written in other styles than those already mentioned (pianoforte and church music); but the majority of these remain unpublished.[1]

---

[1] Amongst these are: a stringed Quartett in F, an instrumental Trio, a violin Concerto in C, a Rondo for the violin in A, a pianoforte Sonata in F, an Adagio and Rondo concertant for pianoforte, the first movement and opening of the Allegro of a pianoforte Sonata in E, two Marches for pianoforte in E major and B minor, Marches with Trio in E major, twelve 'Deutsche' with Coda and six Ecossaisen. On the last there is an expression in Schubert's own handwriting: ' Composed during imprisonment in my room at Erdberg. May.' At the end are the

Of vocal pieces set for various voices, and hitherto but little, if at all, known, may be mentioned : 'An die Sonne,' a grand solemn Quartett, with chorus and pianoforte accompaniment; 'Das Grab,' by Salis (vocal Quartett for men's voices); 'Chorus of Angels,' from Göthe's 'Faust,' for mixed voices;[1] 'Drinking Song'[2] (for tenor solo and chorus of men's voices, with piano-forte accompaniment); 'Der Geistertanz,' by Mathisson (Quartett for men's voices), and a vocal Trio, 'Am Seegestrade.'[3]

In respect of the number of songs, the year 1816 may take rank with the year immediately preceding, and both periods were marked with incessant activity in Schubert's career as a song-writer. Amongst the songs of those days are the 'Songs of the Harper,' 'The Wanderer,'[4] 'Fragment from Æschylus,' 'An

words 'Thank God!' As Witteczek, Mayrhofer, and Spaun lived for some time at Erdberg, the imprisonment story probably refers to some practical joke which Schubert allowed his friends to play on him when they visited him. Ferdinand Schubert, in whose catalogues the above-named compositions are found, mentions a Symphony in C (composed in September), but no trace of this work is forthcoming. The three Sonatas for piano and violin (Op. 137) belong also to this period.

[1] This appeared in the year 1839, as a supplement to the 'Neue Zeitschrift für Musik.'

[2] The 'Drinking Song' appeared in the year 1844, sent by Mecchetti as a contribution to the 'Musikzeitung' of Vienna.

[3] Herr Stadler, of Vienna, has the manuscript of this as well as the 'Geistertanz.'

[4] The original of 'The Wanderer' is in the hands of Dr. Carl Enderes, of Vienna. It bears date October 1816. The actual day has been

Schwager Kronos,' &c., compositions which speak trumpet-tongued for the ripe and full power of this musical poet, now but nineteen years of age. A fine song still remains unpublished, 'Abschied,' [1] by Mayrhofer, a melody for a pilgrim, with a national air about it, and a pianoforte accompaniment.

None can deny that, if a number of letters, diaries, and other memoranda, ranging over a long period of the author's life, can be connected together as a whole, such things are admirably adapted to widen and intensify our knowledge of the character and life of the writer in question. The rich treasure-trove we possess in Mozart's letters, and the lately published correspondence of Felix Mendelssohn, give a deeper insight

erased, apparently by Schubert; some passages, too, in the pianoforte accompaniment have become illegible by the thick marks of alteration, and a fresh accompaniment in their place has been substituted by the composer. A clergyman in Vienna, of the name of Horni, drew Schubert's attention to the poem of Georg Filipp Schmidt, of Lubeck (born 1766, died 1849). Horni probably found it in a volume called 'Dichtungen für Kunstredner,' published by Deinhartstein, in the year 1815, where it is marked as 'Der Unglückliche,' by Werner. Schubert has consequently written on the original, 'by Zacharias Werner.'

[1] The poem is headed 'Lunz,' the name of a place in Lower Austria, and begins thus:—

Ueber die Berge
Zieht ihr fort,
Kommt an manchen
Grünen Ort;
Muss zurücke
Ganz allein,
Lebet wohl,
Es muss so sein, &c.

into the thoughts and feelings common to those artistic
natures, than any description of their outer life would
be able to afford; and whilst such letters not unfre-
quently assist the appreciation and value of the works
themselves, they most materially assist the biographer
in his drawing a correct portrait of him whose features
he intends to represent.   But very few of Schubert's
letters have, up to this time, become known: it may
be because he was not fond of letter-writing (of this,
however, no proof is forthcoming); or, again, his letters
may have been lost or kept back, from a false shame
and aversion to their being seen by other eyes than
those for whom they were originally intended.   Only
a few jottings, taken from diaries of the years 1816
and 1824, are before me.   Some of these shall be inserted here, and others at a later stage of the narrative.   Whether Franz kept memoranda ranging over a
long period, I have not been able to discover.[1]   Neither
these short notices, nor the letters, are calculated by
the intrinsic worth of their contents to arrest in any

[1] Alois Fuchs, the well-known autograph collector, remarks in his
'Schubertiana:'—'Some years ago I found accidentally, at an autograph
collector's in Vienna, the fragment of one of Schubert's diaries in his
own handwriting, but several of the pages were wanting.   On my asking the reason of this, the wretched owner of the relic replied that he
had for a long space of time been in the habit of distributing single
pages of this manuscript to hunters of Schubert relics or autograph col-
lectors.   Having expressed my indignation at this Vandalism, I took
pains to secure the remainder for the following pages.'   Herr G. Petter,
of Vienna, possesses the original relic.

great degree the interest of the reader; for Schubert was never wont 'to wear his heart upon his sleeve,' even for the inspection of his most trusted friends. Still, slender as the resources are which illustrate but meagrely the existence of Schubert, the biographer must be permitted to avail himself of every help he can lay hold on, be it seemingly never so trivial, and give the originals without curtailing a syllable, for these authentic records invariably throw streaks of light on the face of the individual whose portrait we are painting, let alone the thought that small episodes of this kind break in agreeably on the monotonous process of reckoning Schubert's compositions—a feature which will form the chief element in the history of the composer's career.

The discovered fragments of Schubert's diary for the year 1816 embrace only the days from the 13th to the 16th of June inclusive, and run thus:—

'*June* 13, 1816.—This day will haunt me for the rest of my life as a bright, clear, and lovely one. Gently, and as from a distance, the magic tones of Mozart's music sound in my ears. With what alternate force and tenderness, with what masterly power did Schlesinger's playing of that music impress it deep, deep in my heart![1] Thus do these sweet impressions, passing into our souls, work beneficently on our inmost being, and

---

[1] Martin Schlesinger, born 1751, at Wildenschwert, in Bohemia, died at Vienna on August 12, 1818, was an admirable violin-player. A few but insignificant compositions from his pen have appeared in print.

no time, no change of circumstances, can obliterate
them. In the darkness of this life, they show a
light, a clear, beautiful distance, from which we gather
confidence and hope. O Mozart! immortal Mozart!
how many and what countless images of a brighter,
better world hast thou stamped on our souls! This
quintett may be called one of the greatest amongst
his smaller works. I too was moved on this occasion
to introduce myself. I played variations by Beethoven,
sang Göthe's "Rastlose Liebe," and Schiller's "Amalia."
The first met with universal, the second with qualified applause. Although I myself think my "Rastlose
Liebe" more successful than "Amalia," yet I cannot
deny that to Göthe's musical genius must be attributed in a large measure the applause which greeted
the song. I also made acquaintance with Mdlle. Jenny,
a pianoforte-player with extraordinary powers of execution; but I think her wanting in true and pure
expression.

'*June* 14, 1816.—After the lapse of a few months,
I took once more an evening walk. There can hardly
be anything more delightful than, of an evening, after
a hot summer's day, to stroll about on the green grass:
the meadows between Währing and Döbling seem to
have been created for this very purpose. I felt so
peaceful and happy as my brother Carl and I walked
together in the struggling twilight. "How lovely!"
I thought and exclaimed, and then stood still en-

chanted. The neighbourhood of the churchyard reminded us of our excellent mother. Whiling the time
away with melancholy talk, we arrived at the point
where the Döbling road branches off, and I heard
a well-known voice issuing as though from heaven—
which is our home: the voice came from a carriage
which was being pulled up. I looked up, and there
was Herr Weinmüller, who got out and greeted us
with his hearty, manly, cheerful-toned voice.[1] How
vainly does many a man strive to show the candour
and honesty of his mind by conversation equally sincere
and candid!—how would many a man be the laughing-
stock of his fellow-creatures were he to make the
effort! Such gifts must come naturally; no efforts can
acquire them.

'*June* 15, 1816.—It usually happens that we form
exaggerated notions of what we expect to see. At
least, I found it so when I saw the exhibition of pictures
of native artists, held at Saint Anna. The work I
liked best in the whole exhibition was a Madonna and
Child, by Abel. I was much disappointed by the

---

[1] Weinmüller (Carl) was born in the year 1765, in the neighbourhood of Augsburg. At first he belonged to a troop of strolling players,
and at last settled, in 1795, at Vienna, where, step by step, he mounted
to such a pitch of prosperity as to become the chosen favourite of the
public. He had a magnificent bass voice, and his declamatory powers
were very impressive. He excelled also as a lay vicar in the Chapel
Royal. He was pensioned in the year 1825, and died at his villa in
Döbling in the year 1828.

velvet mantle of a prince. I am convinced that one must see things of this sort much more frequently, and give them a longer trial, if one hopes to find and retain the proper expression and impression intended to be conveyed.'

The following somewhat misty and confused remarks were written down by Schubert on the evening of June 16, 1816, after returning home from Salieri's jubilee festival :—

'It must be pleasant and invigorating to the artist to see all his pupils collected around him, every one striving to do his best in honour of his master's jubilee fête ; to hear in all their compositions a simple, natural expression, free from all that *bizarrerie* which, with the majority of composers of our time, is the prevailing element, and for which we are almost mainly indebted to one of our greatest German artists ; free, I say, from that *bizarrerie* which links the tragic with the comic, the agreeable with the odious, the heroic with whining (*Heulerei*), the most sacred subjects with buffoonery—all this without discrimination ; so that men become mad and frantic instead of being dissolved in tears, and tickled to idiotic laughter rather than elevated towards God. The fact that this miserable *bizarrerie* has been proscribed and exiled from the circle of his pupils, so that their eyes may rest on pure holy Nature, must be a source of the liveliest pleasure to the artist who, with a Gluck for his pioneer, has learned to know Nature, and has clung to her in spite of the most unnatural influences of our day.

'Herr Salieri celebrated by a jubilee his fifty years' residence in Vienna, and an almost equally long period of service under the Emperor. His Majesty presented him with a gold medal; and numbers of his pupils, both male and female, were invited to the ceremony. The compositions of his pupils, written specially for the occasion, were produced *seriatim*, according to the date of admission of each pupil, as he had received them when sent to him. The music concluded with a chorus from Salieri's Oratorio, "Jesu al Limbo" ("Christ in Hades"). The Oratorio is worked out in the true Gluck spirit. Everyone was interested in the entertainment.

'To-day I composed the first time for money— namely, a Cantata ("Prometheus") for the name-day festival of Herr Professor Watteroth von Dräxler. The honorarium 100 florins, Viennese currency.

'Man is like a ball between chance and passion. I have often heard it said by writers: "The world is like a stage, where every man plays his part. Praise and blame follow in the other world." Still, every man has one part assigned him—we have had our part given us—and who can say if he has played it well or ill? He is a bad theatrical manager who distributes amongst his players parts which they are not qualified to act. Carelessness here is not to be thought of. The world has no example of an actor being dismissed because of his bad declamation. As soon as he has a part adapted to his powers, he will play it well enough. Whether he is applauded or not, depends on a public with its thousand caprices. In the other world, praise or blame depends on the Grand Manager of the world. Blame, therefore, is balanced.

'Natural disposition and education determine the bent of man's heart and understanding. The heart is ruler; the mind should be.

'Take men as they are, not as they ought to be.

' Happy is he who finds a true friend. Happier still is he who finds in his own wife a true friend. To the free man, at this time, marriage is a fearful thought; he confounds it either with melancholy or low sensuality.

' Monarchs of our day, you see this and keep silence! Or do ye not see it? Then, O God, throw a veil over our senses, and steep our feelings in Lethe! Yet once, I pray, draw back the veil!

'Man bears misfortune uncomplainingly; and, for that very reason, feels it all the more acutely. For what purpose did God create in us these keen sympathies?

' Light mind, light heart: a mind that is too light generally harbours a heart that is too heavy.

' Town politeness is a powerful hindrance to men's integrity in dealing with one another. The greatest misery of the wise man and the greatest happiness of the fool is based on conventionalism.

'A noble-minded unfortunate man feels the depth of his misery and intensity of his joy; just so does the nobly prosperous man feel his good fortune or the opposite.

'Now I know nothing more! To-morrow I am sure to know something fresh! Whence comes this? Is my understanding to-day duller than it will be to-morrow? Because I am full and sleepy? Why doesn't my mind think when my body sleeps? I suppose it goes for a walk. Certainly, it can't sleep!

> Odd questions!
> I hear everyone saying;
> We can't venture here on an answer,
> We must bear it all patiently.
> Now good night
> Until ye awake.'

As we have already mentioned, Schubert, since the year 1814, discharged the duty of assistant-master at his father's school. After three years' torture and endless self-abnegation, and there appearing no prospect of a speedy emancipation from his painful position, he determined, cost what it might, to leave Vienna, in order to stand for a musical appointment. Circumstances created an opportunity for him.

The Central Organisation Commission for the time being had, in the December of 1815, consented to the establishment of a public school of music, to be attached to the Normal School Institute in Laibach. For the post of chief teacher, whose income was fixed at 450 florins and a bonus of 50 more, candidates were invited to compete, and March 15, 1815, was fixed on as the last day on which credentials and testimonials from candidates of Lower Austria could be presented for the consideration of the government. Amongst the aspirants to the office was Franz Schubert. His presentation testimonials were furnished by Salieri:—

' Io quì Sottoscritto affermo, quanto nella supplica di Francesco Schubert, in riguardo al posto musicale di Lubiana sta esposto.

' ANTONIO SALIERI,
' Primo Maestro di Cappella della
' Corte Imp. reale.'

' Vienna: 9 Aprile 1816.'

The petitions were transmitted to the government at Vienna through proper official sources, and Schubert's with the rest. His petition to the Stadthauptmannschaft, the medium of presentation, was as follows:—

' The enclosed petition hereby made by Franz Schubert for the post of musical director in Laibach, is presented to the Superior Court, in addition to the report made from this place on the 3rd of April, 1816, with reference to the similarly framed petitions of Hanslischek and Wöss.'

The candidate was not obliged to give any fresh

---

[1] The original of this certificate is in my possession ; the other dates are taken from official documents belonging to the government, entrusted to me very kindly by Herr Vice-President Riedl v. Riedenau.

proof of his musical capabilities, from Hofcapellmeister Anton Salieri having furnished him with testimonials, dated April 9, 1816, which answered for his fitness as a candidate. As it was Salieri who examined the other candidates for the office, his deliberately expressed opinion in Schubert's favour is very commendable. Not less laudatory was the testimonial of the Privy Councillor and Head Superintendent of Schools, Josef Spendou, in respect of Schubert's method as a teacher:—

' As Schubert was a pupil of the Catholic Convict, was formerly a chorister-boy at the Chapel Royal, and is now actually serving as assistant-teacher at Himmelpfortgrund, these circumstances are considered here as fit to be reckoned in his favour and to his advantage.

' MERTENS, *m. p.* FREIH. v. HAAN, *m. p.* UNGER, *m. p.*
' Vienna: April 14, 1816.'

Schubert failed in his object; the place was given to another,[1] and the school-assistant saw in his mind's eye an impecunious future in store for him. But he had not long to wait for the hour of his deliverance. At the end of the year 1815, a student of the name of Franz v. Schober, then in his eighteenth year, came to Vienna to continue his studies in the University in that place. Born in the year 1798, at Torup, in Sweden, where his father (who had emigrated about the year 1784) occupied the post of an estate-agent, Franz v.

---

[1] Salieri proposed a certain Jacob Schaufl as the fittest person for the post of music-teacher to the Institution at Laibach.

Schober returned to Germany with his mother Catherine
(a Miss Derffel, of Vienna, before she married) and his
sister, after the death of his father in the year 1802. In
1808 he began his studies at the Kremsmünster Institute, and having completed them, withdrew from Upper
Austria to Vienna, where he continued to live for a
long time. Whilst staying with the Spaun family at
Linz, in the year 1813, he happened to fall in with
some of Schubert's songs, which Josef Spaun had
brought with him from Vienna, and the great interest
which these strange and beautiful melodies excited in
his mind urged him to seek out the composer himself.
He found him in his father's house, correcting school
exercises, and so absorbed in his duties, that it was hard
to understand how Schubert could manage at such a
time to compose such heaps of music. What Schober
then and there heard of Schubert's compositions was
only calculated to enhance his admiration for the young
tone-poet. Convinced that, in order to fill his appointed
destiny, he must necessarily be withdrawn abruptly
from the soul-killing situation in his father's school, he
formed the idea of taking Schubert to live with him.
For this arrangement Schober got his own mother's consent, and after the elder Schubert had declared himself
satisfied with the proceeding, Franz withdrew to Schober's residence, at that time in the ' Landskrongasse.'[1]

---

[1] In the forty-second number of the Vienna 'Sonntagsblätter' for the
year 1847, Ferd. Nic. Schmidtler tells a piece of gossip which came from

There he remained for somewhat over half a year,
until a brother of Schober's, an Austrian hussar officer,
came on leave·to Vienna, and laid embargo upon the
only disposable room, whereupon Schubert had once
more to think about getting lodgings for himself.   Josef
Spaun took up the matter, and contrived that Schubert
finally should join partnership with Mayrhofer, who
at that time lived in the Wipplingerstrasse, and was
destined to keep house two years consecutively with the
musician.[1]

Whilst Mayrhofer was busy with his censorship
duties, Schubert toiled with equal perseverance, remaining at home till dinner-time; after dinner he either
visited Schober's rooms, or went to the coffee-house,[2]
where, with Schober and other friends, he would pass

Lichtenthal, to the effect that Schubert, in consequence of having given
some wool-gathering school-girl a stiffish box on the ears, had a violent
scene with his father, who was extremely indignant at his conduct, and
that having received his letters dimissory, Franz resigned his office as
teacher.   How much and what of truth this story contains I have never
been able to ascertain.

[1] For the above-mentioned dates I am indebted to Herr v. Schober.
As Schubert (according to the government certificate) was still in his
father's service to the year 1816, and Herr v. Schober passed the year
1817 in Sweden, and seeing it was only in the year 1819 that Mayrhofer went to live with the musician as joint occupier, certainly it
appears difficult to reconcile Schober's statements, so far as they affect
certain definite periods, with these actual facts.   ·

[2] Schubert used to visit the Bognersche Coffee-house in the Singerstrasse, where a waiter, by the odd manner in which he called out
to the kitchen the customers' orders, used to send him into fits of
laughter.

the rest of the day. The greater part of Schubert's later years were passed under Schober's roof.

Franz v. Schober plays a very prominent part in Schubert's biography, for they were brought together as associates in early days, and, allowing for short intervals and interruptions, Schober remained on terms of personal intimacy and friendship with Schubert up to the time of his death. With the exception of the years 1817, 1824, and 1825, which Schober passed in Sweden and Prussia, afterwards of the two years 1819–1821, during which period Schubert shared a room with Mayrhofer,[1] Schubert's quarters were fixed in Schober's house, or at all events there was a room there always at his disposal.[2]

Of all Schubert's friends, Schober was the one who exercised the most lasting influence over him, and the circle of young ambitious men who surrounded Schober was also admitted to Schubert's confidence and intimacy.

[1] In the year 1816, Mayrhofer lived in the Wipplingerstrasse, No. 420; in 1817 (with Spaun) in the Erdberggasse, No. 97. In the year 1818 he returned once more to 420, where (with Schubert) he remained until 1821, and then withdrew to No. 389 in the Wipplingerstrasse.

[2] Schubert lived next to Schober (Landskrongasse, afterwards Göttweiherhoff), then with Mayrhofer, in the Wipplingerstrasse, then (from 1821 to 1823) once more with Schober (Tuchlauben, near the Music Institute), in the years 1824–1826 on the Wieden, near the Carlskirche, No. 100, from 1826 to 1827 in a house on the Carolinenthor-Bastei, then again with Schober (Bäckerstrasse, Währing, Tuchlauben), and lastly, from September 1828, with his brother Ferdinand, Neue Wieden, No. 694, where he died.

Music, indeed, as a creative art, had scarcely a representative amongst them; on the other hand, a wider field for the cultivation of other arts and intellectual impulses in various directions was conceded to them, seeing that the musical element was so brilliantly represented in Franz Schubert. Later on we shall speak in more detail of the circle of friends which Schober gathered round him—friends who esteemed Schubert as one of the most honoured and beloved members of their society.[1]

[1] Of the prominent members in those social gatherings, there live still, Moriz v. Schwind, Bauernfeld, Spaun, and Franz v. Schober. The latter, after Schubert's death (when just in his thirtieth year), passed some time in Hungary, on an estate of the Count L. Festetics, returning in the year 1833, after his mother's death, to Vienna, where he undertook the management of a property in the neighbourhood of the Residence. After travelling through Italy and France, he entered the service of the Grand Duke of Weimar as Counsel to the Embassy; in 1856 he settled in Dresden, where he has remained ever since. The family of Schober was raised in the year 1801 to the rank of Austrian nobility. One sister of Franz v. Schober was married to the famous singer Siboni. Schober's poems, a considerable number of which Schubert set to music, were published in 1840.

CHAPTER V.

(1817.)

JOHANN MICHAEL VOGL—ANSELM AND JOSEF HÜTTENBRENNER—
JOSEF GAHY—OVERTURES IN THE ITALIAN STYLE—SONGS—PART-
SONGS—PIANOFORTE SONATAS.

To complete the poetical-musical triad which figures so prominently throughout the biography of Schubert, and influenced in so many and noble ways the musician's artistic development, we must here mention with some particularity one with whom Franz became acquainted shortly after he met with Schober, and with whom, during his subsequent career, he contracted a close and, from an artistic point of view, a very important relationship. The young musician found in his friends Mayrhofer and Schober the librettists of several of his most beautiful songs, and at an early stage in his career it was his good fortune to win for these very songs a most admirable interpreter, whose services he permanently secured with hardly any help or intervention on the part of his friends. This enthusiastic friend and devotee of Schubert's muse was the well-known singer Vogl, who, nearly twenty years older than Schubert, and at that time in the full vigour of manhood, had for some years past, as an operatic singer, commanded the warm sympathy and admiration of the young tone-poet.

The first meeting of the two artists seems to have been contrived by Schober; he at least it was who, in Schubert's company, called repeatedly at the house of the singer, coy and somewhat incredulous of the fame of the so-called genius, until at last Vogl determined on paying his respects in person to the two friends, then living in the same lodgings together at the ' Göttweiherhof,' in the Spiegelgasse.[1]

---

[1] In Josef v. Spaun's memoirs I find the following passage respecting Schubert's first meeting with Vogl :—Schubert, who had hitherto for the most part been the interpreter of his own songs, aimed principally at getting hold of the Court opera-singer Vogl, whose powers commanded his warmest admiration. It was of the first importance to get an opportunity for Vogl to become acquainted with Schubert's compositions ; all the rest would follow as a matter of course, so the friends thought. Schober had often spoken to him with enthusiasm about the young composer, and invited him to be present at a sort of trial of his works. But at first all efforts were ineffectual to overcome the aversion of the singer, already wearied with music, and incredulous at the very sound of the word 'genius,' after his many and painful experiences. He was obliged at last, however, to give way to the repeated entreaties of Schubert's friends ; the visit was promised, and, at the hour agreed, Vogl one evening came to Schubert's apartment, and the latter entering with shuffling gait, and incoherent stammering speech, received his visitor. Vogl, quite at his ease, scratched his nose, and taking up a sheet of music-paper, which was near him, began humming the song 'Augenlied.' He thought it pretty and melodious, but not of any great value. Afterwards he ran, *mezza voce*, through several other Lieder, which he took to much more than the first, particularly 'Ganymed,' and 'Des Schäfers Klage,' and, on leaving, he tapped Schubert on the shoulder, exclaiming : 'There is some stuff in you, but you are too little of an actor, too little of a charlatan ; you squander your fine thoughts

Johann Michael Vogl, born at Steyr on August 10, 1768, was the son of a shipowner.[1] An orphan at an early age, he received his education in his uncle's house, and, as a boy of five years of age, attracted the attention of the 'regens chori' of the parish church by the clearness of his voice and perfection of intonation. This gentleman grounded him in music, and by the time he had reached his eighth year, Vogl was admitted as a paid and professional member of the choir. Meantime the other branches of his education were not neglected. The earnest desire for acquiring knowledge, which followed Vogl throughout all his life, was early awakened in him. When sufficiently prepared, he became a member of the Educational Institute at Kremsmünster, where he passed the gymnasium and a course of philosophical studies with distinction. In the monastery he first found an opportunity of giving proofs of his talents in declamation. In small vaudevilles and dramatic cantatas, Vogl and his countryman Franz Süssmayer (afterwards Mozart's amanuensis) were always amongst

instead of properly developing them.' Then he went away, without making any promise of returning. But to others he spoke in favourable terms of Schubert, and in terms of astonishment at the ripeness and freshness of the young man's genius. By degrees the impression made on him by Schubert's songs became weightier and weightier; he frequently came uninvited to Schubert's house, and studied his compositions with him, delighting himself and those who listened to him.

[1] The following sketch of Vogl is taken partly from an essay of Bauernfeld, printed in the year 1841, and partly from information furnished by Herr v. Schober and Dr. L. v. Sonnleithner.

the most active supporters. The audience flocked in numbers, and the two artists shared in the applause which greeted their exhibitions.[1]

But a short interval elapsed before the two lads agreed to make a pilgrimage together to the Imperial City. At Vienna Vogl passed a course of legal studies, and then commenced as a practising lawyer. Süssmayer became Capellmeister at the Theatre Royal, and at his suggestion the young official received a summons, which he obeyed unhesitatingly. On May 1, 1794, he became a member of the artists attached to the German Opera, with which company he was connected for twenty-eight years. Those were the palmy days of singing for German vocalists, and the names of Weinmüller, Saal, Sebast. Mayer, Baumann, and Baucher, Anna Milder, and Buchwieser, Wild, and Forti, mark an artistic epoch of really great singers. Vogl's entry into this circle was followed with the happiest consequences. As a well-educated man, he raised, by virtue of his intelligence and cultivation, a society whose sole excellence was judged from a musical point of view. His gestures and by-play were a good deal cavilled at; on the other hand his imposing personal presence, expressive face, noble bearing, and full rich baritone voice, were incontestably much in his favour.

[1] Franz Xaver Süssmayer, born at Steyr in 1766, died at Vienna in 1803. The musical dramas and cantatas which were at that time performed at Kremsmünster were for the most part set to music by him.

His strength lay in pourtraying some individuality of character, in an artistic combination of truth with beauty. He had a fine feeling for the flow of verse, declaimed his recitatives with great power, and, by virtue of his well-grounded theoretical studies, was sufficiently well versed in the laws of harmony. None, however, allowed him a good vocal method, strictly speaking, and his singing was specially objected to, on the ground that he too often neglected a perfect evenness in his delivery of an air; and in this respect people contrasted him unfavourably with his fellow-artist Wild, although admitting, in a general way, Vogl's intellectual superiority. His greatest performances were Orestes (in ' Iphigenia '), Count Almaviva (in ' Figaro's Hochzeit '), Creon (in Cherubini's ' Medea '), Jacob (in the ' Schweizerfamilie,'[1] and in ' Joseph and his Brethren '). His acting in the first of these operas and the two last made a great impression on the youthful Schubert. His last _rôle_ was said to be the Seneschal, in Gretry's ' Bluebeard,' which was restored to the stage in the year 1821. In this year the Opera House was leased to Barbaja, and at the end of the following year Vogl was pensioned, but only to continue as a Lieder-singer—a second epoch in his artistic career,

---

[1] This opera was given for the first time at Vienna in the March of 1809. Graf Dunois, in ' Agnes Sorel,' the Colonel, in the ' Augenarzt,' (by Gyrowetz), and Telasko in the ' Vestalin,' were famous parts of Vogl's.

which was followed by a long period of success commensurate with that which attended his career on the
stage. As late as the year 1821 his execution of the
' Erl-King ' paved a way of immortality for the youthful Schubert, and four years later we find both men on
a tour in Upper Austria and the Salzburg country,
each contributing as an artist to enliven and spiritualise
the tedium of travel. In the autumn of the ensuing
year, the already aged and gout-afflicted singer was
on his way to Italy, where he remained until the next
spring; but after his return the bachelor announced
to his astonished friends his intended alliance with
Kunegunde Rosas,[1] a woman who had been educated
apart from, and independently of, the world around
her, and towards whom he had, for a number of years,
stood in the double relation of tutor and adviser. The
singer completed this alliance by marrying her when
he was fifty-eight years old, and she presented him in
the autumn of his days with a single daughter. Vogl
was no ordinary man, and the education he had had,
although in a great measure his own, was such as
rarely falls to the lot of theatrical singers. The benefits
he had derived from an early monastic training had
not been without a corresponding influence upon his
character, and had served the purpose of encouraging
in him certain tendencies to speculative thought which

---

[1] Daughter of the former superintendent of the Gallery at the Belvedere, in Vienna. Vogl's widow still lives in Steyr.

contrasted in the strangest manner with his condition
and circumstances. The ruling motive of his being
was a moral scepticism, a nice moral anatomy of self
and of the world; he was haunted through life by a
strong desire to become better day by day, and
when passion hurried him away, like all strong impetuous natures, to dangerous ventures, he was never
weary of self-recrimination, of doubt, nay, almost of
despair; if he made another false step, it was followed by more self-accusation and contrition of heart.
Deep reading and study had a painful influence over
the course and habit of life of this singular being.
The Old and New Testament, the creeds of ancient
philosophers, the observations of Marcus Aurelius, the
Enchiridion of Epictetus, and Thomas·à Kempis'
'Taulerus,' were the constant guides and counsellors
of his life.[1] The religious discipline of his early days
in a cloister affected the whole current of his after-
life. The lessons of 'the porch,' too, suited his way of
thinking, for he could harmonise them with a feeling
for the beautiful, his own perceptions of the beautiful
in artistic works of all kinds being so eminently keen
and intuitive. His favourite German writer was
Göthe, whose influence over him as a thinker and

[1] His favourite writers were the Greeks, and he copied a work of
Epictetus in four languages. In the green-room his leisure moments
were occupied in transcribing the pages of the classical authors of
Greece, and he was held in considerable respect by his theatrical comrades for his knowledge and his solid acquirements.

student was, according to Bauernfeld, of a very marked
kind.

Hints thrown out in his diaries—and these he kept
from an early period in his life—show very unmistakably the motive powers of his life and actions. Amongst
these entries there is one which, from its reference
to Schubert's songs, may here be quoted. 'Nothing
has so plainly shown the want of a good practical
school for singing as Schubert's songs.   Otherwise,
what a prodigious and universal effect would have
been created in every country where our language is
understood by these godlike inspirations, these utterances of a musical "clairvoyance!" What numbers
of hearers would have understood for the first time
the depth of those utterances, words, language, poetry
in music, words in harmony, thoughts clothed in
music! They would have learnt how the greatest
poem of our greatest poet, when translated into such
musical language, can be glorified—nay, outrivalled
by sound. Numberless examples occur to me: the
"Erl-King," "Gretchen at her Spinning-wheel,"
"Schwager Kronos," the songs of Mignon and the
Harper, Schiller's "Sehnsucht," "Der Pilgrim," "Die
Bürgschaft."'

The following incident induced Vogl to use the
expression 'clairvoyance.'[1]   Schubert, one morning,

---

[1] In a letter dated November 15, 1831, Vogl writes to A. Stadler:—'If
the subject be that of manufacturing, production, or creating, I don't care,

brought him several songs for perusal. The singer was busy at the moment, and put off the musician to another time; the songs were laid aside. Vogl afterwards examined all the songs at his leisure, and found amongst the number one that pleased him particularly. But the song in question was too high for him, so he transposed it, and had a fresh copy made. About a fortnight elapsed, and the two artists and friends were enjoying music together. Something new was proposed, and amongst other things the aforesaid song, which Vogl, without saying a word further, placed in the handwriting of the transposer upon the piano. When Schubert heard the composition in its transposed state, he called out with exultation, in the Viennese dialect :— ' H'm! pretty good song. Whose is it then ? ' On this occasion, after the lapse of two weeks, he could not remember his own work.[1]

Vogl also occupied himself with book-writing. He compiled a method of singing, and collected his expe-

I won't have anything to do with it, especially since I have learnt, by my experience of Schubert, that there are two kinds of composition; one which, as with Schubert, comes forth to the world in a state of clairvoyance or " somnambulism," without any freewill on the part of the composer, the forced product of a higher power and inspiration—one may well be astonished and charmed at such a work, but not criticise it; the other is the reflected,' &c. (Herr Stadler, of Vienna, has the original letter.)

[1] Freiherr v. Schönstein told me this story, which was well adapted to justify to himself his favourite notion, that Schubert was gifted with musical clairvoyance. The name of the song he could not call to memory.

riences, which he had gathered as an opera-singer, and subsequently as a singing-master, into a work, which, however, was never published.

As already mentioned, the composer and the active professional musician were closely associated with one another in the year 1817. Vogl soon ascertained the great value of Schubert's songs, and Schubert saw what had long been the unexpressed and ardent wishes of his soul realised beyond all expectation. The singer, earnest, thoughtful, already advanced in years, could not but exercise the most favourable influence over Schubert's musical development. He guided Schubert's choice of certain poems, after he had previously declaimed them to Schubert with passionate expression, and his peculiar appreciation of the intendment of Schubert's songs made his suggestions very influential with the composer.

Schubert generally visited Vogl some time in the forenoon,[1] either to compose in Vogl's house or to try over his new songs with his artistic friend. He had attached great importance to Vogl's opinion, submitted most of his vocal compositions to his criticism, and availed himself in a qualified way of the supposed good advice.[2] Vogl, by his admirable execution of Schu-

---

[1] Vogl lived at this time in the Plaukengasse, afterwards in the Alleegasse, on the Wieden.

[2] Schubert even consented to Vogl's transposing and making all kinds of unjustifiable alterations in his songs, which Vogl, either from posi-

bert's songs, first introduced him to the artistic world, and brought him in connection with persons and families with music-loving tastes, and Schubert's special attention to truth of expression, correctness of accentuation, and even declamation, must certainly be in part ascribed to Vogl's credit. He was a judicious guide, a fatherly adviser, and where and when it was possible, an active promoter of Schubert's worldly interests.

Spite of this intellectual bond of sympathy, cemented by an intercourse of several years, the connection of these two artists, relative to each other, was strange and peculiar. Vogl chose to adopt the air of patron and protector towards Schubert, the younger man of the two, and in many respects less matured in artistic experience, and the latter, fond of liberty and independence, could never get rid of a certain coyness and reserve in the presence of his stern and gifted companion. Owing to this barrier opposed to the two natures, the traces of close friendship, in the strict sense of the word, cannot

tiveness or a wish to make an effect, was venturesome enough to undertake. Several of these have passed, thus metamorphosed, into print, and a restoration of the original readings of all the genuine songs of Schubert would be an undertaking welcomed by all lovers of music, the more recent editions differing in reading from those first issued. Dr. Standharthner and Herr Spina have in manuscript Schubert's songs, with Vogl's clumsy alterations, which, being made in reference to the operatic singer, vary very materially from the original. The 'improvements' in the 'Müllerlieder' alone amount to a dozen. We come across some fearful alterations in 'Der Einsame,' and in the 'Altschottischen Ballade,' and the process may have been repeated with others of the songs.

be said to have left their mark; and regarding this connection purely in a musical point of view, it cannot be
denied, admitting the happy results arising from the
mutual co-operation of the creative mind and the inter-
preting artist, yet that this perhaps unique relationship
in art has also its reverse side. For instance, there can
be no doubt that Schubert, under Vogl's influence, wrote
several songs for a range of voice very seldom met with,
whilst Vogl, whose organs fitted him for these excep-
tional difficulties, could produce wonderful effects by
dropping his intonation and speaking a word, by a sudden burst of falsetto, deviating, in fact, from the natural and, artistically speaking, only justifiable method
of vocalisation. Further, it must be mentioned as an
important fact resulting from this alliance, that Schubert, to please the singer, concentrated much more of
his energies in writing songs of a slight character and
import than he would otherwise have done.

After Schubert's death, his friend, who had already
entered his sixty-eighth year, still sang with vigour and
animation, in private circles, those songs to which he
owed so much of his reputation. He certainly found
it necessary to husband the remains of his voice, and
draw largely on the peculiarities of his method, in
order to create his effects : the result was a certain self-
complacency and affected delivery, which increased in
proportion with the decay of his natural powers, and
ended by making the artist appear downright ludicrous.

The misery of the last years of his life was embittered
by a disease which, at his great age, made him a ter-
rible sufferer, and kept him confined to his room.
Patience was not one of Vogl's virtues. Withdrawn
from the outer world, he still found an alleviation in
his old customary intellectual employment. His inner
world must have indemnified him for the loss of joys
long surrendered, and for the confusion of mind which,
in respect of external things, seemed to be looming in
prospect. The old man became the victim of queru-
lous old age, and a morbid fancy that the end of the
world was at hand haunted him during hours of bodily
suffering; in calmer moments he fancied that for the
first time the meaning of his life became clear to
him, and the feeling overpowered him with rapturous
sensations.

His wife clung to him until his last gasp with intense love and devotion.

Vogl died, in his seventy-third year, on the 19th November, 1840, on the anniversary of Schubert's death,
twelve years before. Shortly before his decease, his
own and Schubert's friends had presented him with a
cup and portrait of the composer, as a memorial of the
intellectual bond that existed between the two artists.
Vogl's name is indissolubly associated with Franz
Schubert's songs. His peculiar appreciation and way
of executing particular songs of Schubert are said, by
the still surviving witnesses of the great days of the

singer, to have been unrivalled—a pattern and model
for all time. That Schubert himself entertained this
view, at least partially, can be gathered from a passage
in a letter which, together with what remains of his
written memoranda, shall be given in the latter part of
our narrative.[1]

Besides Vogl, we must mention several other musical
connoisseurs, whose intimacy with Schubert began at
this period, and brought him soon into friendly relations with them. For instance, there are the brothers
Anselm and Josef Hüttenbrenner [2]—the first a composer, the last a musical amateur—and Josef Gahy,
(a government *employé*), an accomplished pianoforte-
player. In the year 1815, Franz had met Anselm
Hüttenbrenner at Salieri's; in the summer of 1817
he became acquainted with his brother Josef, who—

---

[1] 'It is the way and style in which Vogl sings,' writes Franz (1825)
to his brother Ferdinand; 'and when I accompany, we seem at such a
moment to be one—a quite unheard-of novelty by the people here.'

[2] Anselm was born at Gratz in the year 1794, studied at Vienna, and
subsequently returned to the Steiermark, where he has property. He
was a passionate lover of music, and wrote an immense number of compositions in every kind of style. Of these, however, only a few, and
amongst them the Requiem, have become known, Elected President
of the Styrian Music Association, he undertook, in the year 1834, the
editorship of the 'Heller-Magazin.' Anselm now lives at Gratz, in retirement, and, in the summer, upon his Rothenthurm estate at Judenburg. Josef A. now lives in Vienna, pensioned by Government. With
the third brother, Heinrich, Doctor of Laws, Schubert seems to have
been not so intimate as with the other two; Heinrich A. was also
something of a poet, and Schubert set two of his songs.

at that time acting as steward of the family estate of
Rothenthurm, at Judenburg, in Styria—had come on
a visit to Vienna, and, two years later, occupied the
same house (in the Wipplingerstrasse) with Schubert and
Mayrhofer.   Schubert had already, at an earlier period
sent to him (although personally unacquainted) some
songs ('Minona,' 'Rastlose Liebe'); in the year 1818
he presented him, through Anselm, the song 'Die
Forelle,' composed on the night of February 21.   The
music was enclosed with the following lines: [1]—

'Dearest Friend,—I am overjoyed to find that my
songs please you.   As a proof of my sincere friendship,
I send you herewith another ("Die Forelle"), which
I wrote at midnight for Anselm.   But what mischief!
Instead of the box of blotting-sand, I seize the ink-
bottle.   I hope, over a glass of punch at Vienna, to
become better acquainted with you.   Vale!

'SCHUBERT.'

Franz was always on the most friendly footing with
these two brothers, although he cultivated their friendship from different motives.   For Anselm he had a true
and sincere regard, associated with the interest which he
bestowed upon the musical efforts of his friend.   Josef,
on the contrary, as he grew in the course of time more

---

[1] The original is in the hands of Herr Josef Hüttenbrenner.   I
desire to express my thanks to him for all the information he has given
me respecting himself and Anselm.

intimate with the musician, became an ardent Schubert-worshipper, and showed himself so zealous an admirer, that Schubert was far more anxious to keep away from him than to encourage him; and he would reject his too fulsome adulation with words of irony — 'Why, that man likes everything I do.' [1]   But the active service of this Hüttenbrenner, so far as it related to correcting printed proofs of Schubert's composition, arranging his symphonies for the piano, managing his correspondence with foreign publishers, and other less conspicuous services, suited the easy-going Schubert exactly; and that, to all outward appearance, his relations with Josef were of an appreciative friendly character, we have abundant testimony in the letters of Schubert, now in Herr Hüttenbrenner's possession. In them Schubert honours his willing friend with all sorts of commissions of a musical kind.[2]   Of Josef Hüttenbrenner's con-

[1] Herr Josef H. is particularly fond of pointing to this circumstance of Schubert's refusing to swallow his exaggerated praise. A gentleman, intimate with Schubert and Hüttenbrenner, described to me (perhaps a little overcolouring the picture) the relations existing between these two men, in a manner that tempts one to believe that they only loved at a distance. This is the passage:—'Josef, who would take no denial in his worship and zeal for Schubert, became almost an object of aversion to the musician; he often put him off rudely, and treated him so harshly and inconsiderately, that we nicknamed Schubert "The Tyrant"—of course, good temperedly.'

[2] Here is a note of Schubert's (in the year 1819):—

'Dear Hüttenbrenner,—I am, and ever shall be, yours. I am exceedingly pleased that you are ready with my symphony. Come here this evening with it at five o'clock. I am living in the Wipplingerstrasse, with Mayrhofer.'

stant but futile efforts, at a subsequent period, to get
Schubert's works recognised, and their sale, in and out
of Germany, enlarged, we shall have frequently to speak;
and none will venture to dispute his title to having
done such good service. It may well be instanced, as
a bitter wrong of fate, that, by the misadventure before
alluded to, three acts of operas by his adored master
were lost by this enthusiastic friend of Schubert.

Josef Gahy,[1] besides being an admirable pianoforte-
player, was selected by Schubert to join him in playing
through the duett arrangements of his own and other
compositions, especially Beethoven's Symphonies. Franz
used to play the treble. Gahy's playing was pure and
full of expression, and (a matter of great importance in
Schubert's eyes) he was a first-rate reader at sight. The
two friends were frequently together, especially in later
years, and they met several times a week, at the house
of one or other of their mutual friends,[2] to share a

On another occasion he sends off his zealous friend to Diabelli, 'to
give his dance-music to the engraver, and receive for him the money
he is in such urgent need of,' &c. The symphony here mentioned was
that of Schubert's in D (1813), and a pianoforte duett arrangement was
made, which Schubert and Hüttenbrenner played together on an old
worn-out piano of Milpitz. Schubert also often visited Gross (Court
Chamberlain), who lived in the Wipplingerstrasse, for the purpose of
playing to him, or duetts with him.

[1] Josef Gahy, Sectionsrath at Vienna, died in the month of March
1864.

[2] At Schober's, Lascny's, Vogl's (the last of whom lived, during the
years 1827 and 1828, in the Alleegasse), and at Pinterics', to whom we
shall have occasion again to allude.

pleasure so genial to both. Schubert was not a virtuoso
in the modern sense of the word, but he accompanied
his own songs beautifully, keeping the time very strictly,
and in spite of his short thick fingers he could play the
most difficult of his sonatas,[1] and always with appropriate expression.

Gahy assures us that the hours he passed playing
with Schubert were among the most enjoyable of his
life, and that he can never think of that time without
deep emotion. Not only on such occasions did he
learn a great deal he had never known before, but the
pure rapid playing, the bold free conception, the alternately tender and fiery energetic playing of his short
fat friend raised his spirits to the highest pitch.[2]

Schubert's temper being always at its best on such
occasions, he would make humorous remarks on the
several different compositions before them. These
were sometimes caustic and severe, but always to the

---

[1] Except the Fantasia (Op. 15), which he never could master. On
one occasion, whilst attempting it at a private party, and sticking fast
in the final movement, he jumped up from his chair, exclaiming: 'The
devil may play the stuff if he likes!' (Kupelwieser, Spaun, and Gahy
were present.)

[2] On one occasion Schubert played one of his sonatas to a pianist and
composer of the name of Johann Horzalka (died at Hitzing, in the year
1861), and the latter called out enthusiastically: 'Schubert, I admire
your pianoforte-playing more than your compositions!'—words which
afterwards led to a misunderstanding. Schubert occasionally accompanied his own songs at concerts; for instance, at Jansa's and Salomon's
concert (1827) he played for Tieze the 'Normans Gesang' and 'Der
Einsame.'

purpose. Gahy's almost fraternal intimacy with Schubert lasted undisturbed to the time of the musician's death.

With regard to Schubert's compositions referable to this period, we find orchestral music represented by two so-called 'Overtures in the Italian Style.' Rossini's operas, with their sweet cantilenas and passionate sensuous expression, enjoyed an enthusiastic triumph at that time in Vienna. Schubert was a constant visitor at the theatre, and it will excite no surprise that the tone-poet, with his rich store of songs, should be penetrated by the stream of melodies flowing from Rossini's music; although Schubert yielded to none in unsparing condemnation of the weak side of the genial maestro. Coming home one evening with several friends (amongst whom was Herr Doppler, the responsible author of this story), after hearing 'Tancredi,' there was a general chorus of praise of Rossini's music, and especially the overtures to his operas, whereupon Schubert, who thought the praise overdone, and was moved to contest the point, declared it would be the easiest thing for him to write down, at the shortest notice, overtures of the style alluded to. His companions took him at his word, and promised, on their part, to reward Schubert's efforts with a glass of good wine. Schubert there and then set to work, and wrote an orchestral overture, which was subsequently followed by another, and these, under the names of 'Overtures in the Italian Style,' were given, during Schubert's lifetime, at concerts with applause.[1]

Amongst the songs of this year,[2] those set to poems by Mayrhofer and Schober are pre-eminent in value and interest. Their selection points to the influence of Vogl, some of whose greatest triumphs were achieved in these works.

Of part-songs written at this time we must mention Schubert's setting of Göthe's poem, 'Gesang der Geister über den Wassern,' set for four male voices, as we detect in this work the germ of some of his later and grander conceptions.[3]

The most remarkable event of this period was the appearance of Schubert's Pianoforte Sonatas.

[1] The original of the Overture in D (composed in May), and of that in C (composed in November 1817), are in the hands of Herr Spina. Schubert made a pianoforte arrangement of both overtures. One of these was given on March 1, 1818, at the concert of Jaell, the violin-player, in the large room at the 'Römischer Kaiser,' at Vienna. We read of this performance in the 'Wiener Theater-Zeitung' of March 14:—'The second part began with a wonderfully beautiful overture by a young composer of the name of Schubert. This gentleman, a pupil of the famous Salieri, knows how to move and agitate all hearts. Extremely simple as the motive is, it developed a host of astonishing and delightful thoughts worked up with great power and skill.'

[2] Of unpublished songs we may mention 'La Pastorella al Prato,' an Italian canzonet, written in a graceful flowing style; a song for soprano, with accompaniments for stringed and wind instruments; and the songs 'Einsiedelei,' 'Fischerlied,' and 'Geist der Liebe,' afterwards arranged as a vocal quartett. There is an Italian air also, with a recitative of considerable length, written in the style of Mozart.

[3] Schubert set the 'Gesang der Geister' three times; in the year 1817 as a vocal quartett; in the year 1820 as chorus for male voices, with pianoforte

Few expected, at that time, that Schubert, whilst bringing out song after song suited to the capacity of his favourite singer, would apply with equal facility to the composition of pianoforte music. The same versatile power which had served him in such good stead in the production of his numerous vocal works and compositions for the stage, now befriended him in his later efforts in the department of chamber music. Schubert, in truth, having once selected his particular field of study and invention, set himself to his task with unwearied energy and zeal, never resting until he had satisfied the imperious demands of his genius by creating works of real artistic value. Of this intuitive perception of his own capacity we have evidence in the fact of his sudden rush into a new field of activity, that of composing pianoforte music, and writing in the period of a single year no less than five sonatas.[1] These once finished, he gave up writing for the pianoforte for a number of years. It is impossible to contemplate without emotion and wonder these precious results of quiet honest industry, which, in the majority of instances, were not to be reckoned amongst the artistic treasures of the world until long after Schubert's death.

accompaniment; and afterwards as an eight-part chorus for equal voices, with orchestral accompaniment. Herr Josef Hüttenbrenner has the first sketch, the second arrangement remained a fragment, the last is in the Royal Library in Berlin.

[1] These are the Sonatas in E-flat and A-flat, in A, and F and B minor, and probably, also, the fragment marked in the catalogue as Op. 145.

CHAPTER VI.

(1818 AND 1824.)

SCHUBERT AS MUSIC-TEACHER—THE FAMILY OF COUNT CARL ESTER-
HAZY—STAY AT ZELÉSZ—FREIHERR CARL VON SCHÖNSTEIN—SCHU-
BERT AND THE COUNTESS CAROLINE ESTERHAZY—THE QUARTETT
'GEBET VOR DER SCHLACHT'—THE 'DIVERTISSEMENT À LA HON-
GROISE'—THE FANTASIA IN F MINOR—THE SONG 'DIE FORELLE'—
'ERSTE WALZER'—THE SIXTH SYMPHONY (IN C)—A LETTER OF
IGNAZ SCHUBERT, THE SCHOOLMASTER, TO HIS BROTHER FRANZ.

SCHUBERT, like Mozart and Beethoven, had a special
aversion to giving lessons, and following the routine
and method generally prescribed for musicians. And
yet these three composers were driven by force of circumstances to become teachers (Beethoven only during
his early years).[1] Mozart laboured during a large part
of his life as a teacher; and Schubert, had he wished to
improve his means, at all events for the first years after
leaving his father's house, would have necessarily had to
conform to the usual *régime*. The reasons for a dis-
inclination to this course were the same in the case of

---

[1] In later years, too, Beethoven, as in former days at Bonn, went to
his task like 'a stubborn ill-tempered donkey,' and made it as easy to
himself as he possibly could—notably in the case of his pupil the Archduke Rudolf.

all three musicians, and need no further explanation. Schubert certainly so far disciplined himself as to spend several years in initiating pupils of the lowest class in the mysteries of the spelling-book, and his patience during the ordeal frequently forsook him; but to the restless energetic creator of music, the employment of giving lessons in music seemed absolutely intolerable. It is a fact that he got rid of all obligations of this nature, where such might be supposed to exist, so as to be perfect master of his time and inclinations. He unhesitatingly, however, accepted one, and but one offer, which was in many ways an advantageous one, and threatened in no respect to compromise his longing for independence. Unger, the Wirthschaftsrath of Baron Hakelberg (father of Caroline Unger-Sabatier, who became a famous operatic singer), recommended him at this time to Count Johann Esterhazy as a music-teacher, and the Count proposed to Schubert that he should officiate as music-master to the family, and pass the winter with him in town, and the summer at his country estate, Zelész.[1]

As this position was a properly paid one (according to Herr Doppler, two gulden the lesson), and opened out a prospect of many pleasures, in which persons associated with wealthy families are wont to share, Schubert

[1] Unger wrote the verses for Schubert's well-known Quartett, 'Die Nachtigall.'

accepted the offer very gladly, and in the summer of
1818 went for the first time to Zelész.[1]

Count Johann Carl Esterhazy married the Countess
Rosine Festetics, of Tolna, and by this marriage had
three children: Marie, Caroline, and Albert Johann.

The whole family was musical. The Count had a
bass voice; the Countess and her daughter Caroline
were altos; and Marie had an exquisite high soprano
voice. As the Baron Carl v. Schönstein[2] was an excellent second tenor, and often on a visit to the Esterhazy family, the vocal quartett was complete; and the
four connoisseurs are inseparably associated with one of
the finest of Schubert's vocal compositions, the ' Gebet
vor der Schlacht' (by De la Motte Fouqué). The two
daughters, moreover, played the piano, and whilst Marie
devoted herself more particularly to the cultivation of
her voice with the best Italian masters, Caroline, with
her sweet but less powerful voice, worked diligently and
successfully at accompaniments for the concerted pieces.

Schubert had already completed his twenty-first year

---

[1] Zelész (or Zselics), a property situated on the river Waag, belonging to the divisional district of Barsch and Honth, on this side of the
Danube, about fourteen stages from Vienna. The Esterhazy family
generally passed the winter months at the Residenz, in the Herrengasse.

[2] Born at Ofen, on June 27, 1796, and began his official career in
the year 1813, under the Hungarian Government. In 1831, was
made Secretary to the Exchequer, then Hofrath, and in 1856 retired
on a pension. I am indebted to this gentleman for his courtesy in sup-
plying me with information relative to Schubert's connection with the
Esterhazy family.

when he was first introduced to this family. The Count was in robust manhood. The Countess Rosine was twenty-eight years old, her eldest daughter (Marie) thirteen, Caroline (the younger) eleven, and her son a little boy of five.

It followed, as a matter of course, that Schubert's powers as a composer would soon be discovered by such a circle. He became the established favourite of the family, and, according to agreement, passed the winter with them as music-master, and repeatedly accompanied the family to their estate in Hungary. He passed a great deal of his time, apart from hours devoted to music, in the Count's house, and visited the family frequently up to the time of his death. In the first years of his acquaintance music was sedulously practised: Haydn's 'Creation' and 'Seasons,' his four-part songs, and Mozart's 'Requiem,' were amongst some of the family achievements. A vocal Quartett by Anselm Hüttenbrenner, 'Der Abend,' a great favourite with Schubert, was frequently sung.[1] Baron v. Schönstein, who, up to the time of meeting Schubert, had been an exclusive worshipper of Italian vocal music, now began enthusiastically to study the German Lied, as represented in its zenith of glory by Schubert, and devoted himself from henceforth to performances of Schubert's works, in which he became, like Vogl, unapproachable,

---

[1] This has been engraved, and was performed at a musical club gathering (*Kränzchen*) at Vienna, in 1862.

and actually surpassed that artist in respect of beauty
and quality of voice. The composer became much
attached to the Baron, and was always glad to study
music with him. Schönstein's audience during these
vocal displays generally consisted of the Esterhazy
family, where he was so welcome a visitor, and of which
every member was an ardent admirer of Schubert; but
his social position gave him an opportunity, in course of
time, of bringing these compositions before still higher
circles, and the 'crème de la crème' of society. As a
matter of course, the residence in the country (in the
years 1818 and 1824) was, in the matter of music, by
no means barren of results. Pianoforte pieces for solo
and duett-players, marches, sonatas, and variations, let
alone songs and concerted vocal pieces, originated in
that period, and are ample evidence of Schubert's
unwearied activity. At Zelész he heard, too, the
national Hungarian Sclavonian airs, which, whenever
he heard them, either played by gipsies or sung by
the castle servants, he noted down, with a view of reset-
ting them artistically, and giving them his own exquisite
embellishments. The 'Divertissement à la Hongroise'
(Op. 54) consists mainly of a series of melodies of a
somewhat gloomy character. Schubert got the subject from the kitchen-maid in the Esterhazy family,
who was humming it as she stood by the fireplace,
and Schubert coming home from a walk with
Schönstein, heard it as he passed. He kept on hum-

ming the tune during the rest of the walk, and next winter it appeared as a subject in the Divertissement. Snatches of the national Hungarian melodies are to be found in some of the Impromptus, Moments musicals, Sonatas, and even in movements of his Symphonies. On the occasion of his first visit to Zelész, Schubert remained until late in the autumn, for the ' Abendlied,' ' Du heilig glühend Abendroth ' (by Schreiber), the original manuscript of which is at Vienna, in the hands of the Countess Rosa v. Almasy (*née* Festetics), and niece of the Countess Esterhazy, bears date ' Zelész, November 1818.' Also the Lied 'Blondel zu Marien' (contained in Series 34), composed in September, and Vocal Exercises, filling five pages of manuscript, dated July 1818, are all traceable to the time of this country visit. The exercises, in Schubert's handwriting, which were found amongst the papers of the Countess Caroline, were probably written for her sister Marie.[1]

In the year 1824, six years later, we find Schubert a second time in Zelész. Baron Schönstein happened to be there also, and from this period are dated the grand

---

[1] Amongst the music the Countess Caroline left behind her are to be found the following MSS. of Schubert:—The Trio in E-flat, 1827, two Overtures for four hands, in C and D (December 1817), Waltzes (January 1824), 'Deutsche' (October 1824); the songs 'Abendlied,' 'Blondel zu Marien,' and Vocal Exercises. The Countess Rosa v. Almasy has the MSS. of ' Ungeduld,' and ' Des Müllers Blumen,' from the ' Müllerlieder,' which the lady has presented to Herr Julius Stockhausen. The French Romance in E minor, which Schubert selected as the subject of Op. 10, is also in the possession of the Almasy family.

pianoforte Duett, Op. 140, the Variations (Op. 35), and
the vocal Quartett before mentioned, 'Gebet vor der
Schlacht.' The origin of the last-quoted piece illus-
trates Schubert's surprising gifts of musical invention. One morning, in the early days of September,
1824, the lady of the house, whilst the family were at
breakfast, begged of the master to set De la Motte
Fouqué's poem to music for the family quartett.
Schubert took the book, and withdrew to his study to
think over his music. On the evening of the same day
this profound work was practised from the manuscript
copy on the pianoforte. But the delight at this beautiful music was far greater on the following evening, by which time the voice parts had been written
out and distributed by Schubert himself, and the whole
performance had gained in ensemble, clearness, and
beauty of expression. The quartett was composed
within ten hours, and written down without a single
correction. The composition was not published at
the time, having been written especially for the Esterhazy family, and under the express condition that it
should remain private property, and the Countess
Rosina set great store by her monopoly of one of Schubert's compositions. It was not until some years after
Schubert's death, that Frh. v. Schönstein, with the
consent of that lady, handed over the manuscript to a
house at Vienna for publication.

Schubert very often made himself merry at the
expense of any friends of his who fell in love. He

too was by no means proof against the tender passion, but never seriously compromised himself. Nothing is known of any lasting passion, and he never seems to have thought seriously about matrimony; but he certainly coquetted with love, and was no stranger to the deeper and truer affections. Soon after his entering into the Esterhazy family, he had a flirtation with one of the servants, which soon paled before a more romantic passion, which consumed the inflammatory Schubert. This was for the Countess's younger daughter, Caroline. The flame was not extinguished before his death. Caroline esteemed him, and appreciated his genius, but did not return his love, and probably never guessed its extent and fervency. His feelings towards her must have been clear enough, by Schubert's own declaration. Once she jestingly reproached him for never having dedicated any piece of music to her; his reply was, 'What would be the good of it? Everything I have ever done has been dedicated to you!'

And he clung steadfastly to his purpose; though the dedication on the pianoforte Fantasia in F minor, for two performers (Op. 103), emanates (so I have been told), in spite of the words, 'Dédiée par Fr. Schubert,' not from him, but from the publishers, and only appeared in this form after Schubert's death.[1] A passage

---

[1] Dr. Leopold v. Sonnleithner arranged the Fantasia for orchestra, in which form it now exists in the archives of the Vienna Musikverein. At an orchestral concert in the month of March, 1864, it was given in this form.

selected from a letter to be quoted hereafter (dated
Zelész, 1824), where the 'misery of reality,' 'defrauded
hopes,' &c., are alluded to, cannot be dissociated from
this heart affair which we have just hinted at.[1]

After the year 1824, Schubert never again visited
Zelész, and in 1826 a change occurred in the Count's
family, in consequence of which the musical circle was
deprived of one of its chief ornaments.[2] On December 1,
1827, Marie, the elder daughter, was married to the
Count August v. Breuner.[3] In 1828 Schubert died.

On May 8, 1844, sixteen years after Schubert's death,
the Countess Caroline was married to Count Folliot v.
Crenneville, chamberlain and a major in the army.

Count Johann Carl died on August 21, 1834, the
Countess Marie v. Breuner on September 30, 1837,
at the age of thirty-two years; the Countess Caroline

---

[1] Schubert dedicated to the Count Esterhazy the songs 'Erlafsee,'
'Sehnsucht,' 'Am Strom,' and 'Der Jüngling auf dem Hügel.'

[2] Bauernfeld hints at Schubert's passion in the following verses à la
Heine, the purport of which is but little in accordance with communi-
cations made by Baron v. Schönstein :—

> Verliebt war Schubert; der Schülerin
> Galt's, einer der jungen Comtessen,
> Doch gab er sich einer ganz andern hin,
> Um—die andere zu vergessen.

The 'other' is said to have been Theresa Grob, the singer in the Lichtenthal choir, who in the year 1814 sang the chief soprano part in the
F Mass of Schubert.

[3] Count August v. Breuner, a member of the Finance Chamber, born
on June 6, 1796, also a member of the House of Lords.

v. Crenneville in March, 1851, aged forty-five,[1] their son Johann Albert[2] in the year 1845, and the Countess Rosine, who survived all her children, died in the year 1854, at the age of sixty-four years.

Of the members of the musical circle which Schubert used to meet at the Esterhazy family, there survives still the celebrated Schubert-singer Carl Freiherr v. Schönstein.[3]

[1] In the 'Genealogische Taschenbuch' the year 1811 is given as the year in which the younger daughter was born. This seems to be a mistake. Apart from the fact that it would be difficult to explain Schubert's passion for a little girl of seven years or (even in the year 1824) but thirteen years of age, a near relative of the Esterhazy family has given the year 1806 as the year of the birth of the Countess Caroline.

[2] He was Imperial Chamberlain, and in 1843 married Marie Countess of Apponyi. With the exception of the Countess Marie, who lies buried at Grafenegg, near the estate of the Count Breuner, all the other members of the family lie buried at Zelész.

[3] Herr v. Schönstein was undeniably only second to Vogl as a great singer of Schubert's songs, and had, like Vogl, a particular set of songs which exactly suited his voice; as, for instance, the 'Müllerlieder' (dedicated to him), 'Standchen,' 'Der zürnenden Diana,' &c., whereas Vogl preferred the more dramatic and expressive 'Winterreise,' 'Zwerg,' &c. Schönstein's position in society at Vienna enabled him, as we have already stated, to introduce Schubert's music into the higher circles. In the year 1838 Franz Liszt heard him in Vienna, and wrote an account of the performance to Lambert Massart in the 'Gazette Musicale:'—'Dans les salons j'entends avec un plaisir très-vif et souvent une émotion qui allait jusqu'aux larmes, un amateur le baron Schönstein dire les Lieder de Schubert. La traduction française ne nous donne qu'une idée très-imparfaite de ce qu'est l'union de ces poésies presque toutes extrêmement belles avec la musique de Schubert, le musicien le plus poète qui fut jamais. La langue allemande est admirable dans l'ordre du sentiment, peut-être aussi n'y a-t-il eu un Allemand qui sache bien comprendre la naïveté et la fantaisie de plusieurs

Amongst the vocal compositions in the year 1818 must be quoted the song already mentioned, ' Die Forelle,' several of the ' Geistlichen Lieder,' and three sonnets of Petrarch (translated by A. W. Schlegel).[1] These last-named poems, vying in musical with poetical grandeur, are clothed by Schubert with music of the deepest significance. He wrote also in this year the first set of walzes that appeared in print, amongst them the so-called ' Trauer-' or ' Sehnsuchtswalzer,'[2] dance music which, when once known (in the year 1822),

de ses compositions, leur charme capricieux, leur abandon mélancolique. Le baron Schönstein les déclame avec la science d'un grand artiste, et les chante avec la sensibilité d'un amateur, qui se laisse aller à ses émotions sans se préoccuper du public.' Besides Vogl and Schönstein, August Ritter v. Gymnich and Sofie Linhart must be mentioned as famous interpreters of Schubert's songs during the author's lifetime.

[1] Not by Dante, to whom they have been erroneously ascribed. These are the sonnets :—

1. ' Nunmehr der Himmel, Erde schweigt und Winde.'
2. ' Allein, nachdenklich, wie gelähmt vom Kampfe.'
3. (Recitative) ' Apollo, lebet noch Dein hold' Verlangen,' &c.

The first is in B-flat major $\frac{12}{8}$, the second in F minor $\frac{4}{4}$ (a slow flowing movement), the third in A-flat major $\frac{3}{4}$. The compositions are all, the last especially, on a great scale. The treatment of the music is declamatory, and follows the words very closely. The sonnets are unpublished and unknown.

[2] The ' Trauerwalzer' were written by Schubert, according to Herr Josef Hüttenbrenner, on March 14, 1818, at Anselm Hüttenbrenner's, in Neubad. The ' Walzer,' of the original of which H. Anselm is said to be the owner, is dedicated to his ' toping punch-drinking brother' Anselm H. Questions about the authorship of this popular piece gave rise, like C. M. Weber's ' Last Thoughts,' to the warmest discussions, and were associated with the names of Beethoven, Hoffmann, and Henne-

was in great request, and contained one of those popular airs which test the art of the transcriber and
arranger of variations.[1]

To this period belong the Variations for four hands
(Op. 10), dedicated in the year 1822 to Beethoven by
Schubert, some marches for the piano, an (unpublished)
Fantasia in C (in the possession of Baron v. Spaun,
of Vienna), a lively four-part song, and the Sixth Symphony (in C), which was given either in 1828 or 1829,
in lieu of the seventh, at a classical concert at Vienna,

berg. In the 'Allgemeine Musikzeitung' of July 1829, an anonymous
writer asks, how it happens that Beethoven's 'Sehnsuchtswalzer' is
identical with Schubert's 'Trauerwalzer'—excepting that it has no
trio, respecting which it is said, that Herr Hoffmann, of Breslau, is the
composer. When some variations on the 'Trauerwalzer' appeared at
Haslinger's, a critic in the 'Wiener Musik-Anzeiger' produced an
arietta in the operatic adaptation of the farce 'Der Jurist und der
Bauer,' by the actor Perinet, which the Court organist, Johann Henne-
berg (died 1822) had composed thirty years before, and which was as like
the 'Sehnsuchtswalzer' as one egg is to another. The problem of the
'Last Thoughts' of Weber was satisfactorily solved by Capellmeister
Reissiger, of Dresden, but the question about the 'Trauerwalzer' was
dismissed. Bernhard Kothe pretends to find the motive of the 'Trauerwalzer' in a Graduale of Haydn, in Beethoven's Op. 7 (first movement),
in the Romance (Op. 40), and in 'Adelaide,' not to mention the D
minor Mass of Schnabel, the Overture to the 'Vestalin,' Mendelssohn's
Quartett, Op. 12, Strub's Organ Preludes, and in numberless songs of
the Küken-Proch period. Certainly he has no lack of invention, especially when fancy aids his powers of discovery!

[1] Thus, at the end of 1831, there was published at Berlin a song
called 'Die Sprache der Blumen' accompanied by Beethoven's 'Sehnsuchtswalzer,' arranged for the pianoforte by C. Schütz, not to mention
other transpositions made subsequently.

and received with applause, and the Scherzo of which was performed at a public concert in the year 1860.[1]

This C Symphony is the last but one written by Schubert, and marks the transition state to his grand Seventh Symphony in C, in which Schubert's individuality stands out free of all foreign influence, whilst in its immediate predecessor, here and there, the contagion of the old masters is unmistakable, or, as in the Scherzo, substituted for the Minuett in the Sixth Symphony, the magical power of Beethoven over Schubert is too plain to be mistaken. In other respects this movement, in form and treatment, is worked out with a freedom and mastery that carries away a genial audience.

In completing our review of the year 1818, we may here insert a letter (dated October 12th) from Ignaz Schubert, written to Franz whilst staying at Zelész, in which the ill-humour of the Rossau schoolmaster, his discontent and conscientious gerund grinding, his slavery as a teacher, and at the same time the feeling of love and veneration which he, in common with the other brothers and sisters, entertained for his brother Franz, are the salient characteristics. The letter, the original of which is in my possession, runs thus :—

'Dear Brother,—At last, at last, you will be thinking

---

[1] The Symphony consists of four movements : an Adagio C major, an Introduction to the Allegro in the same key, an Andante F major, a Scherzo Presto C major, with Trio E major, and the Finale Allegro moderato C major $\frac{2}{4}$.

to yourself, here comes my letter. I verily believe you wouldn't have seen a scrap of my writing, hadn't the blessed vacation, for my comfort, been drawing near, when I get enough leisure to write an ordinary letter in perfect peace, and away from all worrying thoughts.

' You lucky mortal! what a thoroughly enviable lot is yours! You live in a sweet golden freedom ; can give full play to your musical genius ; scatter your thoughts about just as you please ; become petted, praised, idolised, whilst one of our lot, like an old cart-horse, must put up with all the vagaries of noisy boys, submit to heaps of ill usage, and cringe in all submission to a thankless public and addle-pated superstitious Brahmins. You will wonder when I tell you that things have come to such a pitch in our house, that not a soul ventures to smile when I tell some absurd superstitious piece of nonsense about the divinity lecture. You can well understand that at such times I lose my temper and get out of sorts, and know liberty only by the name. Now you see you are free of all these things, quit of them entirely ; you see and hear nothing more of all this disorder, you are rid for ever of our " Bonzen," with regard to whom I need only call to your mind the comforting stanza of Bürger :—

> Beneide nicht das Bonzenheer
> Um seine dicken Köpfe,
> Die meisten sind ja hohl und leer
> Wie ihre Kirchthumknöpfe.

' Now for something else. The name-day festival of
our Herr Papa was commemorated with due solemnity.
The whole *personnel* of the Rossau school, women and
all, were bidden to an evening entertainment, so was
brother Ferdinand with his wife, our little cousin and
Lenchen, and the whole kith and kin at Gumpendorf.
We feasted and drank royally, and all went very merrily.
For once, on this occasion only, I put my very scanty
wits as poet into motion, and drank our venerable host's
health to the following toast :—

> Es lebe Vater Franz noch lang in unsrer Mitte;
> Doch vergönn' er wohl uns heut' auch eine Bitte :
> Er stell' auf's Jahr sich wieder ein
> Mit Hendel, Strudel, Confect und Wein.

' Before the feast we played quartetts, but grieved in
our hearts at not having in the midst of us our Maestro
Franz: our music was soon over. The day after, we
kept the festival of our patron and protector, Fran-
ciscus Seraphicus. The pupils, in a body, were obliged
to go to confession, and the elder ones collected at three
o'clock in the afternoon before the crucifix; an altar
was erected, to the right and left of which two school
flags waved ; then came a short sermon, where we were
twice enjoined to learn how to distinguish the good
from the wicked, and that we owed the patient teacher
deep gratitude; a litany was then repeated, and the
oddity of this said litany surprised me not a little;
finally, we all sang, and every one present was allowed

to kiss the sacred relics, and thereupon I remarked that several of the grown-up people, who probably were not very desirous of participating in this act of grace, sneaked away to the door.

' Now just a word or two about the Hollpeins.[1] Man and wife equally send you their kindest regards, and beg to ask if occasionally you have a thought for them They hoped to see you soon back again, although they suppose, on your return to Vienna, you will not be so frequent a visitor as formerly, as your new circumstances may well prevent you. They often lament this, for they love you, as all do most sincerely, and often express the warmest sympathy in your present comfort and happiness. You will unravel our sentiments, and understand why I don't say a syllable about your name-day festival. I love you, and shall love you for ever, and herewith *punctum*;—you know me. Farewell, and come soon, for I have plenty to say to you, but spare myself for a chat when we next meet.

' Your Brother,

' IGNAZ.

' Should you be writing to papa, and me also, mind don't touch upon religious topics. My cousin and Lenchen send you their warmest regards.'

---

[1] Hollpein was a graver at the Imperial Mint in Vienna. Franz Schubert was on very intimate terms with the family, and passed a great deal of his leisure time with them. In a letter (1825) Franz congratulates himself upon the fact.

CHAPTER VII.

(1819.)

AT a time when Schubert was occupied in the composition of vocal cantatas and smaller dramatic works,
the brilliant star of Rossini arose upon the theatrical
heavens. How this genial writer, the inaugurator of
a musical epoch, became the foremost representative
of Italian opera-writers; what triumphs his charming
music won for him, after it had stormed and taken possession of all the large theatres, and how it was in the
excitable Vienna that an intellectual worship of 'the
Reformer' was encouraged—all this is still fresh in the
memory of playgoers who lived through those days,
and saw that unrivalled phalanx of vocalists, whose
successors in their art have yet to be found, and whose
eminent performances helped in a great measure to lay

the enduring foundations of Rossini's supremacy in operatic music. The narrow one-sided taste of the great public, all tending to this one direction, and the increasing mania for Italian opera at Vienna, which reached its highest point under the management of Barbaja and Duport, but culminated in 1822, when Rossini himself convoyed his own troupe of singers to the capital,[1] was, as a natural consequence, destructive to Schubert's dramatic efforts as a composer, and finally disappointed a long-cherished hope he had entertained of seeing one of his grand operas ('Fierrabras' was already licensed for representation) represented on the stage.[2] Although such a state of things was necessarily painful to Schubert, yet, free from all jealousy and miserable prejudice, he never hesitated a moment to appreciate the genuine merits of brother-artists, and

[1] The Italian Opera began on April 13, 1822, with Rossini's 'Zelmira,' and finished in July with 'Corradino.' The unbridled enthusiasm grew more frantic at each performance, until it degenerated into a kind of mental intoxication, which only urged the singers to redouble their efforts, without having any regard for the worth or poverty of the music performed at the time. At the final performance it seemed as if the entire audience were bitten by the tarantula; there was no end to the hurrahs and screams. The year 1823 saw this furore pass into fanaticism. The little respect left for German vocal art had entirely disappeared, and from this year is dated that melancholy falling off which for ten consecutive years has increased in the capital of Austria. (See A. Schindler, 'Beethoven,' Part II. pp. 57–59.)

[2] In letters from and to Schubert during 1822–1825, the distaste of his contemporaries with reference to the performance of his operas is frequently mentioned.

paid his full tribute of recognition of the splendid gifts
of the 'Swan of Pesaro;' nay, his behaviour evidenced
his unaffected admiration for the melodious maestro,
for he frequently went to the Italian Opera, and made
no concealment of the fact, that for many a hint in
the art of delicate instrumentation he was indebted to
the light and flowing Rossini.　Inferentially it may be
stated that he was at issue with those pedants who
regarded the Italian composer exclusively as the de-
stroyer of all legitimate taste.[1]　A letter of Schubert's[2]
hints at his connection with Italian opera and Rossini's
music especially, referring also to the cabals which
existed in opposition to the performance of his own
musical dramas;[3] and in this letter Schubert, usually
so patient and forbearing, vents his chagrin in very
unequivocal terms.　The letter runs thus:—

'You are a rogue,—that's just it.　A whole decade
flown, before you look on Vienna again.　Now flirting
with one girl, now with another.　The devil take the
whole lot of them, if they fool you so completely.
Marry, in God's name, and then the story's ended.　You
can say, no doubt, like Cæsar, Better to be first fiddle
·in Gratz than second in Vienna.　Well, may I be

---

[1] Schubert's sympathy for Rossini's music has been endorsed by
every one I have consulted on the subject.

[2] Herr Josef Hüttenbrenner, of Vienna, has a copy of it.

[3] The Operetta 'Die Zwillingsbrüder' was, however, given in the
course of the following year.

hanged if I'm not driven clean mad at your not being here. Cornet[1] no longer learns the aforesaid proverb. God bless him! I too shall end by coming to Gratz, and acting as your rival. There is very little novelty here; if one hears anything good, it's always the old things.

'A short time since we had Rossini's " Othello." All that our Radichi executed was admirable.[2] This opera is far better—I mean by that more characteristic—than " Tancredi." One cannot refuse to call Rossini a rare genius. His instrumentation is often original in the highest degree, and so is the voice-writing; and I can find no fault with the music, if I except the usual Italian gallopades and several reminiscences of " Tancredi."

'In spite of a Vogl, it's difficult to manœuvre against the *canaille* of Weigl, Treitschke, &c. Consequently, in lieu of my operettas, we have other rubbish, which makes one's hair stand on end.[3] " Semiramis," by Catél,

---

[1] Tenor singer at the Opera in Vienna; he had just accepted a stage engagement for Prague.

[2] 'Othello' was given in the first half of May, at the Kärnthnerthor Theatre, by a German company. Frau Grünbaum acted Desdemona, Forti Othello, Vogl the Doge, and Radichi Rodrigo. Julius Radichi, who sang the part of Florestan in 1814, died in 1846. In the April of 1819, ' Othello' was played at Vienna.

[3] This remark of Schubert's can only have reference to some worthless operettas and musical vaudevilles which were given during 1818 and 1819 at the Theatre in Vienna, for the repertoire of the Kärnthnerthor Theatre shows a large preponderance of classical works. The fol-

we are to have next, with its downright good music.[1]
Herr Stamm, a tenor from Berlin, who has sung in
several operas, will make his *début* in Vienna here.
His voice is rather weak, no depth, a constant scream
in falsetto. I have nothing more to say. Work hard at
composition, and let me have a share too.   Farewell.

' Your true friend,

' FRANZ SCHUBERT.'[2]

lowing musical dramas were performed :—' Cenerentola,' by Rossini ;
' Zelmire und Azor,' by Gretry ; ' Lorenz als Räuberhauptmann,' a light
comedy with music adapted by Kinsky, the Vicehofcapellmeister ; ' Die
Vermählung auf der Zauberinsel ;' a pasticcio ' Ser Marc Antonio,' by
Pavesi ; ' Odin's Schwert,' with choruses, music by Seyfried (unsuccessful); ' La Dama Soldato ' (Orlandi); ' Graf Armand,' by Cherubini ;
the melodrama ' Samson,' music by Tuczek ; ' Richard Löwenherz,' by
Gretry ; ' Euterpens Opfer,' a ' quodlibet ' (failed) ; ' Das Rosenmädchen,'
opera by Lindpaintner ; ' Faust,' by Spohr ; ' Die Thronfolge ' (Seyfried) ;
' Die Zauberflöte,' ' Elisabeth,' by Rossini ; ' Das unterbrochene Opfer-
fest,' Winter, &c. At the Kärnthnerthor Theatre were given :—' Johann
von Paris,' ' Medea,' ' Talente durch Zufall ' (Catél), ' Liebe und Ruhm '
(Herold and Boildieu), ' Joseph and his Brethren,' ' Iphigenie auf
Tauris,' ' Die Vestalin,' ' Cyrus ' (Mosel), ' Ein Tag von Abenteuer '
(Mehul), ' Sargines,' ' Fidelio,' several of Mozart's operas. Spontini's
' Cortez ' and Catél's ' Semiramis.' Treitschke had translated some of
these operas into German, and Weigl directed the performance.

[1] This opera had already been performed in October 1818, after
having been thoroughly well rehearsed.

[2] On the back of the letter there are some lines to Heinrich Hüttenbrenner, at Gratz, which Josef H., at Schubert's suggestion, added,
and in which he begs Heinrich to write a libretto for Schubert. ' Tell
this to Schrökinger ' (a well-known poet in Gratz), exclaims the ever-
enthusiastic Josef, in addressing his brother. ' Besides, there's an
honorarium attached. Your names will be proclaimed throughout
Europe. Schubert will blaze in the musical firmament like a new Orion.
Write soon your opinion respecting him.'

In the summer of this year Franz, for the first time, visited Upper Austria, and stayed for a short time at Linz, Salzburg, and Steyr. This last-named charmingly situated little town figures very prominently in Schubert's life, especially during the time of his pilgrimages from home. It was closely associated with Schubert as being the domicile of Mayrhofer, Stadler, and Vogl;[1] and besides this, many families very intimate with him, and with whom we shall renew our acquaintance six years farther on in our narrative, resided there.

The names of Paumgartner, Koller, Dornfeld, and Schellmann are only less eventful as associated with the history of Schubert's life, than that of Michael Vogl, who first introduced him to these sober citizen circles.[2]

Silvester Paumgartner (died on November 23, 1841) was deputy-factor to the head guild and an owner of house-property in Steyr. One of the most ardent and brilliant musical enthusiasts, himself a violoncello-player (although his powers of execution are said to have been moderate), he opened his doors to every artist of reputation, and men of ripened talents found in him a generous supporter. This fact will explain the intensity of joy with which he welcomed to his hospitality two such artists as Schubert and Vogl.

---

[1] Süssmayer, Mozart's well-known amanuensis, the poet Blumauer, Katharina Gürtler, and the historian F. Pritz were all born there.

[2] I am indebted to Herr A. Stadler for the following notices.

Music, theoretically and practically, was all the rage, especially as the master of the house (a bachelor) had a valuable collection of music and musical instruments, which he was bent upon improving and enlarging.[1] When Vogl retired on a pension, he took up his abode for a considerable time with Paumgartner.

Josef v. Koller, merchant and ironmonger at Steyr, had become acquainted at Vienna with Vogl through Brandeschi (a worker in the iron trade). His daughter Josefine, named the 'Pepi,' sang and played the piano, and usually took the soprano part at any performance of Schubert's concerted vocal pieces.[2] In the letters of this year and the year 1825, frequent mention is made of this lady as well as 'Frizi.' Dornfeld (still living in Linz), the eldest daughter of the former head of the family of Dornfeld in Steyr. On the occasion of his first visit to Steyr, Vogl was quartered at Koller's, and he and Schubert were daily invited to dinner. Father Koller and 'die Pepi' are both still living; the first, a very old man, at Steyr, the latter the wife of the head-steward of the estates of Prince Wil-

---

[1] He frequently set off on foot to Strengberg, a post-town, to give the Paris courier commissions for the purchase of new music and instruments.

[2] At one of their meetings, Vogl proposed that the 'Erlkönig' should be given with the parts distributed. Vogl sang the father, Schubert the Erlkönig, and 'Pepi' the boy. For 'Pepi,' Schubert set an occasional poem by Stadler, which she sang on her father's birthday (March 19, 1820). This musical composition is unknown. A. Stadler, of Vienna, has the poem.

helm of Auersperg, Franz Krakowitzer, at Wels, where she has been residing for a number of years past.

Dr. Albert Schellmann senior (died on March 4, 1844), a house-owner in Steyr, officiated there as Landes- and Berggerichts-Advocat; his son, Dr. Albert Schellmann (died on November 29, 1854), was an advocate and public notary. The house where the Schellmanns lived (No. 117, on the Platz) was composed of two stories; the first was occupied by Schellmann and his five daughters, the second by the treasurer of the district with his three daughters, besides Albert Stadler and his mother (sister-in-law of the elder Schellmann), and finally Schubert, whose room was very near Stadler's. These are the eight ladies to whom Schubert refers in the following letter to his brother Ferdinand. The letter is dated Steyr, July 15, 1819, and runs thus:—

'Dear Brother,—I hope this letter will find you in Vienna, and that you are well. I write to you particularly to send me as soon as possible the "Stabat Mater," which we want to perform.[1] I am uncommonly well just now, and intend to remain so if only the weather will keep fine. Yesterday we had a tremendous storm here about 12 o'clock. The lightning killed a woman and maimed two men. In the house where I am lodging, there are eight young ladies, and nearly all pretty. You see one has plenty to do. Vogl and I dine every day with

---

[1] This work, however, it would seem, was never performed.

Herr v. Koller; his daughter is uncommonly pretty, plays the piano capitally, and sings several of my songs.

'Please forward the enclosed letter. You see I am not so absolutely faithless as you would perhaps think.

'Remember me to my parents, brothers and sisters, your wife, and all friends. Don't forget the "Stabat Mater." Your ever faithful brother,

'FRANZ.

'The country about Steyr is indescribably beautiful.'

A second letter, from Linz, on August 19, 1819, directed to J. Mayrhofer, at Vienna, is as follows:—

'My dear Mayrhofer,—If the world thrives as well with you as it does with me, you are well and hearty. I am, just at present, in Linz. I have been with the Spauns, and met Kenner, Kreil, and Forstmayer. There, too, I made acquaintance with Spaun's mother and Ottenwald, whose "Cradle Song" I set and sang to him. I found plenty of amusement in Steyr. The surrounding country is heavenly, and Linz too is beautiful. We, i. e. Vogl and I, shall go very soon to Salzburg. How I long for ——! I recommend to your notice the bearer of this letter, a student of Kremsmünster, of the name of Kahl; he is journeying by way of Vienna to Idria, on a visit to his parents. Please let him have my bed during the time he stays with you. I am very anxious you should treat him as kindly as possible, for he is a dear good fellow.

'Please greet Frau v. S. heartily for me. Have you written anything? I hope so. We kept Vogl's birthday with a cantata, the words by Stadler, the music by me; people were thoroughly pleased. Now, then, farewell until the middle of September.

'Your friend,

'FRANZ SCHUBERT.

'Herr v. Vogl sends his kind regards. Remember me to Spaun.'

In the middle of September the two artists took their departure from Steyr. This fact is noted up in two albums, in which, on September 14, the two friends contributed prose and verse for 'Kathi' Stadler, sister of Albert Stadler, who was living at the time with the Kollers.[1]

Of the larger compositions by Schubert during this period, may be mentioned the well-known pianoforte Quintett, Op. 114, with the Lied 'Die Forelle,' as the subject of the last movement but one, and the Variations on that theme. Schubert composed this at Stadler's suggestion, and at the special instance of

---

[1] Schubert wrote in the album the following moral apophthegm:—
'Always enjoy the present discreetly, thus will time past be to thee a sweet memory, and the future be no bugbear.' Vogl aspired higher in the following confectioner's motto:—

'In der Freunde Herzen leben,
Was kann's hienieden Schönres geben?'

Katharina Stadler still lives, the wife of the artist Franz Kozeder, in Schwanenstadt. Herr A. Stadler, of Vienna, possesses these albums.

Paumgartner, to whom Schubert handed over all the parts copied out, but not the separate score; further than this, a pianoforte Overture for four hands, in F minor ('written in November, in Herr Josef Hütten-brenner's room, at the City Hospital, within the space of three hours, and dinner missed in consequence'), and' an 'occasional Cantata.'

In August Schubert wrote, as we learnt from his letter to Mayrhofer, during his stay in Steyr, a Cantata in honour of Vogl's birthday, with pianoforte accom-paniment for soprano, tenor, and bass; the words were by Stadler.[1]

Of unpublished compositions must be mentioned, a vocal Quartett,[2] a Salve Regina (in A) for soprano, with accompaniment for stringed instruments, three Hymns by Novalis,[3] a vocal Quintett (for two tenors

---

[1] The Cantata, of which Josef v. Spaun and the wife of Dr. Lumpe, of Vienna, possess copies, begins with a trio in C major $\frac{2}{4}$, succeeded by a soprano solo (Allegretto, F major); then follows a tenor solo, and then another for soprano, and a second solo for the tenor. The finale is composed of a canon (Moderato, C major $\frac{4}{4}$). The poem contains allusions to the most famous parts and performances of Vogl in various operas. Pepi Koller originally sang the soprano part.

[2] The Quartett, probably an occasional composition, written at Steyr, is for two sopranos, tenor, and bass (D major $\frac{6}{8}$), to the words:—

> Im traulichen Kreise
> Beim herzlichen Kuss
> Beisammen zu leben
> Ist Seelengenuss.

[3] These are the sacred songs:—1. 'Wenige wissen das Geheimniss der

and three basses) to the familiar lines, ' Nur wer die
Sehnsucht kennt,' and a vocal Quartett for two tenors
and two basses.[1]

Conspicuous above all others amongst the many songs
which Schubert up to this time had, in lavish profusion,
scattered from his cornucopia, are those set to Göthe's
poems, both for the finished beauty of their form and
the depth and intensity of their meaning. The thought
constantly presented itself to Schubert's mind, of gra-
tifying the prince of poets, enthroned at Weimar, by
sending him some of his most successful songs, and
convincing him that his magical power had inspired
a young Viennese musician with the spirit to fathom
the meaning of the poet's fancies, and reproduce them
in the poetry of the world of sound. But the first
approach to such an act could scarcely have emanated
from Schubert himself, for his shy retiring nature
contradicts such a supposition—he may very likely
have fallen in cheerfully with the idea suggested by a

Liebe ;' 2. ' Wenn ich ihn nur habe;' 3. ' Wenn alle untreu werden.'
The first hymn, beginning in A minor $\frac{4}{4}$, consists of several numbers, and
has additional recitatives ; the second and third (both in D-flat $\frac{2}{4}$) are
not much to speak of. These three hymns are more peculiar than beautiful. The other two hymns belong to the years 1815 and 1820.

> [1] Ruhe, schönstes Glück der Erde,
>   Senke segnend dich herab,
>   Dass es stiller um uns werde,
>   Wie in Blumen ruht ein Grab.

The manuscript of both these concerted vocal pieces is in the possession
of A. Stadler, of Vienna.

well-meaning adviser, of making some advances which
could not prejudice himself; however that may be, certain it is that he sent a sheet of his settings of Göthe's
poetry—doubtless the songs dedicated to the poet,
'An Schwager Kronos,' 'An Mignon,' and 'Ganymed,'
accompanied with an introductory letter, full of awful
respect, to the great man at Weimar.[1] The old master,
whose house was most hospitably open to sociable musical amateurs and professional artists and composers,
although it was only at times that music affected him,[2]
either took no notice of the songs, and put them aside
as 'schatzbares Materiale,' along with written dedications and complimentary presents, which came to him
as matters of daily occurrence, or purposely avoided
coming into near contact with a man personally unknown to him, and at that time still of small reputation.
Neither in Göthe's works, nor in his correspondence with
Zelter, nor in his conversations with Eckermann, do
we find a syllable in connection with Schubert's name,
although the poet might often have heard Schubert's
settings of his own poems performed by eminent artists.
This curious fact is thus explained,—that the strophe

---

[1] Herr Dr. Leopold v. Sonnleithner mentions this circumstance in an
essay upon Schubert, which he has kindly allowed me to peruse.

[2] When Madame Unger, in the year 1796, sent Göthe some new songs
by Zelter, he wrote to her:—'I can form no judgment of music, for I
have no knowledge of the means which music employs for its own ends;
I can only speak of the impression which music makes on me when I
entirely and frequently give myself up to its influences.' ('Göthe's Correspondence with Zelter,' vol. i.)

songs of Reichardt, Zelter, and Ebenwein, popular and naturalised as they had become in North Germany, were better suited to the poet, now in his seventieth year, than the songs of the Viennese tone-poet, written in a grander style, and often containing separate and distinct airs for this or that strophe or verse.[1] Thus it happened that a musical appreciation and understanding of Schubert's 'Erl-King,' a ballad he had already heard sung, was conveyed to Göthe only in the last years of his long life, by the grand dramatic performance of Wilhelmine Schröder-Devrient.[2]

[1] Göthe's confessedly favourite musician was the director of the Berlin Singing Academy, Carl Fried. Zelter (born in Berlin, 1758, and died there 1832), the old German Imperial composer, as Beethoven called him. As early as the year 1796, he was on friendly terms with Göthe, having presented him with his latest songs, and the intimacy was mutually kept up to the year 1832, and found its expression in a lively and important correspondence. A similar bond of union existed between them as between Mayrhofer and Schubert, with this difference, that Zelter the song-composer was no Schubert, and Göthe at that period had already passed the lyrical epoch. Zelter set to music more than a hundred of Göthe's songs, nearly all of them ballads. Göthe said of the first efforts of Zelter in this style, 'that he could scarcely have believed music capable of producing such delicious tones.' In the year 1823, Milder-Hauptmann sang before Göthe four small songs; 'she threw such great power into them, that the memory of her singing,' said Göthe, 'still would bring tears to his eyes.' May not one of Schubert's have been among the number? In the year 1825, Milder, at her concert in Berlin, sang Schubert's 'Zuleika,' with great applause, but Zelter makes no note of the fact. The famous singer at that time was in correspondence with Göthe and Schubert, and we shall allude by and by to the letters.

[2] When Schröder, in the April of 1830, passed through Weimar, on her journey to Paris, she was introduced to the veteran poet by a member

It may be here mentioned, as a curiosity, that at the beginning of this year (on February 28, 1819, and not, as is generally supposed, in the year 1821), a song of Schubert's was heard for the first time at a public concert in Vienna. The tenor singer Jäger sang on that occasion (and again on April 12) the well-known 'Schäfer's Klagelied,' at a concert given by the violin-player Jaell, at the hotel 'Zum römischen Kaiser.' [1] The song, it seems, was received with great applause.

At this period the Cantata 'Prometheus' was performed (for the last time) at the house of Dr. Ignaz von Sonnleithner (at Gundelhof), and on this occasion the host himself, a fine bass singer, sang the part of Prometheus.

The same cantata was to have been given in the year 1820, at the Augarten, under Schubert's personal direc-

of the Royal Opera-House Company, Eduard Genast, and sang to him, amongst other things, the 'Erl-King.' Although Göthe was not fond of 'durchcomponirter' songs, the grand dramatic power of the artist made such an impression on him, that Göthe, laying both his hands on the singer's head, kissed her forehead, and exclaimed, 'Thanks, a thousand times, for this grand artistic performance,' and went on to say : 'I once heard this composition in my earlier life, and it did not agree with my views of the subject, but, executed as you execute it, the whole becomes a complete picture.' (Alfred Baron v. Wolzogen, 'Wilhelmine Schröder, a Contribution to the History of the Musical Drama,' p. 146.) In the year 1821, Schröder took part in the same 'Akademie' at Vienna, where Vogl, for the first time in public, performed the 'Erl-King.'

[1] Jäger (Franz), born at Vienna, 1796, and in active professional life there up to the year 1826, as a dramatic singer, enjoyed great popularity in certain parts. He went afterwards to Stuttgart as teacher of singing at the theâtre, and he remained there to the end of his days.

tion; but the rehearsals were so unsatisfactory, that Schubert withdrew the score. Since the time of this performance in private society, the work has never been given at Vienna, and we have already noticed the mysterious fate which befel this composition.

CHAPTER VIII.

(1820.)

THE MUSICAL DRAMA 'DIE ZWILLINGSBRÜDER'—THE MELODRAMA
'DIE ZAUBERHARFE'—THE EASTER CANTATA 'LAZARUS'—THE OPERA
'SAKONTALA'—'ANTIFONEN' FOR PALM SUNDAY—THE TWENTY-THIRD
PSALM—SONGS AND CANZONETS—THE PIANOFORTE FANTASIA IN C.

IT happened, by a strange freak of fortune, that our
great song-writer was first to be introduced to the
general public of his native town in a dramatic musical
work. Not one of his songs had as yet appeared in
print. He had written a couple of hundred, and some
of them, sung with rapturous applause in private circles,
had increased his reputation every time they had been
listened to. Schubert himself was not in the position to have his works published at his own risk and
expense, and still less did he offer to press them
upon music publishers, as success was hardly to be
thought of with people shy of, and notoriously prepos-
sessed unfavourably towards only 'budding' geniuses.
What pains were taken in the course of the next year
—and all in vain—by persons conversant with the ways
and dealings of publishers, with a view of bringing out
an edition of the 'Erl-King,' will be alluded to in the
proper place.

The singer Vogl, always intent on winning an opportunity for a larger and wider appreciation of his friend
than had hitherto been given him, brought his influence
to bear on the directors of the Opera House, and they
commissioned Schubert to set a libretto arranged from
the French for the German stages, by Hofmann, the
secretary of the theatre.

He seems to have set to work in the year 1818; at
all events, it was rumoured in Vienna that Schubert
was employed in writing music for an opera.[1]

The libretto is a very used-up fashion of stage plot;
it turns upon continual changes of characters, and the
misunderstandings which ensue on mistaken identity.
No doubt a good many absurd situations are contrived,
but, after all, the conclusion is tame and ineffective.
The melodrama was introduced for the first time at the
Kärnthner Theatre on June 14, 1820, under the title
of ' Die Zwillinge,' a farce, interspersed with songs,
·in one act. The characters are: the mayor; Lieschen
his daughter (soprano); Anton (tenor); the under-
bailiff (bass); Franz and Friedrich Spiess (bass), in-
valids, the first of whom wears a bandage over his right
eye, and the latter one over his left.

The story is as follows :—Eighteen years ago, before
the drama commences, an infant daughter has been born

---

[1] On the original score, in the possession of the Vienna Musikverein,
is the date January 19, 1819. Ferdinand Schubert arranged a pianoforte edition of the opera, of which Josef v. Spaun has a copy.

to the mayor. The happy father is thinking whom he shall choose for sponsor, when his neighbour Spiess, coming into the room, tells him that he has made up his mind, now he is of age, to go out into the wide world, and first of all to France, to seek there his twin-brother, who, as a boy, ran away from home. To mark his departure by some signal and praiseworthy action, he volunteers to act as sponsor to the little infant, and, at the same time, lays down a dowry of 1,000 thalers conditionally, that should he return within eighteen years, and be pleased with the young lady, she must accept him forthwith as her husband. Meantime, Lieschen grows up to maidenhood, has chosen Anton for her husband, and on that very day—not, however, until sunset—when the term fixed on by Franz Spiess for receiving his proper indemnity and payment of his claims to the hand of the lady expires. Anton and a chorus of peasants awake, with a serenade, the bride from her slumber. (Opening of the music.) The young couple wait impatiently for the sunset, when the marriage ceremony is to take place. Thereupon Franz Spiess appears, makes himself known to the somewhat disagreeably surprised mayor, tells him of all his adventures, and ends by reminding him of the promise originally made in respect of his daughter. Lieschen is sent for, and as she pleases the new suitor, the latter considers his marriage as a settled thing. The joint protest of the father, Anton, and Lieschen are of no

avail. Franz persists in his claims, and orders the
mayor to prepare a breakfast, but the two lovers to
separate for ever.. In the interim, Franz leaves to
square accounts and official matters with the 'Amtmann.' Considerably put out, but thinking of some
new means to be even with Spiess, the mayor, Anton,
and Lieschen withdraw into the house.

Franz is then succeeded by Friedrich Spiess, who
is so exactly like his brother, as to be mistaken for
him, and greets everything and everybody in the
highest spirits. The mayor, supposing Franz Spiess is
before him, invites him to the wedding breakfast, already ordered, and keeps on energetically filling up his
glass. Friedrich now declares that he wishes to live in
peace and friendship with all his home companions,
and especially with the mayor; he, misunderstanding
him, hurries back to the house, in order to bring the
joyful message to his daughter. Lieschen herself now
appears on the scene, and a further misunderstanding
arises in the course of her conversation with Friedrich,
owing to her declaration 'that he must be married,'
which he takes to mean a necessity for his making the
young lady his wife, a contingency he guards himself
against for various reasons, and particularly because he
is already the father of a grown-up son. Lieschen, in
an ecstasy of delight, hurries off to the village to seek
Anton. The 'Amtmann' appears, to congratulate Franz
Spiess, in the name of the whole parish, on his many

exploits whilst away from home, and to express his sympathy for the loss of his brother. Then he begs him, as his brother's heir, to receive the sum originally lodged in his keeping, and to sign a receipt for the same. Friedrich and the 'Amtmann' then retire to the steward's house.

Lieschen and Anton enjoy the victory they have won; Franz Spiess joins them, and, in blissful ignorance of what has meanwhile happened to his brother, persists in his demand. Lieschen reminds him of his promise to give her up, and threatens him with Anton's and her father's revenge.

The mayor comes out of the house; Franz Spiess calls for breakfast; the mayor replies that already they have been drinking heavily together—a fact indignantly denied by Franz. Finally, the steward joins the company, and asks Franz to add his signature for the receipt of the 1,000 thalers. Franz denies ever having received such a sum, and will not own to his signature. The dispute waxes hotter and hotter; Anton, Lieschen, and peasants come out of the village. The steward, in whose eyes Franz is an object of suspicion, remarks that Spiess now wears the bandage over the right eye, having at an earlier stage of the story had the bandage over his left; forthwith Franz is conducted before a court of justice as a spy and traitor. Friedrich Spiess, with a bag full of money, approaches from the other side, and asks the mayor to watch over

the coin, but the latter refuses. A fresh confusion arises
in consequence of the questions put to the pretended
Franz Spiess. These Friedrich cannot, of course, understand. At last the mayor stumbles upon the brilliant
idea that there must have been two persons of the
name of Spiess, who caused the whole dilemma. Anton
comes with the news that Franz Spiess has, before the
court, renounced his claims to Lieschen.

Franz appears on the scene ; the brothers rush fran-
tically into each other's arms, and the chorus cheer
vigorously the fraternal and the bridal pair.

The musical part of this play contains ten numbers,
besides the overture, the Allegro movement of which
(D major ⁴⁄₄) is a vigorous movement from first to last.
These numbers are : a chorus of peasants (introduction)
leading to a tenor solo of Anton awaking his intended
bride, a lovely duett (Lieschen and Anton), an air for
Lieschen, an air for Franz Spiess, a quartett (Lieschen,
Anton, Franz, and the mayor), an air for Friedrich Spiess,
a duett (Lieschen and Anton), a trio (Lieschen, Anton,
and Franz), a quintett (Anton, Lieschen, the mayor,
Franz, and steward), with chorus and final chorus. A
spoken dialogue divides the numbers one from another.

Schubert applied himself to the music of this vaudeville with but little zest ; the libretto and story failed to
interest him. The music is, as a matter of fact, to be
reckoned among his weaker productions : by which I by
no means intend to say that the performance of the

musical additions to the piece would not amply repay
the trouble of getting up the performance. Vogl had
undertaken the part of the two twins, representing the
military invalid and the peasant, and did his best to
keep them appropriately separate and distinct. The
music, on the whole, pleased the audience ; the introductory chorus was repeated, and the air of Franz
Spiess (in C) was much cheered. At the conclusion the
applause was renewed, and the people called for the
composer, in whose place, as Schubert was absent, Vogl
expressed his thanks to the audience.

The performance was, on the whole, satisfactory,[1]
but no enduring impression was created, and for this
the weakness of the plot and libretto is in part responsible. The operetta survived six representations,
and then vanished for ever from the repertoire. Critics
pronounced the work as a neat elegant trifle, the production of a young composer, who, as the purity of
his operatic style proved, must have pursued his ordinary studies with diligence, and was no novice in harmony. They went on to say, that the music being here
and there old-fashioned and deficient in melody, it may
be taken for granted that Schubert never misunder-
stood the value of the compliment of those friends who
summoned him in front of the curtain.[2]

[1] The other parts, Lieschen, Anton, the mayor, and the steward, were
filled by Fr. Betti Vio, Herr Rosenfeld, Gottdank, and Sebastian Mayer.

[2] A critic in the ' Allgemeine Musikzeitung ' was of opinion that 'the

A few weeks afterwards Schubert completed a far more important melodramatic composition, which was intended for stage representation.

On August 19, 1820, the Viennese journals contained the following notice :—

' By the liberality of His Excellency Count Ferdinand von Palffy, proprietor of the Imperial Theatre, an der Wien, three artists, whose connections and engagements do not sanction their claims to any clear receipts, are now allowed such payments, which the Count has, unasked, now conceded. These artists are Herr Neefe,[1] scene painter, Roller, master of the machinery, and Lucca Piazza, costumier of the said theatre, who, from their important services to the public, are well deserving of so high a mark of consideration. This benefit performance will take place next Monday, August 21, on the occasion of the third representation of the new magic Operetta, in three acts, '' Die Zauber-

work was deficient in real melody, that the music suffered from a confused overladen instrumentation, a painful effort after originality, the constant wearisome modulations, with no intervals for repose. The introductory chorus, a quartett and a bass air, alone entitled us to cling to the hope of a brilliant future for a young man already known to fame from his clever songs, and for this future he has yet to win the necessary self-dependence and solid powers required to form a real composer. His friends may reflect that there is a marked difference between a fiasco and a furore.'

[1] Herrmann Neefe, son of Christian Gottlob Neefe, Beethoven's teacher in Bonn.

harfe;" music by Herr Schubert; decorations, scenery, and costumes by the receivers of the benefit.'

Schubert had been asked by Neefe and Demmer, the *régisseur* of the theatre, to write music for this melodrama, the author of which was unknown.[1] Schubert set to work, and finished his task in a fortnight. On August 19, 1820, the piece was put upon the stage, and with but moderate success. It was several times given, but vanished from the repertoire before the approach of winter. Solo songs were few throughout the work, the main portions of which consisted of choruses and melodrama. The book was utterly valueless, nay, utterly childish, and was eminently unsuccessful. The overture performed on this occasion, a fine orchestral piece, is the same which appeared in a pianoforte edition as Op. 26, and was incorrectly marked as belonging to the drama 'Rosamunde.' There is a beautiful solo for the tenor, a romance of the Palmer, sung originally by Franz Jäger.[2] The critics attacked without mercy the insipid libretto,[3]

---

[1] Neefe and Demmer had certainly thought of Schubert with reference to the music to be composed for the melodrama, but they went for advice to Dr. L. v. Sonnleithner, and thus they were brought into contact with Schubert.

[2] An Andantino in D major, with accompaniment of violins, viola, flute, hautboy, bassoon, harp, cello, and bass (the pianoforte accompaniment arranged by F. Grutsch, formerly second orchestral director of the Kärnthnerthor Theatre).

[3] Hofmann, secretary of the theatre in Vienna, was its author.

a made-up melodramatic affair, and found much to object to in the musical treatment, but, above all, that it hindered rather than helped the action of the piece, and betrayed the absolute ignorance, on the part of the composer, of the rules of the melodrama. The way of treating the music for the magic harps showed a poor 'fade' decayed taste, and was wanting in the necessary power and characteristics which ought always to accompany ethereal spirits.[1]

Many a small grain of truth may be concealed in these criticisms of the time; but on closely analysing their purport, it is impossible not to remark on a certain predisposition unfavourable towards the young composer, who had only just come before the public with his slight efforts in musical drama. It is certain from the testimony of competent musical judges, who were present at the performances, that the music which Schubert had to compose for a senseless libretto contained vocal and instrumental numbers of the greatest interest.[2]

---

[1] The following criticism was published in the 'Allgemeine Musikalische Zeitung':—'The composer gives glimpses here and there of talent; there is on the whole a want of technical arrangement, which can only be gained by experience; the numbers, generally speaking, are too long and wearisome; the harmonious progressions too harsh, the instrumentation overladen, the choruses vapid and weak. The most successful numbers are the introductory Adagio of the overture, and the romance for the tenor; the expression in these is lovely; the simplicity is noble, and the modulation delicate. An idyllic subject would be admirably adapted to the composer.'

[2] In the year 1835, Ferdinand Schubert was still in possession of the

The objections made at the time to the composer, in respect of his 'harsh harmonic progressions, constant modulations, overladen instrumentation,' &c., would doubtless be reversed by the verdict of our times. The music to the 'Zauberharfe' deserves to be unearthed, for there is no doubt in it much that is beautiful, and Schubert himself reckoned it as one of his most successful works.

We have now to call attention to one of those features which prove very strikingly the greatness and versatility of Schubert's genius.

Nearly about the same time that Schubert was employed with the musical setting of vapid tasteless librettos, there came to light one of Schubert's most significant and characteristic musical poems of a religious kind, the result, it should seem, of hours consecrated by Schubert to thoughtful solitude and retirement. The birth of this oratorio is a mystery, and will probably remain so for ever, for not even Schubert's most trusted friends, such, for instance, as Franz v. Schober, who, in the year 1820, was thrown frequently into personal intimacy with the composer, can give any

score of the 'Zauberharfe.' There may very likely have been a copy in the archives of the theatre at Vienna, and one may be there still. The publishing firm of Spina has the original score of two entr'actes, an overture to the third, and a musical after-piece besides. Johann v. Spaun has a copy of the score of the tenor air, and the pianoforte setting of the same. The Overture (Op. 26) was played at Vienna as an introduction to the Operetta ' Der häusliche Krieg.'

explanation of the cause, or other external circumstances, under which the work in question was composed, but it is certain that to many of Schubert's associates the very existence of this work remained hidden. The Oratorio here referred to of ' Lazarus,' or the 'Feast of the Resurrection,' was intended by Schubert as an Easter Cantata, and, as can be seen by examining the original score, was taken in hand in February 1820, probably in the lodgings in the Wipplingerstrasse, which Schubert at that time shared with Mayrhofer. 'The Feast of the Resurrection' is one of the sacred poems written by a well-known teacher and theologian, August Hermann Niemeyer, formerly Chancellor to the Hochschule in Halle.[1]

In the preface to the collection of poems we find the following passage :—' The oratorios, especially the four first, have been frequented by large audiences in the years 1776 up to 1780. They owe their popularity very mainly at that period to the much-esteemed composer, the late musical director Rolle,[2] who gave very perfect perform-

---

[1] A. H. Niemeyer, born in 1754, at Halle, on the river Saale, became Professor of Theology, and Inspector of the royal 'Pädagogium,' and, in 1814, Chancellor of the University, and died (like Schubert) in the year 1828. He wrote religious tracts, poems, sermons, 'Characteristics of the Bible,' &c.

[2] Johann Heinrich Rolle, born in the year 1718, died in 1785, was director of music at Magdeburg, and was known as a correct and tasteful composer. As recently as 1862 appeared 'Lazarus,' an oratorio in two parts, composed by Johann Vogt, the words selected from the Bible, and it was first given at Dresden, on March 19, 1863.

ances of these works at the brilliant Magdeburg concerts.' These words were written on April 8, 1814; six years later (in February 1820), Schubert set Niemeyer's poem to music, and the latter, during the following eight years which he and Schubert had yet to live, never heard a note of the music.

After the lapse of thirty or more years since the composer's death, the world was surprised by the information of the existence of an oratorio by Schubert, although the original score of the first treatment of the subject had for a long time been in the possession of the firm of Diabelli (afterwards Spina) at Vienna. The discovery had yet to be made of this work, contained in Spaun's Schubert collection, by the compiler of this biography, in the year 1860, and in the late autumn of the following year a further important discovery was made of the largest part of the original score of the second part of the subject, in order to bring to the light of day a work so long veiled in darkness, and to give in Vienna the first public performance of the oratorio.[1]

---

[1] As early as the year 1859, when occupied with the 'Biographical Sketch,' I found the Cantata 'Lazarus' in examining Schubert's autographs in Herr Spaun's collection. These are mentioned in the 'Sketch,' and the remark made that Schubert only composed the first part of the subject. I was the more inclined to believe this, as a composition (especially one of such importance) would not easily escape so enthusiastic a friend of Schubert's as Witteczek, and Ferdinand Schubert (whose inaccuracy in this matter is plain enough) speaks in his memoranda of only one composition. I was soon, however, set right by a far better authority. In the late autumn of 1861, I was invited by the esteemed

Niemeyer's poem is divided into three parts, the first of which ends with the death of Lazarus, the second with his sepulture and funeral elegy by his friends, the third with his awaking from the grave. Of these the musical portion of the first part, exquisitely written out (in the hands of the Spina musical firm at Vienna, and also in copies possessed by Hofrath v. Spaun and the Vienna Musikverein), is preserved entire: what was discovered to be the second part, according to the original manuscript, leads through two recitative airs (of Nathanael and Martha) to the double alternate chorus of the weeping friends of Lazarus, with which, as the last sheets of the score are wanting, this part ought by rights to finish. According to the text, the missing fragment contains an air for Martha, several short recitative

musical historian Herr Alexander Thayer, of Boston (at that time attached to the North American Embassy in Vienna) to his lodgings in Neuwien, to be shown some Schubert MSS. I examined the musical memoranda, which my friend had so kindly placed at my disposal, with surprise and delight, and found amongst the collection the original score of 'Alfonso und Estrella,' that of the 'Zwillingsbrüder,' some stringed quartetts, pianoforte pieces, songs, and the second part of 'Lazarus,' but, unfortunately, not complete. I thought it imperative on me to inform the directors and members of the Musikverein, Herr Dr. Bauer and Herr Herbeck, of this discovery; they, too, succeeded in influencing, in the right way, the owner of the manuscript to produce, for a moderate compensation, an edition of these works, and henceforth to incorporate the collected MSS. with the musical archives at Vienna, as a noble addition to the treasures of the Society.. Fortunately the widow of Ferd. Schubert possessed some additional music belonging to 'Lazarus,' which gave the work a more suitable finish. Further enquiries for the lost numbers have remained, up to the present time, without result.

passages, and a chorus of friends.[1]　Whether the third
and most extensive part of the work, in which a prominent part was assigned to the chorus, was also set by
Schubert, we have no clue or evidence at present.

[1] The passages of the poem run thus:—

Martha.

Und stünden selbst der Engel Reih'n
Um seinen Geist gedrängt,
Ich drängte mich in ihre Reih'n
Auf Fittigen der Liebe ein
Und rief: Ihr Engel, er ist mein!

Nathanael.

Einst wenn vom Abend und vom Morgen her
Der Weltenrichter ruft, dann Martha ist er dein,
Dann ist er unser, ewig ungetrennt!
Jetzt gebt dem Staube, was ihm angehört!
Singt, Jünglinge, singt,
Singt Töchter,—ihr vom Tod
Und ihr vom Auferstehen das Lied.

Ein Jüngling.

Mein stiller Abend ist gekommen:
Wo leg' ich nun das matte Haupt?

Jemina.

Im Hügel, der den Hain umlaubt,
Im heiligen Ruhethal der Frommen.

(Man senkt den Leichnam in die Grabhöhle.)

Ein Jüngling.

Ich bin des Pilgerlebens müde,
Wie säumt, wie säumt mein Vaterland!

Jemina.

Dich leite deines Engels Hand
Und über deinem Staub sei Friede!

The characters in the sacred cantata are 'The man
of Bethany,' Lazarus (tenor), Mary and Martha, sisters
of Lazarus (soprano); Jemina, the daughter of Jairus
(soprano); Nathanael, a disciple (tenor), and the Sadducee Simon (bass).[1]

Ein Jüngling.
Wer hat das Feld mit Saat bestreut?

Jemina.
Der Geber der Unsterblichkeit.

Ein Jüngling.
Heil mir, sie ist mein.

Jemina.
Heil dir, sie ist dein.

Beide.
Und himmlisches Entzücken.

Jüngling.
Ganz unsterblich wirst du mich—

Jemina.
Ganz unsterblich werd' ich dich—

Beide.
An diesen Busen drücken.

Chor.
Wiederseh'n! sei uns gesegnet,
Entzückungsvolles Wiederseh'n,
Wenn uns unser Freund begegnet,
Wo Engel liebend um ihn steh'n!
Dieser Tag der Wonne
Trocknet uns're Thränen ab;
Hoch schwebt uns're Seele
Ueber unser Grab.

[1] At the first performance of 'Lazarus' in Vienna (March 27, 1863),

Jemina and Nathanael excepted, who have not much
but very beautiful music assigned them, the other characters are treated very much on the same footing by
the poet and the composer. The latter has allowed
himself to take several liberties with the text, which
much enhanced the beauty of the poem, and made it
more conformable to musical purposes.[1]

The music consists, conformably with the poem, of
airs, choruses, and recitatives. A prominent position
in this musical poem of Schubert's is assigned to the
arioso and appropriate recitative, in marked contrast
to the airs scattered thinly over the work, and two

under the directorship of Herr Johann Herbeck, the soloists were: Frl.
Tellheim (Mary), Frl. König (Martha), Frau Wilt (Jemina), Herr
Olschbauer (Lazarus), Herr Schultner (Nathanael), and Herr Mayer-
hofer (Simon).

[1] It is very probable, although not proved, that Schubert himself
altered the text. The chief alterations refer to some passages in the
first airs of Martha and Mary, in the second song of Lazarus, and the
grand air of Simon. Thus the words of Martha:—

> Und nun gehst du so fern von uns
> In's unbekannte Land,
> Und einsam bleibt die Hütte dann,
> Des Schmerzes und der Sehnsucht öder Wohnplatz.

Thus altered:—

> Und nun gehst du in die Schatten der Gräber
> Ferne von uns, dass in öden Nächten
> In der einsamen Hütte wir dich klagen,
> Dass im Wipfel der Palme unser Jammer ertöne
> An deiner Gruft zu verhallen.

In Simon's recitative, more energetic expressions are used than are
found in the original, the composer wishing to produce a dramatic effect.

others attached to the two choruses which conclude each of the parts of the oratorio. The composer had a strong preference for declamatory songs, and the mastery with which Schubert contrived to dam up the rapid current of melodies which flowed at his bidding, and penetrated, deep musician as he was, with the meaning of a poem breathing the spirit of intellectual beauty, fuse these melodies into lovely recitative passages full of character, gives a special interest to this cantata, and stamps it as one of the most characteristic poems which have been composed in this style. The compiler of the text has by no means lightened the work of the composer. A genius such as Schubert's was necessary to steer successfully past the dangerous rocks and quicksands of monotony incidental to a subject wearisome from an almost unbroken sameness of treatment, and so overweighted with recitative passages. Schubert applied himself to his task not in a descriptive but dramatic vein, as the poem required; and with what delicacy of feeling and admirable skill he availed himself of the opportunity offered by the poet for the development of his dramatic power, the music allotted to the daughter of Jairus (Jemina) and Simon the Sadducee bears the most brilliant testimony. An intellectual piecemeal criticism of a delicate refined work, which rushed spontaneously from the composer's brain with an uninterrupted current, would be like analysing moonlight, and would be of little advantage, although such minute criticism might bring to the surface many a hidden and buried beauty. We shall merely point generally to the more conspicuous beauties of Schubert's musical poem.

The oratorio opens with a short musical introduction to the song and recitative of Lazarus, who has just been conducted by the two sisters Martha and Mary to the garden, and placed on the green grass under a shady palm-tree. To a low, mournful, and soft melody succeeds (in a quicker movement) a recitative of Martha, and after a short instrumental prelude (Andantino G major) a recital song for Mary. The air belonging to this (an Andantino sost. F major ¾, accompanied by stringed instruments, clarionet, bassoon, and horn) is one of the finest of the number, and has a peculiar colouring given to it by the introduction of wind instruments. A recitative now follows for Lazarus full of touching expression, and another for the disciple Nathanael, who has come in haste from the Saviour's side to see Lazarus; this leads to a grand aria (Allegro mod. C major $\frac{4}{4}$), 'Wenn ich ihm nachgerungen habe.' Amongst the recitatives that follow for Martha, Lazarus, and Mary, that of the latter is pre-eminent:—

Wenn nun mit tausendfacher Qual
Der Schmerzen Heer sich um ihn drängt, &c.,

and the air that follows:—

Gottes Liebe; Fels im Meer, &c.,

with its enchanting melody and character.

Jemina now appears on the scene—the daughter
of Jairus, one of the loveliest forms in the Gospel
history, and a character skilfully introduced into the
story of the poet, in order to place before the eyes of
the dying Lazarus a living witness of the resurrection.
The great scene, in which she tells of her death, as-
cension, and resurrection, gave the composer an opportunity of creating noble, impressive music, which
is worthy of our highest admiration.

What now follows—the last words of the dying
Lazarus, the laments and wailings of the sisters and
Jemina, and, finally, the chorus of friends who gradually assemble—is of surpassing beauty and expression.

The second part begins with an orchestral move-
ment of twenty-seven bars (Largo C minor $\frac{4}{4}$); a kind
of funeral dirge, in which the trumpets produce a
powerful effect. The next number is a recitative for
Simon the Sadducee, who moves restlessly about
amongst those who are preparing the grave.[1] This
song and that which follows—'Ach des grausen Todge-
danken!'—are of a dramatic force of which few thought
Schubert's quieter and gentler musical .predilections
capable. Two recitatives are then given to Nathanael;
and a chorus of the friends of Lazarus, following the

[1] The scene is laid in a green field full of grave-stones overhung by
palms and cedars; in the background is a grove, and in the distance a
road to the house of Lazarus.

corpse, with an impressive combination of men's and women's voices, to the words

> Du nimmst ihn auf, er keimt hervor,
> Er wächst zur Ceder Gottes empor,

introduces a grand finale, with the full orchestra. The whole forms a noble close to this part.[1]

A second large work, of a delicate and exquisite texture, is the Opera of 'Sakontala;' which, judging by the original design, might have contributed greatly to Schubert's reputation ; but unfortunately, and for reasons unknown to me, it was laid aside unfinished.[2] The libretto is substantially a version of the famous Indian drama, 'Ring-Cacuntala,' by the poet Kalidasa ; and the verses have a kind of swing and evenness, honourably distinguished from the miserable jingling rhymes which one so frequently comes across in operatic libretti. Spoken dialogue alternates with the vocal and instrumental parts of the drama.

---

[1] The original score contains, as I have already observed, a recitative for Nathanael, one for Martha, and part of an air for the latter, and ends with the words 'Und stünden selbst der Engel Reih'n,' &c. In the third part the poet avoided bringing the Redeemer to the scene of the awakening of Lazarus ; the miracle and the miracle-worker are kept behind the scene.

[2] According to a statement of Herr Josef Hüttenbrenner, Schubert, at the suggestions of some friends, who disliked the poem as a libretto, abstained from finishing the entire composition. The compiler of the book endeavoured, very strenuously, to persuade Schubert to like it, but in vain. 'Sakontala' was fated once again to be arranged as an opera-text by Hugo Ebert, and set to music by Tomaschek.

The characters in the piece are: Duschmanta, King of Hindostan (tenor); Madhawia, court fool, and confidant of the king (bass); Sakontala (soprano); Kanna, first Brahmin, Sakontala's step-father (bass); Durwasas, brother of Aditi, goddess of the Day (bass); Saregarawa, another Brahmin; Gautami, Sakontala's governess; Amusia, Primawada, Sakontala's play-fellows; Menaka, a nymph, Sakontala's mother; two policemen, a fisherman, genii of the light, demons of the night, two maiden attendants, dancers; Aditi, goddess of the Day; Matali, chariot-driver; and Misraki, a demon.

The plot of the piece, and the musical fragments of Schubert intended for the opera, may be thus detailed: —King Duschmanta, whilst hunting in the hermit's grove, sees Sakontala, declares to marry her, and seals the contract, after Indian fashion, with a kiss; and then hurries forward to his capital, with a view of receiving his bride on her arrival. Kanna, returned from the sacred place Somathirta, where he has learned from the goddess' mouth that Sakontala, before her union with the king, will have to go through some sharp trials, prepares her and her attendants for a journey to the residence of Duschmanta. In order to obtain the blessing of the gods, a sacrifice is made to them in 'the Grove of Memories,' and here the opera commences. A chorus, introduced by boys' voices (Andante con moto F major $\frac{4}{4}$), in which the hermits and the attendant maidens, as well as Kanna and Sakontala, take part, hails the light of day and prays the gods for a favourable reception of the proffered sacrifice. The general chorus, 'Nehmet das Opfer,' &c., concludes this scene.

The scene on the stage changes to another part of the grove. Durwasas, the brother of Aditi, goddess of Day, bursts in, in an uncontrollable fit of fury, and adjures the demons to help him in his revenge against Sakontala—whose mother, the nymph Menaka, he loves with an undeclared passion—and against Aditi, with whom Menaka has sought refuge, and whose son he has kidnapped. The demons answer, from the depth of the earth,

> Wir hören dich!

Durwasas sings a song of revenge (Allegro moderato D minor $\frac{4}{4}$), in which the principal passage runs thus :—

> Ein Zauber, mächtig und schwer,
> Senk' über Duschmanta sich nieder,
> Er soll die Sinne ihm binden,
> Dein Bild soll dem Herzen entschwinden,
> Und sieht auch sein Auge dich wieder,
> Er kenne die Gattin nicht mehr!

Amusia and Primawada enter, and implore Durwasas to withdraw his curse. He, however, again calls on the demons for assistance, and they promise they will stand by him ; the maiden attendants, however, he comforts with the following words :—

Doch seine Zauber sollen schwinden,
Und von des Königs Auge falle
Im Augenblick der Schleier ab,
Sobald er seinen Ring erblicket,
Den scheidend er der Gattin gab.

A choral song, sung alternately by the invisible demons and the maidens, forms the ensemble; after which everyone withdraws and the demons disappear. A short dialogue ensues for the two attendants. Then Sakontala enters, and unburthens her feelings in an air (Andante agitato, B minor), full of sinister forebodings and yearning for her husband. The playfellows adorn her before she starts on her journey. Kanna announces to the nymphs of the wood the impending departure of her daughter to the king's palace.

Women's voices (Andantino G major $\frac{6}{8}$, in music for three voices with flute obligato) sound sweetly from the grove. Kanna leads her step-daughter forth, the others follow; the wood-nymphs repeat the last strophe of their song. Durwasas enters, and sends his servant Misraki to the Melini stream, with the order to dive unseen into the water, and, when Sakontala comes to bathe, to wrest the ring from her finger and throw it into the water.

The scene changes to the palace of Duschmanta. The court fool, just waking up from a troubled dream, bemoans (something like Valentin in Raimund's 'Verschwender'), in a long, humorous air (Andante molto,

E-flat major $\frac{4}{4}$), the so-called pleasures of the chase, ending with the refrain :—

> Und das soll Erholung sein ?
> Nein, das geht mir nimmer ein.

Sakontala and her attendants are announced. Finale of the last act (Andante maestoso B-flat major $\frac{4}{4}$).

Durwasas' stratagem has succeeded. Duschmanta refuses again to recognise Sakontala, although married to him; for she, when about to show the ring in attestation of their union, finds with horror that the token has vanished. A series of lively, dramatic, and in parts passionate, scenes succeed one another, in which all on the stage and the chorus take part alternately. The King rejects Sakontala; Kanna leads the despairing woman away from the place; her attendants follow. But a cloud is seen to descend, amidst thunder and lightning, and bear away Sakontala to the skies. Duschmanta, informed of this circumstance, becomes a prey to melancholy and gloomy anticipations. A sudden thunder-clap and a storm of wind, and heavenly voices are heard in chorus (F major $\frac{2}{4}$):—

> Lieblos verstossen,
> Ohne Erbarmen
> Bist du von frommen
> Liebenden Armen
> Gern' aufgenommen,
> Sakontala !

The melody is distinctly heard, and is echoed back in the distance.

This chorus—a song of the spheres, with an harmonious accompaniment — is the only finished and perfectly completed number.

The second act begins with a trio for men's voices. A fisherman, who has found the ring, is taken up as a thief by two policemen, and brought into the front court of the royal palace. The fisherman tells them that he has discovered the ring in a fish, whereupon all three join in this decision:

> Respect für feine Nasen,
> Sie forschen ohne Licht,
> Sie folgen nur dem Dufte,
> Und irren dennoch nicht.

One of the police repairs to the palace, in order to give notice of the progress of the affair; a chamberlain comes out with him, gives the fisherman his liberty and a purse of money.

Then follows a humorous trio. The fisherman offers to treat the two policemen to a glass of wine at a public-house, where they have a jovial time with the landlord and guests, cheering and toasting one another.[1]

[1] *Die beiden Häscher.*

> So, liebes Brüderchen,
> So, so, so, so,
> So sind wir Freunde,
> So sind wir froh.

Fischer.

> Der Hüter der Ordnung muss wachsam wohl sein
> Und wachsam erhält ihn ein Liedchen und Wein,

The scene changes to the garden of the King; Sakontala and Menaka swoop down in a cloud; two maidens
with baskets of flowers approach and greet them with
a song, in which Sakontala and Menaka join (quartett
for women's voices). Madhawia, overwhelmed with grief,
enters, and says that the King, since the ring has been
found, has recovered his memory, but that his heart is
consumed by sorrow. Menaka, however, reminds her
of the promise given to the gods, that she will never
appear before him. Duschmanta appears, and calls
imploringly after Sakontala; her attendants bring him
the picture of his wedded wife; he looks at it with
speechless grief and melancholy longing. Then next
follows a grand duett between Sakontala and Duschmanta, which the chorus, from the moment when the
King bows his knee before the picture, accompanies to
the following tune :—

> Wahnsinn ergreifet ihn
> In seinen Schmerzen,
> Verzweiflung tobet
> In seinem Herzen, &c.

Duschmanta, convinced that Sakontala has not pardoned him, sinks to the earth, overwhelmed with grief.

> So kommt denn mit mir in die Schenke hinein
> Und trinket euch wachsam im goldenen Wein,
> Hoch leben die Gäste, die Seelen so zart.

> *Häscher.*
> Hoch lebe der Wirth, der nicht ängstlich spart, &c.

The picture is carried off, Sakontala and Menaka bid the King farewell, and are borne away to the clouds. Kanna seeks to comfort him and strengthen his heart in the gods.

Then follows an air of Kanna, in which he glorifies faith and piety, and prophesies a final victory after a manfully contended battle. The court fool then invites the King to a banquet, accompanied by song and dance. In the garden a stage is erected, on which a representation of the following story is to take place. Durwasas, passionately in love with Menaka, but rejected by her, swears vengeance on her and her children; Aditi takes the afflicted one to her care, and Durwasas, who has carried off her sister's boy and become attached to him, refuses to give him back unless a daughter of Menaka's family, abandoned by her husband, will consent to love the author of all her troubles. The curtain rolls up, and on the small stage are dancers and singers, amongst them Madhawia with a chorus.[1]

---

[1]   *Chor und Madhawia.*

Töne jubeln, Tänze wallen;
Lasst sie wallen, lasst sie schallen
Zu der heiligen Vermählung
Jahresfest im Feierton.

Wonne schwebe durch die Reihen,
Welche Lust (?) soll sich nicht freuen,
Aditi, wenn du dich freuest
Mit dem Gatten, mit dem Sohn.

The commemoration festival of Aditi's wedding with Kasapa is being solemnised. Durwasas stands lurking in the background. Kasapa withdraws after the dance is over. Aditi follows him, but first of all sends her son Indra to Durwasas, to cheer him. He calls on the demons, and enquires of them how he can be revenged upon Aditi; they point to the boy, and he seizes and hurries him off. The demons caper about in a wild dance of joy, while Madhawia and a chorus accompany.[1] Aditi and Kasapa return and look for their son. Durwasas shows them the boy standing on a hill, to which demons barricade the way. More choruses and dancing. The spectators weep; the genii of light appear, and a prayer arises to heaven. Chorus. The god of love appears on a cloud, and promises comfort. Madhawia and the chorus greet him. To their cry—

> Sendet, sendet bald ihr Götter
> Was die Liebe hold verspricht,

---

[1] *Madhawia mit dem Singchor.*
Seht die Lust der Hölle!
Ihre Freud' ist Wuth;
Nur wo Schmerzen wimmern
Jauchzt die dunkle Brut.
Heulendes Gestöhne
Ist ihr Jubelklang,
Brüllendes Gehöhne
Ihr Triumfgesang,
Giftgenährte Schlangen,
Ihrer Schläfe Kranz
Grinsen ihre Scherze,
Rasen ist ihr Tanz.

voices from the clouds answer—

Bald,—bald,—bald.

Dancers, singers, and spectators look amazed towards heaven. The curtain of the miniature stage falls. All exclaim together, 'What has happened?' 'What sounds!'

Now comes the finale, a lively and elaborate scene, in which the chorus, the voices from heaven, the three genii, Duschmanta, Kanna and the Brahmins, Madhawia, and all the stage take part. The genii present the King with a sword and a shield, to accomplish his intended task of winning back Sakontala, and assure him of their assistance.

Clouds descend on the earth. A chariot and a chariot-driver emerge from the depths of the clouds. Duschmanta mounts; Kanna and the Brahmins call after the King :—

Leb' wohl Freund, den wir lieben,
Dir folget unser heiss Gebet.

Madhawia and the rest join in a parting salutation :—

Leb' wohl, o Vater, den wir lieben,
Für den dein Volk zum Herren fleht.

The King answers them :—

Dank, liebe Freunde, Dank euch Kinder,
Bald wird mein Aug' euch wieder seh'n!

And after these words he drives off to the skies. A general chorus—

Dann Heil und Sieg dem Ueberwinder,
Nun mag dich Muth und Kraft umweh'n, brings the second act to a close, and with it Schubert's musical accompaniments.[1]

Besides more important works referred to, our composer wrote during this year a stringed Quartett (in C minor) and the antiphons for Palm Sunday;[2] these last for his brother Ferdinand, who had commenced his duties in Passion Week as the newly appointed 'Regius Chori' in the church of Altlerchenfelder. Church music found no favour with the Lerchenfelders as a corporate body, and Ferdinand found himself compelled to look to his school-assistants and friends at Lichtenthal; in this quarter, too, there was a failure of music for church ceremonies, and Franz, in the course of half an hour, chalked down the antiphons, composed in all haste two other sacred pieces, and on Easter Sunday conducted the Mass in D (Nelson's) by Haydn.

The Twenty-third Psalm, 'The Lord is my Shepherd,' written for four sisters, Fröhlich, great friends of Schubert's,[3] and the majestic chorus 'Gesang der Geister

[1] The manuscript of Schubert's sketch is in the possession of Dr. Schneider.

[2] These are written with black chalk on a sheet of blotting-paper; Herr Spina has the manuscript.

[3] The Psalm, the original of which is in the possession of Frl. Anna Fröhlich, bears date December 1820. At that time concerts were given in the old music-hall every Thursday; the arrangement was in the hands of Lannoy, Holz, Bogner, Fischer, Kaufmann, Kirchlehner, Dr. Beck, Pirringer, Schmidt, Dr. L. Sonnleithner (afterwards Randhartinger was one of the party) undertook the duty alternately. Anna Fröhlich was the chief singer, and besides the Twenty-third Psalm, the following of Schubert's works were performed there: 'Gott in der Natur' (August, 1822), 'Ständchen,' and 'Mirjam.'

über den Wassern' (by Göthe), both belong to this period. Of the Lieder, the most important are well known and published; amongst the unpublished must be reckoned the 'Nachthymne,' by Novalis, and four Italian canzonets by Monti, set to music for Fräulein v. Ronner (afterwards married to Herr Spaun); to this must be added the grand Fantasia in C for pianoforte, which Schubert dedicated to, and wrote expressly for, the pianoforte-player, Liebenberg v. Zittin. Schubert passed the greater part of this year in Vienna, visiting with Schober at the castle of Ochsenburg at St. Pölten, where they undertook jointly the Opera of 'Alfonso und Estrella,' which we shall allude to in greater detail hereafter.

CHAPTER IX.

(1821.)

SCHUBERT'S CIRCUMSTANCES—PROOFS OF PUBLIC RECOGNITION OF
HIS PERFORMANCES—SONNLEITHNER FAMILY—CULTIVATION OF MUSIC
—'ERLKÖNIG' SUNG AT THE KÄRNTHNERTHOR THEATRE BY VOGL—
THE 'GESANG DER GEISTER ÜBER DEN WASSERN'—'DAS DÖRFCHEN'
—DEDICATION OF THE FIRST SONGS—THE SINGERS OF SCHUBERT'S
FOUR-PART SONGS—SYMPHONY IN E—DANCE MUSIC—TWO CONTRI-
BUTIONS TO THE OPERA 'DAS ZAUBERGLÖCKCHEN'—SCHUBERT'S IN-
TIMACY WITH FAMILIES AT VIENNA—A LETTER OF THE PATRIARCH
L. PYRKER—CIRCLE OF FRIENDS—'SCHUBERTIADEN'—ATZENBRUCK
—SCHUBERT'S CONNECTION WITH THE FAMILY—A POEM OF RUSTICO-
CAMPIUS.

THE year 1821 is one of the most important in the
short span of life allotted to Schubert.   His performances as a song-composer then first became known
to the great world; the publication of several of his
compositions brought him most favourably into public
notice ; and such warm recognition of his great gifts
and musical capacity was paid by men of influence and
high position, that there seemed every likelihood of its
depending mainly on Schubert himself to use to his
own advantage this happy combination of circumstances, and to better his condition perhaps for the
remainder of his lifetime.

As a belief which, up to very lately, obtained credence, that Mozart's embarrassed position was mainly owing to the indifference of the public at Vienna, has been now contradicted,[1] so also must the affirmation that the distressing state in which Schubert was often involved was owing to insincere men calling themselves his friends. Like other masters in his art, he certainly had to fight against the caprice and stupidity of publishers, and the great world itself was not always inclined to estimate his compositions as they deserved; and even to the Musikverein at Vienna—still famous for its support of music of all kinds, and notably for the encouragement of native talent—his obligations were very small indeed; for the Society, as its concert programmes prove to demonstration, took comparatively very little notice of him, and committed twofold injustice in respect of the great C Symphony. Still it has never yet been proved that Schubert was deserted or treacherously dealt with, or that he was constrained to make use of his talents merely for the advantage of others. At no time of his life was he wanting in sympathising friends, who recognised his genius and were always ready to assist him in word and deed. That he did not invariably feel drawn towards these persons, but, following his own inclination, attached himself socially to those who doubtless delighted in his songs, but valued him rather as a boon companion than a

[1] See Otto Jahn, 'Mozart,' vol. iii. p. 210.

creative genius, and who, themselves at war with existence, were not in the position of giving him a strong
arm of support—all this cannot be thrown in the teeth
of either class as reprehensible conduct.   Schubert
knew thoroughly well what he had to expect at the
hands of his associates, and his good easy nature never
hindered him from bearing their weaknesses in harmless playfulness, and making willing use of the officious-
ness of this or that man, as occasion offered.   He let
slip the few favourable opportunities which offered
themselves for ensuring a good position in the world (if
I am to believe in the truth of the statements made
to me on this point).   Perfect freedom of action was
the element in which he, by preference, moved, and for
which he was content to make every sacrifice.   Whilst,
however, on the one hand, he gained and retained this
personal independence, in other respects he was distinctly a loser.   The circumstances of Schubert's en-
vironment had certainly no influence on his artistic life
and activity.   His power of creating was never cramped
by the untoward events of his worldly position ; in spite
of bitter experiences, he fulfilled his mission in the
world gloriously, and found, in the consciousness of his
own value and the happiness of an inexhaustible source
of invention, an abundant compensation for the absence
or paucity of the good things of this world.

In the following documents, emanating from influential people of his time, an ample recognition of

Schubert's merits as a musician finds its proper expression.

In January 1821, Hofmusikgraf Moriz v. Dietrichstein wrote to Michael Vogl :—'I beg of you, my dear friend, to be good enough to hand this over to the excellent Schubert. I trust it may be of some advantage to him; for since I have fathomed the genius of this young, powerful artist—one of such rare promise—it has been one of my most ardent wishes, as far as I could, to bring him sub umbrâ alarum tuarum. Good morning, my dear friend " rara avis in terra "—I ought to say " rarissima." '

The three testimonials were as follows :—

' I certify that Herr Franz Schubert, late pupil of Hofcapellmeister Anton Salieri, as well from his deep knowledge in the theory and practice of harmony as of the auxiliary sciences requisite for vocal composition and distinguished talents, is one of the most promising of our young composers, of whom the Court Theatre and Opera House may expect the most delightful artistic productions.

'IGNAZ FRANZ EDLER V. MOSEL,
'Acting Court Secretary.
'Vienna: January 16, 1821.'

' We, the undersigned, testify that Herr Franz Schubert, on account of his famous and most promising musical talent, which he has proved chiefly in the art of composition, has been employed by the committee of management of the Court Theatre, and served with great distinction and to the satisfaction of everyone.

'JOSEF WEIGL,
'Director of the Royal Opera.

'Vienna: January 27, 1821.

'ANTONIO SALIERI,
'Royal Hofcapellmeister.
'LEOPOLD OFFERSMANN V. EICHTHAL,
'Coram me:
'JOH. GR. BARTH-BARTHENHEIM.

'Vienna: January 29, 1821.'

'My inclinations and my duty inducing me to examine men of distinguished musical talents, especially those found in my own country, and to encourage to the best of my powers their noble efforts, I have particular pleasure in certifying that Herr Franz Schubert, who received the first rudiments of education in the Convict while he served as a chorister-boy in the Royal Chapel, has, in the course of a few years, by native genius, earnest study of composition, and constant preparatory labour, already given the most eloquent proofs of his deep knowledge, feeling, and good taste, and that it only remains for me to wish that an opportunity be offered to this estimable man to unfold the fairest blossoms in the thriving fields of universal art, and more particularly that of dramatic music.

'MORIZ GRAF DIETRICHSTEIN.

'January 24, 1821.'

These testimonials, in which Schubert's merits and

services to the Opera House are the chief theme, sound as honourable as they were encouraging; those furnished by the noble Count v. Dietrichstein speak more particularly in terms of warm recognition of the musical activity and competence of our tone-poet, and would be sure, when the opportunity offered, of serving as an important voucher and emphatic recommendation. I don't know if Schubert ever made use of them, but doubtless he enclosed them in his petition as a candidate for the position of Hofcapellmeister.

Schubert's first public entry into the artistic world as a composer of songs, and the consequent propagation of his compositions, is intimately, nay, indissolubly, connected with a Viennese family, in which the art of music, at a time when chamber and classical music had not that extensive credit and importance which it enjoys in our time, was highly honoured. This was the Sonnleithner family.[1]

Dr. Ignaz Edler v. Sonnleithner, Rath, advocate, and professor at Vienna, in the years 1815–1824 collected together in his house at Gundelberg a considerable number of artists and connoisseurs for periodical practice, which gradually assumed the character of performances.[2] He had inherited from his father, the

---

[1] Dr. Ignaz v. Sonnleithner, born July 31, 1770, died November 27, 1831. Dr. Leopold v. Sonnleithner was born November 15, 1797, and was therefore of the same age as Schubert.

[2] These meetings were held from May 26, 1815, in the third story

esteemed lawyer and musician, Dr. Christof v. Sonnleithner, an appreciation and love of music. He was
also gifted with a sympathetic voice and one of considerable sweetness and compass; and several of the
members of his large family—among them more particularly his eldest son, Leopold, at that time an advocate
at Vienna—showed an inclination and aptitude for the
practice of art, so that in his own house he found the
elements of vocal practice ready at hand, and the never-
failing supply of novelty in the way of songs and instrumental pieces by degrees won such repute for the
concerts, that, as a preventive measure against the constant pressure of hearers, admission tickets had to be
issued. The works of the recognised master-mind in
art were, before all others, honoured and cultivated in
this circle, at the same time other new and clever men
were taken up, and their compositions allowed a hearing. Here the Cantata of 'Prometheus,' by Schubert,
in which Leopold v. Sonnleithner (on July 24, 1816)
had worked as one of the chorus, was given—only with
pianoforte accompaniment, it is true, but still with

of the Gundelhof, where there was room for more than 120 people.
The meetings were held every Friday evening, and continued even
through the summer months; from the October of 1816, on account of
the increasing importance of the performances, they were held every
fortnight during the winter months. They ended February 20, 1824.
The admirable programmes, and the distinguished people who took part
in them, give an idea of the cultivation of music prevalent in this
family.

entire success. Here, too, were given, on November 19,
1819, 'Das Dörfchen ;' on March 30, 1821, the ' Gesang
der Geister über den Wassern ;' and on June 9, 1822,
the 'Twenty-third Psalm,' for female voices. On December 1, 1820, the 'Erlkönig,' by Gymnich,[1] the brilliant
reception of which exercised a material influence upon
the publication of Schubert's compositions. On January
25, 1821, Gymnich sang this song, for the first time in
public, at one of the evening entertainments of the so-
called small Musikverein ('Zum rothen Apfel ') in the
Singerstrasse, on which occasion the composer in person was introduced to the public. On February 8
Josef Goetz sang 'Die Sehnsucht,' and Frl. Sofie Linhardt (afterwards Fr. Schuller) the songs ' Gretchen am
Spinnrad,' and 'Der Jüngling auf dem Hügel,' and,
on March 8, Josef Preisinger gave the ' Gruppe aus
dem Tartarus,' which songs, including the ' Schäfers
Klagelied,' sung by Jäger, at a concert given in the
year 1819 by the violin-player Jaell, were certainly the
first vocal compositions of Schubert's which were pub-
licly performed.

Leopold v. Sonnleithner, whose acquaintance with
Schubert's compositions dated from the early period of
their schooldays' friendship, had copies of the works,

---

[1] August v. Gymnich was a State official and great connoisseur of
music. He died in the following year (October 6); Goetz on March 9,
1822; and Tieze, whose name is indissolubly associated with Schubert's
songs and quartetts, on January 11, 1850, in the fifty-second year of his
age.

which passed from hand to hand, but had now been
collected and fairly written afresh.   When this was
done he undertook to find a publisher for them.   But
Diabelli, as well as Haslinger, refused to publish the
song, even if offered to them as a gift.   The composer,
they said, was so little known to fame, and the difficulty
of the pianoforte accompaniment so great, that they
could not promise the smallest success.   The expenses,
therefore, were defrayed by subscriptions raised by the
two connoisseurs just named, assisted by two other men,
also interested in Schubert, and in February 1821 the
'Erlkönig' was first engraved.   Dr. Ignaz v. Sonnleithner announced this fact one evening to his guests,
and those present immediately put down their names
as subscribers for a hundred copies, and with this the
expenses of the second part were met.   In this fashion,
the engraving of the first twelve parts was defrayed, and
they were sold by Diabelli on commission.   The receipts
were enough to pay Schubert's arrears, and leave him
with a good sum of money in hand.

His first appearance as a composer was under the
most favourable and happy omens.   On March 7, 1821,
Vogl's performance of the 'Erlkönig' at a concert in
the Kärnthner Theatre paved the way to fame for the
genius of Schubert.   This meeting, held in those
days annually on Ash Wednesday, by a society of
noble ladies, under the patronage of the Princess Therese Fürstenberg (née the Princess Schwarzenberg),

'for the furtherance of charity and other useful purposes,' and the Institute was founded for the teaching of music, declamation, and dancing. The Privy Councillor and Secretary of the Society, Dr. Josef Sonnleithner, arranged the concert, and, acting on the suggestion of his nephew, Dr. Leopold Sonnleithner, inserted in the programme three of Schubert's compositions.[1]

The ballad of the 'Erl-King' was encored with a storm of applause. In the quartett 'Dörfchen,' Herr Josef Barth and Goetz (an officer in the service of the reigning Prince Schwarzenberg), Wenzel Nejebse (then Imperial Rath), and the lately deceased President of the Oberlandesgericht Johann Carl Ritter v. Umlauff (at that time a young beginner in judicial office); in the 'Geisterchor' of Göthe, Weinkopf, Frühwald, and two chorus-singers from the theatres were associated with gentlemen whose names we have already given.

[1] The following is the programme:—1. Overture to the Opera of 'The Templer,' by Girowetz; 2. Tableau; 3. Air by Mozart, sung by Wilhelmine Schröder; 4. Violin concerto, by Spohr, played by Léon de Lubin; 5. Recitation; 6. 'Das Dörfchen,' vocal quartett, by Schubert; 7. Variations for piano, by Worczicek; 8. Tableau; 9. Overture to the Opera 'Das Zauberglöckchen,' by Herold; 10. Air by Mozart, sung by Caroline Unger; 11. Recitation; 12. 'Erlkönig,' by Schubert; 13. Rondo for violoncello, by Romberg; 14. Duett, from 'Ricardo,' by Rossini, sung by Wilhelmine Schröder and Caroline Unger; 15. Göthe's 'Gesang der Geister über den Wassern,' by Schubert. The recitations were by Sofie Schröder and Frau Korn, the tableaux by Fanny Elsler; Girowetz conducted the music; Stubenrauch the dances. Seats for this academy representation were procurable at the Fürstenbergs', Himmelpfortgasse, No. 952. ('Wiener Musikzeitung,' 1821.)

This particular chorus had been repeatedly rehearsed, and (according to Herr v. Umlauff) the performance was exact and careful; nevertheless the impression made on the public by this crabbed music was one of the most bewildering kind.[1]

The singers, impressed with the majestic character of the work, expected to be vehemently applauded; but there was an ominous silence, and the eight victims on the altar of musical insensibility withdrew in confusion from the scene, looking very much as if they had shivered from the effects of a cold douche suddenly poured over their heads. Schubert was no less indignant at the fiasco which befell his chorus of spirits.

The 'Erl-King' and the other songs before mentioned had now a rapid sale.[2] The edition was soon sold off, and the publishers were in the best of good humours.

The first-named Lied was dedicated to the composer's friend and patron, Moriz Count v. Dietrichstein; 'Gretchen am Spinnrad,' as Op. 2, to the Reichsgraf

---

[1] See the 'Allgemeine Musikzeitung,' No. 23, of March 21, 1821:—
'The eight-part chorus, by Herr Schubert, was recognised by the public as a farrago of all sorts of musical modulations and vague departures from ordinary forms—no sense, no order, no meaning. The composer in such works (the criticism went on to say) resembles a big waggoner, who drives a team of eight horses, and turns now to the right, now to the left, getting at one time out of the road, then upsetting, and pursuing this game without once making any honest way.'

[2] The 'Erl-King' was announced in the Vienna 'Zeitung,' April 2, 'Gretchen am Spinnrad,' April 30, and 'Der Wanderer,' May 29, 1821.

Moriz Friess. The prefatory words of dedication were undertaken by Herren Leopold v. Sonnleithner, Josef Hüttenbrenner, and Ignaz v. Mosel; [1] for Schubert, as a rule, troubled himself in matters of this kind as little as he did in attending personally at the rehearsals requisite for the performance of his own compositions,[2] unless driven by some necessity to be present. This time the dedication brought in a good roll of ducats to the composer.

[1] On March 17, 1821, Hofrath v. Mosel wrote to Josef Hüttenbrenner the following lines:—'Knowing, as I do, the kind sentiments of his Excellency Count Moriz v. Dietrichstein towards the talented composer Herr Franz Schubert, I do not doubt of his Excellency's accepting the dedication of the poem of the "Erlkönig," set to music by Herr Schubert.' The dedication to Opus 2 appears to have been written by Josef Hüttenbrenner, and the superscription by Sonnleithner. On April 13 the latter writes:—'I have just received the enclosed letter from Diabelli. As you have introduced the subject, I beg of you earnestly to do all that is necessary. Supposing Count Friess accepts the dedication, the title might be as follows:—"'Gretchen am Spinnrad,' a scene from Göthe's tragedy of 'Faust,' set to music, and dedicated with great respect to the noble Count Moriz von Friess, by Franz Schubert." If Count Friess has not yet accepted the dedication, the engraver can begin his plates all the same, and leave a blank space for the name. Please arrange this with Diabelli.—Yours sincerely, L. S.'

[2] Thus we find Dr. L. v. Sonnleithner writing, March 26, to Josef Hüttenbrenner:—'I beg you to take particular care, and see that Schubert comes to-morrow to Frl. Linhardt, to rehearse with her "Der Jüngling," which she sings with me; and afterwards that Schubert comes to me on Wednesday, at half-past twelve o'clock, to try over his "Geisterchor." I count on your good services to get Schubert to be certain and attend these rehearsals. I must honestly confess my surprise that he never comes near me, as I am very anxious to speak to him about his "Erlkönig" and other matters.'

The 'Geisterchor,' so unsuccessful in the theatre, was repeated on March 30 at an evening party given by Dr. Ignaz v. Sonnleithner, and most warmly received by the audience. On this occasion, too, several songs by the genial composer were given. After this performance the 'Geistergesang' seems to have sunk into oblivion; at all events, up to a recent period no trace can be found of any further performances.[1]

To the works just mentioned must be added two quartetts for men's voices: 'Die Nachtigall,' by Unger, and 'Geist der Liebe,' by Mathisson. The first was given on April 27, 1821, at a charitable concert for which the piece was specially written, in the Opera House; the latter on April 15, 1822, at Merk's concert, in the 'landständischen Saal,' sung by Herren Barth, Tieze, Johann Nestroy, and Wenzel Nejebse, and on September 24, by Herren Heitzinger, Rauscher, Ruprecht, and Seipelt.[2] On October 8, Vogl again sang the 'Erlkönig' at a concert given at the Opera House.

Of the vocal quartett party Tieze and Umlauff were

---

[1] In the year 1858 the chorus-master of the Männergesang-Verein, Johann Herbeck, dragged the music out of the dust wherein it had slumbered peacefully for thirty-six years, and at the end of the year, and of the following one also, it was given in public, and received with enthusiastic applause.

[2] After Schubert's death, in the year 1829, Tieze, Grünwald, Schoberlechner, and Richling (April 11) sang one of his quartetts at a concert given by the operatic singer Giulio Radichi. This, up to a very recent period, seems to have been the last quartett, for male voices, which was performed at a public concert.

very intimate with the composer. Tieze at that time was a star at all revivals or introductions of Schubert's songs; as a solo or concerted singer he was in the first rank of artists, and contributed in a very important way to their success. The composer was very fond of accompanying him on the piano.

Umlauff, in the year 1822, withdrew from this male quartett party, whose lot it was to introduce Schubert's concerted vocal pieces to the public. Summoned on legal and official duty in the eastern provinces, he quitted Vienna, but soon found an opportunity, even in those distant regions, of making musical amateurs familiar with the songs of that poet whose star he had witnessed in its first brilliant rise on the artistic firmament.[1]   Of Schubert's operations in connection with

[1] Umlauff, at that time, followed his profession in the Bukowina, where he sang to the Bojaren who had fled thither out of Turkey the earliest of Schubert's songs. In the book entitled ' Life and Deeds of an Austrian Officer of Justice,' written by his son Victor Ritter v. Umlauff, reference is made to Umlauff's connection with Schubert.   ' He (Carl U.) made the acquaintance of the famous tone-poet Franz Schubert as early as the year 1818, when the Lied, his noblest field of musical composition, was scarcely known at all, and soon afterwards their introduction ripened into friendship.   He used often to visit him of a morning before office hours, and found him generally lying in bed, dotting down on paper his musical fancies, or composing at his desk.   He would often on these occasions sing to Schubert his newest songs to a guitar accompaniment, and ventured to argue the propriety of the musical expression given to single words ; but Schubert, who was a man very tenacious of his own views, would never lend himself to an alteration of what once was written down.   Of my father's stories I remember only one controversy he had with Schubert, on the subject of the question in the " Wanderer,"

concerted vocal music, and particularly part-writing
for men's voices, we shall have to speak again in our
survey of the whole collection of his works. The
musical energies of our tone-poet during this year are
represented in the following productions: he sketched
out a Symphony (in E) which, according to Ferdinand
Schubert's own statement, was presented by him in the
year 1846 to Felix Mendelssohn-Bartholdy. In March
he wrote variations for the piano, ' upon a subject
which every composer in Vienna has tried his hand on

" O Land, wo bist du ? " Schubert insisted on emphasising the word
" bist," Umlauff the word " du." Schubert stuck to his opinion, and the
line was published in this form. Umlauff assisted at the first public
performance of vocal words of the great master, in the vocal quartett
"Das Dörfchen," for example, and in the eight-part "Geisterchor," by
Göthe. "Das Dörfchen," a light style of composition, pleased uncommonly. The "Chor der Geister über den Wassern," a deep grandly conceived tone-picture, was earnestly studied and performed by eight accomplished thoroughly trained musicians; but the difficult recondite music
was unintelligible to a public not yet accustomed to the peculiarities
of Schubert's style; the performance fell flat and cold, not a hand was
raised to applaud, and the singers, penetrated with the majesty and
grandeur of the work, having reckoned on a brilliant success, retired as
if they had been soused in a cold shower-bath. They had the courage,
however, a short time afterwards, to give the same piece, when it pleased
in a very high degree, and a repetition was called for. The brothers
Carl and Friedrich Gross were also friends of Schubert's—the first a distinguished violin, the second, a viola-player; the brothers Carl and Josef
Czerny, the violoncello-player Linke, the elder and younger Giuliani,
Barth, and Binder, both tenor singers, and Rauscher, the baritone, of the
Kärnthnerthor Theatre, all of whom, as well as Schubert, met regularly
every week at the house of Frau v. André, and made music there up to
past midnight.'

in the way of variations.' To this time and the three
following years must be ascribed the greater part of
his dance music, which, charming as it often was, in
the large majority of instances was thrown aside by
Schubert. On several occasions he improvised dance
music, in order that he might afterwards write down
the particular dances which pleased him. [1]

Of the more important Lieder may be instanced 'Suleika' (1 & 2), 'Versunken,' 'Grenzen der Menschheit,'
and 'Mahomet's Gesang,' by Göthe. The last of these,
with its grand vocal phrases and rolling pianoforte accompaniment, has remained a fragment. [2]

In the course of this year Schubert received, pro-

---

[1] According to a catalogue shown to me by Johannes Brahms, there
are no less than seventy-nine 'Ländler,' waltzes, and 'Deutschen,' and
twenty-eight Schottische. Most of these dances, if not all, Schubert
wrote for one performer on the pianoforte; the four-handed arrangements
were made afterwards by the publishers. The 'Deutschen,' which were
finished up to the year 1821, were soon engraved by Diabelli, Josef
Hüttenbrenner superintending the business. Schubert asks, in a letter,
the Court composer Gross, who lived in his neighbourhood (Wipplingerstrasse), to hand over to the bearer of the letter, Josef H., all the
'Deutschen,' with a view to their being engraved. Schubert's published
dance music, however, did not appear in the regular order of succession
in which they appeared originally. Thus, for instance, a part of the
'Atzenbrucker Deutschen,' to be found in Op. 9 and 18, and of the
twelve waltzes 'Deutsches Tempo,' 1½, are found in the 'Deutschen
Tänzen.' The autograph copy of the Schottische (May 1820 and
January 1823), the 'Atzenbrucker' (July 1821), 'Deutsches Tempo'
(May 1823), and other dance music not yet published, are in the possession of J. Brahms.

[2] The composition only gets as far as the first verse of the second
strophe.

bably by Vogl's suggestion, an invitation from the
directors of the Opera House to compose two additional
numbers to the Opera 'La Clochette,' by Herold—a
challenge he all the more readily accepted, as he was
exceedingly anxious to occupy himself once more with
dramatic composition, and to obtain a public recognition of his writings for the stage, which had hitherto
been denied him. He wrote a tenor air for 'Azolin,'
which was given by Rosner,[1] and a comic duett for the
Princes 'Bedur' and 'Cedur,' which was sung by Siebert
and Gottdank. With both these musical compositions,
the authorship of which was purposely concealed from
the public, and even Schubert's friends, Schubert wcn
a satisfactory triumph over those who would not allow
him any capacity for writing operatic music, and went
so far as to find fault actually with his Lieder. Both
the additional numbers pleased exceedingly, and if,
comparatively speaking, the somewhat spun-out and
high-pitched tenor air was the least successful of the
two, the duett was thought unexceptionable.[2]

---

[1] Rosner (Franz), born at Waitzen in Hungary, in 1800, died in 1842.
He was first tenor at the Stuttgart Theatre.

[2] The tenor air consists of three parts. It begins Maestoso in E minor,
followed by an Andante C major $\frac{4}{4}$ and an Allegro in E minor $\frac{4}{4}$. In
the first part, Azolin sees his beloved mother threatened with torture
and death; in the Andante, he is consumed with a passionate longing
for Palmira; and in the Allegro, he again gives vent to a passionate expression of anxiety about his mother's life.

The duett, in B-flat major, impetuous in character, with something
'Turkish' in its style, is accompanied by strings, piccolo, flute, hautboy,

Herold's opera, however, found very little favour with the public. It lacked, they said, 'den Klang aus der Zauberwelt,' and so 'La Clochette,' together with Schubert's supplementary numbers, disappeared soon and for ever from the boards.[1]

As a natural consequence of the musical reputation which Schubert already enjoyed, he received constant invitations from music lovers of all kinds, and was introduced to people of all sorts of rank and position in life. He himself never expressed any wish to mix in society, where he was forced to get rid of his innate shyness, reticence, and a good-natured nonchalant manner, but could not escape yielding occasionally to so much friendly pressure put upon him. The number, however, of those families in Vienna to which he, either

clarionets, horn, bassoon, and triangle. Bedur declares he will break the neck of Azolin, a stranger without rank or title, who wishes to rob him of Palmira; and Cedur assents to this proposal. The humour of this culminates in the joint exclamation of both, 'We break his neck!'

[1] This three-act opera, translated into German from the French of Théaulon, by Friedrich Treitschke, was performed for the first time on June 20, 1821, and afterwards repeated seven times. Rosner, Siebert, and Gottdank took parts in it, besides the following artists:—Wilhelmine Schröder (Palmira), Betti Vio (Ariel), Thekla Demmer (Nair), Frau Vogel (Nurada), Herr Vogel (Sultan), Sebastian Maier (Captain of the Calendars), Saal (Head Brahmin), and Weinkopf (Hispel). In the review of the 'Allg. Zeitung,' vol. xxiii. page 536, oddly enough, there is no mention made of Schubert's supplementary numbers. The manuscript of these may still, perhaps, be discovered in the library of the Kärnthnerthor Theatre. Josef v. Spaun, of Vienna, has copies of the score of both pieces and the pianoforte accompaniments; a copy of the duett is in my possession.

from artistic reasons, or the feelings of true friendship, was drawn into close relations for any length of time, was, comparatively speaking, very small. We have already mentioned the names of Grob, André, Esterhazy, Schober, Sonnleithner, and Fröhlich. When we have added the names of Spaun, Hönig, Bruchmann, Witteczek, Kiesewetter, Wagner, Ritter von Frank, Lascny, Pinterics, and Collin, the list of acquaintances of this class of people is wellnigh exhausted.[1]

In the house of Matthäus von Collin,[2] Schubert made acquaintance with the composer and musical reviewer Hofrath Mosel,[3] the Orientalist Hammer-Purgstall, Count Moriz Dietrichstein, the authoress

---

[1] The names have been given me of Wetzlar, Ulm, Oberst Ettl, and others, but I know nothing more about them.

[2] Matthäus v. Collin (brother of Heinrich) was born at Vienna in 1779, became professor of æsthetics and philosophy in Cracow, and afterwards in Vienna. Since 1813 he edited the 'Literatur-Zeitung,' at Vienna, and from 1818 the 'Jahrbücher der Literatur.' In the year 1815, he undertook the education of the Duke of Reichsstadt, and died in 1824. Hammer published his poems.

[3] Ignaz Franz Mosel, born at Vienna in the year 1772, entered the diplomatic service in 1788, and devoted his leisure hours to the most earnest study of music, for which art he had already in his early years shown remarkable predilection. He composed the musical vaudeville 'Die Feuerprobe,' of Kotzebue; the cantata 'Hermes und Flora;' the lyrical tragedy 'Salem,' and the opera 'Cyrus und Astiages,' all of which were performed and met with fair success. Besides this he wrote an overture to Grillparzer's 'Ottokar,' the music to the 'Hussiten von Naumburg,' besides hymns, songs, and dance music. In the year 1821, he was Vice-Director of the Royal Opera House; in 1829, Court Librarian, and died in 1844. His new edition of several oratorios, by Händel, is known, but very unfavourably.

Caroline Pichler, and the Patriarch Ladislaus Pyrker, much esteemed as a poet,[1] who one and all took the keenest interest in his performances. The Patriarch delighted in Schubert's Lieder, as we gather from the following letter, dated Venice, May 18, 1821, which Pyrker sent to Schubert, on the latter asking him to accept the dedication of a series of songs, amongst which was ' Der Wanderer.'

'Most honoured Sir,—Your kind offer to dedicate to me the first number of your incomparable songs, I accept with all the more pleasure, as I frequently recall to my memory that evening when I was so profoundly stirred by your musical genius, more particularly, too, by the music of your " Wanderer." I am proud of claiming with you one and the same fatherland, and remain, with the greatest respect and esteem,

'Your obedient servant,

' JOHANN L. PYRKER, m. p.,

' Patriarch.'

In the year 1825 Schubert met this gentleman at Wildbad-Gastein, when they renewed their friendship, and Schubert set two of his poems to music.

Whilst Beethoven, the man of the world and all-powerful in his sphere, was almost exclusively worshipped in the circles of the high aristocracy, the modest

---

[1] Of Pyrker's poems, Schubert set to music ' Die Allmacht' and ' Das Heimweh;' of C. Pichler's, the poem ' Der Unglückliche.'

Schubert moved, as his fashion was, by preference, amongst the plain and homely citizens around him.[1]

Far more influential with Schubert than any of these families was the circle of young, ambitious men—generally jovial, cheerful companions—by whom he found himself surrounded in his twentieth year, and who clung to him until the day of his death. The centre and life of this circle was Franz v. Schober. It is characteristic of Schubert's artistic nature to observe, that by far the greatest part of these young men were not musicians by calling and profession; and this seems to have been the very circumstance which induced him to prefer their society to that of all others.

With some of these he had been acquainted in earlier days—with Josef Spaun in the Convict, with Franz v. Schober in the year 1816, and with Anselm Hüttenbrenner about the same time. These people, with Johann Baptist Jenger, Moriz v. Schwind, Eduard Bauernfeld,[2] and Franz Lachner,[3] who only came to

---

[1] He only officiated at the Esterhazys' as a teacher of music. A note of the Princess Kinsky, in the year 1827, shows that he had access to the house of that family.

[2] Bauernfeld, born at Vienna in 1804, studied and passed his law examinations during the time of his acquaintance with Schubert, and in the year 1826 entered the diplomatic service, which he quitted in the year 1848.

[3] Franz Lachner, born at Nain, near Donauwörth, was an organist in the Evangelical church at Vienna, and afterwards became Capellmeister at the Court Theatre. Lachner has been, since 1836, Hofcapellmeister at Munich.

Vienna in the year 1823 or 1824, were on close terms of intimacy with Schubert. Next in order may be mentioned Leopold Kupelwieser, Franz Bruchmann,[1] Johann Senn, and the poet Mayrhofer. At some distance from these, but still attached to the circle of friends, were Dr. Sturm (at that time a physician at Wels), Dr. Bernhardt,[2] Dr. Ernst v. Feuchtersleben, Captain Mayrhofer of Grünbühel,[3] the painters Wilhelm Rieder (at that time Custode of the Belvedere), Danhauser, and Ludwig Schnorr v. Karolsfeld, the sculptor Dietrich, the lithographer Mohn, Anton v. Doblhoff, the State officials Witteczek, Enderes, Franz Derffel, Josef Gross, Josef Gahy, and Nagy,[4] Weiss and Bayer, most of whom, at that time, were in the prime of life.[5]

[1] Johann Bruchmann (senior) was a wealthy merchant in Vienna; Schubert often visited his house, where music and recitation were in great vogue. His son Franz, the compiler of some poems set by Schubert, entered holy orders, and still lives at Altötting. The Lieder, in Op. 20, are dedicated to Frau Justina Bruchmann.

[2] Dr. Bernhardt (to whom Op. 40 is dedicated), a very gifted and scientific man, in 1839 entered the service of the Porte, founded the School of Medicine at Galatta-Serai, and died at Constantinople in 1844.

[3] Mayrhofer (Franz), Imperial Field-Marshal-Lieutenant, was an active literary writer.

[4] Carl Nagy still lives, a pensioned officer, at Vienna. There was also a certain Ludwig Kraissle, painter and violin-player, who belonged to Schubert's circle of friends. He has been living a long time at Klagenfurt, in the family of Rosthorn.

[5] Among the artistic souvenirs left by Leopold Kupelwieser are the portraits of Schubert, Spaun, Schober, Bruchmann, Franz Mayrhofer, Dietrich, Rieder, Doblhoff, and Senn.

On considering the whole range of Schubert's companions, we shall find certain groups occupying a prominent place, and that each coterie had its own artistic followers. Besides Anselm Hüttenbrenner and Franz Lachner, the only musicians by profession (and they only remained a short time in Vienna), there were poets, philosophers, artists, and official people, all men of intellectual turn and aspirations. Their efforts and ambitions were very various, their aims were often distinct, but the chain which bound the whole party together was enthusiasm and the yearning for intellectual freedom.[1] That the mutual interchange of ideas and conversations on art-matters, apart from music, powerfully interested Schubert, is a fact which calls for no further illustration. With some of these men, recognised by Schubert as his true friends—and *bonâ fide* friends they were—he remained on affectionate terms to the end of his days, and only regretted that their union, owing to the different pursuits and paths of life pursued by each individual, was necessarily at times interrupted.

We could cite others besides those already mentioned, who having but a slight personal acquaintance with

---

[1] Jenger, L. v. Sonnleithner, Kupelwieser, and Schober were about the same age as Schubert. Next to them came Senn and A. Hüttenbrenner, then Schwind, Bauernfeld, Lachner, and Feuchtersleben, the four last of whom were much younger than the composer. Spaun and Schnorr were each of them nine years older than Schubert.

Schubert, none the less appreciated his value, not to mention a whole tribe of casual acquaintances flitting across his path, like birds of passage, and whose sym pathies with him were only momentary, and consequently exercised no abiding influence over him: such persons were far from being able to gauge the importance and value of such a man as Schubert.

Franz's relations with the members of his own immediate family were peculiar. They loved him, and he returned that love heartily. Of the brothers, however, but one was admitted to close intimacy with the Schubert circle. This was the landscape-painter, Carl, whose commissions to execute works for his brother's friends brought him an introduction [1]; the other relations were too much occupied with their own affairs, or at too great a distance from their kinsman, independently of the fact that they would have felt ill at ease and under constraint in such an intellectual circle as that to which Schubert belonged.

Surrounded by these young, boisterous, life-loving spirits and friends, Schubert, the earnest and reticent, but at times a thorough madcap, passed his happy time. The centre point of attraction to this circle consisted in the 'Schubertiaden,'—social unions of Schubert's

---

[1] Judging by a letter in the year 1818, Ignaz, as well as Ferdinand, was very intimate and happy with his brother. He seems, however, to have avoided the society of 'friends,' for he was much occupied as a school-teacher, and passed his leisure hours by preference with the Hollpeins.

friends, where games were played, dances danced, speeches made, but Schubert's own compositions formed the staple of the entertainment, and more particularly the last new songs from his pen. The 'Schubertiaden' were not confined entirely to Vienna, but came off at other places where Schubert and his companions happened to be together for a stay of any time ; for instance, in Linz, in St. Pölten, at the castle of Ochsenburg (in St. Pölten), and in Atzenbruck, a summer residence in the neighbourhood of Abtetten, in Lower Austria, occupied by an uncle of Schober's, and where, for three days in every year, there was a continued festival, 'the intellectual enjoyments of which (so Herr v. Schober tells me) no participator in those scenes can ever forget as long as he lives.' To this festive scene a large number of ladies and gentlemen were invariably bidden; amongst others, Schwind, Bauernfeld, Anton Doblhoff, Leopold Kupelwieser, and, as a matter of course, Schubert, who paid for his salt with marches, Schottisches, and waltzes ('Atzenbrucken Tänze').[1]

Besides the 'Schubertiaden,' there were all sorts of country parties and picnics organised, into which the inoffensive Franz was dragged *nolens volens*. Occasionally the wine flowed a glass too freely, and the carousals,

---

[1] Heinrich von Doblhoff, of Vienna, has a drawing, dated the year 1821, of a scene in Atzenbruck. An allegory is being represented, in which Schober, Kupelwieser, and several young ladies take part. In the foreground sits Schubert, looking earnestly at the performance. The drawing contains the portraits of sixteen people.

which lasted until past midnight, would rudely disturb the laws of an orderly household, and contrast with the usually quiet proceedings.[1]

Rusticocampius gives a description of the doings in those days, in the following strophes, which point to this episode in Schubert's life :—[2]

Die Sehnsucht zieht mit Allgewalt
Durch alle die Tage und Stunden,
Mein Schubert! wie bist du doch so bald
Dem trauten Kreis entschwunden!

Und war's nach dir so stumm und still,
Wir mussten darin uns schicken,
Ein ewig junger Tonachill
Stehst du vor unsern Blicken.

Gesegnet wer den Lorbeerkranz
Frühzeitig sich erworben,
Und wer in Jugend und Ruhmesglanz
Ein Götterliebling gestorben.

[1] A place of rendezvous, which Schubert greatly affected at this period, was the still existing extra room on the ground-floor of the 'Ungarische Krone' in the Himmelpfortgasse. Amongst the evening guests were the painters Schwind, Kupelwieser, Schnorr, and Teltscher, the poets Senn and Bauernfeld, the officials J. Hüttenbrenner, Berindl and Bernhard Teltscher; the Börsenrath Engelsberg, the pianoforte-player Szalay (still living), and others. Schubert is said to have been nicknamed by these people 'The Kanevas,' because when a stranger was introduced to his society, the first question Schubert invariably asked of his neighbour was 'Kann er was?' In the year 1827 the corpulent Franz was renamed 'Schwammerl.' Gross and Witteczek called him, for the sake of brevity, 'Bertl.'

[2] In the 'Book of Merry Rhymes concerning us Folk of Vienna,' by Rusticocampius. Leipsic, 1858.

Doch früher hast du gelebt—und nicht
Als Musikgelehrter, als bleicher,
Voll war und rund der Bösewicht,
Ein behaglicher Oesterreicher.

Mit Malern, Poeten und solchem Pack
Hast gern dich herumgeschlagen,
Wir trieben da viel Schabernak
In unsern grünen Tagen.

Ein Dritter noch war—an Gemüth ein Kind,
Doch that er Grosses verkündigen
Als Künstler—mein lieber Moriz Schwind,
Historienmaler in München.

Er ist eine derbe Urnatur,
Wie aus tönendem Erz gegossen,
So war auch Schubert,—heiterer nur,
Das waren mir liebe Genossen.

Bald sich ein Kranz von Freunden flicht,
Kunst, jugendliches Vertrauen,
Humor verbanden sie—fehlten auch nicht
Anmuthige Mädchen und Frauen.

Da flogen die Tage, die Stunden so schnell,
Da stoben des Geistes Funken,
Da rauscht auch der schäumende Liederquell,
Den wir zuerst getrunken.

Wer reitet so spät durch Nacht und Wind!
Es rauschen der Töne Wogen;
Bald ach! ist der Vater mit seinem Kind,
Dem Lied, zum Vater gezogen!

Was ist Beifall der Welt, was Ruhm!
Und Zeitungs-Preisen und Krönen,
Wir hatten das wahre Publicum
Der Guten und der Schönen.

Wie göttlich ein Genie im Keim,
Das in höchst eigener Weise
Sich kräftig entwickelt, süss, geheim,
Im traut verwandten Kreise!

Stellt bei genialer Jugend sich ein
Gott Amor mit seinen Waffen,
Da ist viel holde Lust, viel Pein,
Ein ewiges Gähren und Schaffen.

Real das war der Schubert auch,
Kein künstlicher Textverdreher,
Doch freilich des Gedichtes Hauch
Erfasst er als Sänger und Seher.

Der Rhythmus gewagt, die Harmonie
Bisweilen auch zerrissen,
Doch sprudelt ihm reich die Melodie,
Von der man jetzt nichts will wissen.

Oft ging's zum 'Heurigen' zum Wein,
Gleich ausserhalb des Thores
Stellt meist sich auch Franz Lachner ein,
Cantores amant humores.

Und frisch nach Grinzing, Sievering
Mit andern muntren Gesellen,
Zikzak gar mancher nach Hause ging,
Wir lachten im Mondschein, im hellen.

so brach der Chorus aus,
Wir wollen's dem Leser erklären,
Heisst: C. a. f. f. e. e.—Caffeehaus
Und nächtliches Punsch-Einkehren.

Nicht immer ging es so herrlich zu,
Nicht immer waren wir Prasser!
So trug mir Schubert an das Du
Zuerst mit Zuckerwasser.

Es fehlte an Wein und Geld zumal;
Bisweilen mit einer Melange
Hielten wir unser Mittagsmahl,
Mit diesem Wiener Pantsche.

Die Künstler waren damals arm!
Wir hatten auch Holz nicht immer,
Doch waren wir jung und liebten warm
Im ungeheizten Zimmer.

Verliebt war Schubert; der Schülerin
Galt's, einer der jungen Comtessen,
Doch gab er sich einer—ganz Andern hin,
Um—die Andere zu vergessen.

Ideell, dass uns das Herz fast brach.
So liebte auch Schwind, wir alle,
Den realen Schubert ahmten wir nach,
In diesem vermischten Falle.

CHAPTER X.

(1822.)

SCHUBERT AND VON SCHOBER IN OCHSENBURG — THE OPERA 'AL-
FONSO UND ESTRELLA'—A LETTER OF SCHUBERT'S AND SCHOBER'S
TO JOSEF SPAUN — SCHUBERT AND CARL MARIA V. WEBER — A
LETTER FROM ANNA MILDER TO FRANZ—'ALFONSO UND ESTRELLA'
AND THE PACHLER FAMILY AT GRATZ—CORRESPONDENCE BETWEEN
FRANZ V. SCHOBER AND FERDINAND SCHUBERT — THE OPERA IS
PERFORMED IN WEIMAR—CRITICISM THEREUPON—THE B MINOR SYM-
PHONY—THE MASS IN A—PART-SONGS—SCHUBERT AND BEETHOVEN
—PINTERICS—THE VARIATIONS DEDICATED TO BEETHOVEN—BEETHO-
VEN'S OPINION OF SCHUBERT—THE MUSICAL PUBLISHERS OPPOSED TO
SCHUBERT'S MUSIC—FRANZ TRANSFERS THE PROPERTY OF HIS FIRST
WORKS TO DIABELLI—SALE OF SCHUBERT'S COMPOSITIONS—A LETTER
FROM SCHOBER TO FRANZ—EFFORTS OF HÜTTENBRENNER AND SCHOBER
TO SELL THE OPERAS—A LETTER OF HOLBEIN AND PETERS TO J.
HÜTTENBRENNER—SCHUBERT WISHES TO BE A CANDIDATE FOR THE
ORGANISTSHIP AT THE CHAPEL ROYAL—A LETTER FROM THE BISHOP
OF ST. PÖLTEN TO FRANZ—SCHUBERT'S PETITION TO BE ADMITTED
AS A WORKING MEMBER OF THE AMATEURS' SOCIETY.

IF the wanderer, starting from the town of St. Pölten, shapes his course in a southerly direction and advances towards the Styrian mountains along the waters of the Traisen, he will come to the village of Ochsenburg, with a castle of the same name, beautifully situated, half way between St. Pölten and Wilhelmsburg, an old-fashioned place, three hours' distance from St. Pölten.

Ochsenburg is on the left-hand side. The castle, belonging to the domain of St. Pölten, was then a country seat of the resident bishop Hofrath v. Dankesreithner,[1] a relative of the Schober family. In this part of Germany, the two friends Franz v. Schober and Schubert, enjoying town and country life alternately, passed the autumn months of the year 1821, the musical results of which were the completion of the two first acts of an opera—the poetry by Schober, the music by Schubert.[2]

' Alfonso und Estrella,' the hastily conceived work of two intimate friends, and a truthful exponent of their joint intellectual powers, is the first of the two great operas which were composed by Schubert. The libretto, as Schober himself confesses in a letter written to myself, was composed in all the glow of youthful enthusiasm, and in entire simplicity of heart. Schubert, on his part, set himself to his task with his wonted energy, and the genial taste with which the composer turned on the stream of his gushing melodies over the finished fragments and portions of the libretto before the completion of the entire poem, must have delighted the eyes of the poet, as a spectacle of the rarest power.

A letter of Schober's, dated from Vienna, November 2, 1821, written to his friend Josef Spaun, staying in

---

[1] The ' Harfnerlieder' are dedicated to him.

[2] According to the original score (in the possession of the Musik-verein at Vienna), the first act was finished on September 20, 1821, the second on October 20 of the same year, and the third act on February 27, 1822

Linz, contains some allusions to his own and Schubert's doings in St. Pölten and at the castle of Ochsenburg. Schubert, in a short postscript appended to this letter, mentions the opera very briefly. Both letters are here given without curtailment, and, as will be seen, affairs at Vienna are glanced at, independently of musical matters.[1] Schober's letter runs thus:—

' Dear Friend,—Schubert and I have returned from our visit, and look back with delight upon a happy month spent partly in the town, partly in the country. At Ochsenburg we had plenty to do in visiting the beautiful country in the neighbourhood, and in St. Pölten books and concerts absorbed our attention; spite of all this we both worked hard, Schubert especially—he has done nearly two acts, I am upon the last. I only wished you had been with us, and witnessed the birth of those lovely melodies; the wealth and vigorous outpour of Schubert's fancy is really extraordinary. Our room at St. Pölten was exceedingly nice—two big beds, a sofa, and a good fireplace, not to mention a grand piano, gave it a very snug home appearance. Of an evening we always compared notes of what had passed during the day; we sent for beer, smoked our pipes, and read aloud. Perhaps Sofie or Netta would join us, then we had singing. Two " Schubertiaden " were held at the

---

[1] Herr Heinrich Schubert, of Vienna, has the original of both letters, and has been good enough to favour me with a copy.

bishop's house, and one at Baron Mink's, a favourite of mine, and a princess, two countesses, and three baronesses were present, all of whom were delighted in the most approved aristocratic fashion. We have now fallen in with the mother. We had a feast given us at Heiligen-Eich, and for eight successive days dating from that time, we have revelled in lovely weather and skies, sent as a godsend to travellers. The bishop too has arrived, and thus St. Pölten is transplanted to Vienna. He and his mother are quite well. They are uncommonly hearty, and send you their kindest regards. As you may well imagine, we got on very badly without Kuppeln, who had promised to come, and never came. We missed both him and you very much, especially as we should like to have made you judges of our performances. I am like a man who looks at the sun and only sees the fatal black spots darkening everything around, so completely has your absence upset me. We found "Die Krone" completely deserted.[1] Derffel is by this time quite demented on the subject of whist; besides his two regular fixed days at home, he plays as formerly at Hugelmann's. Dornfeld is always a sure find at the coffee-house; Waldl also is possessed by the same demon as Huber,[2] and both become more and

---

[1] The hotel 'Zur Ungarischen Krone,' in the Himmelpfortgasse, where Schubert's friends were accustomed to meet.

[2] Josef Huber, a friend of Mayrhofer, the latter of whom is meant by 'Waldl.' Huber seems to be the same man who was afterwards made General Consul in Egypt. (Chezy's 'Recollections,' vol. ii.)

more impossible to get at, from their living such a way off in the Vorstadt. Gahy lost everything when you went away; I found him regularly down in the mouth; he doesn't know what he shall do, and looks at the whist-table with blank despair. I will try and be of some comfort to him once more. Kuppel is always at the Belvedere, copying the " Ino," and never finishes it, but sleeps at Schnorr's, who is still living in the Heugasse. His "Faust" was bought for 2,500 florins. Yesterday Weber's " Der Freischütz " was given, but did not please entirely. I am very glad Max is so well. Goetz and his wife dote on one another, to such an extent that lately, in a fit of blissful forgetfulness and delirium, they walked through the suburbs, Linie, &c., and went straight away, until at last, when warned late enough by the pangs of hunger, they found themselves in a line of country where they had great difficulty in getting bread to eat. My kind regards to all. Don't suppose that matters will continue as they are now. Whilst working at the opera, I fancy myself incapable of writing anything else. If Ottenwald still has the poem which I originally gave him, with our bas-relief, be so kind as to copy it for me as soon as you can. Max might do it. Hosp's principal has failed; Hosp is therefore free, and must now take to the theatre.

' Yours ever,

' SCHOBER.'

Schubert adds these lines by way of postscript :—

'Dear Friend,—Your letter has pleased me very much, and I trust you will be always happy and comfortable. I must now, however, inform you that my dedications have done their duty; for the Patriarch,[1] at the instance of Vogl, has expended twelve ducats, and Friess[2] twenty—a fact which suits me extremely well. You must also be so kind as to conclude your correspondence with the Patriarch by a suitable acknowledgment made to him and me also. Schober's opera has already got to the third act, and I should much like you to have been present whilst the opera was in its earliest stage of formation. We count a good deal on the work in question. The Kärnthnerthor and Wiedner Theatres are actually leased to Barbaja, and his lease begins to run next December. Now farewell. Remember me to all friends, particularly your sisters and brothers.

'Your friend,

'FRANZ SCHUBERT.

'Write soon to my father and to us.

'N.B.—Send me Ottenwald's "Cradle Song."'[3]

Schober's libretto, 'written in entire simplicity of heart,' suffers from one patent defect, and of which mention will be made hereafter, but the whole plan of the drama with the poetry, generally speaking uniform

---

[1] Schubert dedicated to the Patriarch Ladislaus Pyrker the 4th Op. of his Lieder ('Wanderer,' 'Wanderers Nachtlied,' 'Morgenlied ').

[2] Moriz Count Friess, to whom Op. 2 ('Gretchen am Spinnrad') is dedicated.

[3] Schubert subsequently set this poem to music.

and appropriate, is very favourably distinguished from the other libretti which Schubert used for his operas, and gives unmistakable evidence of a poetical talent which afterwards developed itself. The opera has no spoken dialogue, but in its place a series of recitatives.

The overture, which, as we may read on the original score, was not composed until December 1823, is one of the best of Schubert's orchestral works, and was greatly applauded at Vienna.[1]

The following is the groundwork of the story. Troila, King of Leon, deprived of his throne by Mauregato, has withdrawn with his son Alfonso to a quiet valley in the neighbouring kingdom, where he becomes an object of high honour among the people from his wisdom and active benevolence. Estrella, Mauregato's daughter, is out hunting with her playfellows; Adolfo, her father's generalissimo, has just returned victorious from battle, and, passionately enamoured of Estrella, prays for a hearing, which however is not allowed him. Adolfo, in a furious rage, threatens the coy daughter of the King with vengeance. Mauregato appears; the trophies of victory are delivered to him, and he calls on the general to

---

[1] The overture (which appeared in the pianoforte edition as Op. 69) was performed in the year 1823 as an introduction to the Drama 'Rosamunde,' by Helmina Chezy, and, according to Herr J. Hüttenbrenner, had to be repeated twice; at the Opera House, the overture, in consequence of mistakes being made with the tempi, met with a cold reception. A motive in it reminds one of the Scherzo in the D minor Symphony of Beethoven, which had not at that time become known.

ask for some favour. Adolfo sues for the hand of the daughter. Estrella adjures her father not to hand her over to this man, whom she cannot love; and Mauregato, casting about for some means to save his daughter, declares that he has made a sacred decree, that that man alone shall wed his daughter who will find the long-lost chain of Eurich. Adolfo, again deceived in his hopes, vows he will destroy the king for having broken his word. Thus the first act ends.

In the second act we see Estrella separated from her hunting companions, and looking for some outlet by which she may descend into the valley where Troila and Alfonso are living. Alfonso sees the form of Estrella, which reminds him of a dream which he had the night before, and told (in a narrative at the outset of the act) his father. In an ecstasy at seeing her, he rushes to meet her, and, after a mutual exchange of their feelings, both find themselves head over ears in love with each other. Upon Estrella's urgent entreaty at the hour of parting, Alfonso hands her over, as a souvenir, a chain which Troila gave him as a pledge that he would yet live to free him from his gloomy solitude.

Meanwhile Adolfo collects his conspirators around him, and exacts a vow from them that they will follow him and devastate Mauregato's kingdom. Mauregato sends messenger after messenger, who try to find his lost child and hope to bring her back, but all in vain. At last Estrella appears, to the joy of her father and the

courtiers assembled in the palace. Mauregato discovers
on her breast the ornament, which he instantly recognises as Eurich's chain. Racked by the gnawings of
conscience, he presses Estrella to confess the means by
which she has come into possession of the treasure.
Estrella tells him of the adventure which took place in
the valley, and avows her love for the youth, of whose
very name she still continues ignorant. The chief of
the body-guard then rushes in with the dreadful news
that there is an uproar in the streets of Oviedo, and
that Adolfo, at the head of the rebels, is storming the
palace. Already are heard from without the conspirators shouting for vengeance, but Mauregato is determined to fight them; Estrella will be at his side. In
the midst of general confusion, the second act ends.
The terrors of the now devastating war reach to the very
borders of the still valley, where Troila and Alfonso re-
side. Adolfo, in the tumult of the fight, has carried off
Estrella from her father's side, and drags her away with
him. Once again he tries to win her love, but with no
better success than formerly. In a storm of passion he
draws his dagger, and bids her choose between life and
death. She screams for help, and Alfonso appears with
some hunting companions, and takes Adolfo prisoner.
Estrella thanks her deliverer, but wrings her hands in
agony for her father, of whose fate she is still ignorant,
and who has probably already fallen in battle. Alfonso
now learns from her that she is the daughter of the

King of Leon, and determines to befriend the King by
aiding him with his own troops. He blows his horn
three times, and the rest of his companions appear, at
the head of whom he now places himself, to attack the
enemy. Troila, frightened at the clash of arms, now
appears, and Alfonso gives him the charge of protecting
the King's daughter until the battle shall have ended.
The general, in former days banished by Mauregato,
suppresses his feelings in silence, and blesses his son,
now hurrying forth to fight the rebels.

Mauregato, returning in the haste of flight, sees suddenly the dethroned Troila before him, and, thinking
him a ghost, implores his mercy. Troila approaches
him in a friendly manner, and whilst asking pardon for
his crime, brings his daughter to him. In the distance is
heard a warlike march. Alfonso returns with his army
as a conqueror, and lays his sword at Mauregato's feet;
the latter points to Troila as the rightful king. Adolfo
again recognises the man whom he formerly served, and
for whose supremacy he has undertaken a war against
the usurper. Troila hands over the kingdom to his son
Alfonso, and Mauregato gives him his daughter. The
peasants pray the old king not to desert them, and he
grants their request. The opera[1] concludes with a
general chorus of joy. The first act begins with an
introduction, followed by a chorus of peasants, a melo-

---

[1] The original score (in the possession of the Musikverein at Vienna)
has the metronome tempi marked by Schubert; he had a complete copy

dious movement, interspersed with solo passages for
the tenor (the youth), and the contralto (a maiden).
This is succeeded by a fine bass air for Troila (Allegro
E-flat minor $\frac{4}{4}$), recitatives, and a second chorus of
peasants (G major $\frac{3}{4}$), with solos for Troila and the
youth. The chorus moves in the rhythm and character
of a 'Landler,' which we meet with in Schubert's dance
music, and this peculiar form is telling and effective in
the opera. A duett between Troila and Alfonso (Andante D minor $\frac{4}{4}$) is of the Lied order, and of small
artistic value; but the fine expressive tenor air of
Alfonso, with clarionet obligato (B-flat major $\frac{3}{4}$), and its
lyrical character, outshines all the preceding numbers.
A duett between Alfonso and Troila opens well, but
is lost, as the movement developes, in commonplace
phrases. The hunting chorus of women (Allegro G
major $\frac{6}{8}$) has in some respects the usual freshness and
originality, but owes its charm and value to a beautiful
air for Estrella, with which the chorus is interwoven.

made of the score, for which (according to the testimony of J. Hüttenbrenner) the publishing firm of Diabelli deducted the sum of 100 florins
from the profits resulting from the sale of Schubert's compositions. In
a note written in the year 1822 (in the possession of J. Hüttenbrenner),
are the following lines, in Schubert's handwriting:—

'Dear Friend,—Be so good as to bring me one act after another of the
opera ("Alfonso") for my correction. I wish, too, that you would take the
trouble to square my accounts up to the present time with the firm of
Diabelli, as I am in want of money.'

A copy of the score, in an abbreviated form, by Liszt, is in the hands
of Herr J. Herbeck, in Vienna; the firm of Spina has the original copy.

The bass air for Adolfo (Allegro E-flat minor) is in the outset imposing by its heroic colour and character, but falls afterwards into commonplace prettiness, from which it never raises itself again. The duett between Estrella and Alfonso (Andantino C major $\frac{3}{4}$) is melodious, and the final Allegro movement in C minor, with its passionate character, is an agreeable change to the monotony of the previous number. The finale is introduced by a (musically commonplace) chorus of warriors, which leads into a general chorus of mixed voices for the people. There follow short recitatives and airs for Mauregato, Adolfo, and Estrella; the musical action of the piece widens out into a lively ensemble, with chorus, connected with an interesting orchestral interlude. The music at this point gains materially in dramatic expression, the chorus of warriors summoning their followers to battle, and the ladies their companions to the hunting-field, suggesting fruitful themes of invention to the composer. Recitatives of Troila and Alfonso, with harp and flute accompaniments, introduce the second act. The romance for Troila (a legend of the Daughter of the Skies) does not answer the expectations which one would be disposed to associate with this particular piece, for it seldom rises above the level of a sentimental commonplace cantilena; but Schubert's true romantic spirit breathes in the next duett (in G minor) for Alfonso and Estrella. We scent the blossom and hear the whisperings of the woods, and from the melody and the accompaniment peers out the long-lost face and earnest look of the composer. Recitatives for Alfonso and Estrella, an air for each, but neither of any special interest, a commonplace duett for the same characters, with no ring of Schubert about it, except in the last phrases, form the remainder of the numbers. A double chorus of the conspirators, interwoven with an air for Alfonso (Allegro agitato), is vocally and instrumentally full of character, and must be reckoned among the few and thinly scattered numbers in the opera which have real dramatic value. An air for Mauregato with chorus (Allegro D minor $\frac{2}{4}$), a duett for the same with Estrella (Andantino F minor), are also of a commonplace character, and have nothing of special interest. The Finale (Allegro A minor $\frac{2}{4}$) is a grand ensemble, in which Mauregato, Estrella, the leading sentinels, choruses of men and women, besides one for conspirators behind the scenes, all take part : the constant cry of 'Revenge' contrasts effectively with the voices of the women and the war-cry of the men, the whole scene with its characteristic and vivid colouring giving Schubert an ample field for the development of his dramatic power. The third act begins with an orchestral introduction of some length (Allegro D minor alla breve), which, in strains of a restless and passionate character, tells the horrors of the battle raging in the secluded valley. This introduction is followed by a series of recitatives for the youth and maiden

(Allegro G minor $\frac{4}{4}$), in which they communicate in strains of awe and sorrow their mutual experiences of the horrors they have witnessed in the flight. The cry of fugitive women, ' Weh uns—fliehet!' concludes this number, which is conspicuous for depth of feeling and dramatic expression. The duett, too (No. 3), for Adolfo and Estrella (Allegro assai F minor $\frac{3}{4}$) is conceived in a grand style, and must be very effective on the stage. The ensemble which follows, viz. a trio for Alfonso, Adolfo, and Estrella (Allegro D major $\frac{4}{4}$), preliminary to a septett made up with parts for four Jäger, is very promising at first, but lapses afterwards into the commonplace Italian forms then in fashion. Then we have a series of beautiful and expressive recitatives for Alfonso and Estrella, and a powerful duett (Allegro molto C major $\frac{4}{4}$) set to words of an heroic character, but from the point where the two voices join, the music falls into the unmistakable phrases of the Italian cantilena. A duett for the same characters, alternating with a chorus of fugitive soldiers, is well worked up and full of character and expression. The following double chorus (Allegro E-flat major $\frac{6}{8}$), with a fragmentary introduction of trumpet signals, which peal alternately from two orchestras, although rhythmical and melodious, is yet trivial in form, and at a later period, when the general chorus of soldiers and huntsmen gives a wider scope for musical invention, fails to impress one as a work of any great musical value. But the recitatives for Troila, Alfonso, and Estrella are all the more

effective. The next ensemble, made up of the principals and chorus, is effectively and dramatically worked,
but is entirely thrown into the shade by the scena
immediately following, in which the flying Mauregato
coming on a sudden face to face with Troila, takes him
for the ghost of the dethroned king. The air of the
bewildered and despairing Mauregato (Allegro agitato G
minor $\frac{4}{4}$) and the succeeding interview with Troila are
all written in a grand dramatic style, and would un-
doubtedly produce a great effect upon the stage. The
duett, also, for Troila and Mauregato, treated with great
beauty and originality, is one of the most conspicuous
features of the opera. The voice-writing for the two
parts, moving together so melodiously in the concluding passages, reminds us again of the influence of the
Italian style over Schubert. Lastly, a very pretty and
dramatically effective trio for Troila, Mauregato, and
Estrella, B-flat $\frac{4}{4}$, points to the same conclusion.

The finale is introduced by a march, followed by a
lively but not very interesting chorus for Jäger and
soldiers in B-flat. More recitatives follow for Alfonso
and Mauregato, which are succeeded by an ensemble,
in which the chief characters are joined by choruses
of peasants and soldiers, imploring Troila, in earnest
accents, to stay and help them. There are some exquisitely tender and beautiful passages in this ensemble,
especially an Andante movement, in which Mauregato
and Troila, addressing the lovers (Estrella and Alfonso),

bless the union and invest them with rule over the kingdom. The general chorus, an Allegro in ⁴⁄ time, in the bright key of E major, is a noisy conclusion to the entire opera, and never rises above the level of a commonplace dramatic finale.

The criticisms here offered of the worth and character of the single portions of this opera are sufficient to show that the first work of importance written by Schubert for the stage is by no means wanting in numbers which would be gladly welcomed by Schubert's friends as worthy of the composer. Some individual airs, duetts, and choruses, the finale of the first act, the entire body of recitatives, and the orchestral movements are beautiful, full of expression and dramatic energy; and the fact may be stated that the last act, taken as a whole, being of a higher musical value than other parts of the work, contributes materially to the general effect of the opera. On the other hand, the work has some material defects, which, apart from the musical inferiority of some numbers, must be chiefly ascribed to the monotonous style of lyric treatment throughout the entire poem, and a series of movements open to the same objection. The grand dramatic element is entirely wanting in Schober's libretto, and the blame must be laid rather to the compiler's mode of treating his subject, than the musician's adaptation of his friend's work. There are endless lyric effusions, and none can wonder that the composer, unmistakably influenced, it may be remarked in passing, by Rossini's operatic music, in the absence of some salient point offering scope for bold dramatic expression, contented himself in emptying his cornucopia of melodies over the broad lyrical surface of the libretto, and gave, with a happy consciousness of power, full play to his light and genial muse. Whenever the poet offered him a fit opportunity for any strong dramatic treatment, Schubert never let it escape him; and although 'Alfonso und Estrella' would scarcely satisfy the requirements of the theatrical representations of our own day, there can be no doubt that Schubert, in some scenes of this very opera, showed an extraordinary skill in his mastery over the grand forms of the musical drama.

'Alfonso und Estrella,' as we shall point out by and by, was only once represented on the stage (in the year 1854), and on that occasion the defects we have alluded to seem to have sealed the fate of the opera. Thirty years before, when Schubert and his friends were endeavouring to get a performance of the opera on any of the larger stages, the prevalent taste of the period would have augured a longer existence for the work than that which was actually allotted to it. Apart from the musical contents of the opera, the work has a more abiding external interest in the fact that (according to a statement of A. Schindler),[1] it brought

---

[1] Anton Schindler, Beethoven's well-known friend, was born at Mädel in Moravia, and died, as musical director, at Bokenheim, in January 1864.

Schubert into contact with another great master. The interview, at first not very happy in its results, led to a discussion between the two composers which is too characteristic to be passed over in silence.

Carl Maria von Weber came to Vienna in October 1823, to conduct in person a performance of his 'Euryanthe,' written expressly for the Court Opera House. This work was given for the first time on October 25, but, owing to reasons which we need not do more than refer to, had not anything like the enduring success which had been awarded to ' Der Freischütz.'[1]

Schubert was present at the performance, and his

[1] The first three representations, on the 25th, 27th, and 29th October, were conducted by Weber, the fourth by Capellmeister Kreuzer, the composer attending as a listener, and sitting in one of the private boxes. The success of the first performances was brilliant. Frl. Henrietta Sonntag sang the part of Euryanthe, Frau Grünbaum that of Eglantine, Forti was Lysiart; the other parts were filled by Heitzinger and Seipelt. Weber was called for on the first evening amidst a storm of applause, and, when the performance was over, drove off to the 'Ludlamshöhle,' where twenty-seven poets and artists were collected to give him a triumphant reception. The day following, Mosel and other musical connoisseurs came to congratulate him (see Weber's letters to his wife). ' Euryanthe,' at that time, was given about six times more; it was repeated again at a later period, under Duport's management (when Schröder-Devrient sang the chief part), and again under the administration of Count Gallenberg. Enthusiasm, however, soon grew cold, and Helmina Chezy, the authoress of the libretto, herself confessed, that the success had not answered the high expectations formed by the public. A section of the ' Ludlamshöle ' blamed the libretto; Castelli thought the opera had come into the world half a century too early; others laid the entire blame on the musical setting; in short, the triumph which greeted the birth of the opera was soon metamorphosed into a

opinion of the new work was regarded by many connoisseurs as decisive.　He asserted openly that Weber's
'Euryanthe' certainly contained many beauties of harmony, but no single original melody, and was entirely
deficient in this respect—a fact he was ready to prove
to Weber by a reference to the score.[1]　When he was
met with the assertion that Weber had in some respects
been obliged to alter his style, because the art of music
was about to enter new phases, and from henceforth
must needs produce effects by aid of heavy masses, Schubert argued, 'What good are heavy masses? ('wozu denn
schwere Massen?").　"Der Freischütz" was so genial,

defeat.　On other German stages (Berlin, Weimar, and Dresden) the
opera met with great success, and also in London, in the year 1831,
when Mina Schröder and Heitzinger sang the chief parts.　That Weber
went to Beethoven with the score, and prayed him to make such alterations as he pleased (as Schindler affirms), is not only discredited as
being utterly irreconcilable with Weber's habits of thought, but has been
strenuously and positively denied.　('Neue Zeitschrift für Musik,' vol.
xiii. No. 48.)

[1] 'You have now,' wrote Friedrich v. Rochlitz, on October 4, 1823,
to Herr Tobias Haslinger in Vienna, 'my dear friend Maria v. Weber,
with his "Euryanthe," at Vienna.　He has to conquer a great enemy,
and that enemy is himself in his own Freischütz.　Yet I don't doubt
he will succeed this time also.　He truly deserves it.'　Afterwards,
on December 22, 1823 :—'The fate which our friend Weber's "Euryanthe" has (probably most undeservedly) met with in Vienna does no
honour to the discrimination of your public ; and seeing that for years
past, and with abundant reason, your audiences are credited with sharp-
sighted judgment in musical matters, this result is very injurious to
Weber—a matter I deplore on his account, your own, and that of your
public.'

so full of heart, it bewitched you with its loveliness; but in "Euryanthe" very little geniality can be found!' When this derogatory criticism came to Weber's ears, he is reported to have said, 'Let the blockhead learn something first before he presumes to judge me.' This hasty inconsiderate expression went the round of musical circles in Vienna, and Schubert, who at the time although only twenty-seven years old, was the author of several symphonies and operas, besides a couple of hundred songs, felt aggrieved at Weber's words, and went off with the score of 'Alfonso und Estrella' under his arm to show him that he was ready to fight Weber with equal weapons.

After Carl Maria had gone through the score, he spoke of Schubert's criticisms on his (Weber's) opera, and the latter still adhering to his opinion, Weber, a little piqued, exclaimed, 'But I tell you that the usual course is for people to drown the first puppies and the first operas '—a sentence clearly intended to hint that Weber was of opinion that 'Alfonso und Estrella' was Schubert's first dramatic work, of the puppy species. In spite of this encounter, these two great artists did not keep aloof from one another as personal enemies, and Weber silently withdrew his harsh criticism; for at a later period, acting under the recommendation of Hofrath Mosel, who, along with Salieri, had a very favourable opinion of Schubert's opera, Weber expressed his readiness to have a performance of the work at the Dresden

Opera, and expressed in a letter the personal friendly interest he took in the work.[1]

We have it on the authority of J. Hüttenbrenner, that the libretto was sent to be delivered by Wilhelmine Schröder to C. M. v. Weber at Dresden; the score (only a copy of the original) was sent by Schubert to the singer Anna Milder, who wished to have the opera performed in Berlin, but afterwards gave up the design. The following letter of Milder, given word for word as it was written (addressed to Herr Franz Schubert, at the school-house in Rossau), is more minute on the subject. It runs thus:—

'Berlin, March 8, 1825.

'Most honoured Herr Schubert,—I hasten to inform you that I have, with extreme pleasure, received your Opera "Alfonso und Estrella," as well as the second song of Zuleika. I heartily thank you for your cheerful compliance in this matter. Zuleika's second song is divine, and each time I sing it my eyes fill with tears. It is indescribable. You have managed to introduce in that song every possible spell and mournful enchantment; this you have done likewise with Zuleika's first

---

[1] This letter, according to Herr Josef Hüttenbrenner, was sent him by Weber, and it came subsequently into the hands of Herr v. Schober. Schober told me, however, that he never possessed the letter. As throwing light on the relationship existing between Weber and Schubert, this letter would be of great interest. One would have expected to find in Max v. Weber's published biography of his father a more detailed account of the relationship existing between the two composers.

song, and the "Geheimniss." One can only regret the impossibility of singing all these endlessly lovely things to the public, since all that the common herd care about (alas! that it should be so) is to have the ear tickled. Should, however, by any chance the "Nacht-schmetterling" be unsuited for a brilliant vocal display, I would ask you to choose some other poem instead, and, if possible, something of Göthe's, which might be divided into various movements, to enable the artist to employ different shades of expression. Such poems are to be found amongst Göthe's works. For example, "Verschiedene Empfindungen an einem Platz,"[1] or a similar piece,—I leave it to you. That your success will be brilliant, I cannot doubt.

'For any amount of songs you wish to dedicate to me, I can only feel extremely pleased and flattered. On the 1st of June I leave this place; but could I only have from you the song I should like for my concert tours, I should be exceedingly pleased if you would kindly introduce some passages and embellishments suitable to my particular style.

'With regard to your Opera "Alfonso und Estrella," it pains me to make the remark, but I must do so, that the libretto does not answer the taste of the people here, who are accustomed to the grand high tragic opera, or the comic opera of the French. The public

---

[1] The title of one of Göthe's poems.

taste here being as I describe it, you yourself will
understand that success here would be impossible for
" Alfonso und Estrella." Should I have the happiness
of playing in one of your operas, the character should
be written expressly to suit my individuality as an
artist; for instance, the *rôle* of a queen, a mother, or
peasant-woman. I would advise you to write something entirely new, if possible in one act—an Oriental
subject, with the chief character given to the soprano;
this, as I gather from Göthe's " Divan," could not fail
to succeed in your hands. You can rely on a good
performance as far as the chorus goes, and three characters, the soprano, tenor, and bass. Should you find
such a subject as I suggest, pray let me know of it,
that we may come to a better and closer understanding
on the subject. Then I would make every effort to
bring the play on the stage. Be good enough to let
me know what is to be done with your Opera " Alfonso."

' Pray greet my friend and teacher Vogl very heartily
for me. I am very sorry to hear he is such a sufferer ;
I am not much better myself. Tell him that I am
obliged to go this year to Wiesbaden. I should be
delighted to get a few lines from him. Please give my
best regards to Fr. v. Lascny.[1] I should much like to

---

[1] To this lady, whose maiden name was Buchwieser, the ' Divertissement Hongroie ' was dedicated. Herr Lascny was a landowner in
Hungary, and his wife an accomplished songstress. Schubert and several
of his friends constantly visited them.

sing your Lieder to that amiable and artistic lady.
To your favour and goodwill I heartily commend myself. Your most humble servant,

'Anna Milder.'

In the September of 1827, Schubert, as we shall
have occasion to show by and by, went to Gratz for a
fortnight, where he was quartered in the house of Dr.
Carl Pachler, advocate. On returning to Vienna, he
sent his friend the libretto of the Opera 'Alfonso,' and
the libretto remained in the custody of Dr. Pachler up
to the beginning of the year 1843. Schubert left the
score behind, doubtless with the hope of the work being
performed in Gratz, and every effort was made to have
the work represented on the stage. At the rehearsals,
however, Hysel, the orchestral conductor for the time
being, declared that 'it was technically impossible to
play what Schubert wanted.' The difficulties of the
score seemed to the Gratz orchestra of the time being
absolutely insuperable. An attempt, too, is said to
have been made with 'Fierrabras' (written 1823), and
to have failed from the same reason.[1]

In the year 1842 there seems to have been some

---

[1] Dr. Faust Pachler, to whom I am indebted for these statements, ob-
serves that his father, the alterego of the theatrical manager, Stöger;
would certainly have brought about the performance, had such a thing
been possible. He remembers one or two orchestral rehearsals at the
Gratz Theatre, but thinks it most likely that the first of the rehearsed
operas was 'Fierrabras.'

intention of representing the Opera of ' Alfonso' at Vienna. At least the following letter of Ferdinand Schubert's would seem to indicate this, unless we allow a margin for the supposition that the writer alleged, by way of pretext, his hopes of a coming performance as a motive for reclaiming the score of the opera.[1]

The letter, dated June 26, 1842, and addressed to Dr. Pachler in Gratz, runs thus :—

' I have heard with intense pleasure from my friends at Vienna, that the original of the Opera " Alfonso und Estrella," a composition of my dear departed brother, is still in perfect preservation and in your hands. I venture boldly to ask you, sir, to be kind enough to send me the score, as I have hopes of getting a performance of this opera next winter at the Royal Opera House.'

In January 1843 the opera came once more into the hands of Ferdinand Schubert.[2] There never was any performance of this opera at Vienna. But when, in

---

[1] I cannot remember ever to have heard a word said in Vienna about any representation of the Opera ' Alfonso.'

[2] Hofrath v. Witteczek, of Vienna, in a letter of the 14th of September, 1842, empowered Dr. Franz Schreiner, of Gratz, to take charge of the manuscript, after he had removed Dr. Pachler's doubts and convinced him of its genuineness. About the 30th of October, Schreiner allowed the score to be sent, and on the 19th of January, 1843, Ferdinand Schubert acknowledged the receipt. The original score was, during the year 1861, in the possession of Herr Alexander Thayer (of Boston), to whom it had been presented by the family of Ferdinand Schubert. At present it is the property of the Musikverein of Vienna.

the year 1847, Dr. Franz Liszt took up his residence in Weimar, he expressed a wish to Franz v. Schober, the compiler of the book (and at that time Legationsrath at Weimar), to bring out one of Schubert's operas. Schober called Liszt's attention to the fact, that ' Alfonso und Estrella ' was the only finished opera, and had never been performed anywhere,[1] and pledged himself to write at once to Ferdinand Schubert, desiring him to send the score to the committee of management for the Court Opera House.

After the lapse of two months, he received from Ferdinand Schubert the following letter, dated March 3, 1848 :[2]—

'Noble and highly honoured Herr Legationsrath,'— I am uncommonly glad to hear that Herr Hofcapellmeister Dr. Liszt bears in mind the operas of my dear departed brother, and the more so, as I know that Dr. Liszt, simply from a generous enthusiasm for these compositions, is intent on bringing them before the public. I am extremely sorry on this occasion to be unable to comply at once with your wish, as I am already in treaty with Breitkopf & Härtel respecting the operas, as well as some other works of my deceased brother. That the Opera " Alfonso und Estrella " should so long have remained unrepresented

---

[1] There Herr v. Schober was mistaken, as half-a-dozen operas were finished, but never performed in public.

[2] Herr v. Schober lent me a copy of this letter.

on the stage, and be therefore well calculated to make managers distrustful of its artistic worth, is a circumstance which need not awaken any apprehensions; circumstances are in a great measure accountable for the fact that one of Schubert's great admirers in Gratz, after the death of the composer, so conscientiously and carefully kept the opera in a money-drawer, that he only discovered his musical treasure after the lapse of fourteen years.[1] Besides this, it is no longer possible to get this work rehearsed during Dr. Liszt's stay at Weimar, as the parts are not yet copied out, and the shortness of our time does not admit of that being done. As soon, however, as I have made my arrangements at Leipsic, I will immediately acquaint you, so that you may be able to give other directions for the future.

'It gives us intense pleasure to know that your Honour still continues the true friend of our brother Franz, and co-operates so heartily with those who wish to erect yet another memorial to the departed Schubert. Receive the assurance of my high and distinguished consideration, and have the kindness to give my profound respects to Herr Capellmeister Dr. Liszt, and thank him most especially for the noble enthusiasm

---

[1] This must be a false version of what actually occurred. Schubert had the original score, a copy of which had been sent to Berlin for his friend Dr. Pachler, who was to dispose of it as he chose, and that gentleman wished to bring out the work before the public at Gratz.

which he so actively employs towards perpetuating the memory of my deceased brother.

'Your most obedient servant,

'FERDINAND SCHUBERT.'

In consequence of this letter, Herr v. Schober, on March 18, 1848, wrote a pressing letter to the owner of the score, which some days afterwards arrived at Weimar, addressed to Dr. Liszt. The performance, however, was delayed until the year 1854, when the opera was given on June 24, at the end of the season, as a festival performance on the birthday celebration of the Grand Duke.[1] Liszt directed the opera for this, the first time it was given at Weimar. The work had been well studied, and the representatives of Troila and Estrella were deservedly applauded;[2] the orchestra and chorus also did their duty. The success, however, of the opera was not remarkable.[3]

---

[1] For this reason a 'Jubilee Overture,' by Rubinstein, was given in lieu of Schubert's.

[2] The singers were Milde (Troila), Liebert (Alfonso), Mayrhofer (Adolfo), Höfer (Mauregato), Frau Milde (Estrella).

[3] In the 'Neue Zeitschrift für Musik,' Gottwald thus criticised Schubert's opera:—' I looked forward with intense interest to the performance of this opera by our greatest song-writer, as his special strength lies in the lofty tone-poems adapted to every temperament, in clothing passion with such appropriate musical forms, that the enchantments of his fancy still attract us by their magic power. One was justified, after hearing so many of his rare and dramatically worked-up Lieder, in looking for very important results when he came to deal with the province of opera. Unfortunately, however, the poetical large-hearted

Of the more important works composed in this year we may cite :—

An orchestral symphony in B minor, which Schubert presented, in a half-finished state, to the Musikverein at Gratz, in return for the compliment paid to him of being elected an honorary member of that society. Josef Hüttenbrenner is my authority for saying that the first and second movements are entirely finished, and the third (Scherzo) partly. The fragment in the possession of Herr Anselm Hüttenbrenner, of Gratz, is said, the first movement particularly, to be of great beauty. If this be so, Schubert's intimate friend would do well to emancipate the still unknown work of the

composer found himself in company with a thoroughly prosy librettist; from this reason Schubert's opera will have no vitality in it. The meagre way the subject is handled, destitute of any kind of interest, offering no exciting situations, no good dramatic effects, must necessarily have a tame depressing effect upon the audience, not to mention the lyrical effusions, which are immoderately dragged out and extended. These last are the peculiar features of this opera (which one might correctly designate a song-opera); the consequence is that Schubert, with his pure vein of melody, must have felt a constant sense of restraint, and cannot get beyond the simplest phrases and forms of his Lieder. The inevitable consequence is a kind of suicidal monotony, which Schubert could never succeed, even by his wealth of melody, in entirely dispelling. This is all the more lamentable, as the composer, at any point of the story where he could reckon on support (for instance, at the conclusion of the first act, the first interview of Estrella with Alfonso, with, by the way, its most interesting instrumentation; in the conspirator's chorus, at the conclusion of the second act, besides the scene in the third act between Estrella and Adolfo; the march of victory, and as much besides), has given convincing proof of his great powers of

master he so highly honours, and introduce the symphony to Schubert's admirers.[1]

The Mass in A-flat, one of the most important church compositions of our master; the Cantatas, 'Volkslied,'[2] by Deinhartstein, 'Des Tages Weihe' (Op. 146); the Quartett for sopranos, 'Gott in der Natur,'[3] and the Quartett for men's voices, 'Geist der Liebe' (Op. 133 and 11). The Lieder belonging to this period are nearly all in print, and are widely circulated.

When Schubert's works were already before the public, Beethoven was employed on his two gigantic works, the Ninth Symphony and the D Mass.

The Opera 'Fidelio,' composed and performed in the

---

operatic writing, had the compiler of the book held out to the musician a helping hand.' This criticism squares precisely with the opinion I have just expressed; here, however, too much blame is attributed to the compiler. The composer, P. Cornelius, who was present at the performances in Weimar, told me that the opera contains many beautiful things, but, taken as a whole, the present state of theatrical taste and conditions considered, could not command any lengthened term of popularity on the stage. The thought inevitably suggests itself, that a deal of valueless patchwork in music triumphs in our days in various theatres, whereas theatrical doors are persistently closed to any work of Schubert's.

[1] A pianoforte duett setting of the symphony (which none but a few of the 'initiated' have seen) is in the hands of Josef Hüttenbrenner.

[2] Written at the suggestion of Dr. L. v. Sonnleithner, and performed on February 11, at the Theresianum, on the birthday festival of the Emperor Franz, under Sonnleithner's direction. In the year 1848 it appeared, with altered words, as a 'Constitutionslied' (Op. 157), engraved by the firm of Diabelli. The composition is written in the spirit of Haydn's Volkslieder.

[3] Written for Frl. Anna Fröhlich and the pupils of the Conservatorium.

year 1805, but since the year 1806 consigned to the mouldy shelves of the theatre library, had once more been restored to the repertoire of the Opera House, and from this time up to the year 1823 was splendidly performed by the following troupe of artists :—Milder-Hauptmann ; more recently by Campi, Hönig, and Frl. Schröder, Michael Vogl, Weinmüller, and Radichi.

Besides his magnificent orchestral works, Beethoven had composed a considerable number of masterpieces, especially for chamber music, and all of them incomparable in their way.

He was still, however, to a great extent, unintelligible to the mass, but an object of adoration to those who could fathom the great depths of his genius.

Coupled with the works of the great masters who preceded him, Beethoven's compositions were omnipotent in musical circles, or, at all events, were paving their own way to universal recognition. Brilliant offers from abroad were made him ; and if at home he occasionally had trouble with his publishers, he was still, and had been for a long while, in the happy position of being able to name his own price for his compositions, and in cases where people indulged in nice criticisms, to make his own sovereign will and decision the arbiter of the value of his work.

In this respect matters fared very differently with Schubert. He wrote hurriedly and incessantly, without the smallest hope of disposing of even half of his writings, or seeing the rewards due to his great mental energy. When he died, some hundred or more of his songs had been published, about one-fifth of all his vocal compositions. It was mainly from the income derived from the sale of these Lieder that he was forced to eke out his existence; for his other works, partly from the fact of their having to stand a comparison with those of the old masters, but more especially from the crushing power of Beethoven's position, were, with few exceptions, but little esteemed. Nor were the most strenuous efforts of his friends and well-wishers successful in obtaining, in Vienna itself, much less on the Continent, a quick sale or importation of his larger works, not even of his Lieder. With regard to the Lieder, the publishers observed a studied reserve and coyness, or made proposals to Schubert which he, in the interests of the art he represented, firmly declined.[1]

For thirty years consecutively were two immortal masters of music breathing the atmosphere of the same city. During a period of seven years Schubert, already famous, lived in close proximity to Beethoven, his senior by twenty-seven years, without either coming into anything like close personal relationship. Schubert, in his early years, had the deepest reverence for

---

[1] Thus he was desired to make the pianoforte accompaniment to his songs simpler and easier, as the difficulty of the accompaniment hindered any extensive sale. Schubert disregarded the suggestion, and wrote exactly as his humour dictated.

Beethoven, and told repeatedly, in his Convict days, a story about one of his early works, for the production of which, a few months before he became a pupil in the Convict, the band had been ordered to Schönbrunn, when Beethoven and Teyber, the music-master of the Archduke Rudolf, were present.[1] He was at the time still a mere boy, and after the performance of some of his ordinary Lieder set to Klopstock's poems, he enquired of a friend who had heard them, whether he really thought that he should ever do anything. The friend replied that he, Schubert, was already something first-rate; and the latter answered, 'Sometimes quietly to myself I think so too. But who can ever do anything after Beethoven?'

The accomplished Pinterics, a constant associate of Beethoven's, who either acquiesced with the great musician in their philological and political discussions, or combated his arguments, as occasion served, was well acquainted with Schubert also, and (according to Schindler) is said to have had some influence over him; it would seem, however, that he never undertook to interpose as a go-between, and to bring these kindred spirits together.[2] Beethoven was difficult of access,

---

[1] Teyber (Anton) was born in 1754, and died, a composer of chamber music, at Vienna, in 1822.

[2] Carl Pinterics was private secretary to Count Palffy, of Vienna; his office was in the Count's residence in the Josefsplatz. He was a very accomplished versatile man, an excellent pianoforte-player, and had a curious facility in cutting out figures from cardboard. He lived at the

and probably, until the day when the Variations for four hands by Schubert (Op. 10), with the dedication on the title-page, came into his hands, had taken little notice of the composer of the ' Erl-King.'

Their two natures were essentially distinct and different. If Schubert's easy disposition, his childish naïveté, his guilelessness in the ordinary dealings of life, his delight in a glass of wine and sociable habits, his sincerity, and a good mixture of Viennese geniality, remind one of Mozart's character, these very qualities essentially contrasted with and distinguished him from the somewhat capricious, mistrustful, sarcastic, and haughty Beethoven, whose depth of intellect and greatness of soul, coupled with his vast classical range and versatilty of power, enabled him to tower, in many respects, above both Mozart and Schubert.

As regards the Variations here mentioned, Anton Schindler alludes to their presentation in the following terms :—' In the year 1822, Franz Schubert set out,

time we speak of at the ' Zuckerbäckerhaus,' in the neighbourhood of the Carlskirche. Thither came very frequently Vogl, Schubert, Schober, Gahy, Von Asten, and many others, so that music, as may be supposed, flourished in his lodgings. Pinterics was in the possession of the most complete collection of Schubert's Lieder; but even his catalogue, which contains 505 songs, did not exhaust the number. He and Beethoven frequently went together to the ' Blumenstöckl.' An officer of the German guard made a third in the usual party. Pinterics died on March 6, 1831. He too, like Vogl, allowed himself to make alterations in Schubert's Lieder, and endeavoured, by plausible reasons made to the publishers, to justify his conduct.

to present in person the master he honoured so highly with his Variations on a French song, Op. 10. These Variations he had previously dedicated to Beethoven. In spite of Diabelli accompanying him, and acting as spokesman and interpreter of Schubert's feelings, Schubert played a part in the interview which was anything but pleasant to him. His courage, which he managed to husband up to the very threshold of the house, forsook him entirely at the first glimpse he caught of the majestic artist; and when Beethoven expressed a wish that Schubert should write the answers to his questions, he felt as if his hands were tied and fettered. Beethoven ran through the presentation copy and stumbled on some inaccuracy of harmony. He then, in the kindest manner, drew the young man's attention to the fault, adding that the fault was no deadly sin. Meantime the result of this remark, intended to be kind, was to utterly disconcert the nervous visitor. It was not until he got outside the house that Schubert recovered his equanimity, and rebuked himself unsparingly. This was his first and last meeting with Beethoven, for he never again had the courage to face him.'

Beethoven's biographer, who is now dead, must be held answerable for the correctness of this episode, with all its rather improbable details, so humiliating to Schubert. It should be stated, however, that a gentleman still living at Vienna, an intimate and trusted friend of Schubert's (Herr Josef Hüttenbrenner), shortly after the presentation of his musical work, heard from Schubert's own mouth, that he certainly visited Beethoven, but that he was not at home, and that Schubert entrusted his Variations to the care of the housemaid, or man-servant, and consequently that at that time he neither saw and still less spoke to Beethoven. Hüttenbrenner remarks, further, that Schubert subsequently heard with great pleasure of Beethoven's enjoying these Variations, and playing them frequently and gladly with his nephew Carl.

In the summer of 1822 Friedrich von Rochlitz came from Leipsic to Vienna to visit Beethoven and confer with him on the subject of some musical compositions, especially a proposed setting of Göthe's ' Faust.'

In the second letter which he wrote to Christian Härtel, in Leipsic, on the subject of his interview with the master, the following passage occurs, which we give here, as bearing expressly on the personal relationship and points of contact between Schubert and Beethoven. It runs thus :—' A fortnight afterwards [after the first interview with Beethoven], I was just going to dinner, when a young composer, named Franz Schubert, an enthusiastic worshipper of Beethoven's, met me. Beethoven had spoken to him about me. " If you want to see him cheerful and unconstrained," said Schubert, " you ought to dine in the same room with him at the

Gasthaus, where he always goes to dine." [1] He brought me to the house. The places were mostly taken; Beethoven sat surrounded by several of his friends, who were perfect strangers to me.' The letter contains no further mention of Schubert.

Schubert was familiar enough with Beethoven's works, more especially with his Symphonies, which he heard played at concerts and practised himself as pianoforte duetts; but Beethoven had taken very little trouble about Schubert's performances—an act of omission which may perhaps be well excused in Beethoven. Absorbed in the composition of his profound works for the orchestra and chamber, he had neither time nor inducement to pay attention to Schubert's Lieder, which were only just now beginning to emerge into public notice.

It was not until the close of his life that he learned to know more faithfully the compositions of one who looked up to him as his ideal; and as Jean Paul, who was greatly attracted by Schubert's genius, and found in his declining years of blind old age a consolation in Schubert's Lieder, and asked for the 'Erl-King' only a few hours before his death, so did Beethoven also, in the last days of his life, study Schubert's songs, which up to that time had been almost entirely unknown to him.

Schindler alludes to these circumstances thus :—' As

---

[1] Probably 'Zum Stern' or 'Zur Eiche,' on the Brandstätte.

the illness, which, after four months of incessant suffering, ended by killing Beethoven, had from the very outset made his usual mental activity impossible, they were
obliged to devise some distraction suitable to the dying
man's spirit and inclination. Hence it happened that
I laid before him a collection of Schubert's Lieder
and vocal pieces, about sixty in number, and several of
them at that time in manuscript. I did this not merely
with the view of agreeably entertaining him, but of
giving him an opportunity of fathoming Schubert, of
forming a more favourable opinion of his gifts, which
were regarded with suspicion and distrust by many ec-
centric persons who treated in the same manner others
of their contemporaries. The great master, who up to
this time knew but three or four songs of Schubert, was
astonished at their great number, and could not believe
that before that time (February 1827) Schubert had
written over five hundred. But if he was astonished at
the number, his wonder was at its height when he examined their contents. For several days he could not
tear himself away from perusing them, and he pored
for hours daily over " Iphigenie," " Grenzen der Menschheit," " Allmacht," " Junge Nonne," " Viola," the
"Müller-Lieder," and several others. He exclaimed repeatedly, in a voice of rapturous delight, " Certainly,
a godlike spark dwells in Schubert." " Had I had this
poem, I too would have set it to music ! " He could
not say enough in praise of most of the other poems,

and Schubert's original way of handling the subject. Nor could he understand how Schubert found time and leisure "to undertake so many poems, many of which are extended and subdivided into ten smaller ones," as he expressed it; and of such songs written in the grand style Schubert alone has set above a hundred, not merely lyrics, but lengthy ballads and scenes full of dialogue, which, worked up as they are in dramatic form, were in their proper element even in opera, and were sure of producing their legitimate effect. What would the great master have said had he ever seen the "Songs from Ossian," the "Bürgschaft," "Elysium," the "Taucher," and other great songs, which have only recently appeared for the first time? In short, the esteem which Beethoven felt for Schubert's gifts was so great that he wished to see his operas and pianoforte works; his illness, however, had already so undermined his constitution that he could not gratify this wish. He spoke, however, frequently of Schubert, and prophesied that "some day he will make a great sensation in the world," and regretted that he had not at an earlier period made his acquaintance. As is well known, Anselm Hüttenbrenner, on hearing the news of Beethoven's dangerous illness, hurried off from Gratz, remained alone with him during the last hours of his life, and closed the eyes of the dying man.'

Some time before this fatal event, Schubert, Josef Hüttenbrenner (who vouches for the truth of this episode), and the painter Teltscher (the latter intending, unobserved, to sketch in his album the features of the great master), came to Beethoven's house and stood a long time around the sick bed of the dying man. Beethoven, who had been beforehand informed of the names of his visitors, fixed his motionless eye upon them, and made signs with his hand which they failed to understand. Schubert, most deeply moved, then left the room with his companions; and this, his last visit, may probably have been the first Schubert ever paid to Beethoven, as several of Schubert's most intimate friends, who are still living, cannot remember any more than a chance interview between the two composers.[1]

Schubert followed Beethoven to the grave, accompanied by Franz Lachner and Josef Randhartinger.[2]

---

[1] Ferdinand Schubert, when asked of his brother's relationship with Beethoven, gave the somewhat vague answer, ' They very seldom came together.' Beethoven, as is well known, was often to be met with at the ' Fuchshöhle,' in the Paternostergässchen, kept by Herr Steiner, and there Schubert often fell in with him. Wilhelm Lenz remarks, in his biography of Beethoven: 'Franz Schubert, the Beethoven of songs, knew Beethoven only a short time. People had misrepresented to Schubert the noble spirit of Beethoven, and purposely kept him away from Beethoven. A few days before his death he gave expression to his recognition of Schubert's value, exclaiming: " Certainly, there glows in Schubert a divine spark." All Europe has confirmed this opinion. On an English piano at Cadiz I found the " Winterreise," &c.'

[2] In the journal 'Sammler,' 1827, No. 45, Schubert is named as one of the thirty-eight torch-bearers who stood around Beethoven's bier at his funeral. Lachner and Randhartinger are not mentioned.

On returning from the funeral he and his friends went to a tavern, ' the Mehlgrube ; ' there he filled two glasses with wine, and emptied the first to the memory of him they had just followed to the grave, but the second to the memory of that man of the three who should be the first to follow Beethoven—never suspecting that he himself would be the man, and that, too, in the year following. His often-expressed wish to rest in a grave by Beethoven's side was granted him.

As already mentioned, after the enthusiastic reception given by the public to the ' Erlkönig,' the music-publishers of Vienna expressed great interest for Schubert's compositions.

Besides the firm of Cappi & Diabelli, publishers appeared in the shape of Leidesdorf, Eder, Czerny, Thaddäus, Weigl, Pennauer and Artaria, and there appeared several works of Schubert in these music-publishing firms.[1] With Leidesdorf Schubert contracted for the publication of songs for two years; he seems,

---

[1] These firms have been, for the most part, since the time we speak of, superseded by others. Herr Doppler told me that Schubert would entrust none of his compositions with the publisher Domenico Artaria, because once when Schubert, whilst still a pupil of Salieri's, presented him with three stringed quartetts, bearing as an inscription the words ' dedicated to Anton Salieri by his pupil F. Schubert,' the publisher rejected the offer with the words, ' I never take any pupil's work,' and yet in later times he entrusted him with the publication of several compositions, amongst others the Rondeau, Op. 70. In the contract, in which Leidesdorf surrendered to Diabelli the right of publishing compositions, mention is made of a trio by Lachner and Schubert.

however, to have withdrawn from the bargain. With Peters too, in Leipsic, arrangements were made, by the intervention of Josef Hüttenbrenner, and we shall call attention to these circumstances by and by.

The twelve works published by Cappi & Diabelli had brought in a sum of over 2,000 gulden, and in the first nine months of the year 1821 over 800 copies of the 'Erl-King' alone were struck off, and 50 per cent. profit made by the firm of Diabelli.

Schubert at that time had it in his power to lay a solid foundation for a comfortable livelihood, and to win substantial profits by his published works. But inexperienced in business habits, and only caring for the moment, matched against a capricious self-seeking publisher (who afterwards became wealthy by means of Schubert), the man was defenceless and powerless to adopt favourable circumstances to promote his own interests.[1]

In a weak moment, and probably when he was in

---

[1] 'When I consider,' says J. Mayrhofer (in 'Recollections of F. Schubert') 'the illnesses and pecuniary embarrassments of my poor friend, it invariably occurs to me that he failed particularly in two things, which might have grounded his financial position and made him entirely independent. Contrary to a well-digested scheme, and one actually in the course of operation, he disposed of the copyright in these and other works that followed, and neglected a favourable combination of circumstances for obtaining a good musical appointment, with a regular salary attached. A love of enjoyment, confirmed by deprivations in early life, and ignorance of the world, may have led him to commit such errors. In later times (1827 and 1828), he always made modest offers to the publishers, which they thought exorbitant.'

actual want of money, Schubert suffered himself to be persuaded by Diabelli to part with the copyright of the first twelve sheets of songs for the sum of 800 florins. Diabelli, no doubt, paid him in advance for his future labours ; but by taking this step Schubert lost his independence and the advantage which would afterwards have accrued to him, had he remained the sole owner of his own works. His anxious friends, ignorant hitherto of these proceedings, lamented the fact, but never ceased on that account to look after him with the same care they had always taken.[1]

Franz v. Schober and Josef Hüttenbrenner must be cited as persons who interested themselves in popularising and getting a large sale for Schubert's works, not only in Vienna, but elsewhere. The first endeavoured for eight years, but in vain, to get a performance in Vienna, Dresden, Prague, Gratz, Berlin, or Pesth, of the Opera of ' Alfonso und Estrella.' A letter which Schober sent to Schubert from Breslau, on December 24, 1824, shows how earnestly he thought of his friend's welfare, although they were separated from one another. The passage alluded to runs thus :—

---

[1] The songs he disposed of were ' Erlkönig,' ' Gretchen am Spinnrad,' ' Schäfers Klagelied,' ' Der Wanderer,' ' Rastlose Liebe,' ' Memnon,' ' Antigone und Oedip,' ' Am Grabe Anselmos,' Waltzes (1–3), the Variations for two performers (Op. 10), a sonata for two, and three sonatas for solo players on the piano. The song of ' The Wanderer' is said to have brought to the publishers, from the time it appeared to the year 1861, the sum of 27,000 florins.

'Now with regard to your affairs. How are your operas getting on? Have "Die Verschwornen" and "Fierrabras" been given? Are there no tidings from C. M. Weber [respecting "Alfonso und Estrella"]? Write to him at all events, and if you don't get a satisfactory answer from him, ask him to send back your work. I know how to get at Spontini; would you like me to make an effort to get him to put your work on the stage?—for he is difficult to manage.

'My belief is, it merely depends on something being given in its entirety to revive afresh your popularity with the mass. No doubt the sooner it is done the better. Does it fare badly with Leidesdorf? I am heartily sorry for that; and your "Müllerlieder" too, have they made no sensation? The hounds have no genuine feeling; they do not think for themselves, and surrender themselves blindly to noise and opinions not their own. If you could only get a couple of noisy drumming reviewers, who would for ever prattle about you, all would go well. I know some quite commonplace people who became popular and praised by this means. Why then should not a man avail himself of this assistance, who in the highest degree deserves it? Castelli writes in two Continental papers that you have set an opera by him; he ought to noise this abroad.

'Moriz has sent us the "Müllerlieder;" pray send us all else that has appeared. How glad I am you are quite well again. I shall be well too, very soon. Thanks

again and again for your poem; it is so true and full of
feeling, and has made a great impression on me. Yes,
verily! In crazy old age people go crawling about.
Farewell, and love me. We shall certainly meet. You
will read more in Moriz's letter. Ever yours,

'SCHOBER.'

Hüttenbrenner tried to bring out on the stage the
Opera 'Des Teufels Lustschloss' (its second adaptation),
and for this purpose applied to the directors of the
Josefstadt Theatre, to Count Gallenberg in Vienna, to
Capellmeister Winter at Munich, and to Director Holbein in Prague. None of these attempts, however, were
crowned with success, and Schubert, since the year
1820, was not gladdened by seeing one of his operas
represented on the stage. The directors of the Josefstadt Theatre let the matter rest, with a promise to
bring out the opera; Count Gallenberg declared he
would bring it out in the Hoftheater, if the sum of
10,000 florins were guaranteed as an indemnity for costs
and contingent failure. Matters proceeded no farther
at Munich, and Holbein, the director, professed himself
only ready under certain provisoes to bring the opera
before the public. On October 22, 1822, he wrote thus
to Josef Hüttenbrenner :—

'It gives me particular pleasure in any way to smooth
the usually rough and difficult path for young men of
talent. Be good enough to send me the libretto and score

of " Teufels Lustschloss." If it comes up to your version
of its merits, nothing shall stand in the way of its performance. I regret that during my residence in Vienna
from September 20th up to October 19th, I had not the
pleasure of becoming personally acquainted with you
and your gifted friend.'

The correspondence resulted in nothing further, and
the opera up to this very day has never been performed.

As a proof of the guarded reserve of foreign publishers, and their timidity in dealing even with Schubert's Lieder, we may appeal to the following letter,
written by Peters to Josef Hüttenbrenner :—

' Leipsic: Nov. 14, 1822.

' My constant occupations hitherto must be my apology for the somewhat procrastinated answer to your
favour of October 18th last.

' I am very grateful to you for your communication
respecting Herr Schubert. Several of his vocal compositions are favourably known to me, and strengthen
my confidence in all that you allege in favour of this
artist. I will very gladly contribute to a further ex-
tension of the works of this composer, so far as the
firms in Vienna can manage it. Before, however, I
make any definite and conclusive answer, allow me to
lay before you a short sketch of my own business and
the dealings of the firm.

'Immediately on entering into my present business, I resolved to make my name as a publisher by never printing anything inferior, but by publishing the very best things I could get hold of. It is not possible to carry out my project strictly, since I am unable to obtain from first-class artists alone as many MSS. as I want; and, in the second place, we publishers are often constrained for the sake of convenience to print a great deal which I, for one, would not print, were I free to choose. Certain it is we are obliged to publish much that is superficial, and pay attention to every branch of our customers; for with mere classical works our business would be but a very small one, seeing that the number of classical connoisseurs is now in a minority. Nevertheless, I have not from a love of gain suffered myself to be seduced by the silly trifles now in fashion, which are more lucrative as a speculation than solid works, but I have taken care that our publications, even for the common tribe of customers, should never be utterly bad, and I have always worked upon my favourite principles, my chief aim being the publication of first-class works. The result will, in the course of things, make my efforts plainer than hitherto, since every year I am careful to make only good connections, the steady improvement in my business allowing me to maintain and keep them.

'Two results, however, follow from this state of things, and I have often felt myself a slave to circumstances.

The first is time, in the employment of which I am almost invariably constrained to a stereotyped usage. In order to keep up the largest possible stock of good works, I must make contracts with first-rate artists, and strengthen those alliances in such a manner as not only to make the composers well satisfied with their bargain, but present myself to them always as a willing and cheerful publisher—a proceeding which acts for the mutual benefit of composer and publisher. My intercourse with most of the masters of real value to me, such as Spohr, Romberg, Hummel, &c., &c., has contributed to most friendly relations with them; I feel doubly bound in point of honour to take in hand everything sent by such friends and able artists, even though, as is often the case, I foresee that I shall realise no profit from a good deal they send to me for publication. My time is much restricted in consequence of these obligations; for not only do these artists keep me constantly employed, but I must also reserve some moments for works which come on me unexpectedly. This happens to be the case just now. What time I have to spare seldom suffices for publishing other things necessitated by the demand; so that I am nearly always hindered from forming new connections with new composers, having no time for looking at their works.

'The second point, necessarily involved in what we have already said, and aggravating the difficulty of making a new alliance, is the novelty, and, as far as my

experience of business goes, the still unknown name of
a mere beginner in the composing line. I am often
met with the objection that I will never lend a helping
hand to the publication of works by a new composer,
and that such a one can never become known, if no
publisher will trouble himself to bring out his work.
But this reproof is wrongly grounded. I can't do everything; a man must follow one uniform plan, if an or-
dinarily successful result is to follow. I only want works
by masters already recognised by the public. No doubt
I publish a good deal besides; but assuming I can get
a sufficient supply from these, I must leave to other
publishers the introduction of the work of new composers. These publishers are to be had, and many of
them are very glad to be employed, as they are afraid
of the money demands of the older and dearer artists.
If the new composer be of mark, and his works stamped
as valuable, I am his man; for the publication of his
works squares with my design, based rather on honour
than profit, and I should prefer paying him for his
works an extravagant price, rather than receiving them
on terms at the outset advantageous to myself.

'You will see, therefore, that I find a difficulty in
falling in at once with your proposals respecting Herr
Schubert, my chief reasons being, as I have alleged,
the limited time at my command; whilst, at the same
time, after the opinion I have formed of the young
artist, I do not like absolutely refusing his wish. By

way of compromise, I would therefore propose that
Herr Schubert should send me for examination some of
his works he intends for publication, for I print nothing
of a young and little-known composer without having
first seen it. If some great and well-known master does
anything bad, the blame falls upon him, for his name
was my surety; but supposing I publish anything of a
new artist, and it turns out unsuccessful, I am blamed;
for who forces me to print anything if I am not persuaded in my own mind of its worth? Now, in this
case, the name of the composer affords me no protection. Without doubt, Herr Schubert entrusts his works
in perfectly safe keeping; he is assured against any
possible abuse of trust. If I like them, I will retain
all that I can. On the other hand, Herr Schubert will
not take it ill of me in being perfectly candid if I do
not like anything, and say so at once, for such plain
dealing leads most surely to a thoroughly good understanding.

'I must further request, that he only sends me his
most successful works. Of course he will publish
nothing which he does not reckon successful: be this
as it may, one work turns out better than another,
and I must have the best—I repeat, I must have the
best, if I am to introduce a new composer before an
extended and large public, not for the certainty of
profit, but for my own credit. I have laboured tooth
and nail to make my business as perfect as possible,

and am already reaping my reward in the confidence
and preference given on all sides to my firm. People
are accustomed to the fact of my publishing several
good works, and if occasionally I succeed with a new
composer, he, in his turn, wins a greater amount of
public confidence than before; people believe he must
be good, because I take him in hand. No doubt I have
sometimes been deceived, but I have now become more
careful to maintain and establish the credit I have
gained with so much difficulty. For this reason I desire a new composer to let me have his most successful
works, that I may with propriety at once recommend
him, and my recommendation be justified. A first successful impression often paves the way for the whole of
a man's subsequent career; consequently a good lesson
can never be too often repeated in the ears of youthful
composers—that in the matter of publishing their works
they should proceed as cautiously as possible. They can
venture much, but only have a few of their works published, until their reputation be first well established.
Spohr has only published fifty-eight, Romberg sixty-
six, and Bernhard Romberg thirty-eight works, whereas,
at present time, several other artists, who are much
younger, have already had over 100 published. These
well-known and recognised artists have written much
more, but have not published; and if I am met with
the argument of a prolific and yet solid Mozart, Haydn,
Beethoven, &c., I say these are rare phenomena, and

though they must be taken as patterns, yet experience alone will show if a man is the equal of these men; and what a number of the earlier works of Mozart, &c., have never appeared in print at all!

'Have the goodness to communicate with Herr Schubert upon the subject of my letter, and to act further in the matter as you think fit. As regards the conditions to be made on his side, please let me know of them; it is an unpleasant feeling for me to be huckstering and bargaining for a work of genius. For the rest, we shall not quarrel as to terms, for the constancy with which my employers stick by me, proves that I deal with them on fair terms—that is a praise which I can allow myself. Besides this, the conditions made by the young artist will not be on so high a scale as to make their acceptance a difficult matter to myself.

'That 300 copies of one work of Schubert's might be disposed of in Vienna alone, is quite possible, as soon as it is printed; but I should scarcely get rid of 100 copies, although I am in business dealings with every musical firm. You will easily understand this; nor will I enter into reasons for such a fact, but you will readily believe it is so; experience only too readily confirms this, and there are but very few exceptions to the rule. With best respects, I remain, with great esteem,

'Your most obedient servant,
'B. V. PETERS.

' P.S.—If Herr Schubert sends vocal compositions, let them be songs with a name, such as Beethoven's " Adelaide," or the like.   These I prefer to mere Lieder ; for so many songs and cantatas appear, that people do not pay sufficient attention to their titles.'

Even these efforts on the part of Hüttenbrenner remained barren of result.   Subsequently Schubert entered into direct communication with publishers in Leipsic and Mayence, and these were partly successful.

Herr J. Hüttenbrenner is my authority for stating that an opportunity was given to our composer, about this time, by the acceptance of an office, the duties of which would have infringed but little upon the use of his time—of winning an assured and safe position, which, some years later, might have been of great advantage to him.   The acting Hofmusikgraf, Moriz v. Dietrichstein, made Vogl the medium of offering to the composer, to whom he had formerly been much attached, the post of organist to the Court Chapel choir.   Hüttenbrenner brought the news to Schubert's father, at that time a schoolmaster in the Rossau, who was vastly delighted at the idea.   But Franz, to the grief of his father, refused the place, doubtless from a distaste and dread of sinking into a dependent position, which would deprive him of his entire liberty.   Some years afterwards, he good humouredly assured his friends that the absolute requirement of his art called on the

Government to support him, in order that he should
be able to write freely, and without worldly anxieties;
but this aid not forthcoming, he stood of his own free
choice as candidate for the office of Hofcapellmeister,
which, as we shall have occasion hereafter to point out,
was given to another.

We must here mention a letter of thanks which he
received from the Bishop Dankesreithner, in St. Pölten,
for the dedication of the 'Harfnerlieder' (Op. 12). It
runs thus :—

'Noble Sir,—You have conferred on me a most unde-
served and special honour in dedicating to me the twelfth
volume of your universally esteemed and favourite musical compositions. For this distinction and politeness
receive my best thanks, as also for the copies you have
sent of your admirable work, with your kind dedicatory
letter, for all which I confess myself largely indebted to
you. I have presented my secretary, Herr Giessrigl,
with one copy, and Herr Professor Kastl with another.
God, from whom every good gift comes, has singled
you out in endowing you with rare and noble musical
talents, and has enabled you, by continued industry and
proper use of your gifts, to lay firm foundation for
your future success. Wishing you, from my heart, all
prosperity in life, believe me, with every assurance of
deep respect and obligation,

'Your devoted servant,

'JOHANN NEP., *m. p.*, Bishop.'

Schubert applied about this time to the 'Gesellschaft der Musikfreunde' for admittance as a practising member (as a player on the viola), but was refused, in consequence of a clause in the standing orders of the society, which enacted that only amateurs could be admitted, and not professional musicians.

CHAPTER XI.

(1823.)

THE DRAMA 'ROSAMUNDE'—THE THEATRE 'AN DER WIEN'—WILHELM
VOGEL — HELMINA VON CHEZY—THE OPERA 'FIERRABRAS'—THE
OPERETTA 'DIE VERSCHWORNEN'—CASTELLI AND SCHUBERT—PER-
FORMANCE OF THE OPERETTA AT VIENNA AND FRANKFORT—CRITI-
CISMS—ORIGIN OF THE FIRST 'MÜLLERLIEDER'—'DER ZWERG'—
SCHUBERT IS MADE MEMBER OF THE MUSICAL ASSOCIATION AT LINZ.

THE year 1823 is conspicuous as one of the most productive, and in a musical point of view most important,
in Schubert's life. He passed this time in Vienna, absorbed in work as a composer, several grand works in
various kinds speaking in eloquent testimony to his
ceaseless activity. His splendid attainments as a song-
composer, proved at an early period, were now employed
in new vocal works, and culminated in the series or
chain of songs entitled 'Die schöne Müllerin.' To the
same period belongs the ripest and most successful
works of our tone-poet in the province of dramatic
music, besides the music to Helmina Chezy's Drama
'Rosamunde,' the Opera 'Fierrabras,' and without
doubt the Operetta 'Der häusliche Krieg.' Helmina
Chezy,[1] an authoress much read at that time, but now

---

[1] Wilhelmine Christine Chezy, whose maiden name was Klencke,
was born at Berlin, in 1783, and married in 1805 to the French Oriental

only remembered as composer of the libretto to Weber's 'Euryanthe,' paid her first visit in the summer of 1823 to the Austrian capital, where she had some literary patrons. The odd and capricious lady had intended to leave Dresden, her last place of residence, and revisit the North; but on setting off, and feeling her pocket, she missed her Prussian passport; the Austrian one, however, was safe, and Helmina, looking on the inci dent as a warning of fate, ordered the coachman to go by way of Prague to Vienna. She stayed there only a few days, and then started with her two sons, Wilhelm and Max, for Baden, where she lodged at Count O'Don-nel's. At Baden Helmina wrote the Drama 'Rosa-munde.' A young friend, of the name of Kupelwieser (brother of the painter Leopold K., and compiler of the libretto of 'Fierrabras') asked her for a dramatic poem, which Franz Schubert was to set to music. The piece was intended to be given as a benefit performance for

scholar Antoine Leonhard, in Paris. They separated in 1810. Hel-mina then left France with her two sons Wilhelm and Max, and stayed in various German towns, for different lengths of time, living entirely on her literary efforts. After many wanderings through various parts of Germany, the restless lady came, in the year 1823, to Vienna, where she remained up to 1828, during which interval, however, she made ex-tensive excursions; for instance, in the mountainous country of Upper Austria. Her autobiography appeared a short time before her death, with the title, 'Unvergessenes, Denkwürdigkeiten aus meinem Leben,' Leipsic: Brockhaus, 1858, in two Parts. Quite lately (1863), her son Wilhelm published 'Erinnerungen aus meinem Leben.' I have drawn from both these memoirs.

Fräulein M. Neumann (afterwards Madame Lukas), a beautiful actress at Vienna, for whom Kupelwieser had conceived a tender passion. The part of the heroine, which Helmina selected for herself, does not belong to historically known characters of that name, but an ideal Princess of Cyprus, and the plot of the story is borrowed from a Spanish drama. The work was finished in five days, and sent straight off to Wilhelm Vogel, at that time director of the theatre in Vienna.[1]

There is no doubt that the prevailing taste in the Opera House at Vienna was not quite favourably disposed to such an undertaking as was now proposed for Frau Chezy with Schubert for a coadjutor. The owner of the theatre was Count Ferdinand Palffy, the conductor and irresponsible comptroller the aforesaid Vogel, whose influence on the institution was of the most marked kind, as he provided the theatre with a stock of farces and dramas of his own invention, all of which satisfied in a high degree the naive spectacle-loving public.[2]

It happened that, without Chezy's knowledge, there

---

[1] Wilhelm Chezy mentions this extraordinarily short interval.

[2] Helmina Chezy thus speaks in her 'Denkwürdigkeiten:'—'Count Palffy surrendered to his director, Vogel, the entire management of the theatre, a man thoroughly understanding the public, and knowing how to supply what it wanted. He was specially entrusted with the preparation of pieces sure of a long run and crowded audiences, sure also to be remunerative to the treasury. Directly they ceased to draw, the plays were superseded by new ones. There was the usual stage villain, then a doleful love-story, a stalwart knight and champion, a few clap-trap effects, and the drama was sure to please. The author received,

was also in preparation for the benefit of Frl. Neumann 'Der böse Krollo,' a piece by Vogel, of the pungent sensational character which seemed to have such special charms for the visitors of the theatre. 'Krollo' followed after 'Rosamunde,' and completely carried off the palm from the Cyprian Princess. Helmina, who could not remain ignorant of these facts, gave her poem to the composer with an undisguised feeling of anxiety.[1] Schubert, in his usual easy way, poured out the streams of his beautiful melody over the libretto, which were at the first performance immediately appreciated by the discerning part of the public, and were received with the loudest applause. The first

whether the pieces failed or not, 100 florins. If but a scanty audience appeared, extravaganzas were tried, and other means of attraction.' Wilhelm Chezy draws the following picture:—'The Theatre an der Wien was at that time specially distinguished for the completeness of its mechanical effects and scenery. Magic disappearances under ground, shifting scenery, and metamorphoses were wonderfully managed. The piece which, in the winter 1823-24, drew the largest houses at Vienna, was a melodrama, "Der Wolfsbrunnen," founded on the story connected with the well-known place of resort for parties of pleasure at Heidelberg. The play was one of a class called a "Viehstück," in which a wild beast plays an important part, the animal being represented not by one of his own species, but by a man. The wolf was played so admirably, and was so boisterously received, that after the second performance the actor insisted on his name appearing in the playbill—if not, he decided he would not appear again. His request was granted.'

[1] 'I felt,' says Chezy, in her notes, 'that the book was out of place; for the Theatre an der Wien had its own particular public, and not knowing this public, I could not have written anything likely to please them.'

performance of the play, with band, chorus, and dance
music, took place on December 20, 1823.[1]   The treatment of the story is as follows:—'The Princess Rosamunde, from some fancy of her father's, has been
brought up as a shepherdess. When she has completed her eighteenth year, her nurse reveals her real
condition and rank to the whole nation, and they enter
upon the government. Their term expires on June 3.
A great deal that is wonderful is connected with this
circumstance—such as the arrival of the Prince of
Candia, who, from his childhood enamoured of Rosamunde, rushes off to Cyprus after the receipt of a
mysterious letter, but suffers shipwreck on the coast,
and is the only one saved of the crew. Fulgentius, the
Stadtholder of Cyprus, has in the interval ruled for
sixteen years over Cyprus, and is so little tired of go-
verning, that he hears with indifference of the exist-

---

[1] On December 18, 1823, there appeared in the literary journals of
Vienna the following notice:—'Frau Helmina v. Chezy has supplied
the director of the Imperial Theatre an der Wien with a new Drama
with choruses, "Rosamunda von Cypern." The music is by the popular
talented composer Herr Franz Schubert, and the first performance,
which was given on Saturday, December 20, was for the benefit of an
actress in that theatre, Fräulein Neumann. The names of the authoress
and the composer are a guarantee to this artist of the wisdom of se-
lecting a work safe of an honourable reception—a work which, from its
solid character, claims a place amongst the most remarkable of modern
times.' The bill at the theatre was as follows:—'Rosamunde, Princess of
Cyprus. Romantic play in four acts, with choruses, musical accompaniments, and dances, by Helmina Chezy, née Klencke. The music by
Herr Schubert.'

ence of Rosamunde, believed by the people to have been
dead a long time since. Rosamunde has already seen
the disguised Prince of Candia, and the two, by a sympathetic and romantic understanding, are recognised as
the loving pair intended for each other. The Prince,
who, to prove the loyalty of his lady-love, will not discover himself, and perhaps also because his travelling
companions are tipsy and he cannot rely on any protection, enters the service of Fulgentius and wins his
confidence, having rescued his daughter from the hands
of banditti. Up to this point everything goes on pros-
perously; but Fulgentius falls madly in love with
Rosamunde, and she not reciprocating his flame, he
pursues her with cruel vindictive hatred, accuses her of
having caused his daughter's misfortune, and has her
thrown into prison. Not satisfied with this, he dips a
letter into the strongest and most deadly poison, and
orders the disguised Prince, who is initiated in the
secret of this murder, to deliver the letter to Rosamunde. She, however, has in the interim found the
means of escape, and withdraws to the hut of her old
protectress. There the Prince of Candia finds her, and
tells her of the murderous purpose of Fulgentius. By
bad luck the loving pair are surprised by Fulgentius,
and disasters are imminent, prevented only by the
Prince persuading the tyrant that Rosamunde had
swooned away the first moment she looked at the
poisoned letter—a necessary myth, which the lady

shows by her gestures she perfectly understands, and acts up to. The credulous Fulgentius now entrusts his friend with the care of Rosamunde, and once again all seems to be going well. Now, however, comes a letter from the head citizen Albanus (the man, by the way, who wrote the mysterious letter to the Prince of Candia, and is proclaimed every year on the 2nd of June, the birth-day of the Princess), who is likewise discontented with Fulgentius' *régime.* Unhappily Fulgentius surprises the Prince as he is reading this letter; his incredulity is now at an end; the hypocritical friend's life is forfeited, he must give up the letter and die. But the Prince prefers life and marriage, gives with quick instinct the poisoned letter instead of Albanus's letter to Fulgen-tius : he scents the letter and dies.

The musical part consists of vocal and instrumental pieces. In the first of these is a Romance (in F minor, for alto), a simple, beautiful strophe song of genuine Schubert stamp, and three choruses—a hunting, a shep-herd, and a spirit chorus, the first of which (in D major, for mixed voices) is fresh and melodious; the second (in four parts, B-flat major $\frac{2}{4}$) is like the spirit chorus (four parts, for men's voices, D major $\frac{4}{4}$), a deep and thoughtfully written composition.[1]

---

[1] The above-mentioned pieces appeared with pianoforte accompani-ment, the ghost chorus also, with horn and trumpet obligato, printed as Op. 26, at Diabelli's. The choruses, too, were often performed in public at Vienna. Dr. Schneider possesses a copy of the instrumental

The instrumental movements, according to the statement of competent judges who were present at the performances at the time, are for the most part weighty and beautiful, so that a revival of the musical part of 'Rosamunde,' should it ever be found in a complete state, may yet be advertised in the concert-room.

The overture to the play was that of 'Alfonso und Estrella,' by Schubert, and (according to Josef Hüttenbrenner) it pleased the audience so much that it was repeated twice.   The romance, sung by Frau Vogel, and one of the choruses, were greatly applauded ; Schubert himself met with a more friendly reception than was usually given him on occasions of his earlier dramatic displays.   This was arranged by a compact phalanx of Schubert's allies, who made it a point of honour to do battle at all hazards for the genial tone-poet.

That the artistic freedom and peculiarities of Schubert's music, so effective to musicians of our own day, should originally be found fault with and called 'bizarrerie,' will not, after the experiences common to all times, excite wonder.   The same thing has happened even in our own time.[1]   Certain it is that the drama

music of the first act; the music-publisher Spina has the original MS. of the ballet music.

[1] Thus a critic wrote (in the periodical 'Der Sammler') :—' Herr Schubert shows originality in his compositions, but unfortunately "bizarrerie" also.   The young man is in a period of development; we hope that he will come out of it successfully.   At present he is too

being found, spite of the beautiful music, wearisome, survived only two representations, to give place to the more longlived 'bösen Krollo,' [1] which, by the brilliancy of spectacle and the sensational acting, had those powers of attraction for the public which the director, Vogel, was most anxious to cater for. [2]

much applauded ; for the future, may he never complain of being too little recognised.' On the other hand, Chezy (in the 'Denkwürdig-keiten meines Lebens') remarks that the final failure of 'Rosamunde' must be in part ascribed to the fact that Schubert had quarrelled with Weber on the subject of the 'Euryanthe' performance, and the hangers-on to Weber, enraged against Schubert, had either kept away from the performance of 'Rosamunde,' or prejudiced it as much as possible by their non-appearance.

[1] Chezy thinks that the third representation of 'Rosamunde' would have gained full recognition for the piece, but ' Der böse Krollo' would not allow of its being given. Accordingly the play was performed only twice, and then disappeared.

[2] 'On the whole' (remarks Chezy in the 'Denkwürdigkeiten') ' the Viennese were so well disposed towards me, that I soon got over my disappointment at the small success of my piece. The "Rosamunde" had been very poorly put upon the stage. Madame Vogel, as Aja, could produce very little effect. The public is very gracious to mammas in the best years of their lives, but they ought to look young ; they like to hear, too, the romances of Schubert, and have always been well disposed to accept my own, but they require a fresh voice. Madame Vogel sang bravely, and the accompaniment with wind instruments could not fail to be effective. Fulvius could not have been better se-lected ; Herr Rott played the part. The talent of Frl. Neumann was only just beginning to bloom.' Wilhelm Chezy says of Madame Vogel :— 'If her husband was poor, mean-looking, the wife was round and stately ; he a dry hedge-stake, she a large butt ; he pale and sallow, she glowing red ; he sickly, she bursting with health, although having long passed her teens. On the stage, where her make-up was always good, she played older parts with much skill, and looked the character to the life.'

With regard to the performance of 'Rosamunde,' the authoress of the libretto inserted in the 'Wiener Zeitschrift' of the 13th January, 1824, the following absurd and exaggerated description:—

'The orchestra, which had only been able to play twice through Schubert's fine music, and that in a single rehearsal, did wonders, and the overture and most of the other numbers were given with spirit and precision. A majestic flow of melody, reflecting and glorifying the poetry by the subtle intricacies of music, captivated the hearts of all who were present. It matters not that certain members of the public who, ever since autumn began, have been hunting stage wolves and leopards on the boards of "an der Wien," lost their way in the labyrinths of "Rosamunde," it matters not that a party had secretly influenced the mass of the listeners, this stream of harmony would have swept victoriously over every obstacle.

'H. CHEZY.

'Vienna: January 4, 1824.'

Schubert's second grand opera—or, reckoning the two unfinished works ('Die Bürgschaft' and 'Sakontala,') his fourth—is the heroic romantic Opera in three acts, 'Fierrabras.' This, too, was destined for public performance in the theatre. The libretto had been commissioned in the year 1822, by Barbaja, manager of the Imperial Opera, and compiled by Josef Kupelwieser (at that time secretary of the Josefstadt Theatre, and my authority for this information), who received a handsome sum for his pains. Two years later, however, the administration was dissolved.[1] Nothing more was heard about any performance of the opera, or payment on account of the libretto. Schubert composed the music at Vienna, and, as it would seem, the greater part of it was written at his father's house in the Rossau.

Of the ease and swiftness of Schubert's work, the score of this opera gives the most convincing testimony. Hardly had he received the libretto when he unlocked his ceaseless streams of musical invention, and assuming the correctness of the dates which head the copy of the score, the 300 pages of the first act were composed in seven days.

The entire opera (filling 1,000 pages of written score) was finished in the interval between May 23 and September 26—about four months' time; and yet he had the energy and found time to write, in addition to this work, an operetta, some songs, and pianoforte pieces.

The plan of the opera (which, like 'Fernando,' 'Die Freunde von Salamanka,' 'Claudine von Villabella,' and 'Alfonso und Estrella,' is supposed to take place in Spain) is as follows :—

---

[1] Barbaja's lease, and the administration of the theatre, came to an end on March 31, 1825. Carl then made his first appearance as an actor under the new management.

King Charles has in hard-fought battle overcome the Prince of the Moors and taken his son, Fierrabras, prisoner.

Four years before this time he and his sister, Florinda, had been in Rome, and there met Emma, the daughter of King Charles. Without knowing anything about her, he has been madly in love with her ever since. But, in the meantime, Florinda has cast sheep's eyes at Roland, a knight in Emma's train, and, more fortunate than Fierrabras, finds her passion for him reciprocated. Both parties then leave the holy city to return to their respective homes—Fierrabras with the set purpose of abjuring the faith of his fathers.

The imprisoned Moors are led before the king; Fierrabras sees Emma amongst the crowd, and is told by Eginhardt, a knight in the Court of Charles, that she is the daughter of his father's conqueror. Eginhardt, selected by his master to go with an embassy entrusted with offering the conditions of peace to the Prince of the Moors, appears in the garden of the brilliantly illuminated castle, serenading his beloved Emma with his lute, and telling his parting tale of love. During the song she appears on the balcony, but soon vanishes again; the door of the castle is opened, and Eginhardt admitted. Soon afterwards Fierrabras appears on the scene; startled by a commotion going on in the house before him and the cry of people, who seem to be looking for somebody, he steps aside, to wait for what may happen. Suddenly the door opens, Emma leads Eginhardt out, and covers the fugitive with her veil. Fierrabras then enters, prepared to avenge with his sword the injured honour of the family. Yielding to Emma's entreaties, he allows Eginhardt to continue his flight undisturbed, and offers, with noble resignation, his arm to the king's daughter (beloved by him), in order to lead her back into the castle. But King Charles appears at the gate with his attendants, and on seeing his daughter resting on the Moor's arm, harbours a cruel hatred against him for violating the laws of hospitality, and orders his trusty Eginhardt (ignorant of his passion for Emma) to throw Fierrabras into prison. Fierrabras victimises himself for his rival, and is led away in fetters. Meanwhile the horsemen intended for the ambassador's attendant train collect themselves together, with waving flags, palm branches, and other symbols of peace, to start for the palace of the Moorish Prince.

The opening of the second act introduces us once more to the knights, who have just passed the boundaries of their native land. Eginhardt and Roland bid farewell to their fatherland in a lovely duett, which is afterwards taken up by the chorus of knights.

Eginhardt, dreamily followed by his companion, and longing to be at home again, is, by his own desire, left behind by his knights, and charges his comrade, in case of impending danger, to blow his horn, so that his friends may run to his assistance. They have only just quitted the scene, when the Moors appear, take Eginhardt prisoner, and carry him away. The knights, hurrying forward at the signal given by the horn, disperse in different directions to look for him. Eginhardt is brought into the camp of the Prince of the Moors, who enquires of his son's fate, and, on hearing that he is pining in prison, vows destruction upon the whole tribe of Franks. Florinda learns that Roland is amongst the ambassador's followers. The knights arrive, Roland tells the Prince his army has been beaten, and Fierrabras embraced the Christian faith. The Moorish Prince curses his son, and orders them to confine the ambassador's retinue in the tower, and give them up to the vengeance of his soldiers. Florinda determines she will save Roland and his friends. With a sword in one hand, and a light in the other, she rushes into the dark chamber where the knights are assembled, in order to tell them of an impending attack of the Moors. The muttering of drums is heard, mingled with the clang of trumpets and the cries of the enemy. The knights seize their arms in hot haste to defend themselves. Roland and Eginhardt undertake to cut their way through the enemy and rejoin their companions and relieve the citadel. Eginhardt, mounted on the horse of a fallen Moor, succeeds in passing the boundary; Roland is taken prisoner.

The third act opens in the castle of King Charles. Emma is busy with a party of maidens, weaving garlands for the returning victors. King Charles enters, and his daughter, tormented with pangs of conscience at the fate of her knight Fierrabras, confesses to her father her love for Eginhardt, and the treachery he has practised. Fierrabras is forthwith set at liberty. Eginhardt rushes in, relates all that has passed in the Moorish camp, and implores help. Carl gives orders that everyone capable of holding a weapon should prepare for a rush at the enemy, and bids Eginhardt, if he would redeem his life—already forfeited—to save his friends.

The knights still hold out in the citadel, hoping for aid which they believe to be near at hand. The Moors raise a pile of faggots to burn Roland upon. Florinda, when viewing the agonising scene from a battlement, raises her veil on the point of a lance, and gives the Moors a signal that she will surrender the citadel.

The gate opens, Florinda and the knights come forward. The daughter of the Moorish Prince falls at her father's feet, and confesses to him her love for Roland. He, however, orders her and the knights to be condemned to death.

Brutamonte then rushes in with the announcement that the army of Franks is advancing in full marching order. The Moors rush upon the knights with drawn sabres, but Eginhardt and Fierrabras have already attacked. Roland tears away Florinda from her father, who is about to take her back to the citadel, and on the point of stabbing the Prince of the Moors, when Fierrabras seizes the already uplifted arm, calling out to him to spare his father. King Charles and Emma appear; the vanquished Prince of the Moors is called on to finish the dispute; Eginhardt falls prostrate at the King's feet. The latter forgives him, and leads him to Emma, his affianced wife; but the Prince, softened by the intercession of the son, joins Florinda's hand with Roland's. Fierrabras prevails on King Charles to be allowed to follow from henceforth his victorious standard. The opera ends with a universal chorus of joy and exultation.

The music, including the overture, contains twenty-three numbers.[1] The first is an orchestral introduction (in F Andante $\frac{3}{4}$), a genuine Schubertian movement, full of interest, linked to which is the constantly recurring subject (F Minor, Allegro ma non troppo $\frac{4}{4}$), which runs through the overture like a silver tissue.

The opera commences with a chorus of Court bed-chamber-women, occupied in spinning at the loom in Emma's apartment at the King's castle (Andantino C major $\frac{6}{8}$). There are short solo passages, and the chorus takes up again the first strophe. After a short spoken dialogue Emma sings the same melody (in G minor); the chorus afterwards concludes the piece with

[1] The original overture is in the hands of Herr Spina, at Vienna.

the introductory air (in C minor), which, with its melodious and tuneful character, is admirably adapted to
the situation.[1] To this first chorus succeeds another
for the virgins, crowning with garlands the returning
heroes, and a short and not very striking love-duett
between Emma and Eginhardt (Andantino A-flat
major ¾). The scene changes to the state apartments
of the King's castle. A march (Allegro mod. D major ₄)
is followed by a fine chorus for the knights,[2] beau-

---

[1] *Chor.*

Der runde Silberfaden
Läuft sinnig durch die Hand,
Zum Frommen wie zum Schaden
Webt sich ein Liebespfand.

Solo.

Wie er die Welt begrüsset,
Der Säugling neu belebt,
Die Hülle ihn umfliesset,
Von Spinnerhand gewebt.
    Chor (erste Strofe).

Solo.

Zur Hülle selbst im Grabe,
Zur Klag' im Treuebruch,
Webt sich als Spinnergabe
Von Spinnerhand gewebt, &c.
    Chor (erste Strofe).

[2] *Ritter.*

Zu hohen Ruhmespforten
Klimmt er auf schroffem Gleis (*sic*),
Nicht fröhnt er hohlen Worten,
Die That nur ist sein Preis.

tifully interwoven with the alternate strains for the wives and daughters.[1] Both these movements culminate in a general chorus, in which the march is again introduced. Next in order follow recitatives for the King, fresh from the honours of his coronation; alternate choruses of great beauty, and a general chorus; then recitatives for Fierrabras and Roland, and a charming chorus for virgins, with a soprano solo.[2] These movements introduce an ensemble, in which the King, Roland, Ogier, Fierrabras, Eginhardt, Emma, and the knights all take part.

The introductory march and chorus are again heard, followed by a melodious but not otherwise remarkable duett for Roland and Fierrabras (Allegro maestoso con sforza A major $\frac{4}{4}$) and the finale. This opens with

---

[1]   *Frauen.*

Den Sieger lasst uns schmücken,
Von frischem Kranz umlaubt (*sic*),
Muth strahlet aus den Blicken,
Der Lorbeer um das Haupt!

[2]   *Emma.*

Der Landestöchter fromme Pflichten
Weih'n, Edler, Dir die Heldenzier;
Mir war des Amtes zu verrichten,
Ich reich' für sie den Kranz nur Dir.

       Chor.

Vaterhuld und milder Sinn
Schmückt den hohen Helden,
Seiner Tugenden Gewinn
Bleibt der Dank der Welten.

Eginhardt's farewell serenade in front of the terrace
at the castle—a beautiful romance, consisting of an
Andante in A minor $\frac{4}{4}$). A few plaintive chords accompany the entry of Fierrabras, who, in a recitative and
beautifully accompanied air, bewails his untoward fate.

A shout is heard along the corridors of the royal
castle, and the cry, 'Wo ist sie?' 'Verfolget die Spuren,'
&c., strikes on the ear; this leads to a series of powerful
dramatic scenes, set to beautiful and expressive music.
The trio that follows, and a quartett preceded by a
recitative and air for Emma, are one and all numbers
of high musical value. A loud blast from the horn gives
the signal for the knights to rise. The alternate strains
of the knights and troopers (Allegro vivace C major $\frac{4}{4}$),
concluding with a quartett [1] (Emma, the King, Egin-

---

[1]   *Emma, Eginhardt und Fierrabras.*

Dulden nur und schweigen
Ziemt um solchen Preis,
Und kein Blick darf zeigen,
Was die Seele weiss.

Carl.

Ernst und Strenge zeigen
Ist mein Pflichtgeheiss,
Vor des Frevlers Zeugen
Werd' der Schmach er preis (*sic*).

Chor.

Fort zum Siegesreigen,
Fort auf sein Machtgeheiss,
Eures Ruhmes Zeugen
Bringt des Finders Preis.

hardt, and Fierrabras), admirably worked up, bring the first act to an elaborate close.

The second act begins with a pretty duett for Roland and Eginhardt (Andantino C major $\frac{4}{4}$), as they gaze for the last time on their fatherland. The chorus of knights repeat the melody. They depart, and a characteristic march announces the advance of the Moors. Eginhardt blows a blast on his horn, and the challenge is answered by his friends. In a powerful wild chorus, the Moors,[1] who scent treason in the horn-blast, threaten the betrayer with death. After taking Eginhardt with them, a second trumpet-blast is heard, the knights return to look for him they have left behind, and the next chorus (an Allegro molto vivace in F major $\frac{6}{8}$) is full of energy and interest. Still finer is the lovely duett that follows for Florinda, with violoncello obligato (Andante con moto in A-flat) :[2]—

> Muth und Besinnung schwinden,
> Ein düstres Todesgrau'n
> Lässt mich nur Qualen finden,
> Zerstört ist mein Vertrau'n.

---

[1]   *Chor der Mauren.*

> Was mag der Ruf bedeuten?
> Seid wohl auf eurer Hut,
> Mög' er Verrath bedeuten,
> So ströme bald sein Blut.

[2]   *Florinde.*

> Weit über Glanz und Erdenschimmer
> Ragt meiner Wünsche hohes Ziel,

The third act begins, like the first, with a chorus of virgins collected at the royal castle, and occupied in twining garlands. In this chorus the solo part of Emma is heard prominently above the other parts. A duett for the king and his daughter follows, with a recitative and a lovely trio (Emma, Eginhardt, Fierrabras), in which Eginhardt takes leave of his beloved (Allegro mod. in C). The scene changes to the interior of the tower, which the Moors are besieging. The knights are busily occupied about Florinda. The air which follows for Florinda, accompanied by chorus (Andante con moto F $\frac{3}{4}$), a fine air of a plaintive character, is one of the most successful pieces of music in the opera.[1]

Und jedem Glück entsag' ich immer,
Lohnt mich der Liebe süss Gefühl, &c.

[1]

Florinde.
Des Jammers herbe Qualen
Erfüllen dieses Herz,
Zum Grabe muss er wallen,
O unnennbarer Schmerz! &c.

Chor (als Mittelsatz).
Lass dein Vertrau'n nicht schwinden,
Noch leuchtet uns ein Hoffnungsstrahl,
Noch kann sich Rettung finden,
Und spurlos flieht der Leiden Qual.

Florinde.
Und seines Todes Wunde
Bringt mir Verderben auch.

Chor.
Des Herzens tiefste Wunde
Heilt froher Hoffnung Hauch.

A funeral march is heard close at hand, the prelude to another orchestral movement, and then comes a lively dramatic scene (Florinda and the knights), in which Florinda orders the gates to be opened, and the knights desire to die with their friend. They are answered by the wild energetic chorus of the Moors, an ensemble (Tempo di marcia D minor $\frac{4}{4}$), accompanied by beats on the great tomtom. Florinda rushes into her father's arms, recitatives follow, and an ensemble (Admiral, Florinda, chorus of knights and Moors), and a finale (Allegro moderato B major $\frac{4}{4}$). Warlike signals are heard in the distance, succeeded by recitatives, a short chorus of the knights, more recitatives interspersed with choral passages, and the final chorus with a quartett for the principals (Allegro vivace $\frac{2}{4}$) :—

Vereint durch Bruderbande
Gedeiht nur Menschenglück,
Es weilt im Vaterlande
So gern' der Söhne Blick.

The libretto of this opera belongs to that class of the 'heroic-romantic' kind in which valour and chivalry contend for the palm. Every character is more or less heroic, the passive Fierrabras excepted, who, however, lends his name to the opera in which he plays so poor and contemptible a part. His delight in self-sacrifice knows no bounds; and yet he thanks the King when the latter orders him to be shut up (instead of Eginhardt). There is no lack of brilliancy in the piece,

and the warlike processions, war cries, and heroic
deeds in battle, contrast with the soft lyric element
introduced by Emma and the choruses for women.
The tuneful burden of the Lied makes itself heard
here and there in the opera; whilst ever and anon an
opportunity offers for the development of dramatic
musical effects, which Schubert never fails to avail
himself of. The choruses for men are vividly coloured,
and those for the Moors well in keeping with the
national character. Song alternates with spoken dialogue, which, with the melodrama and recitatives, occu-
pies a conspicuous place in the work.

The opera was never performed in public. Some
years after the death of Franz, his brother Ferdinand
introduced fragments of the work in his concerts; in
the year 1858, at a concert given by the Männergesang-
Verein at Vienna, the overture, the first scene of the
second act (for tenor, bass, and men's chorus), and the
scene in the citadel (for soprano and chorus) from
the third act, were given, and in the year 1862 the
chorus ' O theures Vaterland,' from the second act, was
performed with marked success. Should a revival of
' Fierrabras' ever be contemplated on the stage, it
would be found to contrast unfavourably with ' Alfonso
und Estrella.' In the former the spoken dialogue is
diffuse and wearisome; in the latter, musical recitative
supplies the place. A remedy must be found, either
by improving the text and shortening the recitatives,

or inserting new ones. From the more judicious arrangement and connection of the different numbers, and a more lively dramatic treatment, one would feel disposed to augur confidently a greater stage success for this opera than for the lyric and monotonous drama 'Alfonso.' We have yet to mention a small but delicate and lustrous jewel, which some years ago was discovered and extracted from Schubert's 'Casket,' in the shape of an operetta.

In the eighth yearly series of the dramatic 'Sträusschen,' published by J. F. Castelli, will be found, amongst other compositions, chiefly borrowed from the French, the one-act Opera 'Die Verschwornen.' The author wrote the following preface to his work:—'The complaint, generally speaking, of the German composers is this:—"Well, we should be very glad to set operas to music, only get us proper words to write to!" Now here is one, gentlemen! If you will accompany it with music, pray let my words have fair play, and don't spoil the intelligibleness of the plot, whilst you only look after roulades and flourishes in preference to musical characteristics. In my opinion, the opera should be a dramatically worked piece, accompanied with music—not music with a text specially adapted as an after-thought; and the general effect and impression, according to my view, are of more importance than that of giving an opportunity for some individual singer of displaying the elasticity and power of his

vocal organ.   Let us do something, gentlemen, for the
bonâ fide German opera !'

This preface, which is to be read in the 'Sträusschen'
for the year 1823, whereas the musical accompaniments,
according to a statement on a copy of the original
score, are said to have been composed as early as the
year 1819, leads me to expect that the compiler of the
libretto was ignorant of the fact that his verses had
already been clothed in musical dress, and by no less
a composer than Franz Schubert.   Castelli, in his old
age, remembered once to have heard that Schubert,
whom he knew personally, had taken in hand a setting
of his operetta; [1] but that as the opera never was
represented, and, in addition to this, it having been
whispered to him that the composer, so far from master-
ing the author's humour, had put together a gloomy,
sentimental, colourless toned picture, he had ceased to
take any further interest in the matter.   With regard
to the actual point of time when the musical part of the
work first originated, he could not, at such a distance
of time, give any further information.[2]

It is strange that Ferdinand Schubert (who seems to

[1] This I had in a short conversation with Castelli immediately after
a performance of the operetta at the Concert Hall.

[2] The information would certainly be supplied by the original score, on
which Schubert, as his habit was, would have written the day he began
and the day he finished the work.   The manuscript, however, is not
forthcoming, and has probably, with other of Schubert's compositions,
been sold by Ferdinand Schubert.

have assigned the year 1819 as the date on the copy of
the work made by him) has always in his catalogues
given the year 1823 as the date of the origin of the
opera. The music of the opera itself speaks in favour
of the latter period—a time which synchronises with
the best period of Schubert's power as an original composer.[1] It is a characteristic feature with regard to
Schubert's conduct in this matter, that he never makes
the slightest mention of the compiler of the libretto,
whilst the old Castelli seems to have been glad to
retaliate for such reserve, seeing that after the first

---

[1] Bauernfeld, in his 'Sketches,' compiled in 1829, fixes 1824 as the
year when Schubert wrote the work. Josef Hüttenbrenner affirms confidently that Schubert did not play the opera to him on the piano before
1824 or the year after; and his memory is all the clearer on the matter,
as the composer himself was pleased with his own music and wished the
opera to be performed at the theatre—an event which both he and
Hüttenbrenner made several ineffectual efforts to bring about. In a
memorandum-book (in the possession of the latter) there is the following notice in the year 1824 :—' "Der häusliche Krieg," written at my
father's house, reviewed and passed for representation at the Royal
Opera House.' Schubert, in a letter to Kupelwieser in the year 1824,
mentions the operetta. In a notice of the ' Augsburg Allgemeine Zeitung ' for October 1862, relative to a performance of ' Die Verschwornen ' at Munich, the following words appear:—'A year after Schubert
had given his opera to the managers of the Opera House at Vienna, he
thought the time had arrived for him to make some enquiries after the
fate of his work. Whereupon he got back his score from the library,
rolled up, tied, and fastened—in short, in exactly the same state as he
had sent it thirteen months before to his wise judges and reviewers.'
If this be true, or if any part of the story be true, I have never ascertained : J. Hüttenbrenner has no memory of the circumstance here
narrated.

performance of the musical part of the operetta, he hazarded the extraordinary assertion, ' It's impossible that all the music should have come from Schubert!' However, as to the question of the composer's thoroughly grasping the author's meaning, his prejudices were entirely removed. The original title, 'Die Verschwornen,' was fixed on by a committee of censors, who were for a period of twenty years in the ascendant, and this title became afterwards fused in the less threatening name of 'Der häusliche Krieg.' The operetta consists of eleven numbers of different kinds, interspersed with spoken dialogue. The treatment of the subject—radically nothing more nor less than an adaptation of the 'Lysistrate' of Aristophanes into mediæval Viennese, may be thus described.

Count Heribert von Lüdenstein, a feudal lord, Astolf von Reisenberg, Garold von Nummen, Friedrich von Trausdorf, vassals of Heribert, and several knights with them, have gone forth in the crusade against the Saracens. Their wives, Ludmilla, Helena, Luitgarde, Camilla, and those of the rest of the knights are lamenting for their husbands, and yearning for their return. Ludmilla, angry with her husband for listening to the call of honour rather than the obligations of love, and for his determination to endure a long separation, invites the wives of all those knights who have gone to the wars to assemble at her castle, there to persuade them of the advisability of treating their husbands on their return home with indifference and coldness. The page of the Count, Udolin, who has hurriedly preceded the knights on their return home, hears of this plot from his lady-love Isella, the waiting-maid of the Countess, and, disguised in woman's attire, attends the fore-appointed wives' parliament. Ludmilla's proposal is unanimously voted. The knights arrive at the castle. Udolin secretly informs his master of the vote of the women. The knights speedily resolve to enter the lists with the same weapons, and to meet their seemingly indifferent wives with still greater coldness on their part. In the great hall of the castle the knights meet their ladies. The hypocrisy of both sets is admirably acted, only the knights, without ever having first saluted their wives, go off at once to a state apartment, there to hold banquet and revel. The Countess is amazed at her husband's behaviour, the other wives already begin to make objections to the plot of their own contrivance. Isella then appears in the scene, and tells the Countess that her husband filled his drinking-cup to the brim at dinner, and proposed as a toast, 'Here's to war and the glory of war!' adding, 'Let us only rest a little, and then once more to the field of honour in search of fresh laurels. Until that hour let us keep apart from our wives.' Ludmilla's consternation and that of the other women is at its fever-point. The state of things begins to be unbearable; the Countess is already asking for a secret

interview with the Count, the other women appoint a
meeting with their husbands. Helena is the first to be
seen together with Astolf; the Countess suspects her
cause has been betrayed, and meets her husband very
affectionately, whilst he, scarce able to master his feelings, only escapes by lying, to the effect that he and his
fighting companions have sworn a fearful oath to return
again to the field. He bids a last adieu to the Countess,
and withdraws. Udolin and Isella then enter. The
first of these confides to the Countess the intelligence
that the knights, surrounded by Saracens without any
hope of escape, had taken a vow on themselves of once
more enduring a campaign for the sake of their own deliverance, and further, of showing no symptom of the
smallest affection for their wives, unless they, from pure
devotion to their husbands, would buckle on armour,
fight side by side with them, and do battle for the faith.
The Countess declares she will never do such a thing.
Isella takes a suit of armour down from the wall, puts
it on, but only in jest she says. The Count appears;
touched by the sight of his own wife, he summons all
the knights. The Countess wishes to put off the armour,
when the other ladies step in, all of them clothed in
armour, and compel their leader to remain so in a warlike capacity. The men now give in as being mastered,
the Count tells the story of the vow as having been a
pure invention, Isella and Udolin exchange greetings,
and all come to terms.

Schubert's music contains a duett for Isella (soprano) and Udolin (tenor,[1] Allegro A major $\frac{4}{4}$), a romance for Helena (Moderato F minor $\frac{6}{8}$), a chorus of the knights' wives (Allegro moderato C major $\frac{4}{4}$), consisting of several movements differing in key and rhythm from each other; the plot chorus for the wives (Allegro D minor $\frac{4}{4}$), with a final movement (Andantino D major $\frac{6}{8}$), a march and chorus of knights (Allegro moderato B minor $\frac{4}{4}$), a chorus of knights (Allegro moderato E-flat $\frac{3}{4}$), a chorus of knights and wives (Andantino C major $\frac{3}{4}$), and a duett for the Count and Countess (F major $\frac{4}{4}$), a duett between Astolf and Helena (Andantino B major $\frac{3}{8}$), with the concluding movement (Allegro vivace $\frac{2}{4}$), an air for the Count (Allegro moderato A major $\frac{2}{4}$), another for the Countess (Allegro moderato C major $\frac{2}{4}$), and the finale (Allegro giusto D $\frac{4}{4}$), a movement in several parts very varied in tone and character, of which the march and chorus of women (G major $\frac{4}{4}$), the solo of the Countess accompanied by men and women's voices (Andante C major $\frac{4}{4}$), and the final chorus (Allegro moderato C major $\frac{6}{8}$) are conspicuous features. This charming musical vaudeville is a subject of special interest, as it was the first of a series of Schubert performances in the way of dramatic music, and gave the first stimulus to further efforts in this direction.

[1] The part of the page Udolin is composed in the duett (No. 1) for tenor, in the other numbers throughout the work for soprano.

After the operetta had slept over forty years by the side of other unknown and unused treasures, the music was given for the first time at Vienna on March 1, 1861, at a concert of the Musikverein, and obtained a brilliant success before a numerous and eager audience.[1] The freshness and beauty of the melodies, coupled with the marked individuality of each character in the piece, worked upon the attention of the hearers in the same degree as the power and facility of treatment shown in the vocal and instrumental parts called forth delight and astonishment on the part of those who were incredulous of Schubert's gifts in this particular branch of art. Our tone-poet showed his lyric power here most remarkably. The entire libretto gives no opportunity for genuine dramatic effects, although there are certain portions, as, for example, the finale, which might well excite the envy of artists still living amongst us. We have now before us a series of eleven vocal numbers, each of which is more charming than its predecessor.[2]

---

[1] Herr Johann Herbeck, director of the society, conducted at this performance, and we were much indebted to his knowledge of the operetta in question. The singers who took part were Frl. Hofmann (Countess), Frl. Ottilie Hauer (Helena), Frl. Bertl (Isella), Herr Mayerhofer (Count), and Herr Olschbauer (Udolin and Astolf). At the second performance (March 22) the chief singer at the Theatre Royal, Frl. Kraus, sang the part of the Countess, and Herr Walther the tenor part.

[2] In the spring of 1862, a pianoforte edition, by Dr. Schneider, was published at Spina's with and without the words, and other arrangements of the operetta have appeared.

With respect to the stage performances of the 'Verschwornen,' Frankfort on the Maine got the start of all other cities of Germany. It was in that Imperial city, on the 29th of August, 1861, that the first representation was given with marked success, and other performances followed soon afterwards.[1]

[1] The 'Frankfurter Museum' contained the first notice of the performance, and expressed itself to the effect that 'the charming little work, the sweet music of which' combined in a wonderful way the soothing, melting, southern strains with the rough energy of German music, was greeted by the critics and public with a very friendly reception, and will be valued as an important acquisition to the repertoire of the theatres. The music,' it goes on to say, 'is as delicate, lovely, and charming as one would have expected at the hands of the famous and versatile Schubert. Each number is more beautiful than the other. The opera was admirably put upon the stage, the scenery good, the players took great pains; one felt that they liked the work. The applause was hearty.' In the 'Didaskalien' of the 'Frankfort Journal' this theatrical event was thus alluded to :—'Our directors have done a good stroke of business in taking in hand the "Häuslicher Krieg," a one-act opera left by the genial Lieder-composer Franz Schubert (words by Castelli). This charming work has already been given twice with marked applause, and ought to keep a lasting place in our repertoire. The theatre here is the first to produce this opera before the public, although the music has been first familiarised to Vienna by a concert performance given in the spring of this year by the "Gesellschaft der Musikfreunde." A lapse of forty-two years was necessary to pave the way on the stage for this valuable and poetical work, and in the interim what a quantity of vapid colourless music has supplanted it. Castelli's libretto invites a characteristic and energetic treatment on the part of the musician, it is full of lively situations throughout. Schubert has understood and identified himself with the various lyrical, sentimental, and comic situations offered by the text; the music is very animated and dramatic, the wealth of fresh melody is extraordinary, and the tunes are many and original. Each separate number has its special charm.'

On October 19, 1861, the opera was given for the first time at the Court Theatre. The performance of the music was not on the same scale of excellence as that which had preceded it in the Concert Hall, but the reception of the novelty on the part of the public was very favourable. That 'Die Verschwornen' should have kept its place in the repertoire for only a short time, is attributable to circumstances which have nothing to do with the intrinsic value of Schubert's composition, but rather the management of the theatrical programmes, and the desire of the public to have the entire evening filled up with some grander operatic performance and more brilliant scenic delusions.[1]

At a very recent period (October 1862), the operetta was given at the chief theatre at Munich and also at Salzburg, where it enjoyed a genuine triumph. As already stated, the charming series of Lieder, 'Die schöne Müllerin,' belongs to this period.

One day Schubert visited the private secretary of Count Seczenyi, Herr Benedict Randhartinger (at present Imperial Hofcapellmeister), with whom he was on terms of great intimacy and friendship. He had only just entered the room when the secretary was sent for. He withdrew, after giving the composer to under-

---

[1] The 'Häuslicher Krieg' was given with a dance divertissement, or a second operetta. At the Court Theatre in Vienna, Frl. Fischer sang the part of Isella and Herr Erl that of Astolf; the other parts were filled by those who had sung there at the second concert performance.

stand that he would return in a short time. Franz
went to the writing-table, and found a volume of
poetry lying there; after reading one 'or two of the
poems through, he seized the book and went away,
without waiting for Randhartinger's return. The latter, when he came back, missed his volume of poems,
and went next day to Schubert to fetch away the
book. Franz alleged his great interest in the poems
as an excuse for his predatory performance; and, as a
proof that his theft had not been barren of results,
he presented the astonished secretary with the first
'Müllerlieder,' which he had partly finished in the
small hours of the night. The well-authenticated fact
of Schubert's writing several 'Müllerlieder' and 'Der
Einsame' whilst lying as a patient in the hospital, is a
convincing proof that his powers as a musical composer
were in no way impeded by his bodily ailments. Of
the songs which first saw the light at this time were
'Viola,' 'Der zürnende Barde,' 'Drang in die Ferne,'
'Pilgerreise,' 'Auf dem Wasser zu singen,' and 'Der
Zwerg' (properly 'Treubruch'), fragment of a poem
by H. Collin, one of the most beautiful of Schubert's
compositions in the way of songs. 'Der Zwerg' is allowed to be one of the most animated dramatic compositions—a masterpiece, which the composer, when
pressed by his publisher to write a song off-hand,
dashed down upon paper in hot haste, without any preparation, keeping up a conversation all the while with

a friend who had come to take him out for a walk—a worthy parallel to the calm collectedness of mind with which Mozart, in the midst of a noise going on in the house, wrote down the glorious concerted things in the 'Hochzeit des Figaro.' In this year, too, was written a sonata for piano and arpeggione (unpublished), and the beautiful Sonata in A minor (Op. 143) dedicated by the publishers to Mendelssohn.

After Schubert's early nomination to an honorary membership of the Musikverein at Gratz, both he and Vogl—probably at the instance of Albert Stadler, at that time officially connected with the Musikverein at Linz as secretary, or still more from the proper recognition they met with as artists—were admitted honorary members of the Musical Institute at Linz.

END OF THE FIRST VOLUME.

LONDON: PRINTED BY
SPOTTISWOODE AND CO., NEW-STREET SQUARE
AND PARLIAMENT STREET